MASTER OF ONE

JAIDA JONES AND DANI BENNETT

An Imprint of HarperCollins*Publishers*

HarperTeen is an imprint of HarperCollins Publishers.

Master of One
Copyright © 2020 by Jaida Jones and Dani Bennett
Map art © 2020 by Anka Lavriv
All rights reserved.

ISBN 978-0-06-294145-9

Typography by Catherine Lee
22 23 24 25 26   CPI 10 9 8 7 6 5 4 3 2

First paperback edition, 2022

Printed and bound by CPI Group (UK) Ltd, Croydon, CR0 4YY

MASTER
OF ONE

For Tamar and Alice, our fae Enchantrisks

PROLOGUE

Tomman Hail of House Ever-Loyal was going to die before the sun rose.

It wasn't as heroic as it sounded.

It was a lonely, terrible thing. Made worse by the lonely, terrible knowledge weighing on his chest. The secret he'd uncovered.

It'll be our lives if we're caught, he'd said.

Now, as then, he believed the cause worth the cost.

Even as he heard the pounding at the door announce the Queensguard's arrival to his family home, Captain Baeth at their head. *The middle of the night* wasn't an hour at which anyone bore pleasant news.

They carried torches of fire, not shards of the Queen's mirrorglass. Danger flickered in the wicked orange light that dappled their well-trained faces.

Better them than a sorcerer, Tomman thought.

Father led them into the sitting room. Mother, straight-backed and proud in her dressing gown, asked if Baeth would like some tea.

The captain had already trained her unyielding gaze on Tomman. Having stood opposite that look for countless lessons in sword and dagger, he knew there was no parrying it.

"Tomman Hail Ever-Loyal." The Queensguard stood straighter when Baeth spoke. None of them would look at Tomman, at his parents. "You will be remanded to the Queen's mercy."

Live steel strapped at their waists. Authorized to use force if command wouldn't suffice.

Whether Tomman resisted or not, the result wouldn't change. He'd seen where this path might end—*too soon*—and he'd taken it anyway. Made the path his.

No illusions of being stuffed in a cell to go mad. What he'd discovered couldn't be hidden. It had to be erased.

If the Queen hoped to maintain the pretense of civility in front of his parents, Tomman intended to play along. It would make this easier for them.

"I surrender," he said immediately.

"Like shitfire you surrender." Lord Ever-Loyal came to stand beside his son. "Baeth, I learned the blade from your father before he was pinning your diapers. When the Queensguard take a man in the middle of the night—we know he won't return. What *is* this?"

Captain Baeth shook her head. Her hand must have been forced. She would never have done this willingly, but she was keeping her grief private, admirably stone-faced. Then Tomman saw her eyes, blank and cracked as an old mirror. His fear bottomed out into despair. She was no friend of his, no friend to anyone but the Queen. "Not another step. The slightest resistance could be cause for deadly force."

"What are the charges? Against *my* son?" Father swept the Queensguard with a practiced gaze. "These are no escorts."

Movement from the side and rear. A hiss of steel. Lady Ever-Loyal gasped and the Queensguard whirled with blades in hand to face Ainle, Tomman's nine-year-old brother, who'd stepped into the room rubbing sleep from his eyes. He stopped short, cry cut off, a red stain blooming along the collar of his blue pajamas.

Groundskeeper Eraith entered at the same moment, straight from the stables with pitchfork in hand, to ask what the trouble was.

Tomman yelled to stop it, but it had already begun.

The shouting, the weapons, the smell of fresh blood, and the Queen's lifetime of lies. More than sufficient powder and flame.

Baeth signaled the attack.

Tomman's vision became a blur of his mother's howling mouth, her flying hair. She raced to Ainle's side as his father drew his Queens-guard sword.

Lord Ever-Loyal was an exceptional duelist.

But he stood against thirty swordsmen.

He refused to kneel, so they cut him down, across belly and chest. Blood on the starburst tile Mother loved so much. Tomman didn't see her body lying with the others. Had she fled in time to warn the girls?

Tomman fought, but Baeth had always bested him in practice. Now was no different. She brought the hilt of her sword into the bone of his cheek. He staggered, fell to his knees. She caught him and pinned him to the wall with a knife through his palm. Held the point of her sword, still sticky with Lord Ever-Loyal's insides, to Tomman's throat, forcing his chin up so he had to watch.

They'd never planned to take him alive.

They were merely saving him for last.

Mother's impeccably set dining room was a mess. Three of the seven fae-glass windows were shattered. Tomman broke free, struggled with Baeth, used the knife that pierced his hand to cut her bottom lip and chin. Baeth had the bigger weapon, the longer range. The struggle ended quickly. He was pinned again.

The slaughter continued.

All night there was weeping, begging, servants spitted while Tomman was forced to bear witness. Iron-toed boots in his gut and iron-soled boots crushing his hands.

Despite everything he knew, *because* of everything he knew, he didn't crack. He tried to goad the Queensguard into killing him before a sorcerer could arrive and begin the true torture.

He wasn't dead yet. Unfortunately.

He sat, pinned again to the wall between two broken windows, Baeth's blade neatly lodged between his heart and his liver. Steel sheathed first in muscle, then plaster. The Queen's crest upon the hilt: a golden two-faced sun stained with Tomman's blood.

At last the sorcerer Morien appeared before him.

"I keep you alive because you have something I want," he said. *"You will tell me where it is."*

The sun peered over the horizon. The sorcerer was gathering fragments of silver-polished glass toward him simply by curving his fingers and beckoning them closer. They shivered and shuddered across the tile. Instead of reflecting the pale light, they absorbed it. They showed Tomman a thousand secrets he shouldn't have known, from the eyes of the men and women and children, *his family*, who had died that night. Their wishes, their bargains, their silenced dreams.

Each let him know that he would risk this tragedy again, if he were given the chance.

Tomman could barely move, but he rolled his face away. The

sorcerer wouldn't be the last thing he saw in this life. Cool, damp wind touched his cheek, kissed by the jagged lip of the windowsill. It stirred the hair on Ainle's head—he lay by Tomman's side, otherwise unmoving—where it wasn't plastered to his scalp with blood. Tomman remembered his laugh, how the silly lad had begged to hold Father's Queensguard broadsword, though he didn't have the strength yet to lift it.

Outside the window, in the trammeled grass of Mother's garden, Tomman thought he saw a Queensguard running. Not toward the house—away from it. Flinging his blade into one of Mother's rosebushes. Peeling off layers of his uniform as if they burned his skin. Driven from the Queen's service by the horror of the Queen's service.

Real or hallucinated, it was a sign. No matter who the Queen controlled, no matter what she stole, no matter how she armored herself, there would always be cracks through which the truth would shine.

"No," Tomman finally answered the sorcerer, "I don't think I will."

Holding Ainle's little hand with his broken one, Tomman shifted to the right. Sliced his heart cleanly in two—and smiled.

Nothing left for the sorcerer to use.

1

RAGS

ONE YEAR LATER

Sixteen days. Rags had been in a cell in the dungeon known as Coward's Silence for sixteen days. They felt as long as his sixteen years.

He wasn't planning to stick around for much longer.

But trying to escape blind, without a plan, would double his guard. So he'd taken his time. Thought it through and decided. The next time the Queensguard tried to transport him would be his best chance to make it out.

Rags was no stranger to this business. He'd been in and out of cells since he could flex his fingers to steal. He'd even developed a system of ranking each of the city's seven jails from best to worst on a scale of one to five points.

One: Cell condition. (Down by the docks, after a rainfall, he'd once slept in two inches of water, and nursed a lingering cough for the next two years and seven days.)

Two: Meals. (Depending on where a thief got snatched, he could count on three square a day and cheese with only a little mold on it. Some got caught on purpose, when pickings were lean.)

Three: Bed. (As in, was there one?)

Four: The company. (Local drunks and fellow thieves, or split-knuckles and murderers? Barely ten, Rags had wound up locked in a cell with a rapist who wouldn't shut up about pretty girls and their pretty curls, until one of the guards knifed him during change-of-duty.)

Five: The quality of the guards.

Rags was holding off on giving Coward's Silence a score. He hadn't heard a peep since his arrival, though the quiet didn't mean he was sleeping easy.

He kept track of the passing days by scratching marks onto the stone wall with a fingernail. Dust and dirt and damp grime packed the space beneath his nails so densely that they split, but Rags kept up the practice diligently. Dutifully. Dug deep so there'd be no uncertainty.

For a bastard thief with no faith, this was the god he prayed to.

"You'll give up eventually," the man in the next cell over said, voice muffled through stone and nasty with loneliness and despair. Rags imagined him as more skeleton than living man. "Everyone gives up eventually. Took me three hundred days before I stopped counting. See how long it takes *you*."

Rags ground his teeth and refused to answer. He had his own cell, a point in the place's favor. Coward's Silence knew how to treat its degenerates, letting them ignore each other in peace.

Sixteen days.

The Queensguard would come to transport him eventually. They were famous for their successful interrogations.

That thought coaxed a snort from his nose.

The job was *supposed* to have been *simple*. Blind Kit had finally pinpointed the location of the Gutter King's underground vault. The haul of Rags's dreams—the infamous collection of pirate gold and stolen Ever-Nobles' fortunes, snatched in the chaos when their families fell out of favor and were run out of town. After the Queens-guard burned House Ever-Loyal last year, countless early Radiance forgeries flooded the Cheapside Gray-Market. Rags didn't buy into the frenzy, knew the real loot had already been smuggled deep under-ground. That cache kept the undercity running, kept the Gutter King stroking the strings.

Rags, with help from Blind Kit, was going to relieve the Gutter King of some of it.

Not all. Not enough that they'd become a target, but enough to make life easier for *years*. Rags had even considered the possibility of going soft, of buying a nice house in a cheap part of town. He could take up juggling, or some other thing that took quick hand-eye work but carried fewer risks than thieving.

Rags had made it into the sewers, past the shadowy henchmen and their spring-traps, all the way to the *fucking door of the vault*.

The man who'd been tapped to rig the explosion hadn't lit the fuse.

Instead, the grating had opened. Out had poured dozens of Queensguard in silver and black.

Only one wall had separated Rags from the biggest score of his life. In the blink of an eye, it was gone.

Someone must have sold him out. Not Kit, who'd had a bounty on her head for close to two years, as long as she'd been blind. She wouldn't go near the Queensguard after they'd run the last healers and hedgewitches out of the city.

To Rags, her fear and mistrust made her reliable. Sure, a handful of other thieves in the Clave might risk a run-in with the Queens-guard over a fat score, but Rags was careful not to make enemies with *those* crazy gamblers.

Think about that later. The interrogation was coming, and from the way they'd thrown him in, left him to stew for *sixteen days*, they were planning something extra nasty. Rags ran his tongue over the split in his upper lip—it stung, infected and bound to scar—and set to cleaning the dirt from under his nails. He'd waited too long to be set free, returned to his tools: delicate metal lockpicks that worked in a pinch for cleaning under an infected nail.

He'd have to do it by hand.

Rags set to the task, careful and slow. He couldn't afford to damage the other, irreplaceable tools of his trade: his wicked quick fingers that danced with a hummingbird's speed and could sting like a wasp when called to.

Sixteen days. He wasn't going to lose count. He marked the passage of time by the delivery of his meals, if they could be called that, and chewed the moldy bread, not bothering to spit out the maggots. Protein. Keep his strength up, his mind sharp. The cell stank of his filth, but that honed his senses, kept his teeth bared. He wouldn't rot in this place. As soon as the Queensguard came for him, Rags would get *out*.

The Queensguard finally showed when he was drifting through the vulnerable shadow space between sleep and waking life. The man in the next cell laughed darkly, choked, spat. Rags's eyes adjusted to the sudden fall of light, scanned the row—two rows—of Queensguard for a weak point, and found none.

Hands on him, hoisting him to his feet. No jeers about his condition, no introductory punches. The royal seal on their breastplates.

Rags swore like a dying pig.

The Queensguard ignored his vulgarity and hauled him out.

2

RAGS

They went up, not down. Troubling, because *all* interrogation rooms were down, the better to hide the screaming from civilians. If they weren't hauling him in for torture and questioning, where were they headed?

Rags lifted his head high—he couldn't see over the spiked epaulets in front of him—and readied himself to meet—

Whatever it was.

A long trek through the dismal dark, following the relentless, clanking pace set by the Queensguard. It grew cold enough that Rags's teeth would have chattered if he'd been alone. With company, better not to show that kind of weakness. He had to fight to keep from stumbling.

Rags knew exactly how big Coward's Silence was, and it wasn't this big.

Still the Queensguard continued upward, not a direction Rags had on the map in his head. As they kept ascending, the stink of death faded, and the walls started looking pretty. Wafts of perfume, snippets of song, the distant clink of silver and glass. Coward's Silence was accessible from Queen Catriona Ever-Bright's castle on the Hill, but Rags couldn't be headed for a royal audience. The thought was enough to make him laugh. Or vomit.

He managed to hold both in.

A door opened to reveal windows and chandeliers and beautiful bright moonlight. Rags's muscles strained toward the exit instinctively and the grip on his wrists tightened, held him back, not even a grunt of effort from the Queensguard holding him.

"You'd best not," the one nearest him said. Simple, emotionless, without threats.

It did the trick.

Queensguard had a reputation for being off. The stories only got worse each year. Troops would turn up in the dead of night to evict entire rows of tenants for the Queen's mining expeditions. Whole neighborhoods went down so she could build her silver Hill higher. The displaced wound up beggars, or employed in the same mines being dug under their stolen homes.

Now Rags was in Queensguard custody, a gang of them to take care of one small thief, dragging him through what seemed to be the Queen's own white palace.

It didn't get stranger than this.

They hadn't been so quiet during Rags's last encounter with them. So stiff. In the lineup of a dozen men and women, not one coughed, jiggled, or hummed to make the walk go faster. No one so much as pretended to bait Rags with an insult about his height, which didn't sit right.

Their stark black uniforms, detailed with silver, turned them into shadows. They were all business, as though their mistress, the Queen, could see them everywhere, every heartbeat of every day, so they always had to be on their best behavior.

That thought gave Rags shivers, and he stepped down hard on it. Had to quit daydreaming. If he planned to see this bewildering trip through, figure out how to escape it, he had to pay attention.

A few more halls. The architecture was late Radiance period; this could only be home to a member of the Silver Court, a theory confirmed by the masterpieces—not forgeries—hung in lily-shaped frames between the windows. Then a brightly lit chamber, a chair at the far end flanked by two massive, wire-furred hounds. A lean young man sat dead center, his long black hair seeded with jeweled beads. At his back, another man, stockier, dressed entirely in red. Like a sorcerer.

Like a fucking sorcerer.

Shit, shit, shit.

The Queensguard didn't let Rags go, didn't give him the chance to bolt. One put his hand on the back of Rags's head and said, "Bow."

No choice. Down on his knees in front of some Ever-Noble, staring at his own filth-caked hands, fingers splayed on marble tile veined with silver.

"You need a bath," the young man in the chair said.

And a knife, and a way to turn back time, to be a good boy and ignore the rumors about jewels buried beneath an abandoned bank.

"'Snot all I need," Rags said. ". . . Your Importantness." That last bit earned him a boot to the side of the face—a boot with its toe cased in iron.

"Rise," the sorcerer commanded.

The Queensguard assisted Rags, shoving him forward. They let go of his wrists because they didn't need security, not now that the sorcerer had stepped forward, his eyes just visible between swaths of bloodred fabric.

The sorcerer continued, "We'll kill you if you don't agree to our proposal."

"I agree to your proposal," Rags said.

The sorcerer shook his head. The cloth around his mouth and nose didn't stir with his breath, sending a shiver through Rags's body. The rumors that sorcerers didn't have to breathe couldn't be true.

Was he the last thing the Queen's most recent enemies, the Ever-Loyals, had seen before their eyes had glazed over for good? Someone should've noticed that Rags didn't belong in their noble, deceased company.

"Let's eat first," the sorcerer said. "Shall we?"

3
RAGS

No names were offered, but they were generous with their food. Rags's manners had the wiry hounds looking away in shame, but no one corrected him or was stupid enough to bring out a knife and fork to help him eat. He ate with his hands. At least they had brought him a basin of clean water and scented soap to wash them in first.

He had caught sight of himself in the surface of the water before he disturbed it. Hollows in his cheeks, under his dark eyes. The split in his lip was worse than he'd thought, definitely going to scar. He took in his sharply angled features, the mouth that felt permanently twisted. The posture and attitude of a magpie, with the bird's shifty, quick grace. Black hair curling over the curves of his ears. The lobe of the right had been torn, the hoop that once hung there ripped out in his latest tussle with the Queensguard.

All that work, skillfully avoiding every trap, only to have *Queensguard* waiting for him at the end of the maze. It still smarted. The Gutter King was laughing in his vault somewhere.

And counting his un-stolen jewels.

The memory offered revelation. "*Oh*. You want me to steal something for you. Right?" Rags caught the Ever-Noble's flicker of surprise and kept smug triumph from crossing his own face. "Figures.

Even though I got pinned by your guys, you still think *I'm* the pawn for your special job?"

The Ever-Noble tipped his head back with a faint smile.

Rags's eyes naturally picked out the shiny first: A shimmer of chain against the man's dark skin, connecting the gold ring in his ear and the one in his nose. A whisper of metallic thread crosshatching his midnight-blue tunic. The gilt finish of his smoking slippers, the pure silver signet ring adorning his left hand. All these things told Rags that the Ever-Noble was a mover and shaker. Coming up in the world, doing well for himself, and showing off *too* much, like all new money.

The sorcerer's eyes showed nothing, reminded Rags of polished stone. Reflecting, not revealing.

Rags's throat was still dry. He contemplated drinking the water in the basin he'd used to wash his filthy face and filthier hands.

"You did well in the test," the sorcerer said, and waited for this to sink in. When Rags swore, comprehension dawning, he continued: "Yes, I designed the obstacle course below the bank. You evaded every trap, save for the final one. Had you done that . . ."

"You would have been in trouble, Morien," the Ever-Noble said, a flash of fire in his eyes. "No need to withhold names any longer. He's the one for the job. Let's treat him well."

Morien. *Morien the Last.* Rags recognized the name from rumors only. His mind spun. *Last what? Last in his class, or last thing you see before he tears out your still-beating heart and eats it with eggs at breakfast?*

Morien shrugged beautifully, heavily. "As your will commands, my lord Faolan Ever-Learning. This thief *is* the one for the job."

Rags swore again, curses so colorful that when his voice broke and he fell silent, Lord Faolan Ever-Learning of the Silver Court applauded him for his inventiveness.

Faolan wasn't just your average lily-soft Ever-Noble. Most thieves worth their spot in the Clave knew better than to steal from House Ever-Learning, because young Lord Faolan worked directly under the Queen.

Poor folk kept track of that kind of thing. Needed to know who was too dangerous to be worth stealing from.

Rags's old friend Dane from Cheapside would've eaten this story up. But Cheapside was a long way from the royal Hill, Dane was long dead, and Rags was in the deep shit now.

Lost-Lands help him, he wanted to know how deep.

4
RAGS

They had him clean up first, while also, Rags figured, letting him stew in curiosity for hours, so he'd drive himself wild with the need to know what came next.

He only allowed himself to properly boil once he'd bathed and changed and prodded at the split in his lip in front of a spotless mirror, in a waiting room that would've held half of all the street rats with allegiance to the Clave. With space to spare. Family portraits hung in gilded frames; the window fixtures were wrought from precious metal, the chairs upholstered in the finest velvet.

Of course, the Queensguard was watching, so Rags couldn't make off with the lot stuffed down his pants.

He dressed in clothes that had been left for him: trousers without holes and a belt with pouches. The belt was magnificently useful. Everything else was too much, especially the cowl-necked tunic, fluttering hem so crooked it had to be on purpose. All in black, with a pair of soft leather boots he'd hawk if he made it out of this in one piece.

No harm in wearing them for this job, learning what life without foot blisters was like.

Rags whistled at the picture he made. Tugged the draped fabric up and around to hide his nose and mouth. Looked like a child playing in an older sibling's clothes.

Save for the boots, which were a perfect fit, every item of clothing was at least a size too big. Rags wasn't troubled. Most of the clothes he owned had been purchased for someone else to wear.

He couldn't remember the last time he'd been so *clean*. His skin was pink, tingling from the rough scrubbing. His hair clung wet to his forehead and the back of his neck. His hands were dry and peeling around the nails, but otherwise unharmed.

One of the Queensguard caught him flexing his fingers and examining his knuckles, and cleared her throat. Rags tried to stop looking so suspicious after that. It was dawn when Morien and Faolan returned. Rags watched through the window as the sun began to climb, turning Cheapside's seemingly endless line of tin shanties briefly gold. From the Hill sprawled Westside, where folks were nearly as rich, but their houses weren't as well guarded; and Northside, which was merchant and shop territory, the newly rich, who were about as trustworthy as Cheapsiders and Clave thieves. Sinkholes, a hazard from all the collapsed mining tunnels, pocked the fallen Eastside district.

Didn't stop desperate orphans from trying to take shelter in the rubble. Every month, their corpses were discovered in the shifting dust and cracked stone.

Loss of an entire neighborhood led to more overcrowding in Cheapside—the city's poorest district, and Rags's home. The view from on high transformed his old sneaking grounds into something beautiful, angular, like lines on a map, instead of the familiar, stink-soaked back alleys Rags was so fond of disappearing into.

Then the door opened, the lord and his sorcerer entered, and the Queensguard left. Only the dogs stood between Rags and Faolan.

They cowered aside, made way for Morien the Last.

"My favorite part of the test you designed was the bit with the barbed arrows that came at me from every direction," Rags told Morien. "That was fun."

Had the Gutter King's vault ever lain in wait for him, or had it been a ruse from the start? *Was* there a Gutter King anymore? Rags didn't know what to believe and, as always, decided not to believe in anything, except his quick fingers.

"There's worse where you're going." Morien stood by the window. The sunlight revealed black threads veining the red cloth he wore, like branches against a burning sky. No—like the creep of deadly poison through blood.

"That was my favorite part, too." Faolan patted the head of the dog nearest him affectionately. "What do you know of the Lost-Lands, little thief?"

What *did* one trash-raised, trash-named thief know about the Lost-Lands? The same stories every guttersnitch knew: extravagant lies, elaborate inventions. *Once upon a lost-time, Oberon Black-Boned ruled a glittering court, as beautiful as it was treacherous. His fae Folk were handsome, strong, and brilliant, but inhuman and terribly cruel. Their beauty was the lure, their nails and teeth sharp.*

Through subterfuge or sheer luck, armed with sorcery and shadowy pacts, humanity had managed to destroy them all. Even after their annihilation, the mere thought of them or their Lost-Lands still traced its fangs along the back of Rags's neck, raised the hairs there. As though echoes of fearsome fae remained, ready to enact ghostly vengeance despite being buried long ago.

Instead of letting on how the thought chilled him raw, Rags snorted. "That if I don't finish my vegetables every night, I'll be taken away, replaced in my bed by a changeling, and fed to Oberon's children finger by finger."

Faolan waved a hand. His dogs watched it move, accustomed to treats. "Regardless of what you believe in, we've discovered an intriguing ruin. You'll be brought there—you'll have to be blindfolded much of the way—then charged with leading my explorers through its pitfalls successfully."

"And if I'm not successful?"

"You aren't our first choice," Morien said.

"Or our fifth," Faolan added.

"Seven have already tried and failed."

Faolan sighed deeply. "Poor number six."

So the whispers of the Gutter King's vault had lured more than Rags and his clever hands. Made sense. A big score bred big competition. He should've suspected something sideways right from the start.

Wherever Blind Kit was, Rags couldn't decide whether to curse her or hope she was still breathing.

He settled on both.

"What's the pay?" he demanded.

"You keep your life if you succeed," Morien replied.

There was no reason to assume that was a joke. Rags regretted opening his mouth.

"But"—Faolan offered a weary smile—"if it makes you feel better about your prospects, Morien's tests have grown more difficult with each vaultbreaker. You made it through his hardest one yet!"

"Lord Faolan believes in the importance of hope," Morien said.

"And you?" Rags asked.

"Like any drug, it has its uses," Morien replied. "And like any drug, too much is fatal."

Faolan waved his hand again. "No more theatrics, Mor. It's getting old. Just do the awful thing so we can prepare for the eighth expedition."

Morien turned away from the window, the sun at his back. His eyes had changed color. They were death-shroud white. He held up one hand and said, "Be still."

Rags didn't feel it when he fell to his knees, but he heard the echoes of Morien's footsteps, each strong enough to shatter his bones, as the sorcerer crossed the room. Darkness drew around them like a pair of raven's wings folded against rain. Morien touched Rags's jaw, tilting his face upward. The sorcerer's fingertips traced the large vein in Rags's throat until it stilled. The world pitched gray, became shadow. Rags opened his mouth and no sound came out.

"You will obey," a voice commanded. It sounded like three Moriens speaking at once. A hand on Rags's chest. Something sharp, cold, slid into it, through the skin, past muscle, between bones, lodging itself in his heart.

Mirrorcraft. The word passed in nervous whispers from eave to gutter through the lower city. Only Queen Catriona Ever-Bright's sorcerers practiced the mysterious art.

Then Morien's voice was in Rags's ear: "If you try to run, the shard of mirrorglass I've placed within you will shatter and shred your heart's muscle into a thousand pieces."

As he said it, the shard within Rags vibrated, threatening to slice his heart apart then and there. Something inside him, not a part of him. The wrongness of it was like biting down onto a nail in bread, a mean trick some bakers used when cooling loaves on the sill. Ruining their own goods to punish hungry orphans with sticky fingers.

"You understand." Morien's voice was quiet, but it flooded Rags's head like a chorus. "I've devised a trap you can't escape. We own you. You'll do as I wish, until I decide otherwise. And when you're no longer of value, I will kill you."

In reply, Rags vomited, then blacked clean out.

They gave him a horse to ride. Given Rags's lack of experience with horses, he had told them it would be faster if they tied him to the shitting end of one and let him walk.

But all Morien had had to do was touch the beast's snorting nose, and it bowed its head, pressed its brow to Morien's brow. After that, it gave Rags no trouble.

However, its glossy muscles jostled Rags with every step, and by the end of their first day riding, his ass was bruised, his thighs sore, his fingers cramped from clutching the reins for dear life.

He rubbed his hands together over the campfire, not too close to the flames, cracking his knuckles and easing every ache. He thought about the shard of sorcerer's mirror-magic in his heart and crept closer to the warmth. Nothing could heat his chilled flesh.

Lord Faolan Ever-Learning wasn't accompanying them on their journey, but he'd sent six of the Queen's best Queensguard, led by Morien, and one of his dogs, who had refused to be wooed with half of Rags's sausage at dinner. The hound had eaten it, of course, but didn't get friendlier for it, and he still slept at Morien's side.

Fucking waste of a sausage.

The first night under the open sky, far from the city Rags knew from crooked cranny to cunning corridor, found him sleepless, staring at the stars.

He was worrying a hole in one too-long sleeve, biting where it covered his knuckle. If he tried to run, the shard in his chest would shred his heart to scraps. Not a pleasant way to die. The best he could imagine for his future was a full pardon and being turned back to the streets where he belonged—*with the shard* still *in his heart to ensure he never spoke of this mission to anyone.*

It wasn't much hope, but that was for the best, since hope and Rags didn't get along.

He touched his chest, imagined he could feel the shard through his rib cage, and withdrew his hand. Above, a canopy of stars shimmered, marking shapes he knew from bastardized street versions: the Swan-Slayer, the Sheep-Fucker, the Shitting Lad.

"Those aren't the names *I* learned," Dane had said once, wide-eyed at Rags's filthy mouth, his filthier fingernails, and the impression he immediately gave of being a bad influence. Rags, age twelve at the time, had informed Dane he was simpler than a headless chicken if he didn't think that mess of stars looked exactly like a man bending over and pulling his trousers down.

"And that's where his—"

"I see it now," Dane had said, eager to end the conversation. Sorry he'd started it. Laughing despite himself.

Like always.

Rags blinked, thought he saw one star shake free from the swan's beak and arc downward, brightly burning. Another blink revealed it was a trick of tired eyes. Rags closed them, threw his elbow over his forehead to block out the world, and forced himself to rest.

6
RAGS

Another day of tireless riding through homely farmland, now under ceaseless drizzle. The Queensguard remained eerily silent. Old bruises got banged around, joined by new ones. Farmhouses dotted the fields, smoke rising from chimneys. They passed field laborers—whose lot in life was a fate that made Rags shudder as much as the shard in his heart—farm animals, piles of dung, rotting vegetables for fertilizer.

It was horrible. If he lived through this, he'd never leave the city again. A steamy cluster of stone buildings and too many crowded bodies, with the Queen on her Hill watching them scuttle about like ants: that was his turf.

He missed it fiercely.

Would he ever return to his Cheapside? Now, in the daylight, Rags tried again to envision a way this ended well. Morien the Last was a name that stuck to the darkest parts of the city, whispered in alleyways, swirling on the dockside breeze. It was rumored he'd fought in the Fair Wars, or his master had, yet he looked no older than a man in his early twenties. No one had seen his full face in years, but the straightness of his back and the lack of wrinkles around his fathomless eyes gave everyone pause.

The Queen's sorcerers were technically on the side of the people, but no one liked how they hid their faces, how they used mirrorcraft.

Generations of bred-in-bone fear of the fae didn't disappear. It was slowly transferring to the next obvious target. Morien the Last was just another bogey snatching innocents from the street.

And Rags wasn't above superstition. The stories he'd heard about Morien curled hair, and now here they both were.

Allies?

No, closer to hunting dog and master, the former kept on a short leash. Nothing good would come of pretending he was anything like a partner to Morien.

At least Lord Faolan's hounds got a nip of meat and a warm place to sleep every night, scritches on the head, fond words. Rags was in less cozy a position.

The morning of the third day, Morien woke Rags before dawn. He held a blindfold, a swatch of black-threaded red, the same fabric as the sorcerer's robes. A quick glance around revealed that the six Queensguard already wore them. The fabric didn't look thick enough to keep anyone from seeing the ugly farmland they were bound to pass, but the moment it was tied around Rags's head, sunlight disappeared.

Rags couldn't see or hear or smell. He couldn't open his mouth and assumed that meant he couldn't speak. Panic swelled within him. He fought it down. Panic was the death knell of rational thought, and he *needed* to be able to think clearly in the face of this magic.

Don't pay attention to what you can't do. Remember what you can.

He could still breathe, wanted to keep breathing.

Trapped alone with his heartbeat, his grip on the reins, the queasy rocking of the cantering horse between his legs. The aches and bruises faded from his senses, as though those too were dulled by the sorcerous blindfold. He tried to keep track of time, but without the shifting of the sun's warmth over his skin, he couldn't be sure he hadn't lost count of the hours somewhere along the ride. He began to miss the fertilizer smell. Anything would have been better than the loneliness, than worrying he was the only person left alive in the world, a nasty horse his sole companion.

Time unspooled, lost its structure. All day and into the night— then the next night, then the next. What felt like an hour might've been an hour, but it might've been a minute. Rags had no notion of how long they'd traveled. He lost count of the rhythmic beat of his horse's hooves. Every time he tried to concentrate on them, the blindfold bwith his brain.

The one thing he did know for sure was that the Queen's sorcerers weren't supposed to be able to touch people's minds like this. This was old fae magic, the kind no one living had witnessed.

Except for Morien the Last, if the rumors were true and he *had* been alive during the Fair Wars.

What had Rags gotten himself mixed up in?

Nah. Don't sweat it.

Wherever it was they were going, Morien *really* didn't want him to know anything about it. That made Rags want to know more, contrary as a pissed-off cat facing down a closed door.

The memory of the shard in his heart tamed him.

He kept himself company with rhymes, the scraps and phrases he'd overheard at night in Clave lodging. Tenement stuff, pure trash, but catchy. If he lied to himself, he could pretend to be huddled on a rooftop, catching a grimy glimpse of starlight overhead, hearing rough voices bellowing below:

> *Oberon comes when the moons are high.*
> *Polish your silver, the end is nigh. . . .*

7
RAGS

At some point—day or night, Rags had given up trying to guess which—the horse stopped moving, knelt to urge Rags off. He steadied himself one-handed on the powerful neck, found his bedroll, and spread it out close to the horse's side. He leaned his face against its flank without smelling its sweat or feeling its heat.

It must have been Morien who pressed the hunk of bread into his hands.

Rags shaped the food with his palms and fingertips first, running his thumb over the crumbs, the crust. Then he practiced his craft in total, dead sightlessness, soundlessness, breaking the hunk apart shape by shape and lining the pieces in what he hoped was a straight line on his bedroll.

Good exercise for keeping his fingers limber.

He had to stay nimble, on top of his game, for what lay ahead.

He ate after.

Without the stars to watch, he fell into sleep quickly, and Morien, true to his word, didn't give him any dreams. Rags wasn't used to that. He made his living sticking his fingers into everyone else's business, expecting the same courtesy in return. Maybe Morien really couldn't read minds.

Why bother? He could shred hearts.

The next morning, the blindfold was gone. Rags blinked, staring up into a canopy of silvery leaves dusted with distant sunlight. What had woken him was the hush of life creeping back into his periphery, faintly, a curtain still drawn between him and the world. Only this time the curtain was the thickness of the forest, not a magicked cloth.

Tall black trees flashed an unexpectedly hoary gleam in the corners of his eyes. Thick ropes of spider silk, centuries abandoned by its spinners, cobwebbed their branches. Birds sang somewhere else, but not here.

Not daring to sing here.

Morien held an apple core. The horses were blindfolded, unnaturally still, and the Queensguard's blindfolds hadn't been removed. Only Rags had that honor.

"Morning," Morien said.

The ache of Rags's bruises came back to him, along with a crick in his neck from sleeping twisted. He rolled his thin shoulders. Dirt in his hair. He smelled of rain. His bedroll, damp.

"*Is* it morning?" Rags asked.

Morien stood, setting the apple core aside instead of ensorcelling it to disappear. "Come with me."

Not an answer, but it was go with Morien or stay behind with the Queensguard—spread out, unmoving, like carvings on old graves—and the slow-breathing horses.

Rags knew which wretched choice he preferred.

He rose, stretching his legs, and did his best not to stumble after Morien. He settled for a slow-paced hobble and pretended he didn't see the trees moving out of Morien's way, inching ever so slightly aside to give him a wider berth. The last of the familiar brown and gray branches parted to slender black trunks only, varieties of trees Rags had never seen, whose names he'd never want to learn. They stood in tight clusters, growing gnarled and scattered along the path Morien chose. Sparse red leaves blossomed in violent splashes across the bark, clumping into deeper purple like bruises closer to the roots. Though the growth was weak and small and the wood looked dead, the colors themselves were brilliant, a poisonous warning. Rags's neck prickled. This wasn't natural.

He'd heard stories about the Lost-Lands. Everyone had. It was one thing to hear a tale about a distant place, one lost to human eyes forever. Another to see it unfurling right in front of his nose.

This place was impossible.

Rags standing here was impossible.

His eyes rejected what they saw. If he shut them, would the landscape disappear? Or would Morien simply assume he wasn't ready for this task and kill him where he stood?

Too much of a risk to take.

"Forest at the edge of the Lost-Lands?" Rags's mouth moved of its own volition.

This, Rags understood, was why he'd been blindfolded. Morien couldn't let him know how to get here on his own.

Morien didn't grace Rags with a reply, the answer so obvious, it didn't require confirmation. Rags would have rolled his eyes, only every time he looked somewhere new, the air shimmered, the shadows shifted, and the glowing of the mist-draped bark intensified, all to dizzying effect. Looking at his feet didn't help, since light dappled the moss and roots so it seemed like the ground rippled with constant, liquid movement.

Rags wondered how much he'd get for a handful of those red leaves, if it would be possible to steal a cutting to bring back to the city.

Nah. Bad idea to start plucking magical plants without knowing if they'd curse him for trying.

Rags focused on his hands instead, imagining rolling a coin between his knuckles, distracting himself from the crazy stew he'd landed in.

There were too many legends about the Lost-Lands. Mostly, they concerned what those lands were before they were lost. Home to the fae: heartless kidnappers and baby eaters who'd slice open your pet dog to keep jewels in, quick as they'd give you a second look.

They'd slice you open and use your skin next.

With every step, Rags couldn't shake the conviction that he was intruding on something best left sleeping.

Though Rags didn't have a mother to remember, there'd been plenty of those older and wiser in the dregs of Cheapside offering free advice—most of it bad. He'd grown up knowing what anyone with a bit of common sense knew: there were no fae to be frightened of anymore.

The Queensguard had made crossroads and countryside safe for simple folk. It'd been hundreds of years since anyone had caught a glimpse of one of Oberon's wicked children. Only the Queen's sorcerers used magic these days.

But here Rags was.

Morien watched him as if he could read Rags's thoughts as quickly as Rags could think them.

Rags shifted his focus.

Think about the coin, not the politics behind it. Thieves before him had come this way. Maybe not all of them had disappeared due to the dangerous terrain. Maybe they'd spoken their minds at the wrong moment to an unsympathetic ear.

Under his red scarves, Morien's ears looked very unsympathetic. They also looked slightly too small for his head.

"I can't wait to die in this place," Rags said.

"Remain silent," Morien ordered.

The first sign of ruins resembled a tree stump—it might have been one once—ringed with moss and petrified with age. Then there was a set of steps, a barely noticeable thinning of the trees, an archway, broken at the top and smothered in vines. Rags nudged one leafy branch aside with his elbow to find stone beneath, misty white, and realized as he let the vine fall back that its leaves were part silver. *Real* silver. Half greenery, half precious metal. Break off enough of those gilded things and he'd be rich—

"Can I take things?" Rags blurted out. "Not the treasure you lot are after, but littler stuff? If I see it?"

Morien turned, taking notice of what had caught Rags's attention. "They'll attack you if you try that," he said.

As if in response, the vines stirred, despite the still air. Rags shoved his hands into his pockets. "If that's true, this place won't be easy to rob."

"This isn't the place. It's the first doorway."

Rags peered through the archway. "Aren't the rest of the gang coming?"

"They'll follow when it's safe."

"Any advice from past failures?"

Morien shrugged lightly beneath the bower. "There are door-ways, and we aren't sure how many. Your predecessors have made it past the first five. When one is opened"—Morien handed him a polished pocket mirror—"let me know."

"What's this for?" Rags took the slender compact between two fingers. "Can't you wiggle your fingers and make me dance?"

The second he said it, Rags wished he hadn't.

Morien's eyes betrayed nothing but boredom. "This connection will prove most reliable once you are in the depths of the ruins" was all he said.

So it was true. Not only the fae themselves, but their buildings—their ruins—were magic. What else but magic could interfere with a sorcerer's power?

Rags regretted his quick decision to hunt Lord Faolan's treasure.

Not that he'd had another choice.

"Not gonna tell me how the others made it through the first two doors, huh?"

"Figure it out yourself and consider it practice."

Something twinged in Rags's chest. It hurt, but he wouldn't show how bad. On the streets, any sign of weakness was a signal to others: *Easy pickings.*

He shrugged and stepped under the archway. There he found an enormous flagstone, the first in a path. Veins of ore in the marbled rock thinned into age rings.

There were a lot of rings.

Surrounding him, like judgmental sentinels, the tall trees' needle-thin branches twisted in unnatural shapes, embracing nothing but damp, woodsy air. Like an empty frame, its painting stolen.

There had been something grand here once. The archway he'd stepped under had only been the outer gate of something much, much bigger, the shape of which could still be traced by the way branches bent out of the way of its memory. As Rags followed the path, he tried to imagine the ancient structure, now less than ruin, that had so warped the trees. He stepped lightly, expecting the first trap immediately, but the path carried him forward, footfall by footfall, without trying to kill him.

Lull him into a false sense of security. Get him to drop his guard.

Not going to happen.

A stone missing from the path gave Rags pause, made him look back over his shoulder. Morien waited on the other side of the arch. He hadn't followed Rags through.

Back to the break in the pathway. Rags poked it lightly with one toe, testing if it would hold or open up beneath his weight, if the vines and roots would snarl out at him and drag him away.

Nothing.

Rags stepped over it onto the next stone.

The silence in the ruins wasn't bad compared to the nothingness of Morien's blindfold. Rags could hear the sounds his boots made when they touched the ground. He was fine.

Then the earth began to rise around him and he stopped short. He was descending, the ground he stood on a platform, slowly lowering him. The earth was swallowing him, sort of. Flanking him on both sides were walls of dirt veined with silver and slabs of ghost-white rock. Arches like ribs, or teeth. It was like being guided into the warm, open mouth of a beast from legend. And the beams, or bones, whatever they were, glowed in spots, lighting his way forward.

He wouldn't have objected to having a sorcerer with him for this.

Rags licked his lips, prodding the scabbed-over split with his tongue. The old itch to touch, to *feel* everything around him so he could learn what made it tick had his fingertips twitching, but years of training and better instincts kept his hands at his side. In a place where the vines would kill you for fondling them, he couldn't be reckless. Not even to see if the ribbed wall arches were as smooth as they looked.

Fae-work. Definitely. The real deal, not the knockoffs you could buy for cheap in back alleys: *Chunk off the base stones of the fabled Lone Tower, prevents colds, wards off the plague, cures back trouble, wear it around your neck and impress your friends!*

Swindlers, preying on the superstitious. Not like Rags, who stole honestly, never pretended to be anything more than a thief.

Which had led him here, into this dark cavern, glints of blue light drawing him deeper into the ruin. The shapes they formed were like eye sockets in skulls, rows of teeth, long fingers pointing him on.

A crypt, Rags suspected. Where the dead were buried with their treasures. Legends told of the fae's last stand at the Lone Tower, and plenty of dead fae warriors meant plenty of unguarded treasure.

Treasure Rags was here to find, take, and trade for his life.

Rags didn't know where in the lost fae lands Morien had led him, but wouldn't it be a sidesplitter if he was actually exploring the real Lone Tower—a sneaky flea crawling through the stacked pages of ancient history?

Until the path stopped—was stopped—by a solid silver door. To its left, a few-months-old corpse slumped into itself, knees to chest.

The first test.

Rags folded his legs under him and sat. The door had the answers. *Somewhere.*

And Rags had to find them, unless he wanted to join Corpse-y over there in lifeless eternity.

8

RAGS

Rags knew better than to simply push the door open. After a few proper once-overs, he noticed handprints etched into its silver filigree, a pattern so fine he had to tilt his head to one side, squint hard, to see it. Four pairs of handprints overlapped at the top of the door, while a pair in the center touched fingertip to fingertip, all of them significantly larger than Rags's hands. None of them revealed a clue—not one Rags could read, at least—to how to open the door and not die. Or how to open the door at all, death included.

Rags held his hand up to the last of the prints without touching the surface of the door. His thumb pointed downward, like a sign for *no luck, you're fucked.*

Hands. It had something to do with hands. It didn't take a genius to land on that hope, since there was no visible lock, nothing to pick. Rags gingerly felt his way around the frame without touching the door itself to see whether there were loose parts or a stone he needed to push, like the one he'd stepped on to lower him into the earth.

Nothing.

He was going to have to touch the door eventually.

He glanced, not for the first time, at the corpse. "Wouldn't mind some help."

The corpse, being dead, had no answer. But a worm inched out of its hair, down the fall of black, onto its shoulder.

The corpse was dressed well. Most corpses of Rags's acquaintance weren't. In Cheapside, the dead were covered with whatever cloth scraps their neighbors had to spare. A tattered shirt, a stained old handkerchief, someone's torn trousers. It was traditional to shroud the dead until they were carted off for burial.

It gave the corpses some dignity back after being picked clean by thieves.

The worm approached Rags's boot, then started back slowly the way it had come, inching up a leg and into the folds of the corpse's sleeve. Rags told himself he was better than this, better than getting stuck at only the first doorway.

For the moment, Rags gave up on the door and knelt nearer to the corpse instead, drawn by the movement of fabric that the worm managed to stir. Barely perceptible, but there.

The corpse's pale, silken sheet of long hair spilled like a waterfall over its face, its knees. A bit much for a common thief. All flash and no substance. No wonder they hadn't made it far.

Rags brushed the hair out of the way, then recoiled as he met empty eye sockets and black—*black?*—bone.

He gasped and fell backward onto his ass.

Black-boned.

It couldn't be Oberon himself, but did that make Rags feel better? He was staring at a dead fae.

The corpse wasn't mere months old. Its clothing only appeared to be. There was nothing but more black bone under its sleeves, while its silver gloves, which glistened like wet flesh at the right angle, in this lighting, had deceived Rags for not yet completely rotted hands. They perched and met, fingertip to fingertip, on top of the corpse's bony knees.

Hands.

He didn't have to touch the door. Not risking his *own* fingers.

Rags grinned, calming the racing of his heart after the shock of meeting a fae skeleton. Without flinching—he knew his share of corpses and they didn't spook him, since the dead wouldn't fight you for a day's earnings—he pinched the sleeve between his fingertips. The fabric was cool and sleek, light as gossamer. Some kind of Lost-Lands fae bullshit.

This place was the real deal.

No wonder a sorcerer and an Ever-Noble were so obsessed with it, needed a master thief to break them into the place.

Rags stomped on the urge to shiver. Fae stories were hundreds of years old. No living fae, no new tales to tell.

Plundering a fae tomb should be simple enough. But being in this place gnawed on him like teeth on a bone.

In a setting best suited for myths and legends, Rags was an ant scuttling through a palace.

Keep moving.

He rolled the corpse's sleeves up to its black elbows and noticed neat silver hinges attaching them to the next bones. The metal was warm, as if it had recently been touched. Rags ran his thumb around the circumference, finding and flattening a silver disc. The forearm slid free with a sigh. Flopped into Rags's lap soft as a kiss. Rags set it aside, freed the second forearm, then held both by the wrists as he approached the door.

The gloved hands were unusually large, the perfect size to match the etchings. Rags held them up to the handprints, took a steadying breath, and pressed forward, bony palms to empty outlines.

The door swallowed the gloves like he'd poured water onto hot sand.

9
RAGS

After the door disappeared into the surrounding wall with the same liquid dissolution as the gloves, Rags was left holding two bare bone hands. Warm wind blew over him from the newly exposed path.

Though calling it a "path" was generous.

The room ahead was a chasm once spanned by a broken bridge now little more than a jagged platform. A crooked tooth in an otherwise empty mouth. The walls were decorated with the same style of arches that had surrounded Rags on his descent, only now he was going deeper, and there was nothing glowing to light his way. He could barely make out the knobbed shapes of twisting, metallic vines clinging to the stone.

Rags returned the arms to their owner—not like their owner missed them—and watched with grudging amazement as a force like magnetism drew them back, clicked to lock them into place. He set the hands on the corpse's knees the way they had been. No point in making things hard for the next guy. *Isn't going to be a next guy.* Then he rubbed his chest in thought.

When one is opened . . . let me know.

He fished the mirror out of his pocket, breathed on the glass. Wiped it clean.

"Uh," Rags said. "I'm letting you know?"

Silence followed. Rags couldn't make sense of whatever the connection was. Morien could reach into his head to talk outside the ruins—but not here. And he didn't seem to know what Rags was thinking. Good. Rags couldn't manage politeness inside *and* out, not at the same time.

"Hello?" Rags tapped the glass with one finger, feeling like a wet-brained idiot, when the sound of footsteps in heavy, single-file march revealed his success.

Rags turned to meet Morien and Lord Faolan's retinue of six Queensguard, still blindfolded.

"Funny idea of company you sorcerers have." Rags couldn't help himself, figured he'd earned a smart remark by passing through the first door. "All those swords can't be for *me*. You expecting we'll run into something else that'll need all that steel?"

Although Morien's scarves swathed only the bottom half of his face, his eyes were as cool and blank as mask-glaze as he regarded Rags.

Not impressed.

"I trust you have something of value to show me."

If there was this much secrecy to the venture, could a single shard of sorcery be enough to ensure Rags's silence? *No.* There was no reason to believe death didn't wait for him at the end of this, even if he managed to triumph where the others had failed.

Rags grimaced, pessimism having been his closest companion for the past sixteen years.

"There's a big hole." Rags jerked his chin toward it. "Should have brought a circus acrobat along, too. For jumping."

Trust the fae to lock a door that opened onto nothing. From every whispered rumor and legend about the fae bastards, Rags wasn't surprised they'd let him feel like he'd progressed, only to have him slam headfirst into another blockade.

"You've been nimble in past endeavors," Morien said.

Yeah, without an audience.

Rags turned his back on the sorcerer, facing the next chamber. Pit of agony? It was too dark to tell how deep down the hole went. He edged onto the silver path. Impossible to figure out what supported it. What supported *him*. Rags eyed the vines on the wall. He was slender, skinny. This had aided him in his chosen profession on many occasions in the past. No reason that couldn't continue.

"Question," Rags said. Morien's silence encouraged him to proceed. "How murderous *are* those vines?"

The sorcerer didn't deign to respond.

"Guess I'll find out for myself," Rags said, and reached for the nearest one.

10
RAGS

The vine he chose didn't try to kill him.

But the edges of the leaves were sharp, almost serrated, like a torturer's knife. They also folded, which Rags only discovered after he'd nicked his thumb at first touch. A warning before he discovered the trick to not slicing himself into ribbons.

Lovely and deadly, in keeping with what Rags knew about the fae.

Rags gave the vine a sample tug to see if it would hold—it held—then stepped onto the broken bridge. Its surface was slippery-smooth, like glass. He took a deep breath, wrapped the vine around one arm at the elbow, the wrist.

"This is nothing," Rags lied to himself.

He'd scaled Ever-House spires, their walls slick, purchaseless polished marble. He'd danced around the wrought-iron spikes lining their tiled roofs.

Climbing up was ten times easier than going down.

But there was no preparation adequate for leaping into a fae-made precipice toward your apparent doom. Rags closed his eyes before realizing that didn't help, either, and finally eased himself backward off the silvery edge of the half bridge into the darkness below.

For one terrible moment he hung there, gently swaying back and forth. Then he kicked out once, twice, finding the wall with the balls of his feet.

Hand over hand, like he'd practiced in the Clave, Rags lowered himself down the vine.

It was like being swallowed, traveling down the gullet of an enormous beast. Folklore said the fae had lived alongside the Ancient Ones, made dwellings from their bones. Those massive creatures who had roamed the world in its infancy and left their remains to fortify mountains, channel streams, cup the oceans, seed the forests.

Rags wasn't superstitious about the dead, but a bad feeling followed him in this place like eyes on the back of his neck.

He'd only wriggled down the height of two men before the dark gobbled him whole, abruptly shutting out the sight of Morien and the Queensguard. A lesser thief might've yelped in surprise. Rags held his tongue by biting its tip, sharpening his focus with a touch of pain. Cold, clammy under the collar, like a first-year pickpocket. It followed that he'd revert to one of their tricks, distracting himself from his nerves with a bit of verse.

Oberon comes when the moons are high—

No, that wasn't the kind of rhyme that brought comfort in the bowels of a fae ruin. His bootsoles scraped the pit wall as he rappelled down. Grit fell and vanished into the darkness. The vine flexed, metal supple under his fingers. What would a single polished leaf be worth?

Time for another rhyme, one about shiny secrets, not a litany of terrible things Oberon could do to lesser creatures.

Rags hummed to hear the sound echoing downward into silence.

Not every bit of doggerel about the fae was a warning. Some were promise.

He buried fae treasure, all silver and blood,
Deep in the earth, where sleeping things grow.
Measure by measure comes Oberon's flood,
More precious than gold, so final the blow.

A hidden fortune sleeping beneath the earth was something Rags could get behind.

Pleased with himself and unused to the sensation, he nearly missed the hairline fracture in the wall. He stopped sharp, already past it, running the sensitive pads of his fingers back over the space. The seam traveled in a perfect line.

Cut, not cracked.

Few others would have noticed it, but Rags's fingers were smarter, more sensitive. He'd trained them to pick out intricate but minute differences in any surface. He'd found an important one here, a groove in the stone. A thin, thin break, traveling down.

Rags chased it down to where it stopped at a pointed tip, drawn upward again on either side in a sharp V.

Didn't need to be a genius thief and expert lockpick to recognize the shape.

An arrow.

Rags lowered himself down the vine after it, found a circle of slippery-smooth stone below its point. When he settled his thumb against it, it depressed. Lights flooded on around him.

A lot of them.

His eyes adjusted to the shape the lights made: more arrows. Everywhere. Glowing seams in the stone walls. They filled the pit, flowing together and apart, a flock of identical geometries carved into the rock. Each of them pointed down.

The vine that was Rags's lifeline shifted, stretched, a breathing thing. He yelped as it slithered around his arm and away, spooling out beneath him in clockwork circles around the pit's walls. Rags dropped, scrambling for purchase, before landing on a jutting ledge of stone barely wide enough to hold him.

A narrow crack in the rocky wall to squeeze through.

An obvious pathway. How hospitable.

His time on the streets had taught him to be wary of *too much* help.

"Little eager for me to head that way, aren't you?" Rags said aloud.

In response, a real arrow shot through the air. Made entirely of silver, it narrowly missed taking off the end of his crooked nose.

"Shit," Rags said.

All he had breath for.

The arrows came in volleys of three, fired from every direction. Rags had scarcely ducked one before the next whisked past him, nicking his sleeve, lodging in stone.

The metal barbs left behind something black and sticky on his shirt. Poison? Rags sniffed it, then flared his nostrils at the acrid scent. *Hawkshade.*

If it got into his blood, he'd rot from the inside out.

Rags knew a man in the Clave who dabbled in toxins. The stuff messed with his head and he was always rattling off distracted ditties about his flowers. Silverseal caused shakes and blindness. Powdered redbell could make someone bleed to death inside before they showed a single outward symptom. Felltooth, a tasteless paralytic, stopped the heart last, kept it beating so a man could feel each part of himself die.

Hawkshade offered a quick end, without subtlety or suffering.

Morien wouldn't save Rags if he were poisoned. He'd find another thief, had probably left the bodies of Rags's predecessors to prove that.

Fine.

Rags could save himself. He always did. He squeezed through the crack in the wall, stumbling out into a tunnel.

More arrows.

Bent double at the waist to avoid the first volley, half falling into a crouch and weaving to avoid the next.

Where were they coming from? The walls themselves?

"Poison," Rags reminded himself sharply as he dodged another arrow, this one tearing his shirt at the small of his back. The refrain kept him keen. "Poison, poison, *poisonpoisonpoison.*"

Scrambling down the narrow path, moving without looking at his feet—had to keep his eyes on the arrows—Rags stumbled as the ground evened out under him.

At the bottom already?

Glancing up to see where he'd come from, Rags snapped into a roll that saved him from a skewering. Arrows pinged too close to his face. He rolled back onto his feet and plunged forward, past an archway of glowing arrow shapes cut into the walls, a volley of real arrows firing from them.

No light at the end of the tunnel. The door there sealed shut, same as Corpse-y's door. The constant assault of projectiles meant no opportunity for thoughtful examination. Rags was in constant motion, rappelling off the walls and floors, leaping like a flea from one orphan to the next.

There had to be something that triggered the arrows. They hadn't been firing when he first descended. His presence had tripped the attack.

How?

Rags shifted his attention to the walls and ceiling, spaces visible between the paths carved through the air by silver-fleet arrows.

There *was* a pattern to their firing. Like the steps of a complicated dance, they kept their own time. Rags breathed with their rhythm, fell into it, bobbing and lunging toward the end of the tunnel.

There was a pattern on the walls, too. What had once been a series of jagged V's pointing haphazardly in the same direction now looked like a series of right angles on the left-hand side only. They were still V's, but their tilt and order had grown, mimicking steps carved sideways into the rock.

Rags flung himself toward the nearest one, arms out, hands searching. His fingers caught a groove.

An arrow pinged off the wall near his elbow.

This was either stupid or brilliant. Rags ascended sideways along the wall, not his most graceful climb, until he'd risen bare inches above the many paths the arrows charted. One wrong placement of his hands and he'd drop back into their ceaseless volleying.

"There'd better be something *incredible* at the end of this," he wheezed.

His hands were slippery with sweat as he dug his fingers in tight to the stone grooves, holding on for dear life. No thief wanted to die in the dark, speared like a prize boar.

Hanging in place to catch his breath, surveying the lay of the land, he noticed what hadn't been visible to him below. A narrow ledge overhung the door at the end of the tunnel. A quiet, shadowed alcove. One spot the arrows weren't firing toward.

Rags jumped. Weightless, breathless. Then he landed, half crouched, half kneeling, on the slate.

His knee throbbed, having taken most of his weight. But he quickly forgot about the pain.

Before him, tucked into a second alcove within the first one, was a strange silver sculpture, intricate as the skeletal insides of a termite nest. Every part of it moved, ticking ahead and around with miniature mechanical parts. The effect made it look alive with crawling metal beetles.

Despite the danger below, Morien's mirror in his pocket, and Morien's shitting shard in his heart, Rags couldn't help himself.

He poked the thing.

Delicate clockwork pinched his finger, almost immediately providing the expected punishment for his stupidity. Rags tugged, then began to pry carefully at the spindly teeth that held his finger in place.

Rags had once found a broken, but quality, pocket watch on the street, its casing shattered, the back popped apart. The smooth inner workings of the silver termite nest resembled the inside of that watch, writ large in interlocking silver gears and rotating discs of polished crystal. Each piece flowed in seeming independence from the others, yet they all worked together to power the whole.

It was breathtakingly beautiful.

Beautiful for a thing that was, Rags suspected, controlling the arrows trying to kill him.

Rags reached in, pinching one of the visible gears between his fingers. The mechanism made a wrenching sound as it ground to a halt.

The steady *thwip thwip thwip* of arrows slowed. From the door below, he heard a *clunk*, the telltale sound of a bolt slipping free of its hole.

"Shh," Rags whispered hopefully, lulling the gears to sleep. "Shush now, there you go." The gear fought against his hold. When he let go, the mechanism stuttered back to life. Arrows began firing again. The door relocked.

Rags couldn't stay up here to hold the door open *and* slip through it at the same time. He had to jam the mechanism. Or break it. Do something permanent, so he'd have time to shinny back down, race through the door, and not be shot.

Bend one of the gears, and he'd throw the whole thing out of whack. Rags reached gingerly for another cog, less solid and thick than the first he'd grabbed. A skin-thin sheet of hammered silver. He pinched it between forefinger and thumb, then tried to pry up the edge before it disappeared under the toothy advance of another gear.

The metal fell apart under his hand. Something nipped his finger and Rags yelped, pulling back.

A tiny silver beetle had attached itself to the webbing of his hand, metal mandibles clenched around his flesh. At his touch, the disc had dissolved into a mass of insects, scuttling through the clockwork and buzzing angrily at Rags for his invasion. He reached to crush the beetle biting his hand and it opened its shell, metal wings beating a rapid reprimand. Rags shook his hand, smashing it against the wall in retaliation.

The beetle's humming stuttered, then increased in volume. Bright red drops of blood welled and dribbled down Rags's wrist. He smashed his palm into the wall, slamming the bug against the stone over and over.

Finally, it fell in a flutter of silver. Rags didn't pause to watch it drop between the arrows. He turned back to the gears, beetles swarming in the machinery without gumming up the works.

Another example of dirty fae magic.

Oh, a simple murder chamber with arrows and locks is too easy, Rags imagined them saying. *What's the point of a trap that doesn't fight back every chance it gets?*

Unfortunately, there were no fae left to curse.

So Rags did the sensible thing: grabbed a nearby rock, rolled his sleeve down to protect his bleeding hand, and plunged both rock and hand into the beetle-infested nightmare.

Easy—if you don't mind pain. A good thief could turn his impediments against themselves, spin obstruction into a way to the prize.

Rags wasn't much, but he was a good thief.

With the crunch of splintering metal and a plaintive whine, the machinery ground to a slow halt.

Rags heard the door's bolt slide back once again. The volley of arrows died, replaced by yawning silence in the tunnel. The last of the beetles fell, twitched, stilled.

Rags crept to the edge of the alcove and climbed down the way he'd come.

On the floor amid the scattered black shafts of the arrows lay the first beetle, the one that had bitten him.

"Could be worth something," Rags told himself, and pocketed it.

But the door was open, and that was more important. Heavy stone he didn't trust not to fall as he darted underneath, feeling foolish but relieved when the slab didn't hurtle down to crush him.

On the other side, Rags popped the mirror from his pocket and notified Morien that he was taking a break. Much needed. Completely justified. He'd opened two doors already.

"It's three, actually."

Rags hadn't realized his eyes were closed until Morien's voice alerted Rags to his presence.

The sorcerer was holding out an apple. Rags took it and bit into it, didn't ask where it'd come from.

"What d'you mean, three?"

"Had you not located the switch, you would have continued your descent into a bottomless pit, indefinitely," Morien said coolly. "That too was one of the doors. Now finish that apple. You'll need your strength."

Like Morien needed to tell a Cheapsider not to waste food.

But there was something off about the fruit. Sweet at first, it had a bitter aftertaste that lingered, and it was too rejuvenating to be a normal, nonmagic apple. Rags hated to think of the trouble he'd gone to to avoid being poisoned by fae arrows if he was only going to ingest Morien's willingly.

But Morien had more efficient ways of killing Rags, if he wanted Rags dead.

"You'd better go back for the Queensguard," Rags said around a mouthful of apple. "Unless your boys in black have some immunity to hawkshade us commoners don't know about?"

Morien's reaction to that statement was a blank expression, not even a rippling of the cloth around his nose and mouth. It told Rags all he needed to know about the sort of person he was dealing with. It didn't matter to Morien who stepped on a poisoned arrow as long as *he* got to where he was going.

Still, when Morien disappeared and Rags was alone again, he felt a strange sense of loss.

It wasn't loneliness. Easier to account for only one set of hands, one mind with a purpose. Getting other people involved was, without fail, where Rags's plans *always* went sideways.

He whistled roughly, pressing back against the weight of the walls closing in on him. Straightened his shoulders in a display of fake defiance. He didn't have a fear of tight spaces, but he *did* have the sense that this place *really* didn't want him around.

Rather than swallowing him up, the walls wanted to spit him out.

It was the rejection that ruffled his feathers.

11
RAGS

It wasn't long into his search for the fourth door, along underground paths illuminated only by the dimly glowing fae carvings in the walls, that he found the next corpse.

Impossible to guess the age on this one, because its face and chest had been chewed open and hollowed out like a Lastday turkey.

Decidedly not a fae this time. The air around the body stank of dead meat. Rags had smelled worse, but not much. He swallowed back a gulp and marched forward, determined not to meet the same fate, showing the dead thief the same respect they would have showed him.

None.

He rounded a corner—and nearly ran into himself.

He stopped short, breath catching, to avoid breaking his beak on the iridescent surface in front of him. Fae glass. Thicker yet more brittle than human glass. As multicolored as opal, as tricky as an oil slick.

The Rags in the glass wavered, looking startled as he swayed from side to side. When Rags turned away from his reflection, it was to find another wall of glass sliding into place behind him.

"No going back." Rags watched his reflection's mouth move. No sound echoed outward.

Creepy. He turned his back on it to continue down the glass-walled path.

At the end of the mirrored corridor he turned another corner. Just ahead, the path split right and left. He paused. Risked a glance at his reflection.

"Don't suppose you know the way?"

The Rags in the polished glass shook his head. Slowly at first, his pupils expanded, then all at once devoured his eyes, filling them with blank, eerie black.

"Yeah. Never mind. Never doing *that* again." Rags returned his gaze to the floor, fending off a shudder. "I'll figure it out myself."

He took a step to the right but sprang back immediately as the heavy stone tile beneath his boots started to sink, then fell away like a broken trapdoor. Only blackness, like his reflection's eyes, stared up at him.

The chasm was too wide to jump. Rags had no choice but to go left.

"In case anyone's listening, I hate this." He reached into his pocket and felt the slippery surface of the mirror there. If he held it up, had Morien face the fae glass, what would the sorcerer see?

Cheering himself by imagining something that could give Morien the same heebies he gave everybody else, Rags slid his booted foot forward along the floor, paying closer attention to the seams between the tiles. The silence was starting to make his skin crawl when a warped laugh cackled its way across glass and stone. *"Hate this, hate this."*

That was his voice. His laugh, though he hadn't laughed like that, open and full-bellied, since— Had he ever laughed like that? Rags squeezed his eyes shut, then forced himself to open them. He needed to keep watch on that shifty floor. Literally shifty. It had already opened up right under him.

When he came to the next fork in the path, he was presented with three choices. Straight ahead, left, or right.

It was a maze. A fucking fae maze, made of fucking fae glass, with a fucking fae reflection giggling like a madman at him from the darkness.

Rags was going to compose a new lullaby poem inspired by the fae. It started like:

> *Fuck the fucking fae forever.*
> *Spelunk in their fae caves never.*

A work in progress.

A hiss snapped across the floor behind him. Rags jumped like a brandscale snake had ankled him. Forward, straight ahead, his choice made by gut instinct more than skill. The stone beneath his feet dropped and he lunged desperately back, just in time to avoid being plunged into darkness. Off balance, Rags stumbled instead toward the left-most corridor, where a pair of hands caught him before he could hit the wall, gave him a hard shove between the shoulder blades.

Whirling to face the culprit, he locked eyes with the Rags in the mirror.

Mirror-Rags's jaw dropped and lengthened. Cavernous mouth. Row after row of pointed teeth. His fingers dripped to an obscene length, tipped with wicked claws. He cocked his head, inquisitive, like a sparrow. But then his head continued to tilt, twisting as his neck stretched and spiraled out.

Rags spun on his heel and ran, praying he was speeding toward the path *without* the trapdoor tiles. He waited for the mirror-thing to lunge, to bite him like the snake it had been transforming into.

Now he understood the corpse he'd seen. His predecessor must've been murdered by his own reflection.

Rags tripped on nothing, went down. Skinned his knee, yelped like a kicked dog instead of swearing like the full-grown thief he was. He cringed, waiting for the *whoosh-snap* of teeth around his neck.

It never came.

Rags's heart rabbited frantically against the cold ground. Throat dry and tight with fright, Rags felt his breaths skitter warm along the clutch of his fist. He rasped in stale air, then opened his eyes.

Gray stone beneath him. Good news. He wasn't in the belly of a fae-dreamed horror-beast.

He knew what he'd seen, though. That *thing* with his face, moving faster than light.

Footsteps sounded behind his prone body. No, not behind. *Beside.* Was his reflection still in the glass? Or was this merely a trick of echoes, of reflected sound? Rags scrambled to his feet, scurrying forward with his eyes fixed on the stone floor.

He couldn't look in the glass, see the thing that wore his face and wanted to kill him. But he couldn't run away properly if he couldn't look up, see where he was going.

He'd been privy to tricks with mirrors before he saw the sorcerer's mirrorcraft up close. From street performers to paranoid Ever-Nobles, who had all kinds of safety precautions set up to guard their vaults. Men and women who didn't trust a simple lock because people like Rags could pop them open.

Was the monster nothing more than a fae illusion?

Worse: a fae illusion that might kill you, despite not, technically, being real?

Rags slammed hard into a glass wall with his shoulder, bounced off, hit the floor. Startled by the pain, he made a mistake. He looked at the mirror he'd run into, and the thing in the mirror met his eyes.

A long-fingered hand reached out of the glass and grabbed his ankle.

Not an illusion.

Rags wrenched free and darted left. This time, when the floor bottomed out, he was almost expecting it. He had enough momentum to pivot and throw himself back the way he'd come.

There was a way through this maze. *Had* to be.

Other saps had been savaged and left for dead. Didn't mean Rags had to suffer the same fate.

His reflection monster wasn't on top of him yet. How had Rags avoided being torn to shreds immediately?

He glanced over his shoulder. Mirror-Rags shimmered free from the glass and sprinted toward him. By instinct, Rags flinched and turned away.

The sound of bootfalls skittered around him, but no hand touched him. Mirror-Rags made no contact.

Now you see it, now you don't.

Maybe Rags had to be looking at the mirror in order for it to come out and attack him. For the thing inside it to exist outside it.

"Shit." Rags exhaled, dug for the mirror in his pocket. Didn't look at it while hissing, "Morien, I need one of your witchy blindfolds.

Don't ask. And if you're going to do the thing where you poof into existence, uh, be careful."

Bad news if the sorcerer saw his own reflection and it devoured him. Rags didn't think Lord Faolan would take too kindly to that, to say nothing of what would happen to the shard in Rags's heart.

He was covering his eyes with his own sweaty fingers when he heard Morien grunt. A light swatch of fabric fell out of the hand mirror and landed across Rags's bare wrist. Morien didn't follow.

"Not so tough when it's not *your* mirrorcraft, huh?" Rags asked.

Only silence met his joke. A sensitive subject.

Had the sorcerers suffered at the hands of the fae and their magic before learning to best them? Rags didn't know. But because he was a thief, he couldn't help wondering if the sorcerers had stolen the magic for themselves.

No, he wasn't here to wonder. Rags tied the scrap of red around his eyes, felt his heartbeat slow as the world around him faded.

Wherever Mirror-Rags was, it couldn't get him now. Rags couldn't hear it or see it. By his theory, that meant it didn't exist.

Rags bent to take off his boots. Mirror-Rags couldn't get him, but the floor could. He was going to have to find his way to the end of the labyrinth by toe-touch alone.

He made slow, torturous progress through the maze, bumping into glass, quickly shifting his weight backward the instant he felt the first crumble of stone giving way beneath his bare toes.

He only knew he was finished when he pushed through a panel of something cool, harder than glass, and heard the *thunk* of a door falling shut behind him.

Rags fumbled with the knot at the back of his head and pulled off the blindfold. Took a deep breath, blinking back his eyesight.

He stood in a room the size of a massive dining hall, only instead of housing feasting tables and chairs, there were rows upon rows of crumbling suits of armor.

Armor made from black bone and fae glass.

Rags would have scoffed at that, but he'd seen what fae glass could do. An entire enemy army could be felled by glancing into a polished breastplate, captured by their own deadly reflections.

What was this place, that it had once held an armory that would have outfitted every Queensguard on the Hill? And why was Rags so determined to think up questions that, if asked, would only get him into trouble?

Clear across the end of the hall waited another door. This one had only one handprint on it.

"Gloves again?" Rags did his best not to look over his shoulder. A cold wind lingered behind him where the door had shut, and he couldn't shake the image of Mirror-Rags prowling on the other side, trapped behind glass.

Waiting.

Just like Morien the Last was waiting for news of Rags's progress.

Rather than face the horror of Morien after dodging the great ax swoop of terror that had come with outrunning his murderous mirror twin, Rags decided to turn his mind toward getting the next door open.

It didn't matter what happened between those doors. All that mattered was surviving to the end.

Eventually Rags discovered he needed to find the *one* crumbling suit of black-and-silver armor equipped with a glove bearing a special pattern, which worked like a key to open the fifth door—all while a polished juggernaut made of black bone rolled after him, hungry to squish him flat.

And so on.

"How come you can't just pop to the end of this place?" Rags asked Morien when the sorcerer appeared with a pittance: another bitter, metallic, stomach-numbing apple.

Morien looked at Rags like he wasn't going to answer. But, to Rags's surprise, an answer did come.

"The rooms beyond do not fully exist before the trial to enter them has been solved. I can do many things, but I can't send myself somewhere that doesn't exist. Yet."

The bastard vanished after that, and Rags was alone again. More doors awaited, his sole choice to learn how to open them, or die.

Down was the vague trajectory Rags sensed, when he had any sense of direction.

The sky became the earth, and the earth became the sky. He was swallowed in darkness, its mouth, throat, belly. Weak light pulsed from the strange symbols on the walls. They were neither mathematical nor naughty pictures, the only two picture languages Rags recognized. These were fae and fancy and infuriatingly vague, lines that merely suggested shape and movement. As his eyes adjusted to the markings, he'd catch a glimpse of something familiar: a reptile tail carved to slither up the rockside, or a wary feline eye glowering from above.

Living door to door, disarming traps, subsisting on Morien's magic apples. Resting, occasionally, in the safe spaces between. Brief naps to restore energy, *somehow, no nightmares*. He began to wonder if he'd ever feel sunlight on his skin again, or breathe the smoky, sultry, stinking-but-alive air of Cheapside.

Soon, he had to stop wondering.

When Rags stepped through the seventeenth door into a round room, he found that the eighteenth door was actually seven doors, lining the room's walls in a half-moon.

At first glance, the doors were identical. All seven were carved from dusty white rock and narrowed to arches at the top. But different etchings covered each. They were separate parts of a series of small images ordered for the eye to follow their story.

Rags couldn't read, but this story he followed over the seven archways of the doors. Each offered another fragment of the tale. Figures knelt before a regal form, taller than the rest, wearing a high crown. It gestured with the length of its spindly arm, and the figures set off. Soon, the figures split into separate directions. One, its geometric tail switching behind it, ventured underground, while one with a wing traveled to a smoky city and one with a fang traveled to a great lake. And so on. Six figures departing to six different locations.

Six: one shy of the number of doors Rags currently faced.

That had to mean something. Seven minus six left one correct door. He needed to use what was in front of him to decide which door he wanted.

He ran his fingers over the delicate figures on the center door, tracing the shapes under his callused skin. Nothing gave. No hidden mechanism, no secret dial camouflaged amid the carvings.

Nothing on *this* door. Six more to examine.

"Not gonna think about what might be behind the wrong ones." Rags's mouth quirked as he glanced over his shoulder.

Of course there was no one there.

Silence in the round chamber as he moved from one door to the next, focused and ready to catch any little difference, his touch hesitant against the stone.

Just then, a voice whispered, "You left him."

It wasn't Rags's voice.

He whipped around.

Didn't sound like Morien, but the sorcerer had a way of showing up silently and when Rags least expected it.

Still alone. He hadn't opened the door yet and he hadn't given Morien the signal.

Rags shook his head like a wet dog, like he could clear his thoughts as easily as drying himself off. Then he went back to his examination of the doors, drew his fingertips over the etched head of the figure who'd wound up in the hilly countryside.

"He buried fae treasure, all silver and blood." The voice singsonged like wind through a crack. It cut Rags cold. *"Deep in the earth, where sleeping things grow."*

Was it coming from beyond this door?

"Time to move on," Rags told himself, speaking out loud to hear what a real voice sounded like. To drown out the fake stuff. He gave the second door a little push to test it, then stepped sideways to the next.

"Measure by measure comes Oberon's flood," the voice started up again, this time before Rags had the chance to put his hand to stone. It seemed to be coming from everywhere, with no single point of origin. It melted from the walls and through the seven doors, slithering into Rags's ears. *"More precious than gold, so final the blow."*

It *was* his voice, he realized, but a younger version, warped by reflection or recollection. The laugh that burbled after it was softer, fainter. Familiar somehow, though that didn't matter.

This was more underhanded fae nonsense meant to dissuade and disarm him.

They wanted to get into his head because they didn't want him to think clearly.

"You're already buried." The whispers crackled louder, like fire roaring in a steel drum. "Who will look for you in this place? Dirty little thief in the halls of legends. Dane might have cared. But Dane is gone."

Dane. It was Dane's laugh. A memory that throbbed like a bad tooth if Rags probed too near it.

"Shut up," he said. "You don't know anything. You're a door."

"And you don't belong here." The whispers swelled to raucous howls. Rags flinched as they echoed, distorting in his ears. *"You don't belong anywhere. You don't belong."*

"Enough!"

He couldn't examine the door like this. Shoulders hunched defensively, Rags rummaged in his pockets, touching the broken beetle before finding Morien's magicked blindfold. He tied it around his head like a ribbon, covering his ears instead of his eyes.

The effect was immediate, like plunging his head underwater. The world of sound receded, leaving him in total quiet.

Rags gave himself to the count of ten to steady his shaking fingers. Then, using only his eyes and his hands, he set to studying, feeling, the etchings in the seven doors.

One of them was the right one. Those voices had been sent to distract him from discovering the truth, to drive him mad before he looked closely enough to solve the puzzle. They hadn't counted on Morien and his sorcerous cloths.

Rags searched in silence until he found one inconsistency, barely the size of an eyelash, the slightest crescent at the base of the sixth door counting from Rags's left. It sat tucked into the door's keystone, like a falling star.

None of the other doors had one. All had identical, unblemished arches, smooth as clean sheets.

"You," Rags said.

He held his breath, stuck his nail into the crescent, and turned.

Nothing but an open hall awaited him. It was almost a letdown.

The nineteenth door was peaceful, or deceptively so. Plain black wood, with bark that flaked and glinted the way the trees in the forest had, as though the chamber had a beam of sunlight trapped inside its stuffy darkness. Rags checked the walls, crawled on his hands and knees over the floor searching for secret traps that would set off explosions, swinging blades, a host of treasure defenders that were just mouths with claws dropping from the ceiling.

But there was nothing.

"Safe," Rags called into his Morien-summoning mirror after removing his Morien-summoned blindfold. This was only a room. The door ahead had a proper knob, shaped like a sun crowned by its beams.

Rags squinted at it.

"I don't trust you," he muttered.

Morien coalesced out of the surprisingly fresh air. "Your mistrust of everything may have been the key to your survival to this point."

Rags grinned despite himself. It wasn't flattery. It was the truth. Morien had told him the rooms in this place didn't exist until the doors opened. Rags would be a fool to trust something that well hidden.

His only consolation was that it had to be getting on Morien's nerves worse than his. An all-powerful sorcerer depending on a Cheapside prowler to escort him to the ribbon at the end of the race. It would've been a great story, if that Cheapside prowler had been anyone other than Rags himself.

He ate another magic apple as he cased the door, flattening his ear against it, listening for noise on the other side. Hearing deathly silence.

The start of a feeling in his heart—around the shard, which he'd come to accept he'd *always* sense, a pinprick with every breath—thrilling bolts of excitement through his arms, down his legs, to his toes. One of his hands was shaking. Not with fear, but with excitement.

That was unusual.

Feelings meant nothing. Instinct, experience, and wariness were his only true friends.

Rags couldn't shake the shiver that jittered down the length of his spine, jerky motions like a spider's weight vibrating a cast thread. It filled him with breathless fire that honestly scared him. He didn't have the right name to call it, although it felt dangerously close to hope.

"Whatever." For himself, not for the sorcerer. Louder, he added, "Stand back. I have a good feeling about this one."

Could the fae leave a spell behind that would inspire false optimism in whoever entered this room? Again: It was just their twisted style.

Rags grabbed the doorknob and turned, fully expecting the mechanism to catch and hold, the doorknob to sprout rows of teeth and gnaw his hand off, anything to stanch the flow of excitement echoing outward from the center of his chest.

It didn't. The knob turned. The door sighed, a wise, old sound, and creaked slowly but inward.

"We'll await your signal," Morien said.

Rags made a rude hand gesture where Morien couldn't see it.

He stepped into the waiting chamber, and the door swung shut behind him with a *whoosh* that stirred the grime on the floor. The *click* of a lock.

What came next was bound to be bad.

12

RAGS

Only it wasn't.

Rags's eyes adjusted to the dark. There was a light somewhere close. He was in another tunnel, not a room—and he wasn't in full control of his legs. His steps quickened without his permission until he was practically running, stumbling as he went. Something drew him forward with the same magnetic insistence as the first corpse's bony arms snapping back where they belonged, re-forming the whole out of its forcibly separated parts. Though his feet dragged leaden and sluggish, he couldn't feel the impact when they hit the ground.

The light in front of him grew, resolving itself into a shape like the lid of a coffin. As he drew closer, he realized it *was* a coffin, made of glass.

Rags stopped in front of it, feet scraping to a halt. He was staring down at another murky reflection of himself.

Only it was too tall, too broad in the shoulders. The coffin wasn't actually mirrored—the top was like a windowpane, and Rags was looking at another *person* within it, their figure distorted through the sheet of nearly liquid glass. Over their chest, a fist-sized hole had been melted through the lid.

A quick glance upward showed a hole in the ceiling about the same size.

How deep down was he? Had something living burrowed its way in from the surface?

Rags longed to take a step away but couldn't. His gaze slid back to the coffin. Radiating rolling heat like forge fire, the shape inside undefined, warped and wavering. Rags didn't trust that touching it wouldn't sear his hand off at the wrist and leave him with an oozing stump.

But how much he *did* want to touch it outweighed all rational fear.

He couldn't explain it. Both hands went up, discovering the same shapes on the surface as on the first door. Handprints.

"Daring as ravens, rich as magpies," Rags whispered, reciting the old Clave prayer for luck, and set his palms against the handprints in the glass, meeting the figure's hands below it fingertip to fingertip.

Rags's hands fit perfectly into each groove. He discovered that the surface itself wasn't burning hot, or, like the rest of the fae technology in the ruins, it reacted to his presence, his touch. The glass began to cool, and as it cooled, it hardened.

As it hardened, it began to crack.

One fissure ran straight down the center, between Rags's fingertips. He was vaguely aware of the coffin shattering open, of its shattered pieces burying themselves in his palms, though no pain accompanied the fact, only mild amazement. One fragment sliced his cheek, another his chin. But instead of blowing him backward with the final force of its destruction, it sucked him inward, so that he met the figure within chest to chest.

The figure sat up, then slumped forward. Rags caught it in his arms, but it was dead heavy, an anchor dragging him to the floor. He managed to slow the fall, to soften the impact. His bloody hands smeared red stains along its bare forearms, a bare chest. Long black hair, save one silver-white shock, tumbled everywhere. The body sagged down, down, and Rags fell back, pinned under its weight.

Then the body began to scream.

13
RAGS

While the screaming continued, too loud and too close and drawing on a depthless well of emotion beyond human comprehension, Rags remained stunned. He spiraled in and out of the scream's pain with dizzying speed, no room left for thoughts in his head, only the echo of the noise.

At the point when Rags suspected his head might split apart at the straining seams like an overstuffed moneybag, the screaming stopped.

The silence in its wake proved worse, leaving Rags empty and adrift. His palms began to sting. Blood dripped down his fingertips. The weight of the other body pinned him to the ground. Gusts of trembling, cool breath stirred his hair.

Something round rolled across the floor.

The body moved. Jerky, awkward movements from limbs trying to remember how they worked, what their purposes were. The weight—thankfully—lifted. Rags stayed put, flat on the floor and staring upward. He watched the body relearn itself, watched it hold up its hands and spread its tattooed fingers apart and stretch each in turn. Strong, tawny arms, with black bones tattooed on the skin. *Everywhere* on the skin. That long hair reminded Rags of the first fae corpse. It fell over the body's face, hid it in endless shadow, until suddenly the body's large hands pushed it back and all its features were revealed.

Looking not entirely majestic.

The face over Rags's was baffled. Bewilderment stamped on majesty, a contradiction amazing enough to make Rags attempt a weary laugh.

"I am awake," the bow-curved lips parted to say. At the corners of the mouth sat twin black X's. No, they were crossbones. The rest of the face was golden skin unmarked by black ink. Big, silver eyes without whites; a nose that reminded Rags of an eagle, or pictures of eagles, which were all he'd seen.

"Yes." Rags's voice emerged in an ugly croak. "The screaming made that obvious."

"A side effect of the Sleep." The fae—because he was fae, *had* to be fae, looking everything and nothing like a person, like so much more than a human could hope to be—bent over Rags again. The intensity of his fae gaze burned. Rags flinched. The fae noticed the blood on Rags, squinting at it until recognition crossed his features. "You are injured."

"Yes," Rags said again. "That happened when the, uh, glass exploded."

"Your touch awakened me." The fae sketched a formal, if cramped, bow with an impossible combination of near-liquid agility and steel-hard strength in his shoulders. The awkwardness he'd suffered at first was nowhere to be found. He'd rediscovered his mobility quickly and was already a master of it. Graceful, beautiful, powerful. Part of a vanished race of superintelligent beings obsessed with their superiority.

The same beings who'd created an obstacle course that had nearly killed Rags to get through. The same beings who'd been declared enemy forces by a queen dead for centuries before Rags ever slipped out of his mother's womb. Humans and fae didn't mix.

This obstacle course might still kill him.

"Okay," Rags said.

Was this the part where he got turned on a spit and roasted for breakfast?

From the shimmering pool of broken glass, the fae extracted a shirt. Or Rags thought it was a shirt. The garment was spun from a fabric so light, it hovered in the air between them, delicate as spider silk and practically transparent. The fae pulled it on over his head. Once on, it clung to his form like it had been made for that purpose.

Maybe it had been. Who was Rags to comment on fae fashion?

Dressed, the fae took one of Rags's hands, his touch startlingly cold. At once, feeling rushed back into Rags's fingertips. He yelped, cursed. His hands were all that stood between him and starvation. If these cuts got infected, if they ran deep enough to sever muscle or affect sensation, he was fucked, he was *so fucked*—

His thoughts devolved into cursing after that, so deeply private and pained that he didn't realize he was speaking them out loud.

"What does it mean?" the fae asked, beginning to diligently clean the blood from Rags's right palm with his hair. "*'Pissing balls of fucking fire'*? Is it your name?"

Rags tried to laugh but choked instead. His hands hurt, his back hurt, his face hurt, and he wished his name *was* Pissing Balls of Fucking Fire. It would suit the mood he was in.

"That's not—no. It's not my name. That's some other guy."

"My apologies to have confused you for someone else." Rags searched the fae's tone for signs of sarcasm but found none. "You who have awakened me have my respect and my loyalty. I would know you. What is it that you are named?"

Rags swallowed. "Uh." This was going to be embarrassing. "Call me Rags."

Instead of laughing—could fae laugh?—the fae simply nodded. "A short name, but one that is strong. In return, know me. I am Shining Talon of Vengeance Drawn in Westward Strike, and I am honored to be met by you."

"Shining what of huh?" Rags pulled his hand back, alarmed by the way the fae's touch had begun to numb it. He shook it out, winced as feeling and pain returned, then began to study the slices and gashes with grim focus.

"Shining Talon of Vengeance Drawn in Westward Strike, my lord Rags."

"Oh, is that all?"

Somber resignation momentarily tugged the X's tattooed at the corners of the fae's mouth. He bowed his head. "It is all. I am young and have not yet proven myself."

Rags sucked at a particularly deep gouge in his thumb, tasting blood. In the pause that followed, he levered himself up onto one elbow in order to look over the fae's broad shoulder. He was met with the sight of cracked glass, the jagged remains of the coffin, its glow dulled by its collapse, and a small, grave-sized hollow in the wall. No chamber beyond. No further challenges, from the looks of it. No more doors.

No treasure.

Rags worked a chunk of glass free from his flesh with his teeth and spat it, stained pink, onto the floor at his side. Although his body tingled at the edges, a fuzzy feeling of uncertainty at the boundaries of his own skin, he got to his feet. The fae moved aside but watched him as he went. Rags swayed but managed to stay upright, lurching toward the thing that had rolled free of the coffin. Maybe it was a diamond. A big, not very sparkly, mostly dirty diamond.

He scooped the lumpy thing up in his hand. Because that was what it was. A lump of twisted ore, like raw silver before a silversmith got hold of it. Worth *something*, sure. There was never a shortage of men and women who wanted swords, and people who needed the materials to make them.

But it was hardly treasure.

Trying to shake off his growing despair, Rags turned and wobbled toward the spot where the fae had been resting—how long? Rags was no scholar, but he tallied something like a couple hundred years, before Rags showed up and busted the guy loose. Accidentally.

Rags poked his head inside the coffin's alcove anyway, figuring there had to be a hidden compartment somewhere. Maybe this test was the hardest yet, the most baffling. And maybe the fae would kill him if he failed it. He'd said *You who have awakened me have my respect and my loyalty,* but legend had it that the fae were known to lie like anyone else, probably the only thing all races had in common. Rags had never met an Ancient One, but he suspected that if they too could talk, they too must have lied plenty.

"What do you seek?" The fae's voice was closer than it should have been. He'd crept up on Rags in complete silence. Rags jerked back at the realization and slammed into the fae's extremely solid chest, practically dislocating his elbow in the process.

Rags cursed. The fae closed both hands over Rags's biceps to steady him, which felt more like a trap than anything else, and Rags thrashed, knowing those hands were too strong and he'd never pry himself free. That didn't stop him from trying.

The fae let go of him the moment his panic manifested. He took a step away, leaving Rags to sway precariously, caught in the channels of his own wild momentum without anything to steady him.

He was alive. Maybe the fae thought he was too scrawny to bother with, not worth the stains his blood would make.

The fae observed him the entire time with blank eyes and slightly parted lips. His expressions were too foreign, the color of his eyes too unchanging, to translate.

Rags sagged against the nearest wall in order to remain upright. "Don't just grab someone like that!"

The fae bowed. "I will not just grab someone like that as you have requested."

It had been half desperate plea, half pathetic command. Rags didn't believe the easy agreement. He stared at the fae through narrowed eyes, waiting for his nerves to calm so he'd make a better showing. So he'd be *slightly* less of a screaming, flimsy human in the face of . . .

This.

Shining Talon of . . .

Shit.

"Shining Talon." Rags poured confidence he didn't have into his voice, an attempt to *bluff a fae, like that'll work, Rags*, into believing he remembered the full name but couldn't be assed to say the whole thing. The fae—Shining Talon, still a mouthful in shortened form—looked up, his face brightening. Was he glowing? Was the essential radiance of his being what lit these tunnels?

The veins of light in the walls flickered with his movements, his breaths, indicating *Yeah, maybe*.

"My lord Rags," Shining Talon replied.

"Right." Rags had to brush that off, pretend it was normal. He stood straighter, as tall as he could in the small space, remembering Lord Faolan's posture, as though Rags was the lord who Shining Talon, for whatever ass-brained reason, believed he was. "Where are the goods?"

A tough exterior was one of the vital tools of living Cheapside. It wasn't difficult if he told himself this was just another job.

Even with all his senses snarling to the contrary.

Shining Talon blinked, still expressionless. Impossible to tell his age. Was he supposed to be smaller? Rags had always pictured the fae smaller.

"The . . . goods . . . ?"

"Treasure chests. Spoils of war. Incredible piles of riches. Jewels. Coins. Precious metals. In there?" Rags stabbed a still-bloody finger at the ruins of the glass coffin. "Secret door? Next challenge?"

"It may be that you hit your head upon your fall, my lord Rags," Shining Talon said.

"I definitely hit my head upon my fall, Shining Talon, but that's the least of my problems with a sorcerer out there waiting for me to *deliver. The. Goods.*"

Shining Talon's brow furrowed briefly. The tattoos on his chest were visible through the open collar of his shirt, black ribs inked over his flesh, reminding Rags of armor. Gray boots in the shape of sylvan moth wings hugged his calves over black leggings of some impossibly soft weave. He looked out of place and big and unbelievable in the cramped tunnel. Because the ceiling was fractionally too low for him, he had to hunch to keep the top of his head from grazing dirt. The bad posture was all wrong, made no sense with his graceful body.

Even when he did hit the ceiling, the dirt didn't stay in his hair. Instead it showered off him, granting him the reverence he deserved—the reverence Rags couldn't seem to muster, though he knew he should. The only reason he was staring was because there was a living, breathing, definitely dangerous, beautifully deadly fae in front of him.

Probably Rags should have been flat on his face in front of the fae begging for mercy. But the pounding of his heart and the dawning suspicion that there might not be a treasure—or worse, that Shining Talon *was* the treasure, not an incredible but otherwise unrevolutionary stash of gold and jewels, and Rags was *so, so fucked*—made anything beyond panic impossible to summon.

This was how he'd felt when Morien the Last had first appeared, only ten times worse. He'd discovered a secret that should have stayed buried. Stolen knowledge he couldn't put back into the earth, that was now his burden to carry.

Was he *sure* Shining Talon couldn't go back into the earth?

New plan. There was no way Morien and Lord Faolan were going to let an unreliable like Rags live. Going out into the world to blab about a *living fae among them*.

No, the treasure had to be something else. Something less world-changing. Otherwise, Rags was going to die. He was a loose end who'd served his usefulness.

Daring as ravens, Rags reminded himself. The slug that was his heart oozed down into his stomach and sank deeper as he looked back at the fae.

"You speak of the Great Paragon?" Shining Talon asked. Rags's throat constricted. Shock, then disbelief. Beneath that, wild hope. "The Great Paragon may be considered a treasure."

"Great treasure." Rags laughed hoarsely. "Yes. A great treasure would be . . . *great*."

Shining Talon's smile made the X tattoos dance. "A great treasure. It is here."

Relief making him dizzy, Rags waited.

So did Shining Talon.

Rags waited a few moments more, but Shining Talon wasn't blinking, had his eyes fixed on Rags with such intensity that something needed to be done to stop him. "Here where, exactly?"

"Here." Shining Talon touched the wall at his side with veneration. "In this earth and on this earth. A weapon to be found piece by piece by those who are worthy, led by one who is worthiest." Another blank, impenetrable, yet somehow expectant look. Silver pools of eyes unblinking and fixed on Rags.

Like Shining Talon thought . . .

Like he thought—

"Ha ha ha," Rags said. "You can't think . . ." *You can't think any of that applies to me.* He squeezed his eyes shut tight—*forget that.* "What's this Weapon, exactly?"

"You . . . do not know of the Weapon?" Rags shook his head. "Built as a gift of alliance, given by the fae to humans, only to have them turn it against us?" Again, Rags shook his head. "So that we were forced, in our final days, to scatter it throughout this world, so it could not be used for cruelty again?"

Rags shrugged. Shining Talon gave him a sharp look.

"But you are holding a piece of it in your hand."

Rags looked down at the lump of—rock? He'd been sure it was metal ore a second ago, but in the dim lighting of the tunnel, he couldn't be sure. The only rocks and metals he knew were ones that'd already been set and stamped by a jeweler.

"This is a rock." Rags held it up in reply.

Shining Talon shook his head. "It is but the first piece of a greater whole, my lord Rags."

Rags shrugged helplessly. "Sounds crazy to me, but—"

Pain in his chest, faint but warning, and Morien appeared at Shining Talon's back. It should've been impossible. Rags hadn't called him.

Or was Morien able to force his way into any room, so long as Rags opened the door first? Was that the only invitation Morien required?

No time to wonder about that. Shining Talon's face darkened when he saw who stood behind him, and Rags's fingers hurt, and suddenly his back did, too, since he'd been thrown to the ground.

Shining Talon's golden face twisted in a feral snarl. He stood as shield between Rags and the sorcerer. Furious heat rolled in waves off his skin, like the way Cheapside tar streets reflected the burning punishment of a cloudless sun.

He'd thrown Rags *away* from danger.

"Lying One," Shining Talon said, the first hint of emotion registering in his voice. Dark as a storm. Darker than Rags had the scope to describe. Fae dark, and terrifying. "Leave this place. I require neither lance nor sword—I shall tear you asunder with hands and will alone."

14
RAGS

Shining Talon had dropped into a crouch, one arm flung out to keep
Rags in relative safety behind him. His bulk stood between Rags and
Morien like a living shield—not that it mattered, because Rags was
bound to the sorcerer by mirrorcraft. Morien could snap his fingers
and slice Rags's heart open from the inside out.

The only good thing about the situation was that Morien hadn't
done it yet. And there was a fae in the mix who might be able to prevent the heart slicing from happening.

Or he might cause further, unfathomable damage.

It was impossible to read Morien's face, hidden behind swaths of
red cloth. But he definitely didn't look as shocked as he should have
to see a real live fae standing next to Rags.

Standing in front of Rags, to be more accurate.

Rags slipped the rock into his pocket. The instinct to hide what he
could was still stronger than fear for his life.

"Rags," Morien began, "you should have called—"

"Silence," Shining Talon said. The word rippled through the air,
twisted it into something solid, like it too could be used as a weapon.
"My lord Rags, I shall protect you from this foul creature with my
life, if necessary."

That might be useful. Rags thought of his assets, and the fact that the fae seemed fonder of him than of Morien was going in the plus column.

Morien took a step back, holding up gloved and empty hands. "It will not be necessary. Rags and I are friends."

"Lord Rags would not trust a Lying One with his oath of friendship and alliance." A pause. Shining Talon's shoulders tightened at Rags's silence. "The Lying One speaks false, Lord Rags?"

Rags wet his dry lips with his tongue. "It's a complicated situation that, uh . . ."

"Oh." A hint of sorrow beneath a wealth of anger. "The Lying One has bound you to his cheating will with wicked mirrorcraft."

As opposed to the really *good* mirrorcraft that had tried to eat him in the glass maze, Rags thought.

Recognizing the potential value of not speaking up in the situation, he kept his lips buttoned.

"I effected an act of security against my interests, to which Rags agreed," Morien said.

In a manner of speaking.

"Against this I cannot protect you fully," Shining Talon told Rags. "I am no master of the lying arts. I am a warrior only. If I could protect your heart—"

Nope. First things first. If they were on the same side, that meant Rags needed to make Shining Talon stop talking. He was only going to get the pair of them into trouble. "Not necessary. Heart in one piece currently, so if you're dead set on helping me, you could start with more specific directions to the Great"—what was it called?—"Paramour?"

"Paragon."

"Right, the treasure . . . thing," Rags agreed. "It's the deal I made with the Lyi—the *sorcerer*. The issue here is if I don't deliver."

"For a Lying One to possess the Great Paragon—"

That sharp pain again. On the other side of Shining Talon's devoted collection of coiled muscles, Morien had a hand lifted in the air, tracing invisible symbols. Commands. Rags's heart answered by slowing, shuddering, stopping. His face paled, his fingertips turning blue. The blood that still oozed lazily from his open cuts dried up at once, and he pitched forward into Shining Talon's back, gasping for breath that didn't answer his call.

Rags gurgled a wordless sound, begging despite himself. He'd made it through all those *fucking* doors, had been so clever, and what did it matter? At the end there was no treasure, only a pissed-off sorcerer, and Rags was the most likely target for said sorcerer to vent his frustrations.

No, it was smarter than that. He was being used. No one in the Clave would've stopped to spit on him if he were dying of thirst, yet here he was, tormented by mirrorglass in his heart into forcing a fae to give up his fae secrets.

There was no way Shining Talon would fall for—

"Very well. I will lead you to the Great Paragon, however I am able," Shining Talon said.

Rags's pain vanished.

"But it will be perilous," Shining Talon concluded.

"Anything worthwhile tends to be," Morien replied.

"What *hasn't* been, lately?" Rags muttered.

"And Lord Rags will be required each step of the way," Shining Talon concluded. "Alive."

Moment of surprise at the stipulation aside, Rags liked the sound of that part.

"I accept," Morien agreed. "You may return the mirror and the blindfold," he said, holding out his hand to Rags, "and I will accompany you the rest of the way out."

15
RAGS

Shining Talon led the two of them through the ruins of the fae complex—underground palace, vault, bathroom, whatever it used to be—with veins of light blinking into existence on either side of him as he went. He took a new path, one Rags hadn't fought his way through. Everywhere Rags looked, massive arches supported the underground tunnels. The more he studied them, the more they reminded him of bones. They really could be the rib cages of the Ancient Ones, for all he knew. They gleamed white and mysterious, threaded with silvered vines.

The lump hung heavy in his pocket. Shining Talon had told him it was a piece of the Great Paragon, but he hadn't mentioned it to Morien.

Which meant they were keeping it a secret. Rags didn't know how he felt about that. They couldn't trust each other, what with Rags being a liar and Shining Talon's entire people being known for their deceptions.

Their alliance was doomed.

He just wasn't planning to be the first to tell Morien about the rock.

Rags and Morien followed Shining Talon in silence, Rags not

asking where the Queensguard were, Morien not mentioning how he'd recently tried to kill Rags.

Shining Talon was aware of, and capable of commanding, doors that previously hadn't existed. They weren't there at all until Shining Talon glanced meaningfully at a bare wall, and a door obligingly appeared. Rags couldn't catch the trick, couldn't figure out how he was doing it. Shining Talon's light found invisible entrances and opened them, and Rags understood with dawning amazement that they were traveling through the remnants of a structure larger than any human palace, bank, or amphitheater. It was the shape of a tower in reverse, burrowing deeper into the earth rather than rising upward from it.

"Stay close," Shining Talon warned only once. "It is dangerous here."

Rags held up his hands, spattered and bloody to the sleeves. "I noticed."

"Yet more dangerous with a Lying One in tow."

Rags wished Shining Talon would stop calling the sorcerer that. Morien couldn't appreciate the name, and anything that made Morien cranky made him more likely to exercise his power over Rags. That wasn't in Rags's best interests.

Didn't mean it wasn't funny.

Then Rags remembered the way Splints the Obscure, an old street acquaintance, had died: loss of blood from a run-in with the Queensguard had made him giddy, giggly. He'd laughed all the way to his last breath, but he wasn't laughing when they shoved him into Old Drowner and set his soul drifting.

The memory put a stop to Rags's good humor.

A moment later, when Shining Talon threw out one solid arm to halt their progress, Rags regretted not having more padding as he collided throat-first with the fae's elbow.

"Be still," Shining Talon whispered.

Rags found himself captivated by the hard, unforgiving tension in Shining Talon's body. He wondered if that was natural for all fae. He hadn't noticed it before, but now that he had, he couldn't *stop* noticing it.

Rags had heard, in a secondhand city dweller's way, about the beauty of wild things. He'd never understood what was being described until now, though it was still impossible to think of the fae as anything other than a nightmare creature.

As Shining Talon disabled a series of whisper-thin blades descending from above, Rags lingered behind to examine one where it dangled, harmless, against the wall. It had sliced a growing root system into sheets of veggies delicate enough for a queen's salad. The blade resembled a musician's instrument string but thinner, spider-silk supple. Nearly invisible, until it was too late.

"Keep up, thief," Morien said. "We wouldn't want any accidents to befall you."

The way he said it made Rags shiver, and he hopped to.

He wanted to thank Shining Talon for preventing them from being cut into flesh ribbons, but when Rags drew closer, the set of the fae's jaw, the steely glint in his eyes, were enough to make Rags's insides curdle.

To witness Shining Talon leading a sorcerer through the old fae ruins was like looking into the deadened gaze of one of those newly bridled stallions, freshly broken from the wilds of Ever-Land—which was as close to lost as one could get without venturing into the Lost-Lands and never being heard from again.

Only a matter of time before a horse like that bucked and broke his master's noble neck. Shining Talon had the same glint in his eye.

Living on the streets, Rags had learned young how to read people, and everything about Shining Talon screamed danger. Not a matter of *if*, but *when*.

Sorcerers had defeated—destroyed—his people. And now, because of Rags, he was being forced to lead one through a place the fae had once called home. Forced to guide him to the fae's greatest treasure.

Rags didn't think a quick *thanks* would do it.

"This your home?" His mouth ran out from under him as usual, driven to distract by the spike of tension in the air.

Remnants of pennants tangled with overgrown roots. Carvings on the walls and floors flashed blue light in acknowledgment of Shining Talon's presence.

Shining Talon seemed surprised Rags was talking to him. Rags was a housefly starting a conversation with a human about the furniture.

"No." Shining Talon's hair shimmered like black rain, hid half his face as he shook his head. "My brothers, my sisters, and I were raised in the Bone Court. The days were warm and the nights lasted twice as long for festivities."

The words seemed to cast a spell. Rags felt sunlight on his face, heard laughter and footsteps clattering down the hall.

Morien grunted and the spell was broken. Rags couldn't tell if he'd done it on purpose.

Decided he had.

"Uh, sounds great," Rags offered. Couldn't stand the silence, though it would've served him better. His words were dust motes settling in the ancient ruin. He turned to Morien and offered his biggest shit-eating grin. "You're not impressed, obviously. Just another day in the Queen's service, twice-long nights and a *living fae* to tell you about them."

"As a sorcerer to the Queen, I have witnessed many miracles," Morien replied. "When Lord Faolan presented his plans for the expedition, I knew it was only right that I should be the one to see them through."

They passed an otherwise empty chamber holding only a toppled tall chair in the center, and door after door after door, all the same shape, with an onion-top peak and no knob or handle.

Shining Talon merely had to approach one and it opened.

He strode onward without looking back at his companions. Rags got the impression he was trying to pretend Morien didn't exist.

So Rags trudged along in silence again, grudgingly respecting the flourishes and details around him being eaten away by dirt. No loose trinkets or half-buried jewelry boxes he could nab to sell. His fingers stung, the air wasn't stale enough for how deep in the earth they were, and the guy who'd hired him was pissed.

All in all, a bad job.

"Leading us to the execution chamber?" Rags asked. His voice echoed over the bare walls.

Shining Talon paused in his self-assured stride and turned with a question shadowing his face. "For what reason would I do that? I cannot kill the Lying One as long as he has contract with your heart. He will destroy you, and I cannot allow that to happen."

Haha. Power fit Rags like a shirt borrowed from a man twice as big as him. A shame. From everything he'd imagined, pulling the strings was supposed to be magnificent, a thrill to kill for.

Rags forced himself to shrug. "Just making conversation. So there *is* an execution chamber in this place, huh?"

"Five of them," Shining Talon replied.

Rags should have stopped asking questions. Didn't. "What kind of a place needs five execution chambers?"

It was near impossible to catch Shining Talon's gaze when it shifted, light reflecting off milky silver. But Rags got the sense Shining Talon had looked at him. Rags always knew when he was being watched.

"This, the Lone Tower, was one of the Bone Court's great military strongholds." Shining Talon's explanation was mild, like it didn't cost him anything to offer. "Even in defeat, it was safeguarded against invasion."

Right.

Except Rags had broken through all those safeguards.

All those *Lone Tower* safeguards.

Rags was almost too numb to the impossible to feel the confirmation of where they were hit, settle, sink in deep.

You don't belong, the door had shouted at him. Maybe it hadn't been a threat. Maybe it'd been a different kind of warning.

Rags *truly* stopped asking questions after that.

He counted another room with a lone tall chair, this one upright, and noted the scorched marks—*shit, handprints*—stamped on the arms. Then they passed through another room with an empty bed, preserved like a held breath, in perfect condition. A third room with a dining table set, plates and goblets and chairs and untouched food that hadn't rotted, waiting for its diners to return. Rags's fingers itched to grab something so he could pretend this was any other job.

But it wasn't.

At about the time Rags suspected they were being led in circles, Shining Talon guided them through a final door and out into the light.

They were in a forest. Stars glittered above. A river of molten silver passed in front of them, reflecting the sky. Or ceiling. Rags stared until his eyes burned, trying to determine what he was really seeing.

Morien lingered on the threshold. Was he unable to cross? Or did he know something Rags didn't—that once someone entered this place, they'd never be able to leave?

Rags tested the theory, putting one foot on one side of the door and the other back into the chamber. He wasn't torn apart or struck by lightning. A good sign. But Shining Talon stared at him with what would have been curiosity on a human face, and that made Rags feel stupid.

"Never spent time in a fae ruin before," he muttered, the heat in his cheeks driving his gaze to the floor.

Fucking. Fae. Ruins.

"It is much changed since before I Slept," Shining Talon agreed.

Without dwelling on that statement, the fae knelt by the side of the river of silver and, whispering what sounded suspiciously like "excuse me," plunged both hands into the rushing water. At his touch, it hissed. Steam rose from the rippling surface. Shining Talon grunted, gritted his teeth, and held his position. His shoulders were so taut, Rags wondered if he'd snap in two.

Despite himself, Rags leaned closer.

The river dried up, all its liquid silver drawn together with and against the current, bubbling and boiling into a single shape beneath, then around, Shining Talon's hands.

When it was finally at rest, Rags could see that Shining Talon had pulled a silver creature from the river.

16
RAGS

It looked, Rags thought, like a lumpy snake. But seeing as how it was a magic river beast that operated with indescribable power, he didn't want to insult it.

It hissed one last time as it rocked into its edges. The lumps became delicate legs.

It was a lizard the size of a pony.

It regarded Rags with one silver eye and Shining Talon with the other. A third blinked open on its forehead, discovered Morien, and narrowed.

"Your pet?" Rags asked. Someone had to say something.

Shining Talon withdrew his hands. They had blackened unevenly from fingertips to wristbones. The sight reminded Rags of his own injured palms, and he scowled.

"Pet?" Shining Talon repeated, like he didn't understand the word.

The big silver lizard put one clawed foot on the edge of the now-empty riverbank and heaved itself out. The way it moved made Rags's breath catch in his throat. It was beautiful, each joint feline in its grace, precise and delicate. Its hinges turned beneath a silver webbing of translucent scales that served as skin.

It was a machine.

Dane would've loved this. The thought echoed unbidden before

Rags could stop it, his old friend's laugh still ringing in his ears. As boys in Cheapside, they'd spun all kinds of tales about fae silver and gold, the wonders of Oberon's lost kingdom, how someday they'd find it together. Rags kicked those thoughts away.

"Her name is One," Shining Talon said. "She is the first fragment of the Great Paragon. Neither of us is her master, and she is impatient to meet the one who is."

"Oh, is that all," Rags replied.

They stared at each other for a brief moment before he suddenly became very interested in checking the maybe-rock in his pocket.

It wasn't moving. Still and cold, even to Rags's hot touch.

Shining Talon had referred to One as *the first fragment*, which meant that they were definitely keeping Rags's piece their secret. A little too much like working with a partner for Rags's liking, but he was still alive, his heart in one piece, and he'd seen treasures kids from Cheapside only *thought* they dreamed about.

The only problem was that Rags couldn't think of any story or rhyme where a human shook hands with a fae and came out on top.

17
RAGS

If such a thing was possible, One liked Morien less than Shining Talon did. As their trek through the fae palace continued, she kept her distance, third eye constantly narrowed to a slit. Morien seemed unbothered, although it was impossible to tell what the bastard was thinking under his scarves. Rags's heart didn't hurt, so he had to assume they'd done something right.

The lizard was indifferent to Rags and, after sniffing Shining Talon's hands—which had begun to cool, the blackness receding toward his fingertips—paid him little attention. The only time One acknowledged their presence was biting the back of Shining Talon's leggings when he came too close to what Rags assumed was a wrong door. Were they now following the lizard? Rags snuck a look at Morien and found him as inscrutable as ever.

When they met up with the Queensguard, Rags was struck again by their silence. Like toy soldiers left unattended between the first and second doors, they lined the dark corridor at eerie and empty attention, still blindfolded by Morien's scarves.

Shining Talon bared his teeth at the sight of them but said nothing. They were backtracking now.

Heading out.

Rags was nearly free to get back to the city, find out who'd sold him into servitude to the Ever-Nobles, and make them pay. After that, he'd settle back into his old life. He'd never swear in the fae's name. He'd get better at being bad and make sure he wasn't caught again.

Yeah, and if he believed that, he'd believe anything.

There'd been a total lack of shock in Morien's eyes when presented with a living fae. Had he been expecting this, not fae-glass lances or star ruby diadems?

"Guess it'd be too easy if one of these guys was the picky silver lizard's master," Rags muttered.

Shining Talon nodded solemnly. "The search could take decades, perhaps a century."

Something about the way he said it made Rags wonder if he was stalling for time. Inflating Morien's expectations.

Nah, it was a mistake for Rags to try to read him like a normal person.

"It would be in Rags's best interest if you would share more information about this Great Paragon," Morien told Shining Talon.

The only point of brightness piercing Rags's foul mood was the way the sorcerer kept his distance from One, putting all six Queensguard, Rags, and Shining Talon between them. His posture wasn't scared, but that detail suggested otherwise.

Rags snorted and sat. "Figure it'll be a long story. Might as well get comfortable."

Shining Talon settled beside him on his knees, his back straight, looking like a wary cat ready to leap at the first shifting shadow. "For the sake of my lord Rags, Lying One, I will answer your questions with words rather than steel."

It would have been nice if Rags could genuinely not care about whatever fae secrets Shining Talon revealed. But he listened, breathless, with mounting appreciation for the light kindling in Morien's eyes at the tale.

Because there *was* a treasure. The greatest treasure, if you valued unparalleled power above all else.

"Forged from the heart of all fae silver," Shining Talon began, "the Great Paragon took an age for our best smiths to create. A second age passed while our Enchantrisks wove their magics over it. Then came the third age. . . ."

And it went on like that. Six ages to complete the Great Paragon, six fragments created together, which, when joined with their individual masters, would form an unstoppable whole, some kind of symbol for unity.

"Hang on." Rags felt a stab of guilt at interrupting the flow of Shining Talon's story, but also, his mouth had always worked a smidge faster than his brain. "Unity like, fae and humans working together? *That* kind of unity?"

Two pairs of eyes, one silver and one black, stared in his direction.

Rags fumbled with the hem of his shirt. "Didn't know unity was ever an option."

"There was peace," Shining Talon continued, "promised between our rulers. The Great Paragon was a gift, five parts united under the command of five humans, with a sixth from the fae to guide them. It was too powerful to entrust to one wielder alone."

So this thing was in six pieces. Of which One was . . . one.

Shining Talon was vague about what happened once all six beasts had found their masters and what happened when they were brought together—Morien seemed especially keen to learn that—but Rags suspected it was because Shining Talon didn't know, maybe hadn't seen it for himself.

"Wait, though," Rags broke in again. "There's a fae master of one of these beasties, obviously that's fine. But the rest—the humans—they're all dead by now. Ancient worm food."

Morien cleared his throat, impatient about the interruption. Rags tried not to let it bother him. If he was going to be at someone else's beck and call, he planned to make it uncomfortable on both ends.

"There is a master born every generation," Shining Talon acknowledged, "to accommodate the realities of your brief, fragile human existences."

"Sure," Rags said. "That makes sense."

"It was many lifetimes ago when the Great Paragon was scattered," Shining Talon concluded, "to remain so until such a time as it was needed."

Rags snorted softly. "Should've brought it back into play before the Lost-Lands became lost. Might have turned the tides."

Shining Talon lowered his head until his face was hidden by his dark hair. "Of this I cannot speak. After the Great Paragon was sundered and its fragments hidden, I was chosen to remain in this place until I was awoken by one worthy of command."

"Of command," Rags repeated.

Shining Talon lifted his eyes to Rags's face. His shining eyes. All of him shone. Rags resisted the urge to squint but felt like a stubborn child staring directly at the sun. He'd always pictured the fae as being as ancient as they were wise, as wise as they were cruel. He'd pictured them as weapons sheathed in shadows, with less of a dazzling glow.

"My lord Rags, though these are not the circumstances I might have envisioned—"

"Do you know the location of the other five?" Morien cut in.

Rags watched Shining Talon's hands work over his thighs, the black bone tattoos shifting with every clench. What had he been about to say? Why did he care? The less Rags knew, the better his odds of survival got. He felt queasy from all the magic apples he'd eaten.

"Such knowledge could not be given to any one being. It would have been too dangerous," Shining Talon replied.

"But you knew where the first"—One hissed menacingly at this, and Morien corrected himself—"where One could be found."

"One knows how to find her master," Shining Talon said. "After that, my instructions were . . . unclear. I believe that One's master may be able to lead us to Two. Somehow."

"Somehow." Morien leaned closer to Rags, and Rags braced himself for the pain to begin again.

"What I know," Shining Talon began—and did Rags detect the first note of familiar emotion in his voice, like fae could feel fear as keenly as humans?—"is that I was intended to be Master of Six. And the one who woke me would be Master of Five."

Rags nearly choked on his own laughter, then had to pretend he'd swallowed a cobweb to explain his sudden sputtering. No one else laughed.

"But it's not *true*," Rags said, dragging them stubbornly by the nose to see the joke. "It can't be me. I wasn't even supposed to be here." Suddenly, he was in shackles again, pleading his case before a magistrate. "I'm more a means to an end. . . ."

"A tool," Morien supplied.

"I know nothing of your human arrangments," Shining Talon said, in a tone that made perfectly clear that he also had no interest in learning. His gaze landed bluntly on Rags, without the sharp steel he reserved for Morien. "Nor does it matter what brought you to me, my lord Rags. Only that it was you who came. You alone possessed the skill to find me."

Morien hissed. It was a sharp, unpleasant sound, and when Rags looked at him, he found the sorcerer glaring his way.

"You imply that Rags is of unexpected importance to our cause," Morien summarized.

Did Rags imagine the way Shining Talon seemed to grow larger, filling his space more thoroughly as he straightened? Or had Rags's mind finally snapped like a rope stretched too tight?

"He is vitally important," Shining Talon said. The finality in his tone left no room for argument—even from a shitty, sneaky sorcerer like Morien the Last.

Rags had to admire how their new roles kept them both safe. Morien or Lord Faolan would want to bring the pieces of the Great Paragon together, to control such a powerful weapon for themselves. Or for the Queen.

Regardless, the sorcerer couldn't off Rags with a wave of his hand. Not unless he wanted to wait for another Master of Five to be born and reach a useful age. A beastie master only came along once every generation.

Morien could have blindfolded Rags and Shining Talon but chose not to. A glance at One explained why. The sorcerer needed someone to stand watch between *her* and *him*.

"If you would spare two of your sorcerous cloths, Lord Rags is injured and would benefit from bandages." Shining Talon thought he was in the position to ask for anything, when this partnership was balanced on the point of a needle.

But to Rags's surprise, Morien handed two red blindfolds to Shining Talon, then roused the Queensguard with a twitch of his fingers.

Shining Talon knelt at Rags's feet. Rags stared down at the fae, aware that he was making an ugly face—distaste, stress, confusion, *why are you treating me like something more than a stain on the bottom of your boot*—but not willing to wipe it off.

He was only alive because of Shining Talon, whose entire people had been done in by sorcerers. Sorcerers like Morien. Morien, whom Rags had led straight to Shining Talon's doorstep, whose orders Shining Talon was now following.

At this point, if Shining Talon had been practical and killed him, Rags would've welcomed the sense it made.

He didn't. Instead, he held up the bands of red fabric, draped like open wounds across his palms. "I know that these are not ideal, or uncontaminated by the Lying arts, but allow me to do what I may, in order to bring relief to you."

"Why?" The question was out before Rags could stop it.

"Because, my lord Rags—"

Someone had to disabuse Shining Talon of this "lord" misimpression. Even if it was the only thing protecting Rags from Morien.

"Not a lord," he said.

Shining Talon paused. "I was told—"

"I don't care what you were told." Rags turned his focus to one of the cuts on his thumb. "I'm a thief. A good one, but fuck it, that's all. I came here to steal some kind of treasure, and I was tricked into it, made a bad deal, in service to your least favorite guy, Morien the Last. So quit it with the 'lord' shit. Unless you're a condemned murderer, *you* outrank my sorry ass."

The X's at the sides of Shining Talon's mouth twitched, then stilled, the only hint Rags's words had hit home.

"I might be a thief," Rags finished, "but I don't lie." Well, there had been a few times. ". . . much. Not enough to be a Lying One."

Another twitch of the X's. "Your honesty reveals a strength of character—"

"Ugh, enough." Rags felt scratchy between the shoulder blades.

"Do whatever you were going to do with those *sorcerous cloths*."

Curiosity was the main cause of death for a thief, but Rags hadn't managed to bury his. He'd grown up rubbing shoulders with Cheapside hawkers, selling hen's teeth and gutter water as cure-ails.

Real magic was for the Queen and her sorcerers. So far, Rags wasn't a fan.

Shining Talon went about his business, weird even by fae standards. It involved packing warm dirt onto Rags's skin, which quickly cooled it, then tying the makeshift bandages tightly. The stinging faded. Rags's hands felt unnervingly numb.

"Dirt isn't supposed to be good for scrapes. You know that, right?"

Shining Talon didn't look up as he replied, "Fed with the corpses and blood of my ancestors, this dirt is different."

"Ew," Rags said.

But his hands did feel better. Couldn't argue with that.

Shining Talon's job done, it was time to leave the ruins. Relief surged in Rags's chest. He wanted out of this place. For good.

If Shining Talon harbored misgivings about departing, the only sign was a faint dulling of his features. He glowed less, and the color of the lights veining the walls in their unreadable patterns faded with him.

19
RAGS

They traveled upward. Rags recognized each of the tunnels but didn't have the opportunity to sit back and inspect his handiwork, appreciate the skill it had taken to get through them. He wasn't in his profession for the glory.

He was in it because it was less pathetic than faking a limp and begging on a corner. Not to mention more profitable.

Rags wiped the dirt off the front of his torn shirt, noticed some bloodstains he hadn't taken stock of before. Before he knew it, they were passing his old friend the first corpse.

"Pal of yours?" he asked Shining Talon.

"My brother," Shining Talon replied.

That shut Rags up. He hadn't been thinking about what kind of people left one of their own to sleep while their world, their way of life, burned down around them. Crass to ask *what happened here* when it was so obvious. Death, ruination, the fae wiped clean off the map.

Save for one.

Rags gulped. "What'd he do to get slapped with a punishment like that?"

Shining Talon looked confused. "Our family was always first in service to the crown. His assignment was an honor."

Shining Talon didn't share how *he* felt about *his* position, but fine.

Rags didn't need to know. He didn't fully understand why he'd asked. Everyone already knew the fae were crazy.

Rags didn't think about Shining Talon or his brother. Instead he focused on the treasures he was leaving behind and how rich they would have made him, giving him something to do until the first breath of fresh air touched his face. Couldn't help grinning as he stepped into daylight, shielding his eyes until they readjusted to the sun.

He'd missed sunlight, the freedom of open sky, a lack of centuries-old traps firing poisoned projectiles at him and walls made of bone that seemed to breathe around him . . .

Shining Talon too stared upward, unblinking, stopped in his tracks.

Morien, when he noticed this, doubled back. "I must request you remain close," he said. "The forest is treacherous. I would not be pleased if I were to lose you. Either of you." This last for emphasis, with a pointed look in Rags's direction.

"But the trees . . ." Shining Talon's voice nearly broke on the last word. "What has happened to the trees?"

Rags tried to follow his gaze, found nothing amiss. The trees grew densely around them, tall and ancient, shimmering at the corners of his vision whenever he switched focus. Other than that, not a stump in sight.

"Don't see anything wrong with them," Rags said.

At Shining Talon's feet, smaller than she'd seemed before, One whipped her tail back and forth, reminding Rags of a wary street dog who'd run into a pack of kids who had once kicked it for sport.

"They are diminished." Shining Talon swallowed, a bob of the black ink bands encircling his throat. He shook his head, shook something unseen off his shoulders. "I will not lag behind again, Lying One. On this, you have my word."

Rags caught him staring at the trees as they continued, occasionally reaching out a hand as if he wanted to rest his palm on the bark, then pulling back at the last moment. There was something sad about it. Rags felt like he was interrupting a mourner at a gravesite.

"What are you doing?" Rags hissed at last. "He's not going to be happy if he has to come back for us again!"

"My apologies, Lo— Rags the Thief," Shining Talon replied, "but the trees do not speak to me."

"Yeah, trees don't speak to anyone."

"They should," Shining Talon insisted. "They used to."

Rags had to bite. "What did they say? 'Fuck, there's a worm in my roots, tickles like a sonofawhore?' 'Wish that sparrow would stop taking a shit on me?'"

"Yes," Shining Talon admitted, "those were the most common complaints. But they phrased it so beautifully. Through their language, you could understand a little more of the living world."

Rags gave up talking to him after that.

20
RAGS

Morien took them back through the forest, past where the black trees faded to brown bark laced with silver, then only brown, dull moss and wet dirt that didn't hum or glow. He had them set up camp close to a stream, where Rags could just barely detect signs of a previous camp, only a few days old. Had they stopped here when Rags was blindfolded and he couldn't remember?

Would the still-blindfolded Queensguard discuss this trip among themselves when it was over? Rags couldn't picture them gossiping. Even before the blindfolds, their silence had been eerie, all-consuming.

At least that didn't matter anymore. They had a lizard to follow, and she had chosen her own path.

The sun dipped below the tree line. Rags sat moodily by the fire. The cuts on his hands, beneath their tenderly wrapped bandages, had begun to itch, the good kind of itching, the kind that signaled skin knitting together and scabbing as it healed.

It was too soon for that to be happening yet.

Rags had the decomposed flesh of Shining Talon's ancestors to thank for his rapid recovery—and for the fact that he wouldn't sleep without nightmares for a while.

Think about something else—like how One stared with three

unblinking eyes at the campfire. Each leaping flame illuminated the mechanisms underneath its only mostly opaque scales. Rags studied the cogs and gears and perfect hinges shaped into One's muscles and bone. He thought of the pride in Shining Talon's voice when he spoke of the Great Paragon, and all the good it *hadn't* done him or the other fae.

"Rags the Thief." Shining Talon's voice, coming from Rags's side without warning, made Rags jump. "There is no need for you to maintain watch. I require little sleep and will act as your guard. You may rest safely."

"You require little sleep, huh?" Rags's moodiness filtered into his words, making him spit them out more bitterly than he'd planned. "You *could* be angling to make me let my guard down."

"*I* do not lie." Shining Talon was so deliberate in this rebuttal that Rags had to assume he'd taken offense. "Rather, I should say that the fae do not lie. My people are incapable of deception."

"Sure." Rags sat up, engaged despite himself. "Except there's plenty of ways to deceive someone without lying to them."

He could've sworn there was a flicker of something like amusement on Shining Talon's face. Or was it only firelight reflected in his eyes?

"Yes," he agreed warmly, in a way that chilled Rags to his bones.

He would've let the silence swell up to insulate him, but Shining Talon spoke again. "Have I done something to displease you, Rags the Thief?"

Nothing. That was the problem. The real source of Rags's frustration was Morien, but he wasn't stupid enough to take it out on the sorcerer. He couldn't talk to Shining Talon about anything real with Morien haunting their steps. Besides, Rags knew Shining Talon's respect couldn't be infinite. It would end sooner or later. Better if Rags didn't get used to it, cut it off at the pass before he started to *like* it.

He knew where this road stopped, and it wasn't anywhere good.

"I wish you'd been a pile of gold," Rags muttered. "Would've made my life easier."

"And once you had delivered what the Lying One asked for? What then?"

Morien's head lifted. He knew he'd been mentioned. If he'd looked at them across the fire in challenge, it would have been preferable to the sense of foreboding in his profile, swathed in scarves.

"He'd've killed me," Rags admitted. "Left me to rot in the ruins with the rest. And someday, maybe somebody comes along and thinks I'm another of the corpses guarding the place." He shrugged. "Could be worse fates. Currently, this suspense is a pain in my ass."

"Allow me to offer my clothing to ease the discomfort," Shining Talon began, reaching to pull off his gossamer shirt, probably made of moonbeams and maiden's kisses, so he could give it to Rags. Like it was nothing.

Rags swore and flung himself down on his back, grimacing when a twig stabbed him in the ribs. "Keep your clothes on, Shiny. I've slept more soundly on worse beds than this."

But despite the confidence in his statement, Rags lay awake for a long time, eyes obstinately shut.

Shining Talon knew he wasn't asleep.

It was the principle of the matter. Which was all Rags had left.

21
SOMHAIRLE

TWO MONTHS EARLIER

It was another perfect morning in Ever-Land, except all the birds were dropping dead.

Perhaps it was a curse.

Prince Somhairle Ever-Bright was familiar with curses, having been born one to his mother: a living reminder of the words Oberon Black-Boned had murmured to the wind in his final moments, a blight on House Ever-Bright.

The royal womb was doomed to lie barren. As long as an Ever-Bright queen wore the crown, she would never bear heirs.

At first, this was manageable. One sibling in every generation was trained for the coronation. Soon, different factions of the court sought to control the queen from an early age. Depending on their advisers, certain queens ruled more wisely, more nobly, than others. All of them died violently, of illnesses that arose out of nowhere, or accidents that could never be explained. They were replaced by the next in line, though she was never a daughter but a cousin, a niece, a favored relative. Always whispers of *the Ever-Bright curse* shrouded the brightness of their power in gray grief.

Somhairle's mother, Catriona, had ascended to the throne during a time of great mourning and terror. When she bowed her head for the crown, she was the sole surviving Ever-Bright. The last of her name.

Historians recorded that on that day, her courtiers' weeping nearly drowned out the celebration bells at her coronation.

Hail, the last of the Ever-Brights. Farewell to their legacy, to the once-sunlit heroes of the realm.

The Queen's supporters believed that she dedicated herself so ruthlessly to her kingdom because she never wanted to hear her people weep again. She worked tirelessly, some thought single-mindedly, with her sorcerers to discover a cure to Oberon's blight.

She awarded her favored courtiers with estates and acreage on the Hill. Ever-Nobles counted their place in the Queen's esteem by how high along the slope their homes were located. Her palace was spotless perfection, without flaw or fault. Rooms of white marble veined with silver, black tiles to mimic the ancient fae frescoes. It was glorious, though at times disturbing, to recall that these black tiles were indeed black fae bone.

Somhairle once asked his mother why she had ordered the palace decorated with fae motifs and fae art when she so hated the Folk.

"Dear boy." The Queen rarely called her sons by name, for she had too many to keep track of. Yet when she was with Somhairle, sadness clouded her eyes—a sadness he knew, even as a child, was reserved personally for him. "There is beauty in cruelty. Beauty is what survives when everything ugly is stripped away. And one must be cruel to triumph against ugliness."

It was then that Somhairle had first understood how someone could fear the Queen.

He hadn't been certain if she was talking about him, or the fae. Her own child, or her most hated enemy.

In the end, Catriona had triumphed by doing what no Ever-Bright queen had done since the Fair Wars ended: she had borne blood heirs.

Despite her triumphs, her people feared her. It was believed that the spell the sorcerers had mirrorcrafted to return life to Catriona's womb had unnaturally extended her life-span in the process.

It was true that although Somhairle's mother had not borne her first heir until the fiftieth year of her rule, she still looked as young as the day she'd taken the throne. Her reign had lasted nearly two hundred years now, more than twice that of any Ever-Bright queen before her.

Fourteen hale and healthy sons had come into the world before Somhairle arrived, one side of him withered from head to toe, piercing the royal fantasy of perfection. Queen Catriona might have been able to cheat death, but there was no cheating Oberon's curse.

Fourteen sons who allowed the kingdom to believe the curse had at last been broken—and Somhairle, whose existence implied otherwise.

Catriona's world was a diamond that would sustain no faults.

While Somhairle's half brothers resembled their respective fathers, Somhairle alone took after their mother. Perhaps this made it worse for her: that, looking into Somhairle's face, she saw only a warped reflection of her own.

If the Queen and her youngest son had ever posed together for a portrait, their artist would have painted two rosebud mouths, full and unsmiling, and two pairs of pale blue eyes the color of summer rain. Somhairle's round cheeks made his face less of a blade than Catriona's, but the same curling gold hair framed their faces. He shared her long lashes, too.

This resemblance only made his flaws stand out more starkly. The muscles in Somhairle's right arm and leg were shriveled and useless, similar to a book left out in the rain, its pages wrinkling toward the spine.

His first memories were of nurses with averted eyes, of hushed whispers cupped behind the same dough-soft hands that had wiped his tears and dressed his scrapes. He was a message. A token. A symbol more than a boy. Somhairle understood this early on. He watched and listened as his brothers brought accolades and honor to their mother's legacy.

The Queen trusted Adamnan, her eldest son and a natural diplomat, to hold stewardship of the Hill whenever she was absent. Diancecht had founded the city's archival restoration, dedicating himself to scholarly pursuits, dredging lost histories up from the muck and into the light. Each year the twins, Coinneach and Comhghall, climbed higher through the ranks in the Queensguard. And Laisrean was popular at court, always dancing late into the night with someone beautiful from one of the Ever-Lasting Houses, netting gossip more precious than pearls.

Of these, it was only Laisrean who was more than mere stranger to him. Owing to their mother's unusual longevity, Somhairle had half brothers old enough to be his father or even his grandfather. He'd been schooled alongside those princes closest to him in age: Laisrean, Prince Murchadh, and Prince Guaire. Among them—in their little cadre Somhairle was the youngest, Murchadh the eldest—the greatest gap was a mere five years.

Another seven years between Murchadh and the next-eldest prince, Prince Lochlainn, who was the only playmate Murchadh had considered worth his time.

In the end, age wasn't the dividing factor, but health, Somhairle's failing and his brothers' hale. Five years ago, after his thirteenth birthday—and his thirtieth life-threatening fever—Somhairle had finally been sent away from court, beyond the far reach of his mother's Ever-Bright corona. The Ever-Land manor bristled with lavish gifts like unburied treasure: a carousel nestled in the woods; a silver skiff in the shape of a dragonfly docked in the boathouse; a hidden cave beneath the cellar with only gemstones buried in the walls for light.

Reminders of the Queen's affection, in the only way she knew to show it.

For the first year, his next-eldest half brother, Guaire, had visited monthly, making no secret that it was duty and not pleasure, to confirm how Somhairle was settling in. After the first year, he visited twice. He hadn't returned since the third year.

The rest of his half brothers carried on, undisturbed by Somhairle's absence, riding a courtly carousel upon which no mount remained for him.

Only Somhairle's half brother Laisrean had visited frequently, together with Laisrean's friend Tomman Ever-Loyal, because Laisrean knew Somhairle got on well with the Ever-Loyal girls. He'd always wanted sisters, and thought he'd found them, until even they grew old enough to forget their youthful summers together and ceased returning to Ever-Land's idylls.

Laisrean still wrote, but infrequently.

Somhairle refused to begrudge them their freedom.

Regardless, it had been years since they'd traipsed through sunlit fields together. Years since anyone, friend or brother, had come knocking at Somhairle's door.

The Ever-Land manor and environs were built to resemble a fae dream. No roads or walkways traced the grounds. Instead, summer gardens grew wild between the estate houses, framed by lakes and rivers, the occasional rocky outcropping leading to a waterfall. One could stumble across a gathering of vine-and-marble statues hidden amid a grove of lemon silkwoods, or an orchard hung with floating globes of sorcery-light. It had once served as the Queen's private holidaying grounds, though after she made it Somhairle's world, she hadn't once returned to visit.

For Somhairle, it was exile.

He should have hated it, should have felt natural disgust at his predicament. Out of sight, out of the story.

But he loved the sprawling country manor. Its uncomplicated, old-fashioned wood-plank roof, upon which the patter of spring showers echoed like laughter; its white stone walls bathed in drowsy sunshine. Waking late and reveling in the slow creep of country life, the solitude of pale sunbeams peering through his leadlight window. Somhairle's court was composed of birds, whose gossip was sweet song, who came and went freely in and out of open windows. No cages. They made their perches on the sturdy branches of Ever-Land's undying trees, built nests, chattered to one another between breezes.

Then, one morning, Morien the Last had appeared with Lord Faolan Ever-Learning in tow.

When last Somhairle was at court, House Ever-Learning had been ambitious but unsuccessful in the ruthless hierarchy of Ever-Families jockeying to gain favor with the Queen. They'd moved up in the world, he noted, if they now had access to one of her most powerful sorcerers.

"Here on the Queen's orders," Lord Faolan had explained, flashing the Queen's seal. Somhairle had limped down the steps to greet them, tousle-headed, wearing only a dressing gown with his steel-and-silver brace and crutch, which steadied and straightened him from ankle to hip and chest to shoulder.

The birds had already stopped singing.

Morien the Last hadn't bothered to explain his presence. Sorcerers rarely felt the need to explain themselves to anyone. They answered to Queen Catriona alone, trusting the lesser princes to stay out of their way and usually affording them the same courtesy in return.

Before the hour was out, Morien had commandeered the dining room, locked the doors, draped a bolt of red linen over each one and curtained the room's many windows.

Somhairle gave him a wide berth. It had been nearly a decade since one of his mother's sorcerers had tried to impress her by curing him of his unacceptable flaws, yet the memories held a keen edge no matter how many years they'd lain idle.

If Morien had come to adjust the enchantments that kept Ever-Land alive and hidden, which sorcerers occasionally did, he'd complete that business and be gone within a week. Somhairle could manage the metallic taste the sorcerer's visit left in his mouth for seven days. He'd have to.

As a lesser prince, without political value as an heir—he was nowhere close to ascending the throne, and even if he had been, he wasn't the image of perfection Catriona would choose to crown—he demanded respect, but wielded no significant power.

He was a prince royal who couldn't so much as ask his houseguests to leave.

So he avoided Morien the best he could and minded his own business, trusting it would all be finished soon.

Three days later, the doves nesting on Somhairle's windowsill began to lose their feathers. The following day, his canaries refused to leave their roost. Treetops once filled with birdsong hushed silent as fresh graves, as if the hardening grounds were holding their breath. The balmy air chilled and thickened.

Somhairle woke in the first night, having dreamed he was choking on liquid silver.

And the next night. And the next. More silver, gushing forth from under the ground, flooding Somhairle's bedchamber. The birds flapped their wings, but one by one, they drowned. Somhairle drenched in cold sweat, like he had during the fevers of his childhood.

Every night he was reminded, by the light of a single candle in his study, that there were invaders in his sacred court.

According to that candle, Lord Faolan never slept.

Usually, neither did Somhairle. But the study was intended to be where he spent his *own* sleepless nights.

Somhairle resented the change at first, then found himself unable to resist the pull and promise of company. Of conversation.

Whether Morien was awake on these long nights was a puzzle Somhairle didn't risk solving.

Lord Faolan was different. Somhairle soon mustered the courage to join him.

Maps had piled up like dirty laundry in the study over the passing nights, gradually devouring a once neatly ordered desk. Tea stains everywhere. Faolan drank a dark, smoky brew that made Somhairle's nose burn, though sometimes Somhairle poured a cup simply to have something warm to hold on to.

On top of the maps rested several open books—some from Somhairle's collection of classical plays—though it was impossible to tell whether they were in the midst of being read or being employed as paperweights.

Morien never made any attempt to join them. Fortunately.

"I have to say, I admire your pluck," Faolan confessed one night, legs flung over the arm of a cream-colored settee, long black hair unbound around his shoulders, resembling a fae prince of legend. "I've never seen anyone dare to *sneeze* in Morien's direction, let alone scowl at him. Are you the formidable secret weapon of the Ever-Brights, kept safely hidden here until such a time as needed?"

Somhairle, who had a short lifetime of experience in keeping his expression blank, forced a rueful smile at the appropriate moment.

"You must offer my forgiveness to Morien for my poor manners. Having been away from court for so long, I must have forgotten myself. I am merely in awe of his magnificence." He sipped his tea. Too strong and unrelentingly bitter. It wouldn't help him sleep, but he hadn't gathered the courage to face his dreams again. He let it warm his cheeks so he could blush sweetly. The innocent cripple: a useful archetype. "I would speak with him directly, but I'm afraid I have an aversion to sorcerers. You might have heard . . ."

"Rumors aren't what interest me." Faolan allowed a courteous moment of hesitation to pass, staring at the curved toes of his pointed slippers, before he continued. "One hears all sorts of things at court, regardless of whether or not one wishes to."

A story. That was all Somhairle was to other people.

If he imagined himself onstage at the old Gilded Lily theater, an actor telling someone else's tale, he could get through what came next without feeling like a specimen on display.

He began to explain his past experiences.

There had been Dyfed the Quick, who'd "painlessly"—his description—inserted a series of mirrorglass needles into Somhairle's side. As Somhairle soon discovered, this procedure caused brief but blinding agony intended to reinvigorate his stunted growth.

After the fourteenth unsuccessful attempt, Dyfed had been removed from service.

Aibhilin the Asking had better luck in pretending she'd come to Somhairle seeking friendship before she lowered him into a mirror-bright pool in one of the palace bathrooms.

She'd held him under until he nearly drowned.

Saraid the Ready had produced a reflection of what Somhairle could have looked like whole to mock him from the safety of a looking glass. That Prince Somhairle had existed solely on the other side of the mirror, an image of himself that should have been, forever out of reach.

In the end, the Queen forbade anyone else from using any magic on any of her sons.

When Somhairle finished speaking, his cup was empty, though his throat was dry.

Faolan shivered theatrically, the way all good audiences should. One of his hands hung at his side, fingers twitching rhythmically as if to scratch a dog that wasn't there. When he caught Somhairle noting the detail, he pretended he'd been playing an invisible instrument.

Somhairle waited. The purpose of oversharing personal, perhaps tragic details from his life—to him, they were merely *what had happened*; to others, they were tales of horror and fascination—was to prompt pity. If Faolan pitied him, he wouldn't respect him. Wouldn't consider him a threat.

Might let slip some useful information someday, with a tongue he would have guarded more closely otherwise. Nearly all Somhairle's contacts at the palace had ceased to reply to him—so if he was forced to undertake a little subterfuge to get news of his own country, that hardly seemed without justification.

"You needn't worry, Your Royal Highness," Faolan said. There were miniature dogs embroidered on his slippers—no doubt the ancestral Ever-Learning hounds. "I expect we'll be out of your hair soon enough."

After two weeks, Morien was still entrenched, Faolan was eating all the cheese, another mourning dove had been found dead in the rosebushes, and Somhairle was no closer to divining the reason for their presence in Ever-Land.

Something had to be done. Somhairle needed to try a different tactic.

He buried the dove with the others, whispered his useless apologies to the roots, and, though it felt like too little too late, wrote about the mysterious deaths to his mother and brothers, the few he thought might bother to write back.

Although the four youngest princes had been schooled together, they weren't close. Each had his friends, his favorite advisers, all of whom were convinced the other princes wanted *their* prince dead.

Somhairle expected to hear from Laisrean if he heard from anyone, but it was Guaire who wrote back first, surprising him.

Don't be a child. Though at nineteen he'd lived only one year longer than Somhairle, Guaire never lacked for confidence. *Our mother has more important lives to consider. She doesn't care about a few sick animals, nor should she.*

Perhaps the best solution is to stop feeding them. Then they'll die elsewhere, and won't disturb your sensitivities?

The backhanded accusation revealed by Guaire's suggestion reminded Somhairle of the many ways he'd proven unsuitable for his mother's Silver Court. He imagined the other chidings that would arrive. He was a fool to have bothered with letters.

Then, the next morning, his mother granted him an audience.

Moments past sunrise in the solarium, when the light was softest, gilded. To keep birds from flying into the glass and snapping their tiny-boned necks, Somhairle's few servants had hung flowering plants along the windows. Bright orange and yellow honeyflower, vibrant scarlet trumpets—all the sweet nectar the birds once loved.

Catriona Ever-Bright appeared resplendent in the midst of the blossoms. The sight of her filled him with awe and fear. Her full white gown, so encrusted with diamonds and pearls that it could have stood on its own, shone with the reflected color of a thousand far-off flowers. She looked younger than Somhairle remembered, but also more distant.

The portrait of a queen, not the queen the portrait was based on.

For she wasn't really there, flesh and blood, in the solarium. The Queen loved her sons best when they gave her time to miss them. What Somhairle saw sitting across from him was merely a reflection, the creation of one of her sorcerers.

Still, it was rare that she could take time to speak privately like this, even with the assistance of mirrorcraft.

"We would never allow any harm to befall our own." Catriona's voice rang like struck steel in the tiny solarium. She pitched for great halls and grand pronouncements—too grand for these more humble surroundings. "It is admirable that your care for Ever-Land extends to even its most insignificant details, but do not allow your dovelike heart to mislead you. The land prospers."

The difficulty Somhairle often felt in speaking to his mother was that she was responding to a different son: the one she wanted rather than the one she had.

The birds weren't insignificant to him. Perhaps Guaire had been trying to spare him the embarrassment of bringing his small concerns before their mother, whose kingdom consisted primarily of actual people, not doves and starlings.

Somhairle shifted on his overstuffed velvet chaise. It was a chair best suited for afternoon naps and late-night reading, less so for receiving one's mother, the Queen. He'd dressed for the occasion, white shirt fastened high around his throat, a gauze flower opening under a delicate waistcoat wrought in filigree silver. The pattern of scrolling vines tinkled when he moved, creating visual and aural distractions from his leg brace.

On his head was a silver circlet. Around his throat, the sun-sigil medallion of House Ever-Bright.

It was too hot. He'd never felt his station less. He missed his loose gardening trousers, the drowsy bumble of bees, the smell of warm dirt.

"I'm not afraid for Ever-Land." He was too aware of the crooked set of his shoulders, the relatively short span of his eighteen years compared to his mother's many decades. Worst of all, he sounded childish. Proving Guaire right was the dread that forced Somhairle to press on. ". . . though, in your wisdom, I'm sure you understand how it might feel unsafe. Morien arriving, birds dropping out of the air around me . . ."

For the first time, Queen Catriona looked at Somhairle instead of the plants. Her attention was total, terrifying. It always had been.

Silver flashed in her stare, then disappeared with a langorous blink.

"Our young, wounded bird." Catriona shared Somhairle's blue eyes and fair complexion, but her features were hewn without sentiment. As a magical reflection, she looked almost ghoulish, as though she had silver bones and silver blood. His mother's court took its name from the wealth of ore in the Hill's bedrock, but sometimes, Somhairle thought she took her ornamentations too far. No other queen in their history had been so garish. "How we hoped that you, of all our children, might escape a life haunted by death. . . . Your beloved father was so lively."

Somhairle's father had gone questing to bring back an antidote for his twisted son. Before his child had had a chance to know him, he'd vanished.

This wasn't unusual. Few of his half brothers had living fathers.

Sun winked off his brace, reminded Somhairle that he too had an unusual silver accessory. Instead of ceremonial crowns, the Ever-Bright smiths had wrought a series of strong, lightweight models fitted expertly to Somhairle's growing height.

He hadn't received a new one in a few years. But now wasn't the time for that thought toward comfort, a base distraction.

"Then I may speak to Morien about the situation?" Somhairle asked gently.

While in name and birth he outranked the Last, both knew who held more power at court. Morien was the Queen's arm; Somhairle, barely a ring to adorn her littlest finger.

Catriona's eyes snapped back to attention. "The Last must not be disturbed."

The blood drained from Somhairle's face. He'd misjudged Catriona's tenderness, employed to placate, perhaps nothing more. The bitter taste in his mouth stung his tongue.

He'd forgotten how quickly his mother's mood could sour.

Catriona held up one graceful hand. "We would not see you honed like a blade toward purpose. Remain carefree, and we shall intervene on your behalf."

It would push Somhairle's luck to exaggerate the issues of his health, but that was his only weapon. He'd buried thirteen birds. His pride was nothing compared to their lost lives.

"You are gracious as ever." Somhairle covered his mouth to cough, forcing a shaky smile.

It didn't matter. Catriona was already gone. The mirror in front of Somhairle showed only a blurred stain, the Queen's lingering profile like a cameo silhouette.

Outside the solarium, dressed as though he was waiting for his own audience with the queen, Faolan straightened quickly to prevent the door from opening directly into his nose. Morien was nowhere to be seen, an implication more powerful than physical presence.

"You look well!" Faolan said with the false cheer of Silver Court conversation, and also its lack of self-respect. The swell of a plum pearl drop dangled from one ear on a rose-gold chain, rather than a silver one—an intriguing, if minor, rebellion against the Queen's favored metal. "Feeling better?"

"I am," Somhairle agreed. "We've lost some of Ever-Land's other residents, however."

"Oh." Faolan's face flickered, was too steeped in court artifice to fall. "Yes. I heard about the birds."

Somhairle wasn't in the mood to be outright mocked—or worse, humored.

Alas, when Faolan fell into step beside him, his brace made graceful disengagement impossible.

"Forgive me, Your Royal Highness. Though it's incredibly unlike me, it seems I've misspoken." Faolan worried away at a wedge of salty white cheese Somhairle hadn't noticed he'd been holding, eating the pieces that crumbled freely into his fingers. "I haven't slept for days. Not that it's any excuse, but I assure you, I wasn't listening at keyholes. I waited for you outside the solarium because I bear glad tidings."

"Oh?"

"I came to find you as soon as I heard," Faolan explained. Acknowledging, without directly expressing, that he needed *some* excuse for being flattened against the door when Somhairle had exited. "You've seen *the last* of our friend Morien. *At last,* eh?"

It was early enough that the house was yet slumbering. They'd traveled through the main corridor, past two unoccupied guestrooms and a sitting area that cradled a dusty piano. Out of habit, Somhairle averted his gaze from the mirror in the entryway as he opened the front doors for Faolan. A warm breeze blew in with the scents of the tea garden, green and floral, with a whiff of—was that cinnamon?

His breakfast awaited him.

Somhairle hesitated, feigned pain as the explanation when it was confusion. He needed a moment to consider.

If Morien was gone, why did Faolan remain?

"Your purpose here, Lord Faolan," Somhairle murmured meekly. "May I be so bold as to inquire . . ."

"Oh?" Faolan turned, sharp and beautiful as faceted, precious stone. Colder than Somhairle had seen him in the soft glow of candelight, bleak and hawk-eyed under Ever-Land's morning sun. "The Queen didn't tell you when you spoke why it is so necessary that we disturb your idyll with our dirty work?"

"She believes my constitution too besieged already. That I mustn't be troubled by matters of court and country." Somhairle cast his eyes down and leaned against the doorframe. His brace's ankle joint struck the hinge, to remind Faolan that he was limited, harmless. "Though it's meant in kindness, it makes me feel like a useless child."

"Well." Faolan gazed at something, anything other than Somhairle, angling his face until he was all aquiline profile. Cheekbones like daggers. Patrician and remote. "We're here on the Queen's business. The business of thwarting the Resistance."

Although Queen Catriona heralded a time of miracles, she'd also weathered her share of disasters. Most recently, the former Eastside district had collapsed after the launch of a contentious tunneling project to build new sewer systems, and the people blamed her bitterly for their loss of land and livelihood.

Somhairle hadn't minded leaving sour rumors and unpleasantness behind when he'd left the Hill. But why should trouble with court malcontents, the Queen's grumbling detractors, have brought Lord Faolan and Morien the Last *here*, of all places? "That's still a concern, is it?"

Faolan's lashes fluttered. "More threat than ever, Your Highness, since their agents were discovered amid the Queen's favorites. In House Ever-Loyal."

Somhairle, who had a lifetime of experience in receiving ill news with a glass smile, felt the world drop out from under him.

22
RAGS

PRESENT DAY

Morning showed up, shivery and wet. Rags had dreamed no clever solutions to his shit situation during the night, had spent most of it sleepless, pondering dangerous questions.

The type of questions that got little thieves killed.

Just how much had Lord Faolan and Morien known before they sent Rags down into the fae ruins? They couldn't be after a weapon the Queen wasn't aware of, not right under the Queen's nose. *The Queen was after the Great Paragon all along,* Rags thought.

He opened his eyes to darkness. A looming form crouched over him, a canopy of—was that hair?—like an umbrella, sheltering him from the drizzling sky.

"The human body is artlessly built," Shining Talon explained from above, "and susceptible to disease in the simplest of weather conditions."

"Argh," Rags replied.

He managed to wriggle free, wrinkling his nose as the drizzle fell on his skin. He stumbled to the stream's edge to wash his face, clean the dead fae remnants off his hands, rebandage them, relieve himself, *escape Shining Talon.*

His hollow cheeks stared back at him from the clear waters,

rippling but distinct. Dark hair matted, darker eyes hard. He plunged his head under the current. Pulled it out, cursing, streaming wet, *cold*.

"Allow me to assist." Shining Talon was beside him again. He'd approached soundlessly and handsomely, an irritating shadow Rags couldn't shake.

"I can wash myself—" Rags began.

Shining Talon cupped stream water in his hands, lifted them without losing a drop. As Rags watched, steam began to rise from the water's surface, like Shining Talon was offering Rags a mug of hot tea on a midwinter day.

"Now it will be less offensive to your tender human flesh," Shining Talon explained.

"Stop that." Rags shoved ineffectually at Shining Talon's arms in an attempt to make him spill the heated water. He didn't budge, and Rags choked down a gurgle of impatience. "I swear, it's not necessary. I've bathed in puddles of city water—which isn't all water, if you catch my meaning. This is fresh. Clean. Besides, the cold clears my head." He clenched his jaw, sticking said head back under the current to prove his point.

Damn piss balls ass shit, it was colder the second time.

Getting the dirt out of his ears with warm water, letting it sluice over his tense shoulders, would have been more comfortable. It'd also make him sloppy, hungry for luxury. Once his edge dulled, that was it. A ruined weapon that wouldn't drive home.

He held his head under the current for a ten count before he emerged, pink cheeked and sodden to the collar, shaking out his hair.

Shining Talon dodged each droplet of water with a speed Rags didn't want to think about.

"See? My *tender human flesh* made it through the experience in one piece, thanks." All he had to do was keep his teeth from chattering, and he might pull off the act. "But if *your* tender fae flesh needs the pampering, don't hold back on my account. . . ."

Rags trailed off. Shining Talon had a hand plunged into the stream, eyes shut, the faintest wrinkle of concentration on his forehead like he was listening to something.

"Uh . . . ," Rags said.

Shining Talon's dark lashes fluttered, his eyes opening. "Seven hundred years." He removed his hand and held it in front of him, staring at his palm. "The stream says it has been seven hundred years since it has seen one of my kind."

"That specific, huh?" Rags asked.

"Water is not known for its specificity, no, but it is accurate enough. It was necessary that I ask the stream. The trees would not answer."

"Right." The trees. "Hey, when are we gonna have a talk about the rock in my pocket?"

Shining Talon's gaze narrowed, and he glanced over his shoulder, back in the direction of their camp, his meaning clear enough to anyone accustomed to deceiving people: *Not while Morien's around.*

Except Morien was gonna be around for a while. Rags didn't have a solution to that problem. *Yet.* He rocked back on his heels, thought about asking Shining Talon to apologize to *the stream* for him—*sorry I plunged my dirty head into you*—then shook the idiot idea away and left the riverbank.

Returned to the fireside, where Morien was waiting.

Sure, the sorcerer wanted to kill him, but at least he wasn't talking to water.

23
RAGS

A half day's riding and the forest began to thin. Shining Talon paused near the edge of the woods, something Rags noticed because he was watching for exactly this kind of mold-for-brains behavior from their fae companion. It was already strange enough that he easily kept pace with the horses, though he was on foot.

Shining Talon needed to quit being bizarre so they could both stay alive. Rags had no doubt of Shining Talon's ability to over-power Morien, especially with One the lizard on his side, but the big fae didn't seem to think it was worth shredding Rags's heart in the process.

A bad bargain any way you sliced it.

Right now, Shining Talon was simply gazing at the trees with a fierce look fixed on his face. Something about his expression made Rags feel like an intruder just by watching. Nothing in that silver gaze was remotely human. It should have made Rags tremble. Instead, he couldn't help but notice the sharp, wolfish beauty in the golden planes of Shining Talon's face. Looking at him, Rags got that same feeling he'd get when he caught the glimmer of untended coin. An excited twist in his gut. Pleasure so unexpected it was almost pain.

Any good thief knew when he'd glimpsed something he shouldn't. Something that should have stayed in the safe.

"Quit staring at the trees and shake a leg," Rags hissed, stomping the feeling flat.

Shining Talon looked at him, startled. The moment was broken. *Good.* "But I am saying goodbye."

The wind shifted, and with it the clouds, which cast the long, ragged shadows of the tree line across them both. It was more than the trees he was saying farewell to. It was the Lost-Lands themselves, and all the fae who'd lived in them.

"Is there a problem?" Morien's voice, when it came, was near enough that Rags could blame his gooseflesh on the sorcerer.

"Nothing." Rags fixed his best I-haven't-got-a-string-of-pearls-down-my-pants smile on his face.

Rags could see Morien's frown even beneath the scarves. The sorcerer's gaze passed to Shining Talon, but Morien didn't say anything. Rags figured he didn't want to talk to the fae any more than he had to.

"I must ask that you keep pace," was all Morien said to Rags.

Then they were riding again.

Rags quickly noticed that while he'd been distracted, Morien had removed the Queensguard's blindfolds. They seemed unimpressed with the new members of their party. Either they'd been working with the sorcerer long enough that nothing surprised them anymore, or they were well trained enough to keep their thoughts about a fae and an enormous silver lizard to themselves. Either way, when Rags looked around to see if he wasn't the only one knocked on his ass by current events, he caught not one of the Queensguard offering so much as a startled blink.

In fact, they barely spoke to one another. Eerie. Like being surrounded by marching tin soldiers come to life. When presented with an audience of one captive thief, one impossible creature from a long-extinct race, and one monstrous silver lizard, the Queensguard ought to have been crowing about another noble victory over Shining Talon's people, shoving Rags's face in how easily he'd been caught in an Ever-Noble's game, and so on.

And yet, not a jeer.

Rags didn't like that.

The twisting, lonely patches of road they traveled hadn't been proper thoroughfare in decades, but were still leading them toward civilization, one hooved step at a time. Morien disappeared from the path once or twice to report to his master. Whether that was Faolan or the Queen, Rags wasn't sure.

Soon enough, they saw the first humble signs of human life: an abandoned hut; a filthy shepherd girl who stopped and gawped as they passed.

Morien waved a hand in the girl's direction. "She won't remember the lizard," he said distantly, by way of explanation.

From the way the sheep stumbled over themselves to get away, he hadn't bothered ensorcelling *them* to forget the shit they'd seen.

"We require additional resources for our return trip," Morien said sometime later, "and must stop in the nearest village in order to restock our supplies. However . . ." He spared a glance for One, who lifted her chin defiantly, her third eye flashing, then nodded at Shining Talon. ". . . that will prove difficult, with certain more conspicuous members of our party."

"In this, Lying One, you do not lie," Shining Talon replied.

"Cloak for him," Rags suggested quickly, with a glance at Shining Talon, a look he hoped conveyed the sentiment: *Enough with the "Lying One" shit before it pisses Morien off for good.* "But the lizard . . ."

He couldn't think of a fix for that problem.

Morien affected a half bow, still in his saddle. "With its permission, I will take care of that matter."

"Her," Shining Talon murmured softly.

Morien didn't appear to hear him.

Rags did.

A cloak for Shining Talon was pulled from a Queensguard pack, and another was procured for the lizard and draped over the majority of her bulk. She shuffled beneath the fall of wool. For a time, Morien's hands traced the signs of his craft in the air above his horse's mane, until Rags realized that when he wasn't paying close attention, the brown cloak made the silver lizard look like a shaggy herding dog. If he let his attention wander, he started to believe the illusion, despite knowing the truth. He shuddered.

Shining Talon pulled the hood of his own cloak over his face, hiding his hair beneath. The cloak took care of the major details—the glow of his skin, the tattoos, the whiteless silver eyes, the pointed ears.

Rags didn't believe that disguise as easily as One's.

"Don't you want to know where we're going?" Rags asked him, unable to keep it in any longer.

The expression of calm on Shining Talon's face was downright infuriating. "As long as I am by your side, and we are by hers, I do not question that I am where I am needed."

Rags envied him.

His confidence was stupid, but it must've been pleasant.

When they came to it, the village was exactly what Rags expected. One stable, a few unfashionable shops for necessities, and a public house with half its roof in need of rethatching. Homesteads neighbored the town's center—not that it could be called a "town" with a straight face—and dotted the surrounding fields. The sun, a low red gash, kissed the hills as it set.

Morien instructed them to wait at the edge of the village while he negotiated terms of their stay with the owner of the public house.

The sun was not yet gone when Morien returned. "We have the run of the place tonight," he informed them curtly. "Stable for the horses in the back. Queensguard, see to it. As for the rest . . . some of us must remain upstairs in private quarters for the duration of our stay."

"Meaning the dirty thief, the tattooed fae lunatic, and the dog who's actually a silver lizard?" Rags asked, and grinned recklessly. Some of his humor had returned with the thought of sleeping in an actual bed. Morien stared him down until the grin faltered. It dropped altogether as Rags dismounted.

"Remain upstairs. Got it." He handed his horse's reins to the nearest Queensguard. "Want us to scale the outside wall while we're at it? I'm good at sneaking into places."

Morien tossed Rags a cloak, which he caught against his chest. "That won't be necessary. All details of maintaining discretion have already been taken care of."

He wasn't lying on that point, either. Nobody looked Rags's dirty-thief way when he entered: the barkeep polished the same spot on the bar top over and over, while the lone barmaid faced a far corner of the taproom and didn't turn, didn't seem to breathe.

The emptiness of the public house was odd enough, but this many royal horses being put to stable should have meant a taproom quivering for Hill gossip, especially with House Ever-Loyal's treason and destruction last year still shadowing everyone's thoughts. Soon the bones of that carcass would be picked clean, and scavenging Cheap-siders would have to turn their eyes upward again, waiting for the next House to fall.

So his city churned, grinding the poor under its wheels so roughly compared to the rest. Rags put his kicking pulse down to homesick-ness, not fear, and scurried up the dusty stairs.

24
RAGS

Staying out of sight in the ramshackle inn meant Rags was alone in a small room under a low ceiling with only Shining Talon and One the lizard for company.

To keep himself occupied, he fished the lump out of his pocket, followed by the silver beetle. Excluding One, this was all the actual treasure he'd come back with out of the fathoms-deep fae ruin, submerged within the Lost-Lands.

No one would ever believe him.

The beetle would be his keepsake for this job, stored in the hidey-hole alongside a dull arrowhead from House Ever-Bold's Heroes of the Fair Wars collection, Lady Blodwen Ever-Striving's silver earwax cleaner, and three bent coins Rags had found after they'd buckled under carriage wheels.

He would have tried to sleep, but there was Shining Talon's tendency to creep up noiselessly beside Rags to consider. Rags would never know if he was alone or if Shining Talon was standing obsessive vigil, eyes unblinking, *staring* at him.

He couldn't deal with that.

Instead, he poked at the beetle. His fingers still stung from where its buggy brothers had bitten him, but the pain was definitely receding, thanks to Shining Talon's magic dirt.

"I don't know what I'm supposed to do with this thing." He held the lump aloft. It was the size of an overripe apple, left to grow on its branch too long. The lamplight caught the lumpy, silver blobs twisted around its base like a gloppy coating of tar, making the object glow in Rags's hand.

Even this, a thing that looked like ossified dung, was too beautiful a fae treasure for Rags to hold on to.

Shining Talon came to stand by the bed. He didn't reach for the rock, which made Rags realize he'd been hoping *he* would relieve him of the important artifact.

But Shining Talon, irritatingly, merely gazed at it, leaving both of them staring like yokels.

"It was in your coffin," Rags prompted, like Shining Talon was a watch that needed a wind to get going. "With you the whole time. You sure you don't have any tips?"

Shining Talon shook his head. His hair moved like a black river, shimmering as it flowed down his back. Absurd, to see someone this elegant and noble in a cramped, backwater inn. Against the grim backdrop, Shining Talon was so beautiful, it hurt worse than any infected splinter under Rags's skin. Comparing himself to the unearthly creature next to him ached like the shard in Rags's heart.

"Forgive me," Shining Talon explained. "I must have been unclear. The artifact was not placed into Sleep with me. Rather, it was . . . stored somewhere safe, until such a time as it was meant to be found."

Rags didn't need to see the uncertainty in the thoughtful set of Shining Talon's lower lip to hear it in his words. Fae might not lie, but he knew when someone was loitering around the edges of untruth without crossing its threshold.

"Somewhere safe?"

Shining Talon blinked. The crossbones at the corners of his mouth twitched. "It is said that our queen placed the artifact among the stars. That she alone would know when it was time for it to fall."

"Great," Rags said. "I get a fragment that's not going to lead us anywhere."

Shining Talon nodded, halting. It was clear he didn't want to admit it, but there was no other conclusion to be drawn. "It is said that one fragment must be led, not do the leading. That this is a test of its master's worth."

There were those words again. *Test, master, worth.*

Did they have thieves from the gutter in the fae court? Did they have gutters?

Nah, Rags thought. *Fae probably didn't shit.*

"If that's true, we're gonna be waiting a long time." Rags tossed the lump from one hand to the other, testing its weight like a juggling ball. "I'm not worthy. I'm as lost as anyone. Don't think I'll be leading anything anywhere any time soon." He set the lump on the bed, then patted his thighs mockingly. "Here, boy!"

Naturally, the lump didn't move.

Shining Talon's brow wrinkled in confusion. Rags didn't feel like explaining the joke. Mostly because he was afraid of pulling the thread that revealed that he, *Rags,* was the only joke in the room.

If fae were so smart, Shining Talon would figure it out.

In the meantime, Rags unwrapped the red bandages on his hands, had to keep himself from exclaiming when he saw how the scabbed-over flesh had healed cleanly. After that, he didn't know what to do with Morien's red scarves—which, despite having been packed with dirt, weren't dirty—so he stuffed them in a pocket and did his best to forget about them. They might be worth something someday, more than the beetle and the fae lump anyway, if he lived long enough to sell them.

Then he set to poking at the lump. To his surprise, the silver stuff moved. Not easily; it wasn't fragile. But with dedicated pressure under the pad of his thumb, he found he could push it aside, like globs of not-quite-dry paint. Rags tried and failed to ignore Shining Talon's attention on him as he pushed at the stuff, discovering that he could pull the silver away in layers, like peeling a piece of fruit. As he gently tore aside a thick strip, he caught a glimpse of something white and gleaming beneath. On its surface were intricate etched patterns, like the ones he'd seen in the fae ruins.

Rags hesitated. There *was* something special under there. Why keep peeling when it was obvious to him, if not to Shining Talon, that he *wasn't* the one meant to hold on to it?

Better to leave it in its protective coating until they ran across someone *actually* worthy of the thing. Like One's master. Whoever that was.

"What about your fragment?" Rags asked. Shining Talon's silence was wearing on him, dragging him down like his nails clawing the lump's surface. "You and the lizard"—One didn't look up at this, deeming Rags unworthy of her attention—"were in the same place. Wouldn't it make sense for her to be yours?"

Shining Talon looked at Rags as if he were trying to decipher the question.

It wasn't that tough a puzzle. Rags had unlocked worse to get to the fae.

"What?" Rags asked finally, less demanding than he'd intended. Whinier. "Something on my face?"

"I do not see anything. I must look closer." Shining Talon rose to his feet in an instant, taking Rags's chin in both hands and turning it toward the meager candlelight before Rags had the chance to yelp a wordless protest. "All is well with your face," Shining Talon concluded.

"Then what about my question?" Rags demanded, warning flares burning to life in his gut.

"Ah." Shining Talon's gaze slunk away like a kicked dog. "I sought to answer without offense. Because of the uncertainty inherent in human nature, it was decided that my fragment should be the last uncovered."

"Okay." Rags waited for more. There had to be more.

Shining Talon lifted his eyes to meet Rags's. "It was thought that if I were to be found alongside my own fragment—if gathering the fragments was without appropriate difficulty—the Great Paragon might fall into unfit hands. Arranging it in this fashion allows me to study the other masters and judge the quality of their character before the Great Paragon can be completed."

Rags's mouth struggled to find the right scathing remark. Typical fae, making something as complicated as possible, not appreciating the shades dappling the space between *truth* and *lie*. Now Shining Talon had to pin all his hopes on Rags, who carried a sorcerer's shard in his heart.

Rags was no expert in fae lore, but his had to be the exact definition of *unfit hands*.

The urge to run pierced him. Once, while he was sneaking through a storehouse at thirteen, a stray nail had gone through the leather sole of his boot. The pain had been so sudden, the resulting rush of adrenaline so heady, that he'd finished the job quicker than a cat, without leaving a single drop of blood on the floorboards.

Pierced by a rusty nail was how Rags felt now. He wanted to bolt out the window, flee down the street. He'd figure out the rest on his way to the city.

A snort of laughter escaped his lips, followed by a convulsing peal of the damn stuff. If he ran, he'd be killed.

Being the best at thieving was his favorite thing. It was also what had trapped him.

"Are you unwell?" Shining Talon asked with real concern.

"Do fae not"—hysterical wheeze—"laugh?"

"They do. It does not look like . . . this."

"Ugly, you mean?"

"I did not say—"

Rags waved the unnecessary apology off before it could ruin the moment. "Don't sweat it. You were staring, I used a figure of speech, you're gonna have to work on not taking everything at face"—another chortled snort—"value."

There was a knock at the door. Rags tucked his treasures away and answered it.

Two trays of food waited for them outside. Rags pulled them in. One waited for him to close the door again before she sniffed warily at the bowls of steaming stew-slop, wrinkled her finely carved nostrils, and recoiled with a shake of her head.

"More for me, then." Rags sat on the edge of the small room's small bed, balanced a tray on his knees, and dug in.

He didn't bother with the spoon at first, using a hunk of stale-but-not-seasoned-with-maggots bread. He hadn't realized until the first bite how hungry he was, and he wasn't satisfied when the bread was finished and the crumbs slurped messily off his fingertips.

Bread gone, the edge taken off his hunger, Rags reached for the spoon, no longer needing to plunge his face directly into the bowl.

He had the spoon halfway to his mouth when something flashed in his peripheral vision. A hard force stung his wrist, startling his fingers open from their grip and sending the spoon flying across the room in an arc of meat, potatoes, and brown gravy.

"Fuck!" Rags scrambled to keep the tray from sliding off his knees, bowl clattering on wood. He gripped his stinging wrist, leveling his accusation at the asshole who'd *slapped the spoon out of his hand*.

That asshole was Shining Talon.

"My lord," Shining Talon said, distressed enough to forget what minimal progress they'd made, "are you all right?"

"You hit the spoon out of my hand! Do you think I'm fucking all right?"

"Yes, I did remove its fell presence, and not a moment too soon." Shining Talon crouched at Rags's side in a warrior's position, ready to pounce. He was staring at the spoon as if *it* were the great weapon in the room, not the giant silver lizard.

Speaking of, her three eyes were tracking the proceedings with what looked like amusement.

Could lizards chuckle?

Rags groaned in irritation. "What are you talking about, Shiny?"

"That dangerous contraption—" Shining Talon began.

Rags put the tray aside on the bed, where it would hopefully be safe from Shining Talon's "instincts," and stalked over to the spoon. Shining Talon shouted as Rags bent to retrieve it, already at Rags's side again. How did he move so fast without stirring the air in the process or making any noise?

Shining Talon gripped Rags by the wrist, real distress on his face. It made him look less unfamiliar, and also kind of funny.

"If it will not release you from its spell," Shining Talon said, "then I will sacrifice myself to its command in your place. Will you accept the substitution, Iron Thing?" This last bit seemed to be directed to the spoon.

Nothing happened in reply, because Shining Talon was talking to a spoon. An ugly one, as spoons went, iron and old, but harmless.

Rags pinched the handle and wiggled it experimentally. Shining Talon's lips parted, baring his sharp teeth.

"Me," Rags said. "I did that. I moved the spoon."

"The Spoon," Shining Talon repeated darkly. "A foul name for a foul item."

Rags tried to pull his arm free of Shining Talon's grip, knowing from the start that it was pointless. "You don't know what a spoon is?"

"I know now, and that is enough. I will not be tricked by it a second time."

Rags patted the back of Shining Talon's hand. "Could you maybe let go of me so I can eat my soup? Because that's what spoons are for. Eating soup."

Incomprehension. Shining Talon still regarded the spoon like he was waiting for it to sprout barbed tentacles and lash out.

"Your people seriously didn't have spoons?" Rags asked, growing tired of the stalemate.

It actually worked, or seemed to, because Shining Talon finally took his gaze off the hated spoon. "You truly know *nothing* of our kind?"

"I truly don't," Rags mugged. Then he regretted going for the easy mockery, realizing a split second later what was going to happen as a result of his bullshit.

Shining Talon was going to try to patch the holes in Rags's knowledge of fae stuff.

Sure enough, his fae companion moved to stand by the window. Although it was shuttered, Rags couldn't shake the sensation that the fae was looking at the village below, could see straight through the wood boarding the windows to the scenery beyond.

Was that something the fae could do? Rags had been honest when he'd told Shining Talon he knew shit-all about them.

"Hundreds of years ago, you would have heard my people in every breeze, seen the flicker of our hair in every rippling brook. Our laughter rustled in the tall grass. Your time held no meaning for us. We were ageless, fearless. No blade could kill us, save for one made of iron. One made by man."

That sounded a lot like what Rags had already heard. The fae had once lurked around every corner, ready to lure children away with sweetsong to sleep for a century. While the children slept, the fae stole their youth and beauty, sucking it from their bones, leaving their clean-picked skeletons tangled in lush vines.

The queen and her sorcerers had at last driven them back, making the countryside safe for travelers and trade, for families and newborns.

Rags looked at Shining Talon. All he could think about was how swiftly he'd sniffed out Morien's spellwork on Rags's heart. He'd sensed that Rags was bound without having to ask, and had grieved it instantly without even knowing Rags.

None of the stories Rags knew about the fae suggested they put their *own* kind to sleep for hundreds of years. A restless mind might dart around wondering what else had been left out of those tales.

Weird. One moment Rags was trying to cram as much food as possible into his mouth without choking, and the next he was too aware of the fae in the room with him to swallow. Shining Talon was probably the last of his kind. Someone mourning an *entire race* of people.

"Your people should've realized *a weapon* doesn't make the best peace offering." Rags knew it was horrible the moment he said it but couldn't take it back. He waited for Shining Talon to look at him with loathing—or worse, with the resignation of total disappointment.

Beneath the heavy fabric of the cloak, Shining Talon crossed his arms. He didn't move more than that, but he somehow looked wearier than if he'd slumped against the wall. When he turned away from the window to look at Rags, his gaze wasn't miserable. It was distant.

"More than a few of us expressed our concerns," he said. "After the Lying Ones had killed our best warriors, they began closing in on the Bone Court. Our king and queen sued for honorable peace. *Your* queen had other ideas."

That explained why the fae had been soundly wiped out by sorcerers. *Honor* wasn't worth the breath it took to say the word when you had to choose between your blood being spilled or someone else's.

Rags had been both teacher and student of that particular lesson. Dane's dark eyes and hopeful, bruised face rose from the depths of memory where Rags kept him banished.

Rags banished him again.

The room's lone window creaked open, snapping Rags out of his reverie.

Rags peered over Shining Talon's massively broad shoulder. The fae had already whipped around to face the source of the noise.

One stood on her hind legs, front claws between window and ledge, levering it open in its rickety track.

"Is it—she—supposed to do that?" Rags asked.

"One acts on her own only if she's caught the scent of her master."

In a blink, she'd shouldered the window completely open and slithered with weightless grace over the ledge. Her tail swished once. She was gone.

"No," Rags said, brain catching up with him. "Uh-uh, we're supposed to stay in here, and we're definitely not supposed to let the big silver lizard leave this room. If the locals see her, we are all—"

"You are Rags the Thief." Shining Talon paused with one hand on the windowsill, one leg already outside. "Do you not flout authority with your very vocation?"

"With my very— Shit, Shiny, listen, we can't—"

"We cannot stop her," Shining Talon said. "For this reason we must accompany her. To mitigate panic, should it arise."

Rags rubbed his chest, thought about how pissed Morien was going to be, and quietly said, "Fuck it."

Then he followed Shining Talon, climbing out the window into the dark, horse-dung-smelling street.

25

Somhairle's favorite spot in Ever-Land was a copse of birch trees near the lake at the edge of the grounds. Surrounded by purple hopswitch, flowering smokebranch, and ancient cat's-a-roses, this was where he slipped into other worlds countless times, huddled over a book or a fresh play from the city, another of Laisrean's occasional presents.

Thinking of you. Laughed when the princess turned into a donkey. Missed your laughter joining mine.

There hadn't been one of those for some time. Laisrean had never replied to Somhairle's letter about the birds. Had it not been delivered?

The silver glimmer of his carousel across the water beckoned, or mocked, daring Somhairle to return to a more dangerous realm of fantasy: the nostalgic past.

How could he do otherwise, after he'd learned this terrible news about House Ever-Loyal?

How delayed the news had been. He was mourning nearly a full year too late.

This terrible answer to the terrible questions he'd purposefully ignored since Faolan and Morien turned up on his doorstep.

When had House Ever-Learning grown so beloved by the queen?

When had House Ever-Loyal turned against the Silver Court?

When had his mother determined he should receive no news of past friends, of the city's shifts and struggles?

Somhairle once counted the House's eldest daughter, Inis Ever-Loyal, as his truest friend among the Ever-Families. Had she been an active agent in their betrayal or a victim of her parents' scheming? The friends of Somhairle's childhood, the brightest memories he treasured of weightless laughter and acceptance—which of them were buried deep in traitor's earth, never again to feel the warmth of the sun?

It frightened him to think such hatred for the Queen lurked even in the hearts he'd thought he knew best, had certainly loved most.

No word of it from home. No warning. If the Queen had thought such news would distress her weakest son, of course she would prevent it from reaching him.

Her total power and keen gaze, once a little boy's great comfort, suddenly reminded him of the worst of his fevers, a chill gnawing him ragged from within.

If only Somhairle could have flown off with the few surviving birds who'd escaped Ever-Land. They hadn't returned yet, though Morien had been absent two days.

Somhairle approached the house more determined now to don the courtly gear of gossip and learn all he could from Lord Faolan. What had happened to House Ever-Loyal, every painful detail. He'd swallow every bitter draft to the last.

Only Morien's horse was back in the stables, all haunch and trembling bone.

Red fabric shrouded the windows.

Storm clouds knit direly above the nearby trees, growling closer.

Black leaves blanketed the front steps. They shattered, rather than scattered, when Somhairle tried to brush them aside with his silver crutch.

Inside, Faolan lingered before a locked door, gaze fixed intently upon the empty keyhole. Somhairle, perhaps too kindly, let his lame foot knock against the wall in warning.

Faolan whirled with a tinkle of ornamental gold. Several chains of varying lengths hung around his neck, one bearing a medallion imprinted with the quill seal of House Ever-Learning. In a thigh-length tunic and fitted breeches in complementary shades of muted sage, his thin shirt a whisper of cool lilac beneath, he looked like a summer hillside.

How many outfits had he packed for this purportedly brief visit?

"For all there is to recommend him," Faolan said quickly and with brittle cheer, "Morien the Last is a uniquely difficult houseguest."

"That sounded nearly apologetic."

"On my honor, I would *never* apologize."

Believable. On the Hill, kindness was misinterpreted as weakness, an unwelcome reminder of frailty in Catriona's Silver Court, where the Queen was forever young. An apology was capitulation.

Catriona did not capitulate.

"I wondered if you might dine with me tonight." Somhairle's lines came out as smoothly as if he'd rehearsed them with more than a statue troupe in the glen. "I'd welcome the chance to hear more of your exploits on the Hill."

"Your hospitality overwhelms this servant of your mother's crown." Faolan affected a bow, though it didn't appear to mock. A dappled pattern of shadow dogs hunting ghost deer cavorted across the back of his jacket. "I hope Your Highness isn't offended by my transparency, but after an hour with Morien the Last, I'd *kill* for a *real* conversation."

Somhairle's laugh drowned out the imagined jeering of his brothers, some of whom must have warned Faolan against expecting too much from the youngest prince.

Though Faolan cast a narrow glance over his shoulder as they left Morien alone to his private business, he didn't appear to find anything lacking in Somhairle's company. He even refrained from pointing out, as though Somhairle might not have been aware of it, that there was no meat at dinner.

The dining room was built for a cozy twenty, white walls and dark wood. Through the windows in the daylight, the dying garden would have been visible. In Ever-Land, the greenery had ever remained fresh as first blooming.

Until Morien's arrival.

Currently all one could see of Somhairle's cultivated shrubs and flowers was a gaunt scattering of haunted, hunching shadows.

"I take it working closely with Morien is a marked departure from your usual affairs, Lord Faolan?"

Somhairle had no love for deceit. But he *was* very fond of stories.

"My honored mother," Somhairle continued, while Faolan waged a battle with a particularly tough country vegetable, "believes I've too sensitive a constitution to learn the extent of her concerns about her enemies. She doesn't wish to burden me. But if anything should happen to her, and I knew nothing of it . . . that would be the true burden on my heart."

He busied himself then with folding and twisting his napkin, worrying his bottom lip. When he lifted his eyes, he made sure they were moist.

He found Faolan observing him closely, as if he were an ancient tome written in fae.

The instant their eyes met, Faolan's hardened, jewel-like. His lips were smiling. "What is it you wish to know, Prince Somhairle? I've no similar concerns about your constitution, and not so gentle a heart as Her Radiance."

In some regions, Somhairle's mother was called Diamondheart for her unyielding strength. If Faolan was being wry, his tone gave no indication.

"Tell me everything you know," Somhairle suggested. "Everything that's happened since I left."

"*That's* asking a great deal. Fortunately, I find myself equal to your challenge." Faolan gestured magnanimously. "Who loves to talk better than the son of a lawyer?"

By dessert, Somhairle had learned the current state of the Resistance.

He'd been sent to Ever-Land too early to have much memory of what life at court was like, but there had been murmurs of discontent even then from those who believed his mother's reign had lasted too long.

She's the first queen to have heirs, yet she won't move aside for them. Somhairle remembered with a flush of sympathetic embarrassment the night Murchadh had had more drink than he could hold and had repeated this scandalous secret a bit too loudly to Lochlainn, who'd cuffed him for repeating it. The party, like others before it, had devolved into brawling.

That was the extent of it, Somhairle had thought, but in his absence, the murmurs had organized themselves into a unified Resistance. They disrupted Her Majesty's mining operations, causing collapse and destruction throughout the city. They sowed rancor and fear among the good men and women of the Queensguard.

None of that compared to the killing blow they must have struck when House Ever-Loyal's eldest son chose to champion their cause.

It had been Tomman, Somhairle learned, not Inis. Inis was, as far as Faolan knew, still alive and well banished, thanks to the Queen's beneficence.

Somhairle recalled Tomman, Laisrean's oldest friend, as slightly too serious, always marching at a dignified pace while Ainle, Inis, and Ivy Ever-Loyal gamboled ahead. Try as he might, he couldn't picture Tomman as the fiery head of a rebellion, a deadly threat to order and the Crown.

Was Tomman's betrayal the reason Laisrean had stopped visiting? The reason he hadn't written Somhairle with the news? Laisrean's big heart must have broken to lose Tomman twice. Once to treason, again to the blade.

However, regardless of personal sentiment, even as sheltered a prince as Somhairle understood the threat. House Ever-Loyal led the Queensguard. If they turned against the Queen . . .

They could not be allowed to turn against the Queen.

"Ever-Loyal was *so* beloved," Faolan said. "Her Majesty hasn't been the same since. I saw the aftermath for myself. I'll always remember the violence I witnessed that dawn."

So it had been bloody, as Somhairle feared.

Traitors to the crown forfeited their right to trial. What had happened at House Ever-Loyal provided public warning, a demonstration of a traitor's ugly fate.

"I mean that as a compliment to Her Majesty," Faolan added shrewdly. "I strive to be as heartless as she, in all things."

Somhairle had to pretend he was choking in order to mask his startled cough.

Too far away from the Hill for too long. He'd lost his edge.

He'd been grateful to lose it.

After reassuring Somhairle that no similar large-scale deception had been ferreted out since—strict measures had been taken to ensure no such plots could similarly fester—Faolan escorted him upstairs. On the steps, Faolan explained that the Queensguard had proven loyal to the Queen by leading the raid on House Ever-Loyal. Allegedly, one of the Queensguard had herself brought evidence of Tomman Hail Ever-Loyal's treason to Catriona.

Once he'd been encouraged to start speaking, Faolan seemed unable, or unwilling, to stop.

Somhairle's heart felt heavier than his head. He wanted only to trudge to bed and mourn in peace.

"I lied to you before," Faolan charged on, with such cheerfulness that it pulled Somhairle from his inner realm. "I suppose I *do* have gentler feelings, and I *don't* want you to worry. Know this." Faolan's features sharpened, every bit the young lord orphaned early yet shrewd enough to lead his house to glory. His words were like hammered metal. "At present, the Last and I are researching something that will crush all treason, all memory of treason, down to its final gasp."

They stopped in front of Somhairle's bedroom door. With one

gentlemanly flourish, Faolan the blade vanished behind an air of coy amusement. He wore again the expression of an insouciant dandy as he opened the door and stepped aside.

"That's supposed to *prevent* me from worrying?" Somhairle asked.

Faolan bowed. This time, it *was* mocking, but Somhairle didn't get the feeling he was the target. Who was? "All your birds are dead, I miss my damned dogs—might as well do *something* to enjoy myself."

"Or you could do something to make things better," Somhairle murmured wearily, but Faolan had already left, having provided Somhairle with more new questions than old answers.

26
CAB

Cabhan of Kerry's-End had defected from the Queensguard for a number of reasons. Reasons he'd since forced himself to stop chewing over in the hopes of sleeping decently for a change.

He'd put the promise of promotion, all the bloodlust and murder disguised as patriotism, behind him. He'd chosen to live on the run, and he hadn't glanced back.

He figured adventure was likewise behind him, the price he had to pay for his freedom. Nameless and unrecognizable as the lad he'd once been, he'd returned to Kerry's-End, wearing clothes he'd gathered from three separate drying lines.

If his shirt scratched him at night because it'd been sewn with quickbeam seeds for protection, well, that was what he got for stealing.

For abandoning his post. For returning to the superstitious countryside.

Cab hadn't looked anyone in the eye since he'd been back. He'd taken on odd jobs for minimal pay in order to keep his body busy. He had to tire it out so well that he could stumble straight to sleep when he finally lay down for the night.

So he could forget the things he'd seen.

Or pretend he forgot.

For three nights now, he'd slept in Tithe Barley's barn while he cleared the weeds from her sowing fields. The endless repetition—pulling and digging, stooping and gathering—numbed his head and his heart just fine.

"Most boys leave Kerry's-End, don't show up here asking for work," Barley'd said on Cab's first day. Squinting at him like she imagined she recognized him, then squinting at him like she realized she didn't.

"Thank you," Cab had replied. Her offer of work was a kindness, and Tithe Barley had been good to his ma before widow's lung took her.

They hadn't shared more than two words since, but someone left cooked meals at the barn door morning and night. Cab guessed that meant Barley was satisfied with his work.

People in Kerry's-End kept to themselves, to their private, difficult lives, which was what he liked best about them. He craved the bluff, glancing nature of his country folk, already too full with their own secret sorrows to probe after their neighbors'.

His boots were the only thing he'd allowed himself to keep from his Queensguard uniform. They were battered and muddy now, unrecognizable, but the soles had good years left in them. Couldn't toss them. Practicality trumped sentimentality. Needed to, for a man's survival.

Time might have sweetened the sour taste left in his mouth by politics on the Hill. Maybe he would've found a way to return to the boy he'd been: a lad with no more complicated aspirations than serving his Queen and country. He might have forgotten the startling warmth of a stranger's fresh blood on his skin. It wasn't particularly noble to want to move past something like that, to bury it. But it was human.

People lived. Living was moving on.

Cab was startled out of his lull by the frantic lowing of Tithe Barley's four cows. He'd tucked in for the evening, eaten the meal laid out for him. Now something had spooked the cows badly. From the nervous *hssh* of restless hooves on hay, Cab could tell the old mare was none too pleased, either.

"Hey now." He hauled himself up ungracefully, aches in his muscles making him clumsy. Both hands ahead of him, he shifted into a soldier's stance by nature. "You're all right, hush. You'll wake the house with that noise."

It'd grown dark while he drifted in and out of rest that never quite reached sleep's comforts. The barn was lit inside by beams from the two moons above streaming through three uneven windows. A quick scan of the shadowy piles of hay revealed nothing out of the ordinary.

Probably one of the cows had seen a rat, or been startled by a shifting cloud and riled the others.

No matter what Cab told himself, old instincts gripped hard, wouldn't let go. He slid his boots along the ground, slippery with hay and hay dust, advancing toward the pen. Silent and powerful, like the soldier he once was.

By the barn door, the old mare whickered softly.

Something outside the barn. Something coming. Not here for the cattle, the old mare, or Tithe Barley.

For him.

No time to prepare a defense. Even if there had been, the notion of spearing a royal bounty hunter on a pitchfork, watching him bleed out in the barn, bringing that violence to Kerry's-End, was more than Cab could stomach.

Then came the voice.

It wasn't quite a voice—half flute-song and half writhing collection of hissed syllables—but something out there was calling him.

Not with his name.

Almost sounded like it.

For the first time since he'd abandoned the uniform, Cab wished he had his sword.

The Queensguard had asked too much. Like a coward, he'd run. Not because he was too moral, too meek, but because he was too frightened.

He couldn't outrun his fear. It had come for him.

A silver beast broke through the barn door. Collided with Cab in a blur of lightning-fast power. Knocked him to the ground so hard that the world disappeared, memories bad and good, confusion, fear, and anger.

The oddest part of the experience was, surprisingly . . .

That Cab had been expecting it. He'd known the voice was calling him. He'd been ready.

Flat on his back in old, musty hay, two massive, clawed feet on his chest and three eyes staring into his own. Pure calm flooded him. He didn't feel afraid, even when the flute-hiss of the almost-voice slithered through him from his toes to the top of his head.

Something wet trickled over his upper lip. Blood from his nose. The lizard darted a silver tongue past its pointed fangs, through what looked like smiling lips. The tip forked over Cab's bloody skin. Cab stared as that blood traveled up the tongue, sucked into the lizard's throat, resting where the clavicle should be. A single red dot, part of Cab's life force, hung there, barely visible through the slightly translucent scales. A part of him inside this thing.

This amazing thing.

If this was his death by sorcery, he welcomed it.

Words began to congeal like mending stitches inside Cab's head, formed from the disconnected syllables that had been haunting him.

He . . .

. . . ll . . .

Hell . . .

. . . o . . .

Hello.

Cab panted to catch his breath, lungs fighting the weight on his chest. The weight eased. The lizard sat back, though both front feet remained solidly pressed over the spot where Cab's heart was ricocheting against his ribs. Possessive.

Not in a bad way.

Was Cab supposed to answer that greeting? Was he out of his mind? Had the mushrooms he'd cleared from Tithe Barley's field that morning been the kind that made you see fae and Ancient Ones and wake up five days later in a ditch with no underthings?

No one runs from their oath to the Hill and lives, Cab's fear insisted.

No, not that. He felt peaceful in a way he wouldn't, if this meeting had been thanks to sorcery. Whole in a way he hadn't since he'd put the Hill behind him for good, and damned himself with the consequences. Right in a way he never had. His lips twitched, tugged into a smile of their own accord.

Hello . . . ? the voice tried again.

Faint lilt of a question, the word more certain of itself. Three silver eyes peered into Cab's face.

Hello, master. Did I break you?

The lizard was talking to him. It wasn't a surprise. It made all the sense in the world, as natural as breathing.

Did . . . I . . . break . . . you?

No. Cab simply didn't know how to answer. Opening his mouth to speak a reply out loud seemed wrong, and he didn't want to blunder in this. It felt too important for him to chance mistakes.

Cab squeezed his eyes shut. Pushed aside the flush of foolishness from his uncertainty, and concentrated as hard as he could on forming each word in his thoughts: *Hello. There. Not. Broken.*

Not broken, despite how close Queensguard life had come to breaking him.

If that hadn't done it, nothing could.

Answering laughter, as sweet and high as an innocent child's giggle. *What are you doing? Why have you shut your eyes?*

Cab opened them again, heat in his cheeks, too amazed for proper embarrassment. *I'm not sure how this is supposed to work. Forgive me.*

I would forgive you anything. Anything but death.

The world fell away beneath Cab's back, swooping in a pitch of joy and belonging. It took him a moment to realize he was weeping. The lizard was licking his tears from the corners of his eyes.

I have waited so long for you, the lizard told him. *So many of your short lifetimes. And I have missed you every moment of every year until we met. Hello, Cabhan of Kerry's-End. I am the One Who Will Serve You.* A pause. A flicker of fresh but sadder laughter as the lizard swallowed Cab's tears, glowed faintly as a result. *You are as attractive by flesh standards as I expected!*

Compliment aside, Cab wanted an explanation for that part about serving.

Before he could request one, a figure darkened the opening in what remained of the barn door, and Cab's instincts made him tense once more. "Who's there?" he demanded in a croaky rasp.

Oh, these. The lizard didn't appear disturbed. Cab found he trusted that more than his own instincts, and that realization didn't disturb him by a fraction of what it should. *The big one is Shining Talon of Vengeance Drawn in Westward Strike, last fae prince of Oberon the Black-Boned. The little one is Rags, who steals things. They are unimportant compared to me.*

"Ah," Cab said softly.

He had no problem believing it.

27
RAGS

Rags didn't know what he expected to see inside the barn. Shining Talon held him back from entering long enough that he wondered if One was in there devouring a still-living human, or something equally gruesome.

Rags settled for standing guard outside the ruined door with Shining Talon—not that he had a choice—telling himself it didn't sound like devouring was going on. In fact, it was completely silent.

Was that worse?

"Don't you want to know what's happening in there?" Rags tried appealing to the thread of nosiness he knew lurked in the core of every heart.

Every heart except Shining Talon's. He merely looked down his long nose at Rags.

"I was not chosen for my curiosity," he said, like that explained everything.

"Does that mean your brother was chosen because he was real good at keeping watch?" Rags's nose wrinkled, obscuring a wince. "Sorry."

He couldn't help sounding coarse. This was merely how he talked to other thieves in the Clave. He'd already figured the fae didn't have gutters, so why would they have need for gutter talk?

"Ignore me," Rags suggested when Shining Talon didn't respond. "Just tell me when it's time to steal something."

"You speak the truth." Hesitance hung like heat haze around Shining Talon's words, almost as though he couldn't believe Rags had been insightful. "My brother was chosen for his vigilance. My sisters for their wisdom and courage."

"How many of you were there?" Rags asked, to distract himself from thinking about an entire family consumed by a greater purpose. Maybe it really *was* an honor. Shining Talon *was* still alive, and they weren't.

Though that seemed like punishment to Rags.

"Five in total." Shining Talon seemed to grow taller for a moment, swelling with pride. Then let some of the air out. "Though my sister Quick Heart—Black-Boned, Strong Hands Ready in Westward Strike—died in the war with the Lying Ones before her duties to the king could be fulfilled."

"Oh." Rags nodded, like he could possibly understand, then resolved to stare at the ground after that.

They kept their focus away from the barn until Rags's twitchy impatience grew too overwhelming for Shining Talon to ignore. Shining Talon glanced into the barn once, then nodded and stepped inside. Rags followed, pushing all thoughts of Shining Talon's family and destiny out of his mind.

In the barn, One was licking a young man, sitting half on top of him and half curled against his side. The young man had a look like bliss and absolution on his face. Rags understood why Shining Talon had refused to let him inside. Whatever had happened in this barn was too private for intruders, so private that Rags looked away from the scene, despite his burning curiosity.

"Ah." The stranger getting a tongue bath from One had a country lilt to his voice. "I think I know which of you is the fae prince and which of you is the little one who steals things."

Rags whirled around at that. "Fae *prince*?"

"It's the prince part that surprises you?" the country stranger asked. "Not the fae part?"

"We have much to discuss," Shining Talon said. Rags could still feel the warmth and the weight of his hand, could easily believe that this fae was a royal member of the long-lost Bone Court, could have laughed at the ridiculousness that someone like that would want to look after someone like *him*. What Rags couldn't do was form any words with his mouth. Or close it. It hung open, gawping. *Fae prince?* "But not here. Let us return to our quarters, where we will have more privacy."

28
RAGS

They got back into their room the way they'd left it, climbing the wall and in through the window, only this time Shining Talon led them. One was busy nuzzling her new friend's throat, sticking close to his side and giving Rags the side-eye whenever he got too close, or snorted in confusion, or waved his hands at no one to release his overwhelming feelings of *fuck you, fuck him, and fuck me most*.

No need to convince their new friend to come with them. He went where One did.

No one came out into the streets or caught sight of them. Morien had concealed them well. Rags didn't care.

Catch them, don't catch them, what did it matter?

Shining Talon was a fae prince.

That made perfect sense, except in all the ways it made no sense whatsoever.

In the room, One's new friend asked, "Something happen here?" He nodded at the stew splattered on the floor, the spoon in the corner. In reply, One hissed, a sound that was suspiciously close to a mocking chuckle. "Oh. I see."

"See what?" Rags fixed the stranger and One with a glare, hoping to be accusatory, landing on puffy and indignant. "Is that— Are you— Can One talk?"

The stranger shrugged and refused to meet Rags's eyes.

Rags shifted his focus to Shining Talon. "A prince?" Shining Talon nodded. "And you call *me* 'my lord'? Ha!"

The chaos, the indignation, flooded out of Rags in a single gust. He slumped onto the bed, leaned back against the wall, hit his head a couple of times half-heartedly. Wished this whole trip was something he could knock out of his skull.

No luck.

He was still in the room in the public house, Shining Talon the fae prince still staring at him with a mixture of regret and adoration, One the silver lizard still cozying up to the stranger's nearest hand like a dog reunited with its beloved master.

"It is the proper form of address," Shining Talon explained, "for the one who woke me."

The sincerity in his tone left Rags chilled.

"Okay, and who are *you*?" Rags asked the stranger at last, the fight sapped from his blood. A closer study of him revealed posture too good for your average farmhand, brown skin, dark hair lustered nearly auburn from the sun and grown long with neglect, a faint hint of stubble on his chin, and a light scar curving over his eyebrow. Stern gray eyes, a hardened mouth, an air of wariness— and weariness—that seemed more city than country. Calluses on his palms from years of swinging a sword, Rags guessed. He held himself as though the sword he'd once carried was gone from him like a missing limb. His gray shirt was speckled with dirt. "Who *are* you?" Rags asked again, more pointed this time, narrowing his eyes as he leaned forward.

Might have milked an answer out of the guy if the door hadn't opened, bringing icy air with it.

Rags's shudder let him know who was there without having to look.

"Hello," Morien said. "Are we having a party?"

One snarled. The stranger dropped back into a defensive fighting pose that reminded Rags of every Queensguard he'd ever met, the formal style taught on the Hill.

Give me one reason, One's three eyes seemed to challenge Morien, *because I've been waiting to tear your throat out.*

Shining Talon stepped between them. "One," he said firmly, looking at Rags.

Rags didn't think that One was as vehement about keeping Rags alive as Shining Talon was, but after a tense moment, she backed down. Rags grinned shakily, didn't feel it reach his eyes. "Did you not get your invitation?" he asked the sorcerer, voice cockier than he felt.

"This is One's master," Shining Talon said. If feeding information to a Lying One pained him, he didn't let it show on his exquisitely blank face. A fae fucking prince, so devoted to Rags's scrap of a life that he'd surrendered to a sorcerer without a hint of resistance. It made Rags furious for reasons he didn't want to explore, hurt his chest in a different way from the shard of mirrorglass buried in his heart.

"Then you are welcome, One's master." Morien didn't bow, didn't sound welcoming. An invisible wind stirred the scarves around his face and throat. Morien was doing *something* magical. "It is my understanding that there is no way to determine when another master might be chosen—might be found. Therefore you must believe I will not harm you. You are invaluable to my interests, which are the interests of the Queen."

"And if your interests mean nothing to me?" One's master asked.

Then I die horribly and painfully, Rags thought.

"I insist," Shining Talon said, "that we respect one another's interests."

One's master met Shining Talon's eyes and held them. His focus flickered after that, his expression distant. He was listening to something no one else could hear.

Yeah, One was definitely talking to him.

The gaze he leveled at Rags next was scathing—pitying. Rags rolled his eyes and looked away.

"'Respect one another's interests,'" One's master repeated. "What would those be?"

"A full pardon for you, Cabhan of Kerry's-End," Morien replied. "A rare gift for a deserter from the Queensguard, wouldn't you agree?"

A deserter? Queensguard were famous for having no fear—nor any other emotion.

This one had run away. Intriguing.

Rags didn't miss the flash of anger in Cabhan's eyes over his introduction. Definitely not emotionless.

"And in return?" Cabhan asked.

Not a total idiot, either.

Morien took a look around the room. "I think it is time for you to meet my employer, before this situation grows out of hand."

29
CAB

Cab's past had caught up with him.

Fine. He told himself he'd always known it would. Told himself he'd been waiting for it. Told himself it was a relief to see it done. He'd never have to look over his shoulder again, or trail the next stranger who came to town, unseen, until he was certain they hadn't been sent to take him.

Told himself he was lucky he'd stayed away, hidden from the Hill, for a full year.

He didn't believe any of it. Not even with how practiced he'd become at lying to himself.

His greatest fear to this point had come to a head after haunting his footsteps and corroding his soul, but it wasn't the most important thing in his life anymore. Even if he hated every second of this, he could bear it.

Cab stole a glance at One and nodded to let her know it was all right.

She needed to let Morien handcuff him without trying to snap the sorcerer's head off.

As satisfying as it might have been to watch her try—to watch her succeed—he didn't want to be the catalyst for the wholesale slaughter that would follow.

Kerry's-End folk still carried salt and iron in their pockets while walking at night, though no one had seen fae in hundreds of years. Superstition ran deeper than tradition, *was* their tradition.

Unlike them, Cab wasn't afraid. After One, even shocked seemed too strong a term.

The Queen has more secrets than you know, he thought.

And the fae prince had a vested interest in keeping some fool of a thief alive. While Cab didn't know why, he did know—from the set of Shining Talon's jaw—that the fae was committed.

Since the thief had been bound by a sorcerer, the same sorcerer who was clapping Cab in irons . . .

There'd be no escaping the situation without making an ugly mess.

Cab wasn't confident he'd be of any use if One made a move and Shining Talon was forced to protect his interests.

Innocent blood would be spilled, and Cab was done with that.

Back when he was in service to the Queen, he'd fled before having his heart sharded by the mirrorcraft he'd come to suspect, nearly too late, made every member of the Queensguard an unquestioning, murdering slave. Escape hadn't been enough to make him feel like a free man.

I do not like to see you this way, One told Cab.

I don't like to be this way. But we have to be smarter than the sorcerer.

Oh, if that's all. One's lips twisted in what Cab recognized as her smug smile. *I think we can manage that.*

Creeping dread didn't consume Cab as he was led downstairs, noting the lack of an audience for his procession out of the public house and out of town. He was empty of emotion, just as the public house was empty of patrons. He should have been afraid of what was to come, desperately bargaining for control of his fate. But he didn't feel anything. Except for resignation, and a soft glow beneath: the knowledge that One existed in this world, and they'd managed to find each other. A piece of himself he'd never known was missing.

Compared to that revelation, his newfound captivity seemed a small burden. There was an inevitability to it, like he'd have wound up on this path no matter which turns he took.

He didn't examine the Queensguard's faces too closely, hunched his shoulders, and hid his expression behind his too-long hair. He let a Queensguard strong-arm him onto the front of a nervous mount, then gave One the look again that meant she needed to stand down.

You're accustomed to giving orders, she said.

I was a rising star on the Hill. No use for Cab to hide anything from her. In fact, he had the suspicion that she already knew everything, and he was surprised only by how much of a relief it was to share his experiences with someone, *anyone* else. *Until the raid on House Ever-Loyal. After that, I ran.*

Smart boy, One replied.

30
RAGS

Four days of riding, two of those in sheeting rain. Morien had cast a spell to shroud them in fog that not only protected them from view but also kept the group uncertain of the scenery around them. Rags felt as though he hadn't yet returned to his own world from the fae ruins.

When the fog cleared, Rags found that instead of arriving at the city, they were on the grounds of a fancy country house, where Morien had them stay on the border of the grounds until nightfall.

Rags sneezed for the fifth time that hour and wiped his nose savagely with the back of his still-damp sleeve.

If Shining Talon said *anything* about the human body, disease, and the simplest of weather conditions, Rags was going to . . .

Going to what? Sneeze in his eye?

Bitter helplessness flooded his belly. He glowered at the country house, waiting for them across a well-manicured lawn, entertaining himself by picking out all the ways he'd sneak in if this were a normal job. Where a window might be cracked open or a cellar door might be unlocked. He settled on climbing up a cypress tree to the second floor and in through a window left temptingly ajar.

Once he'd finished that, he listed off the shit he could have stolen from a fancy place like this one, full to the brim, if Rags knew the type, of pointless, expensive tripe nobody needed. Porcelain piss-pot, because Ever-Nobles wanted only the finest receptacle for their shit. Fancy candlesnuffers with gold-inlaid handles. Diamond candelabras. Pokers carved to look like wild animals of the hunt. Maybe a collection of polished spoons to spook Shining Talon with.

Rags grinned.

"It is good to see you smile," Shining Talon murmured.

Rags stopped grinning immediately.

The twin moons had risen to a point directly overhead, flooding the grounds with gray-white light. They were nearly round, what some called *full*, on account of how a double moon could look like an Ever-Lady's heavy silver bosom hanging in the sky.

He'd already stopped smiling, but now Rags was filled with new depths of irritation. They couldn't cross to the house in the bright open, not after waiting through dank twilight for the sun to set. Night on this heath was cold and cruel as a gutterwench's tongue. And who knew when a proper cloud cover would sweep in and end their—

An unnaturally quick grumbling of clouds appeared over the moons as Rags started thinking about them—*Right, we've got a sorcerer with us, doing sorcerer shit.* On Morien's command, they made their way to the house in darkness so black, Rags couldn't see his hands when he raised them in front of his face.

However, the horses knew where to go. When the darkness finally broke with the sound of a slamming door, Rags found himself inside a stable with the others, Shining Talon standing too close for comfort.

"I could barely see you in the aberrant dark."

"I'm fine," Rags muttered. "I don't disappear when the lights go out."

"You are no Lying One," Shining Talon agreed. "But a thief may vanish when it suits him."

"Nothing about this suits me," Rags growled. Then, because he got the sense that Shining Talon wouldn't leave him alone unless he offered more, he added more affably, "I'm not going anywhere."

It was true. Not merely because he didn't know where the fuck they were and didn't relish wandering through open dales and rambling fields alone, unsheltered, and on foot, but because he was necessary the same way their new pal Cabhan was necessary. Another silver animal waited for Rags, according to Shining Talon's account, and if Shining Talon had lied about that, Rags would be the one to pay the price.

He wondered what his piece would look like. Were they all lizards?

He was getting ahead of himself.

One and Cabhan made a perfect pair. She'd reacted so strongly to Cab that it was hard to ignore the silence of Rags's lump. Logic would naturally conclude that the thing wasn't meant for *him* after all. A mistake had been made. Rags was stuck with it only until they found the right poor bastard to be its proper master.

Why couldn't you have been a diamond? he thought in the direction of the lump in his pocket. *A really big, expensive one?*

Anyway, Morien hadn't killed the ex-Queensguard for defecting— a crime punishable by slow, public, excruciating death. He wouldn't kill Rags for the same reason. Morien needed them alive to form the Great Paragon.

Rags was tired and shivery and about to sneeze again. He didn't expect to get the rest he needed tonight, and Morien confirmed his suspicions when he dismissed only the Queensguard.

Morien didn't instruct them to follow. He turned and exited through a different door than the one the Queensguard had taken, leaving Rags and the rest to trundle after him.

31
CAB

Cabhan knew where they were when he saw the crest above the stable door. The book and the pen meant this place belonged to House Ever-Learning.

The architecture of the place was much like that of House Ever-Loyal. Cab couldn't help but remember his last sight of those halls, also in the dead of night.

A piercing scream that lanced through him with equal parts horror and determination. The distant shatter of glass. The crunch of smashed bone—

What an ugly home. One's voice sliced through the memory, dispersed its fragments like a cloud of dust. *Has too many doors. Its walls are too narrow. And it's far too high above the ground for decent company.*

Thanks, One.

One sniffed, said nothing more.

Cab's shoulders ached from riding cuffed. He was wet and tired, but his mind was just beginning to stir itself from restless slumber. Waking from the stupor he'd induced deliberately at Kerry's-End, choosing not to think or feel.

Ever-Learning had lost its Head of House some years back when Judge Ever-Learning died of fever, followed only days later by his wife. Their young son had risen to take the reins of the House and had done well, a savvy political player by the young age of twelve. Owned one home in the city and another in the countryside, if Cab remembered right.

With a rush of relief, he realized they weren't going to be presented at court. This place reeked of the artifice of simplicity, an Ever-Noble simulacrum of humble country life.

They'd dismounted and entered through another door, another Ever-Learning crest above the lintel. Too small to open onto a great room. More like a private study.

Much of his training for the Queensguard had been learning about the Silver Court. The Houses, their crests, their hobbies. Cab had been a dutiful and dedicated pupil.

Lots of recruits were like him. Village folk, with no ties to the nobility. Being forced to learn everything about the Ever-Nobles made devotees of soldiers. You fought harder to protect what you knew. Simple.

The door opened onto cases of books, a low desk, and two wiry-furred wolfhounds. The Ever-Learning family dogs were a lean-faced hunting breed. Cab had seen Lord Faolan walking his more than once when they were pups.

They'd grown.

Dogs. How bothersome, One said. *They're always barking about something.*

True. After they got over their initial shock, the hounds began to growl, then broke into defensive woofs. One's forked tongue darted out. Tensions might have exploded if Lord Faolan hadn't risen from his seat behind the desk and issued a single command: "Sit."

The barking stopped. The dogs stepped backward to flank their master, then dropped into twin wary crouches.

Was Faolan Cab's own age? He couldn't remember, felt very big and dirty in the fine room regardless.

"Morien," Lord Faolan continued, "care to explain what you've dragged in?"

Lord Faolan had a wicked tongue, for sure, but Rags almost admired its skill, especially when Faolan asked Morien if this was what passed for treasure back in Oberon's day. Rags turned his answering laugh into a cough, muttered something about wind and rain, and shut his trap while Morien brought Shining Talon forward.

"Explain to my lord Faolan what you told me," Morien said.

Rags winced and looked away, not wanting to see Shining Talon's glance at him—*all your fault somehow, Rags*—before he began.

"The Great Paragon," Shining Talon said, "was designed from the heart of all fae silver."

"Sounds like a treasure to me." Lord Faolan's honeyed murmur gave Rags a good idea of what he was like when court was in session. Making anyone who listened feel good about the guy fucking them in the eye. His shirt had fluttering yellow cuffs that nearly covered his hands. Rags tried not to fantasize about how much he could steal with sleeves that ridiculous hiding his fingers.

"More than a treasure," Shining Talon continued, "the Great Paragon is a weapon. But it can only be wielded by those destined to use it."

"Pesky fae caveats. A key element of your society, as historians understand it."

Shining Talon glanced at Rags again, something Rags wasn't expecting. It hit him like a blow. What did Shining Talon want from him?

He had to want something. Couldn't be looking at Rags simply because he liked what he saw.

Rags busied himself thinking about the jewels set into the hounds' collars, how long it'd take for Lord Faolan to notice one missing.

Lord Faolan cleared his throat, then shifted his weight to lean on one arm of his chair. "I'm a student of the law, and we love the little details. Indulge me. How often does one of these *destined masters* come about? If one of ours were to, say, die. Unexpectedly."

Rags laughed.

They were supposed to laugh, right? He glanced around. For some reason, everyone was staring at him.

Nobody else acknowledged that Lord Faolan was asking outright whether he could make them disposable mirrorcraft slaves. Fine, fine. Rags could have this crisis all by himself.

A muscle jumped in Shining Talon's jaw as he clenched his teeth. Too quick, Rags had the sensation that Shining Talon had been looking at him again.

"With the Great Inventors having perished, only the fragments know how to locate their masters." Shining Talon stared hard at a place on the wall above Lord Faolan's head. "But it is my understanding that there is only one master for each fragment living at a time. Should one die, a new one must be conceived, born, and raised to the appropriate age before their fragment can locate them."

His muscles stood so stark and rigid that Rags was sure he'd break his foot if he tried kicking the fae to make him stop talking.

Rags couldn't help thinking again how Shining Talon, this ageless being, had said goodbye to his entire people, and he was *still* trying to protect Rags's short, fleeting horsefly of a life.

No one spoke, though Rags suspected Morien was frowning beneath his red scarves, and Shining Talon continued.

"So it was that the Great Paragon was divided into six fragments, each of which retained its own personality. They are alive"—Shining Talon spared a nod for One, who licked her lips with her forked tongue and winked her third eye—"and also implanted with the knowledge of how to seek out those who were meant to master them."

"And what happens to these beasts when their master dies?" Lord Faolan asked more plainly. "Surely that's an important element of the . . . what to call it—mechanism? Do they self-destruct, or waste away like maidens in a bard's tale, or simply cease to function until their next heir comes of age?"

Shining Talon's hands tightened imperceptibly, not all the way into fists. Rags saw the motion, felt its ache. "Because the fragments of the Great Paragon would accept only those most worthy for the bond, there was no need to fear that the immense power in their bond would be used for anything other than good. But . . ." Another probing look into Rags's eyes—he *had* to stop doing that—followed by an inclination of his head in Cabhan's direction. "I know only that when the Great Paragon was fashioned as a gift, it was intended for human partnership. More than that I was not allowed to know."

Rags found himself staring at Lord Faolan, whose mouth was pressed into a tight line. Showing discomfort in place of the triumph Rags had expected.

House Ever-Learning must have played a part in the war against the fae, though it had happened hundreds of years before Lord Faolan's time. Maybe he was whip-clever enough to know that smiling in the face of your utterly defeated enemy was in poor taste.

Shining Talon continued, ignoring the expressions in the audience. "I do know that the fragments do not like to be alone. When awake, they seek completion."

"Do you know where the other fragments are?" Lord Faolan asked.

Shining Talon shook his head. Rags almost detected a note of hesitation. "What knowledge I was given had to remain vague. No single master can know too much. It is my understanding that One would lead us to her master, which she has done. After that, the instructions become less clear. In some way, One's master should be able to point us toward the Master of Two . . . and so on."

"*Fascinating.*" Lord Faolan turned to Morien. "Like links in a chain. Not sorcery as we recognize it today, but that incredible fae technology whispered about in ruined texts, splinters of a past found only on the most ancient battlefields. . . ."

"Fascinating." Morien's voice didn't shimmer with quite the same amount of wonder. Instead, his eyes burned into Cabhan.

A knot in Rags's throat told him what Morien needed to do to maintain control over this weapon.

If none of the fragments like One chose Morien or Faolan for mastery—who had no reason to rely on such a wild card—there was still a way for the sorcerer and the Ever-Noble to remain masters of the operation. Who wouldn't want that?

The solution to the problem was already buried in Rags's heart.

Rags shouted, stupidly—he didn't know what it was he hoped to effect, who he was warning, if it was even a warning, not a yelp of pointless protest—as Morien made his move, reaching Cabhan's side with lightning speed. One opened her mouth, bared what looked like

ten rows of teeth sliding into position for the occasion, bracing herself
to leap for Morien, flay his skin off his body, suck the marrow from
his bones—

Morien held up his hand. Rags fell to his knees. Lord Faolan shook
his head as if weary of theatrics, and Shining Talon drew himself to
his full height, eyes suddenly blazing.

STAND DOWN!

Later, Rags wouldn't be able to say if he'd heard the words spoken
out loud or if he'd felt them echoing in his veins. The room shook
with the force of its warring tensions, mostly with the strength of
Shining Talon's voice, rattling Rags's teeth in his jaw.

Rags tasted blood. He'd bitten his tongue.

His heart shuddered, needle-thin shards of mirrorglass lancing
through muscle—

Do it, Rags thought. *Do it anyway, you crazy fucking lizard, who gives
a shit, don't stand down—*

Reared and ready to strike, One paused as her resolve wavered.
Rags's eyes watered. He couldn't make a sound, blood bubbling past
his lips instead of words. Maybe he hadn't bitten his tongue and this
was blood from deep in his chest, where Morien's sorcery had begun
to shred him into ribbons—

One lowered herself to all fours, casting Shining Talon a withering
look brimming with impotent fury and betrayal.

Cabhan tried to twist his body into a fighting position despite
everyone in the room, Cabhan included, knowing it was too late.
Morien had Cabhan in his grip. One couldn't protect her master
because it would have harmed Rags, and Shining Talon refused to
let that happen. Cabhan was about to receive the same dirty sorcery
treatment that was ruining Rags's life. About to be gifted with a shard

of mirrorglass in his heart to ensure his obedience to Morien.

Rags's vision swam at the edges. Morien's fingers moved and mirrorglass dazzled. Shining Talon dropped to the floor, hands over his ears. The lizard shape of One's body rippled at its edges, lost certainty, reminding Rags of how she'd been when they'd first met—a formless river. It wasn't worse than being sharded, but being in the room as it happened to someone else wasn't pretty, warping to unrecognizable horror all perspective, distorting the world itself.

As soon as it had started, it was over. One didn't melt onto the carpet. The air stopped trying to suffocate them. Morien released the front of Cabhan's shirt, wiped his hands neatly on a fold of his robes, and turned to Lord Faolan with a slight bow.

Lord Faolan shrugged apologetically. "We learned from experience that such insurance *is* necessary."

Cabhan gasped to regain his breath. His hair was soaked with sweat, his eyes wide and sightless. He swayed on his feet but hadn't collapsed. Had to be one strong bastard to remain standing. One prowled, belly low to the floor, to settle by his side, a grinding noise keening from her throat. Cabhan sagged against her.

Rags bowed his head.

"Morien, what about Shining Talon?" Lord Faolan asked his sorcerer. "Is there any way to know if that insurance will also work on someone with his . . . anatomy?"

"To my knowledge, it has never been tested," Morien replied. "It is something I intend to pursue. But for now, I don't believe it will be necessary."

"Yes, that display did prove as much." Faolan sighed. "Very well. They can rest in the guestrooms while they recover from their arduous journey—and your welcome, Morien. After that . . ." Faolan approached Rags, then passed him like he wasn't there, halting in front of Shining Talon. ". . . we'll discuss how to find the other five fragments. We don't intend to be barbarous. I really *do* want you to be comfortable, to extend every possible hospitality." Lord Faolan lowered himself to one knee after touching Shining Talon's shoulder sympathetically. Shining Talon didn't shake him off. "Forgive our drastic measures. Your people would have done the same—*did* the same, as you can see, by making this Great Paragon so tricky to assemble under one commanding body."

"That was the point," Shining Talon said dully.

Rags was going to be sick.

"Caveats, caveats." Lord Faolan rose to pat the fae's shoulder companionably. "Fortunately, as a student of law, I'm adept at pinpointing loopholes."

His hounds followed him out, only too happy to leave that fucked-up room.

33
RAGS

Lying on what had to be the world's biggest, fluffiest bed, Rags still felt like a pile of shit.

Any other day of his life, Rags would have been able to luxuriate in his sudden, incredible fortune. He'd have rolled around like a happy piglet in silks and velvets, figured out what in the room he could steal, and gone to blissful sleep feeling like a prince. Everything smelled clean, and there'd been a tub of steaming-hot water for bathing, a platter of delicacies for his indulgence. It was better than anything even Clave *leaders* had in their private rooms. It was every street kid's best fantasy come to life, and Rags was living it.

It tasted sour.

He took his lump out of his pocket and set to peeling it free of its silvery cocoon. He tore off strips of the dark, tarnished stuff, revealing the brighter, near-white silver beneath. The etched designs covering it were like those on the seven doorways he'd seen in the ruins, only these depicted no scene Rags could discern, just a repeating geometric pattern. Interlocking diamonds and sharp arrowheads traveled in a spiral from the tippy-top to the fat middle.

Eventually, he couldn't stand it anymore. Into the silence that was driving him out of his skin with frustration: "I'm sorry, all right? I'm fucking sorry, Shiny."

Rags practically felt Shining Talon blink. "Why do you feel the need to express remorse?"

Rags groaned, a hoarse growl. "Why? Why would I? I'll tell you why. Because I'm *nobody*. You don't have to act like *my* shit's worth protecting—for a fae prince, you're an *idiot*. No wonder you were all conquered, if you're like this, *stupid*—"

"It does not sound as though you blame yourself," Shining Talon said.

"That's 'cause I don't apologize," Rags muttered. "Never had reason to, until lately."

"The apologies should be mine. I have failed in my duty to protect you."

"Shut up, Shiny." Rags grabbed a pillow, intending to throw it, then pulled back at the last second, mashing it over his face. Perfumed. He grunted and threw it away. "I *told* you, I don't need that. You should apologize for not listening, if you want to apologize so bad."

"I do listen. But I cannot act on your instructions when they conflict with what must be done."

What must be done. Rags forced a cracked laugh, rolling onto his side and putting his back to Shining Talon. He wished he *had* thrown the pillow at the fae prince's big golden tattooed head.

"Everything's gone to shit," Rags said.

"As I said—"

"I remember what you said." Rags remembered everything Shining Talon had said, every damn word since the start. "And like *I* said—shut up, Shiny."

Shining Talon shut up.

Despite being the one to request—demand—it, Rags regretted it the moment he was left alone with his thoughts, missing the steady fae voice distracting him from everything he didn't want to be thinking.

In silence, Rags practiced the techniques he knew to keep his fingers steady in a tough situation. Couldn't be a thief with shaky, sweaty hands. Not if he wanted to keep those hands.

"Something troubles your heart," Shining Talon said finally.

Rags snorted. It was rude, but he couldn't help himself. "No shit."

Shining Talon shook his head. "Something beyond the Lying One's mirrorcraft. Like a shadow on your soul."

Rags crossed his arms over his chest, feeling foolish as he did it. It wouldn't help him hide.

"Stop looking into my soul," he instructed bleakly.

"This is not something I can help," Shining Talon confessed, a new, mournful note to his voice. Rags was behind that. Great. "My eyes work as they always have. There is no changing them."

"Of *course* not." Rags dragged his hands through his hair, tugging at the ends to jolt himself back to reality. He had to shift the topic, come up with something to keep from talking about himself. If Shining Talon expected an explanation for Rags's behavior, he wasn't about to get one.

"So." Rags hoped the ragged snarl to his voice sounded husky and mature, not like he was completely out of his depth. "Next fragment of the Great Paragon, huh? You said something about how Cabhan can lead us to it?" Rags thought about One, who was an it but also a she, and how little he wanted to offend any of those creatures. "Or to her?"

Shining Talon remained shut up.

Was he sulking? He'd spoken before, so it wasn't that he *always* followed Rags's commands this strictly.

Rags rolled over to face the guy where he sat: in the room's least-comfortable-looking chair, elbows on his thighs, hands clasped, eyes fixed burningly on Rags's face.

"Stop worrying about me, will you?" Rags waved his hands to indicate health and energy. "I'm fine. Nothing wrong. Having a bad day."

Shining Talon waited a moment longer, checking Rags's expression to be sure the admission was genuine, then nodded. "You blame yourself for the fate of a companion. A noble sentiment."

Remind me, how did noble sentiments *serve your king?* Rags bit back the words. Didn't like being read so easily. Fae could probably see into minds, open them like Rags opened locked doors without needing keys.

And if they could, Rags didn't have to tell Shining Talon that that kind of responsibility—that guilt—chewed a Cheapsider up into nothing.

He couldn't survive on the streets *and* get this worked up over every sad-sack stranger who crossed his path. He'd buried those feelings deep, same as how the fae had hidden all their best shit.

"Whatever," Rags murmured. "This is why I work alone. Hey, we were talking about the Great Paragon."

"In answer to your question, my instructions are—were—vague." Shining Talon bowed his head. "All I know is that One will be able to draw the truth from her master . . . somehow."

"Somehow." Rags shoved one pillow aside, only to bury his face in another. "Fucking great."

The quiet went on long enough that he was nearly asleep before Shining Talon spoke again.

"You work alone to protect others from having to share in your fate," he said. "I believe I understand you a little better, Lord Rags."

"If you did," Rags told him, "you'd stop calling me that."

"I prefer your company to being alone," Shining Talon confessed. "I have spent too long in the Sleep to bemoan companionship."

Even that of a lowly thief? Rags didn't know how to respond to that, couldn't handle the weight of replacing *an entire race* of people, even if he wanted to.

Too tired to correct him, or acknowledge the statement, Rags exchanged his misery and hopelessness for a few hours of dreamless sleep.

Slipping away like a thief in the night.

Inis Fraoch Ever-Loyal didn't mind banishment as a concept. Banishment kept her away from court, away from the constant wheeling and dealing of power. The gossip, the wickedness, the flirting.

The relentless backstabbing.

It was how banishment had come—brandishing unsheathed swords in the dead of night, weapons trained on unarmed children—that remained an open wound, still refusing to scar and heal. *Treason*, a magic spell, which, once cast, permitted soldiers to murder her family and servants indiscriminately.

Only her eldest brother, Tomman, had been named as guilty in the writ-of-summons, but Inis knew that was as ludicrous as if she'd been named herself. Tomman had done nothing wrong. One of Lord Ever-Loyal's enemies at court must have whispered enough poison into the right ears to have Inis's father removed from the playing board, no longer a threat, a worry, or anything else, other than garden mulch. They wanted his lands, or his influence, or the rare books he owned, and thought his life—the lives of his *children*—would be a fair price to pay.

It had happened to other families. Sometimes Inis wondered how many. But she didn't think about it as often as she used to.

Memories of her brothers' laughter, stilled in their slashed throats, her father's refusal to kneel before they slit his, visited her with the same patternless frequency as rain on the heath. Aches came and went. She refused to be too grateful about the fact that she was still alive, thanks to the generosity of the Crown. The Queen's royal compassion.

During the massacre, little Ivy had found Inis hiding in a wardrobe. She'd crawled in beside her, buried her face in the collection of their mother's dresses. They'd wrapped stiff petticoats and jeweled sleeves around their heads so they wouldn't have to hear the servants screaming.

Mother only survived, Inis later learned, because they had kept her alive specifically to make her suffer. They'd forced her to watch every moment of torture, every instant of death.

When morning crept in through the flame-licked windows, a rider brought the survivors' pardon—with stipulations.

Leave the Hill. Go to the Far Glades.

Never return.

Inis had no desire to return.

The pardon was a gesture at apology, blaming the overzealousness of the Queensguard, who hadn't been instructed *on paper* to kill *everyone they saw*. Yet those had been their orders, if not officially.

Eradicate anyone who might pose a threat to the Queen.

No one shed a tear when traitors were slaughtered.

The Ever-Loyals had grown up alongside the Ever-Bright princes and called them friends. Inis had spun fae tales with Somhairle while Tomman and Prince Laisrean dueled with sticks nearby. She and Ivy had provided surrogate sisterhood to the Ever-Bright family as it firmed its foundations.

Not one of the princes came to the Ever-Loyals' defense when the

Queensguard marched on them in the night.

Who was living in the Ever-Loyal mansion now, tending its blood-soaked earth? Whose hounds roamed wild on the grounds of Inis's childhood?

Inis didn't know and forced herself not to care. In the cottage that was the new home of House Ever-Loyal, she read to her silent mother and Ivy each night, an attempt to fill her sister's head with better fodder for her dreams, and spent her days walking up and down the heath, even when rain broke suddenly and drenched her to the skin.

Good country air, breeding a strong constitution.

Her boots had holes twice mended by her own hands with scraps of unwanted leather. She sold their purple mourning silks. She cut articulated lacework from sleeves and organza petticoats from underskirts and sold those, too. She gathered piles of heather, dried them in bundles, filled the cottage with them. She opened windows and beat dust from the curtains. She went to town with their faithful manservant Bute on every errand, learning to haggle over the price of eggs and check loaves of bread to be sure they weren't moldy *before* she paid for them. She no longer gave the village people a fine laugh at her expense. She cooked, cleaned, hated sewing but sewed anyway, managed their budget, kept track of Ever-Loyal's banishment stipend when it arrived, and never asked the couriers for news from the Hill. She'd helped Bute repair damage to the roof thatching. They'd all gotten lice, but she was the one to get rid of them, going through Ivy's hair, then Mother's, with a fine-tooth comb out in front of the cottage. Because she couldn't give herself the same treatment and couldn't trust anyone to do it for her, she'd wrapped her head in lye-soaked rags to kill the vermin.

It had worked.

She didn't smell good, but she didn't care. The lye had burned her scalp, but she had no one to complain to.

She walked and walked until the blisters on her feet hardened to calluses. She grew to love the view from the hills that twisted and tumbled themselves higher, crawling toward the mountains. She thought sometimes she could see Lost-Lands treetops from her highest climbs, could catch the shimmering hint of black trees where the fae Folk had made their final stand and burned, and burned, and *burned*.

Stories of the Fair Wars, of the wicked Folk and their defeat by House Ever-Bright's clever sorcerers, had thrilled Inis as a child. They'd been a favorite escape back when the worst thing to sour her days was a six-hour dress fitting, or a piano lesson from their tutor with the garlic-laden breath.

When Inis thought of the fae now, she imagined screaming. The scent of her father's blood as it pooled on the blue-tiled floor of their audience hall. The shrill roaring in her head that insisted none of it could be happening, though all of it was.

It had happened. To the fae first. Then, hundreds of years later, to House Ever-Loyal.

Was it better to be cut down alongside your family? Better to die with than to survive without? Inis set her furious questions into a steel box within herself and locked it tight. Her sister and her mother—what remained of her family—needed her. The answers to her questions didn't.

She tired herself out so well each day that sleep came easily, without any of the bad dreams that haunted Ivy.

Thinking it might help to talk about those dreams, to banish them the way the last of the Ever-Loyals had been banished, Inis took Ivy to the sunniest spots she knew, built her little sister bowers of heather, and told her to share her ghosts as though they were part of someone else's story.

Close her eyes. Feel the sun on her face.

Tell her big sister everything.

One Queensguard chasing her through the halls of—home. (Ivy always stumbled over that word, her expression losing focus with a loneliness that made Inis want to split trees in twain with her bare hands.) In her dreams, instead of letting her go, the Queensguard did to her what had been done to Papa.

"That's enough, little egg," Inis had whispered, pulling Ivy close. "You don't need to say it."

The nightmares continued.

So did life.

35
INIS

Change arrived when Inis was shouting like a haunt-cat about two broken eggs Farmer Brogan insisted hadn't been broken before they went into her basket, which was a lie she wouldn't swallow.

"Perhaps they were crushed by the rest of your dinner, my lady?"

"They're the *only* things in there." Inis's black skirts formed a waterfall over her gray petticoats. She'd tucked them into her belt to create a pouch for carrying the rest of the day's fresh produce. Green beetradish stems swayed with her anger. She smelled and looked a wildfields fright. "You might think I'm a fool, but have the good courtesy not to treat me as such."

Bute stood at her side, embarrassed but refusing to abandon her.

Inis had learned from her mistakes of the first few months. She wouldn't raise trouble now without irrefutable reason.

A crowd should have formed around them to watch the fuss, but hadn't.

A squealing passel of barefoot children tore off away from them down another street, followed not far behind by the village carpenter and his wife, Fishmonger Anthea. Only a few spared a glance for wild-haired Inis Fraoch Ever-Loyal, who was probably cursed, and definitely a pain in everyone's ass. There was a time not so long ago when she'd have died before putting her mended boots and under-things on display.

Now nothing mattered except keeping the heath from growing over and burying her family. Another unmarked gravesite.

"Have it your way, my lady." Curiosity had succeeded with Farmer Brogan where Inis's stubbornness hadn't. Whatever the children were running to see—likely a cockfight—he didn't want to miss it. "Take your eggs for replacement, save your shouting for some other luckless bastard, and have a *fine* day."

Inis turned to Bute blazing triumph, seeing the helpless shrug he gave Farmer Brogan and the grin in his eyes reserved for her alone, the only praise necessary. She made the switch, stood straighter, and started back to Ivy.

Not home. She wouldn't ever think of it as home.

It was the place where what was left of home slept at night.

The cottage granted to the Ever-Loyals in their banishment was larger than any of the village's other houses and far removed from the main thoroughfare, sitting atop a low hill overlooking the market-place. Some long-ago magistrate's family had lived there, separate and above his constituents. Plenty of room, but bare to scrutiny, never a true part of village life.

Under Inis's supervision, and with Bute's guidance, the front gar-den blossomed, the door no longer hung off one hinge. The windows were clean and the roof had been repaired.

But right now, there were horses approaching the cottage, two handsome mounts with a rider each. Someone led them on foot, and an enormous shaggy dog walked beside them.

It wasn't stipend day. Their last had arrived less than two weeks ago.

Didn't matter. This entourage was no courier. Couriers came alone like clockwork once every double moon. They never bothered with ceremony.

Inis dropped the basket of eggs even before she heard Ivy scream.

One of the riders dismounted.

Inis started to run.

FOUR DAYS EARLIER

The raid on House Ever-Loyal had taken a month to plan, based on good intelligence that key members of the family were plotting to harm the Queen.

The irony of the Ever-Loyals acting against their namesake quality wasn't lost on those included in the innermost circle of the Queens-guard's most trusted young recruits. Bright-eyed, fiercely devoted, brutally trained, too eager to serve their country.

Their Queen was threatened. They marched to save her.

Midnight, the night of the raid. Cab led a squad of recruits he'd trained beside, had been taught to trust with every breath. They felt the same about him. The massive mansion loomed over them while their captain knocked on the main door.

Cab couldn't pinpoint when *rounding up traitors* had ended and the slaughter had begun.

It hadn't been by his order but by their captain's. An innocent child's throat was slit. One old groundskeeper, wielding a pitchfork, had entered at that wrong moment, sparked a frenzy that for Cab had ended when he found himself throwing *a little girl* to the floor, his blade to her throat.

He blinked.

He'd seen her eyes.

She wasn't crying. Not because she wasn't terrified. Her fear had carried her somewhere else. Cab stepped back and slipped on a torn curtain trailing through a pool of hot blood. He went down, fingers suddenly unable to keep their hold on the hilt of his sword. It had clattered away from them.

"Run," he'd told the girl.

Then he'd taken his own advice.

In the chaos and carnage, he shouted to one of his bloodstained, glass-eyed cadre, beating a corpse to pulp, that he'd seen someone flee out the window and he intended to follow. His voice had sounded as cool and certain as steel.

Out into the dawn.

Shedding his bloodstained armor, tossing it aside in the trampled garden.

Didn't look back to see the first line of smoke rise, the first flame tonguing out a smashed window, as House Ever-Loyal began to burn.

How many of the Queensguard had followed their orders because they had had no other choice? How many had been like Cab, not yet under the thrall of mirrorcraft, but blinded by love for their Queen? How many had decided, like him, that this was the last Queensguard order they would follow?

Like any true coward, he was terrified of the answers.

They were a haunting. They prowled the perimeter of his guest room in Faolan's summer mansion, drawing ever closer as he recovered from Morien's mirrorcraft.

No matter how far he tried to run, there was no escaping this: Cabhan of Kerry's-End, Master of One, was the only person who could lead Morien the Last to the next master, the next fragment of the Great Paragon.

After he'd recovered from the initial side effects of the mirror sorcery planted in his heart—this involved hours of vomiting—his first instinct had been to kill himself rather than be a sorcerer's puppet. But One was there to stop him.

I'd prefer it if you don't. I've waited a thousand years to meet you. Only getting to be with you for mere days would be a slap in the face.

Cab was imprisoned. All his running had led to nothing.

Except it wasn't nothing. He'd found One, and One had found him.

Can't die yet, Cabhan admitted. *Not before the sorcerer gets his.*

That's the spirit, my soft little fighter.

Cabhan laughed darkly, pressing himself against One's cool scales and trying to sleep. This close, he could hear the ticking of her inner workings. Like a heartbeat, only more reliable. He shut his eyes, pushed his face into hers, and drew new depths of strength from being with her. Felt whole again, more peaceful than he had in years.

Felt less peaceful when her mind clasped his like a handshake, met his like ocean kissed river.

What are you doing? Trying not to panic. Knowing he could trust her.

Looking for something, One replied.

Cabhan lay back, tension tossed away by the tide of One's sentience. Let her look.

She flowed through him, beneath his skin. The only acknowledgment of Morien's presence was how she kept away from his heart.

It was Morien's fault that they couldn't complete each other.

Though they came damn close.

The tickle of her claws tracing his veins, the flicker of her tongue behind his teeth, the throb of her pulse in his temples. His breathing eased and he floated, serene. He slumped into the bed, forgetting where his flesh met fabric. His fingertips tingled, went numb.

One traveled the inside of his skull, his memories, his marrow. She saw everything, knew everything, and embraced all without the stabs of guilt that still woke Cab, sweating and snarling, most nights. She watched what he'd done, the mistakes he'd made, the false steps taken and the right ones, without judgment.

So. This is who you are, her voice whispered.

Somewhere along the way, Cab began to weep.

This was what the fae could do, and they were all but lost now.

He drifted out of consciousness, entering a state more restful than sleep. When he opened his eyes again, it was morning. One was curled up by his side, sharp teeth and scaled chin resting on his knee. He stared at her for a long while, recognized what her face looked like when she smiled instead of grinned.

Good. You survived.

More than that. Cab couldn't remember when last he'd slept without jerking awake to fight or flee a dreamed-up enemy. He sat up, without dislodging One, and stretched his shoulders. Only the faintest twinge between his ribs, like the mirrorglass was the last remaining shard of regret he possessed. He rubbed his stubbled cheek and pushed his hair from his eyes.

Better than survived, Cab thought.

One's chin dipped, eyes flickering. *Yes. We are an excellent match.*

He stood, was halfway to the door—he needed a bath, every inch of his skin too warm and metallic-smelling—when she added, *I know what we must do to find Two's master.*

Cab paused, one hand on the doorframe. Resting at eye level, a scar on his knuckle from his final night as Queensguard.

Think we can find where the last of the Ever-Loyals are lately? One asked.

It had been so long since Cab had let anyone or anything under his armor, he'd all but forgotten the pain of a gut-punch, blooming its bruise in him now. Leaving him breathless as a dead man.

He hadn't realized moving forward would mean he'd have to come to terms with what he saw when he looked back.

37
CAB

So there it was. Unavoidable.

Having to face the surviving Ever-Loyals, having to look them in the eye, would prove too much for the craven to swallow.

But to disobey the sorcerer would be ending his life as surely as if he'd done the deed with his own hands. And even though he'd noted a letter opener and razor while taking stock of the assets in the guest room, killing himself wasn't the solution to his reckoning.

Cab went to Morien instead. What else could he do?

The sorcerer's eyes pitched black in the dim light of Faolan's study. The windows had been obscured with bloodred fabric hung like shrouds, obscuring the glass, blotting out all natural light. A fire crackled angrily in the hearth, though Cab detected no heat in the air.

"You look hale, Cabhan of Kerry's-End." Morien hovered the way a spider hovered, pleased as one with a web full of prey. "An incredible recovery. Queensguard training *does* make a lad strong."

"Right," Cab agreed, because *Thank you* didn't seem appropriate. There was something venomous about Morien's goodwill, considering he'd been the one doling out the punishment. The agony. "I remember how to follow orders."

One's tinkling laughter chimed in his head. He hadn't meant it as a joke. He was trying to placate, to show he wasn't a threat and could be relied on to do as instructed.

In short, he was lying through his teeth. Thankfully, One approved of who he was lying to, which didn't leave room for guilt.

Morien refused to fill the silence, waited for Cab to explain why he'd come, wouldn't move on until he got what he wanted.

Cab's hands felt empty without a tool of some kind. He clasped them behind him after a second's uncertainty, aware of how the position made him stand too straight, almost at attention. "I have a destination for us."

"Oh?" Morien betrayed no interest beyond that syllable.

It was enough.

"Did any of the Ever-Loyals survive?" Cab tried to ignore the voice that told him he'd know the answer if he hadn't deserted.

"Their ancestral home burned." Morien stirred the living coals with an iron poker. No wisps of light rose in the shimmering air. He turned, owlish, to meet Cab's gaze with his. "But you already knew that."

Cab deserved that jab, but it stung, poisonous, coming from the sorcerer.

"The survivors," Cab said. "What I mean is, we should head to see them next. On this mission."

"Very well," Morien replied. "You'll be provided with a map to the Far Glades, and horses to ride out early tomorrow. Should your intelligence prove fruitful, I will rejoin the party. I don't think I need to tell you the trouble there shall be if your intelligence proves less than fruitful."

Easier than Cab had thought it would be to convince him.

Easier than he'd hoped. They'd leave tomorrow.

That didn't give Cab much time to resign himself to what he was riding toward: the survivors of the Ever-Loyal massacre, in which Cab had played a bloodstained part.

Three days on horseback to reach the Far Glades, which on the map was even farther removed from city life than Kerry's-End.

The first day, Rags kept Cab from sinking into his thoughts by raising a wild, hairy stink about having to head back to the countryside.

"What is that *smell*?" He had rolled his eyes, then pretended to faint off his horse. Immediately lost his balance for real. Prince Shining Talon of Vengeance Drawn in Westward Strike trotted up quickly to the skinny thief's side and righted him in one smooth motion before Rags could be trampled by his horse's hooves.

The poor mount wanted to trample him *badly*.

Prince Shining Talon received a thunderhead glare in thanks for his effort. Much how an alley cat feigned aloof dignity after an embarrassing fall.

"Cow pasture up ahead," Cab explained in answer to Rags's question. Trying to be amenable.

After all, they were allies until further notice.

Later, Rags rode up alongside Cab and asked if he thought sheep were evil.

"Not particularly," Cab replied.

"You're wrong. They are. You can see it in their eyes," Rags insisted.

The second day, and the storms it brought, overwhelmed even Rags's capacity for unceasing complaints. Silence fell with the water. They pulled on waxed cloaks and disappeared beneath their hoods, Cab and Rags riding between the drumbeat of rain and the drumbeat of horses, while Shining Talon strode beside them, offering comfort to Rags's miserable mount.

Cabhan nearly missed the stream of Rags's curses and complaints. They'd distracted him from where he was going and why he was going there, serving as barricade between him and their destination.

But, One said, *there's no avoiding it.*

I don't think House Ever-Loyal is going to be inclined to work with me, he told One as they made camp the first night.

Cab-my-heart, that's a problem for later. You've seen how delightful communication can be between us. You'll bring bliss to an Ever-Loyal. Perhaps it might be enough to atone for these sins you obsess over.

Maybe. Maybe not. I'll be bringing Morien and his foul arts.

One suffers for love, One replied.

Cab rode on with Rags in tow, Shining Talon still soothing Rags's long-suffering horse, following the map provided by Lord Faolan's cartographer. There was no other choice.

Time to face the consequences of his actions.

Riding up to the Ever-Loyal's cottage door was no different from the past few days of riding, Cab told himself.

Save that when the cottage door opened an inch, eyes peering out to fix on him, a girl had started to scream.

One sighed. *Oh, you've been recognized!*

Cab swore and dismounted, unslinging the sword belt Morien had provided him with and dropping it to the grass. He held up his hands, began to say something like "I intend no harm," but the screaming didn't stop.

He wanted to scream, too.

He froze where he stood, attempting to make himself look smaller, rooted in the front yard like stone.

He'd prepared himself to accept Ever-Loyal hatred, their curses, as his earned punishment. He wasn't ready for all this screaming.

Cab was still standing like a statue of guilt when something crashed into him from the right and knocked him to the earth. A cloud of dust and pollen rose at the impact. Hands gripped Cab's collar, hauling him upright. Cab noticed with chagrin that One didn't step in to interfere.

"This is going great," Cab heard Rags grumble.

Cab went limp instead of bracing himself for a blow about to land. And it did land. A fist swung in with a *whoosh*, connected with his cheek, sent him sprawling onto his back. He stared up at the sky, relishing the burst of bruise stars he deserved.

Heavy panting, his own and someone else's. The screaming continued. At last One stepped between Cab and his attacker, but as a barrier. She wasn't going to fight back. His attacker battered One's flank, but it was no use.

Stalemate.

Don't protect me, Cab thought. *Let it happen. I deserve—*

Humans. One sighed again. *Skewed sense of right and wrong, what matters and what doesn't.*

Finally the screaming stopped, leaving Cab empty, his ears ringing. There was a crash, Rags sputtering vile curses. Then—

Silver everywhere, an entire dining set exploding through the nearest cottage wall. It hung suspended in midair, cups and platters rippling in and out of recognizable shapes, reflecting the sunlight in blinding, scattered flashes.

Then they melted.

Masquerading as antique cutlery all this time, Cab heard One say, though it wasn't directed at him. *How clever of you, Two.*

Cab blinked.

In that instant, the Ever-Loyal family silver turned into a One-sized cat.

38
RAGS

Everything about their search for Two had been act after act of misery. The grand finale came when a girl with streaming brown curls and a face like an arrow had dashed up the hill to whale on Cabhan.

Worse, Cabhan had let her do it. He wilted, flopping around like a fish, instead of acting like the trained fighter he was. Clearly the girl was mad as a rabid cat, but did that mean Rags's ears had to suffer for it? Who would stop the screaming?

Worst of all, dishware had broken through the wall of the nearby cottage and flown through the air.

Flashes of silver. An amorphous oozing of plates, goblets, knives, forks. They wobbled and shimmered over Cabhan's and the girl's heads. Rags realized what was about to happen with new instincts, ones honed to the weird and impossible since he'd arrived at the fae ruins' first door.

The dishware was about to turn into one of the fragments, *had always been* one of the fragments. Lying in wait for its master, carrying soup, meat, sodding vegetables, letting strangers dribble over it for centuries.

Fuck if that wasn't the craziest shit yet.

All this time, it had been waiting for One to appear, to remind it how to re-form into its true self. Rags almost cackled, hysterically, to think that the silver lizard was getting an earful about how late she was, how long the silver cat had been forced to stir porridge.

The forks joined to form arms, the knives legs. Three ladles became a tail, while two bowls fused into a headlike shape. More blobbing of silver, flickering in and out of recognizable forms.

Then it was a cat, missing an ear and squaring off against One with teeth bared, its features crooked, still resolving.

Rags couldn't help it.

He laughed.

"What is humorous?" Shining Talon asked.

"The cat's nose is still a spoon," Rags wheezed helplessly.

"Many of your lifetimes of suffering," Shining Talon said, "weathered in the shape of an iron thing. How brave."

"Nose-spoon," Rags countered. He wouldn't be cheated out of a laugh when he needed it most.

It hadn't found its way to form nostrils yet, most likely because the cat, Two, was busy protecting its master, the angry girl who'd punched Cab.

"Much of the fae silver was scattered as a safeguard," Shining Talon explained. Missing the humor, as usual. "Save for One, none of the fragments is likely to be found in its original form."

"Sure," Rags said. "Dishware. I'm thrilled," he added. "I'm laughing because everything is definitely not fucked in the eye."

"I do not understand how that—" Shining Talon began.

Rags shook his head. Better not to get into the logistics.

The fighting, like the screaming, had ceased. One and Two watched each other, maintaining their positions, preventing Two's master from lunging at Cab's throat.

Finally, Two reared up and butted its large head against the fighting girl's cheek. Not an attack. A greeting.

Saying hello.

Two's master found her voice. "What is the— Why did the— How did that—"

She didn't get any further. One nodded and Two placed its paws on her shoulders, swiping her face with a lick that left behind no moisture. Its mechanical tail switched under the control of minute gears, just visible near its hip joints. The girl's lips parted in a soundless gasp. Her hazel eyes watered with unshed tears.

Rags crouched by the nearest splintered plank of wood, wanting to look elsewhere. He hunched his shoulders and did his best to ignore everyone, aware that Shining Talon was smiling at him.

Wishing he wasn't.

Rags nudged the root of his thumb against the lump in his pocket. It had shown no signs of transforming into anything magnificent. It remained stubbornly bloblike, the protective outer coating he'd begun to peel off still wrapped around its lower half, waiting for him to finish the job.

If what Shining Talon had said was true, then it'd been waiting hundreds of years. Surely it could afford to wait a little longer, until they found someone worthy to bear it.

What a joy *that* would be.

39

INIS

Inis had told herself she would have killed him because he held himself like a Queensguard and carried a royal sword. Because Ivy's screams told her all she needed to know about who he was. It didn't matter that she didn't recognize him—Ivy did.

Inis would have torn him to pieces with her bare hands.

Then the voice had stopped her in her tracks, made her weep despite herself, hot tears pricking the corners of her eyes.

It wasn't painful.

It was pain's opposite.

It was wholeness, light, and hope. It soared through Inis in a single burst. Tasted like the first sweet raspberry of summer, felt like the first melting of hoarfrost when spring conquered winter, looked like the first leaf dancing in the autumn wind, red and gold.

It came from the silver beast in front of her, a cat with four eyes and a nose the shape of a spoon.

Hello, master, it said. A lilting voice with a masculine edge. Young, playful. A voice that sounded like one of her little brothers', like Ainle's, so similar that she almost thought he stood behind her in the garden.

He didn't. Inis forced herself: *Remember.*

Ainle was dead. Inis didn't know how to answer this voice that sounded too much like his.

Four cat eyes, reflective as silver-tinted glass, mirrored Inis's face, her splotchy cheeks and swimming eyes. The face of someone who had no idea whether to scream or cry.

"You have four eyes," Inis said.

The better to see our enemies with, my dear. The silver cat nuzzled her face, her throat, a touch that eased her pulse where it raced. It petted her with saucer-sized paws, butted its cheek into her cheek. With each touch, peace followed.

She still didn't know how to answer. None of the forms of address she'd memorized over her years of etiquette lessons on the Hill seemed appropriate.

Searching its feline face for answers, Inis found only her own refracted image in each silver facet. A wave of panic overtook her, breaking against the blanketing calm. She *needed* her rage, had donned it like armor every morning to survive the loss of her brothers and father. Rage, so much hotter, so much lighter, than grief.

Anger had kept her strong when they'd lost their mother. Not in the massacre, but afterward, when she'd fled to safety in the far reaches of her mind.

Inis couldn't lose her armor now. Not that, too. If she tried to remove it, it would come off with skin, muscle, bone. It was fused to her. *She needed it.*

Inis, the cat said, *I know your name. And your favorite kind of soup.*

Inis opened her mouth, croaked a wail.

You have good table manners, the cat added. *I am Two, and I am yours.*

Inis shook her head to clear out the last of her warring emotions. That voice held trust and warmth and safety. Just because these things had been taken from her didn't mean they had ceased to exist. Or that she'd ceased to long for them.

The peace Two offered her settled on her shoulders like a cloak.

She turned to face the strangers who'd brought this with them, the Queensguard she hated and the others she hadn't bothered with at first.

A short, scrawny boy with a tangle of black hair and an equally black, thorny gaze. A scar on his upper lip. Wiry arms and graceful hands.

The Queensguard—Inis passed over him, preserving the peace for as long as she could make it last. *Stay strong.*

A third man, or was he a boy? Inis couldn't decide. He was taller than most full-grown men and broad across the chest, observing Two and the silver lizard with a shining, opaque gaze, his black hair long with a shock of white at the front. Tattoos in the shape of bones were drawn everywhere on his golden skin. Their ink caught the sunlight with a blue-black sheen, the color of a crow's wing unfurled at mid-day. The bridge of his nose, his jaw, the long, tapered points of his ears, didn't feel human.

He looked as though he hailed from the Lost-Lands.

Not that Inis had ever seen a fae in the flesh. But there were tales passed down in legend, images scrawled on ancient stonework and in equally old books, and while the picture might have been distorted over the hundreds of years since the fae's extinction, the truth remained, a grain of sand at the center of the embellishment.

The *long, tapered points of his ears* were the main giveaway.

Inis took a step back. A frightened child inside her wailed at her to *run!* Protect Ivy, before the Folk kidnapped her for Oberon's Bone Court.

She should have felt her astonishment. If disbelief was going to register as an emotion outside of anger, it should have arrived precisely now.

It didn't.

The only other nod toward surprise her body gave was the faint flutter of her heart skipping a single beat. She accepted it as no more and no less strange than the talking silver cat who knew her, who'd changed her with a single touch, and no less real.

She turned back to the Queensguard, who knelt in the dirt behind the lizard, his head bowed. Rust-black hair, the back stained with dirt from when he'd hit the ground. Inis hadn't seen his face, didn't know or care what it looked like. All that mattered now was the real child in all this, likely terrified out of her wits.

"Ivy," she said. The name cracked between her tongue and teeth. "Did you—"

Your little egg is fine. Two's voice hushed her the way her mother's had, when Mother could still chase away Inis's childhood nightmares. *This soldier-smelling boy is not your enemy. My sister One, whom you recognize as a lizard, says that he is strong of heart and pleasing of face, and that he has come bearing a heavy burden on his shoulders.*

Inis snorted. A heavy burden? No heavier than what she'd carried for the past year, and *his* burden had been his choice.

"Get up," she ground out. Louder, toward the broken pieces of the cottage, she added, "Ivy? Little egg?"

Silence, but movement stirred on the other side of the door. Ivy's eyes peered out from behind a splintered plank.

Inis held up her hands. "See? All's well. No one's here to hurt us. No need to be afraid." She could hear that her voice had changed, strong city vowels lilting back after a long absence. The sound of a true smile.

"Cat," Ivy whispered.

"His name is Two," Inis replied.

40
RAGS

Despite missing a wall from their cottage, the Ever-Loyals knew their hospitality from their assholes. After belated introductions and explanations, they'd invited Rags and the rest inside for tea. A steady-handed butler had poured it straight from the pot, asking, *One cube or two?*

A cursory glance around the room told Rags what he'd already suspected: nothing in this house was worth stealing.

Especially since all their silver was currently cat shaped and sentient.

A closed door on one side of the kitchen, a sitting room on the other, and a perilous staircase leading up to the second floor. The furnishings were so plain as to be anonymous. Even the ladies—both the tiny one who'd screamed and the one who looked like she could break Rags over her knee—wore unadorned mourning weeds.

What he wouldn't give for *one* black veil embroidered with jet beads. . . .

Silence since the tea was poured. Since Shining Talon had given Inis the Great Paragon speech, explaining her new silver beastie. The only person who seemed to be having any reaction to the situation was Cabhan, who kept staring at the wrecked wall: a calculating look, responsible and guilty, like he was planning how to fix it.

"So there you have it," Rags said. Couldn't take the silence any longer. "Surprise! You've got a fae-entwined destiny. And a really big cat."

This was more or less exactly what Shining Talon had told Inis Ever-Loyal, but Lady Inis hadn't warmed to the big guy. One might say she was outright ignoring him.

Could she teach Rags how to do that? He'd welcome being less aware of every swelling breath in Shining Talon's chest, every silken lock of hair stirred by the breeze streaming in through the gaping hole in the wall.

"I'm *mostly* sure it's true about him being a fae prince," Rags added, mouth running to fill the quiet. "I've seen him in the rain. The tattoos don't run off. They're legitimate."

"How can you *joke* about something as serious as collaboration with the fae?" Color flowed hotly into Inis Ever-Loyal's voice.

Rags hid his triumph. Got her talking, hadn't he?

"But," Cabhan's voice was a dull, rusted sword, and he wouldn't meet anyone's eye, "there's something else you should worry about. Not pleasant, like . . ." His hand strayed to One and, finding her by his side, stroked the scales on the back of her neck with a callused thumb. "Not like this."

"There's more, is there?" A glint in Inis's eyes suggested she was planning the best way to murder Cabhan *and* his lizard. "Out with it."

"I believe I can answer that." A shadow fell from the opening in the wall across the floor and sent the crawlies jittering up Rags's spine. Morien stood at their backs, blotting out the sunlight. Two the cat hissed. Something wordless passed between him and One, unspoken explanation. Rags shuddered. Cab clenched his jaw.

Morien's eyes surveyed the little hovel and its contents, mock pity in his eyes. For a moment, everyone remained frozen in time and place, the sorcerer's captive, disgusted audience.

"Traitors to the crown, rejoice." Morien gestured with a red-gloved hand. "Your Queen has found a new use for you. Or rather, for *one* of you."

Inis reached over to her little sister, pulling her close to cover her eyes and ears.

And Morien did what had to be done.

41
CAB

Once again, Cab was present to watch darkness descend on House Ever-Loyal.

"Was that necessary?" he asked Morien.

If he thought he was making up for what he'd done to the Ever-Loyals by expressing helpless concern for their eldest daughter, a shard newly lodged in her heart, he was fooling himself.

The little one cried. Their manservant tried and failed to comfort her.

Cab had to get out of there. Couldn't breathe under the weight of his guilt. Told himself he'd done what everyone expected of a deserter. Hadn't let anyone down except himself, who didn't matter.

"Everything I do is in service of the Queen," Morien replied. "Would you question Her Majesty's will?"

Yes, Cab thought, but that road led only to a yet thornier mire. Morien was implying it was the Queen behind their quest, not House Ever-Learning.

"What about Lord Faolan?" If Cab had learned anything of politics while in the Queensguard, it was always to answer questions with more questions. Made for a miserable conversation, but at least one you might survive without surrendering valuable intelligence.

"I will leave to inform him of these developments," Morien replied, looking pleased to have won their minor standoff. His expression darkened when he glanced at Cab. "Never forget that I see all. Escape from me is impossible. Whether I am here or elsewhere, I am watching—through this."

He touched his own chest, stared at Cab's.

After he left, while Inis Ever-Loyal recovered, Cab set about finding the wood he needed to fix what he could mend: the wall. Rags wouldn't go with him. "These hands aren't for hard labor or swinging clumsy *chop-chop* blades around," he'd said, and Shining Talon had refused to leave the thief's side, so that ruled his assistance out.

Cab would have been alone, except the manservant—"Name's Bute. It seems you've brought harm to my doorstep twice, *sir*"—had insisted on coming along. Together they trundled to the heath and chopped down slim-trunked trees, stripped them of their branches. Cab tore into the work with a dedication that made his palms bleed.

Felt nothing.

My silly boy. One's voice floated to him from the cottage, across the clearing. Her chin rested on her front feet as she surveyed his work at a respectful distance. *That's a flaw of your kind. Always building, destroying, then destroying to rebuild . . .*

This has to be done, he replied.

Does it? An artful, serpentine shrug.

Cab wiped sweat off his brow with his forearm, taking stock of the materials. The pile of wood was nearly waist high. Enough to start.

Bute clamped a hand on his shoulder before Cab could head back up the hill.

"If you bring more death to this family," he said under his breath,

"I don't care who's on your side, what sorcerer's working with you, or"—he gestured to One—"what *that* thing can do. I'll hold *you* accountable. You understand me?"

"On my life," Cab replied.

They worked through the night. By sunup, they had the basic structure of the wall back in place.

On shaky feet, Inis stepped out to join them at work. (Anything, Cab suspected, to ignore the mirror in her heart and the voice in her head until she was ready to face both.) She was handy with a hammer, and Cab stayed out of her way, letting Bute move between them and settle there.

The wall got fixed.

Ivy came out with breakfast. Cab wouldn't take food from an Ever-Loyal's mouth; there was enough left in his pack to satisfy him. He ate outside by the horses to avoid more discomfort under the Ever-Loyals' roof.

Your attitude might be misinterpreted as sulking, One told him. *Or worse, cowardice.*

Cab shrugged that aside. Went to bathe off the night's dirt, sweat, and blood in a nearby stream. He stripped out of his shirt and plunged into the cold water, shocking everything but shivers from his thoughts.

He stayed under the surface until the pain in his lungs sliced through the numbness everywhere else. Then he rose. Water in his eyes and ears, his nose and mouth. Not to mention every cut and scrape he'd earned while repairing the cottage. He waited for them to sting so he could feel again. Feel anything he was supposed to.

He'd fled from House Ever-Loyal and unswerving loyalty to the Queen. Somehow, he'd wound up back where he'd started.

But with a new purpose. He couldn't let the Queen get her hands on One and the rest of her kind.

The bruises on his jaw and the back of his head were both thanks to Inis Ever-Loyal. Cab deserved them. Deserved more.

And Inis deserved better.

He couldn't put things right; he could only do right from now on. One knew best—he should stop worrying.

Cab swiped the water out of his eyes with his hand.

He heard the rush of air behind him and understood what it was— *large object, about to connect with my head*—too late to do anything but let it hit him.

And the world went black.

42
RAGS

Rags managed to hang on until just after breakfast before he knew: He had to get out of that house. Had to get away from everything, everyone, in it.

Including Two, locked up with Inis in her room since breakfast.

Including the woman sitting motionless by the fireplace in a rocking chair, her face younger than her gray hair suggested, who hadn't spoken a word to anyone or looked once at her unexpected guests since they'd arrived. Hadn't glanced at the missing wall or acknowledged the loud, sweaty efforts to fix it.

And the little girl hiding under the table, staring at Shining Talon from beneath the tablecloth.

And the manservant who kept aggressively asking Rags and Shining Talon if they wanted more tea, as though he believed the next cup could pour life back to normal.

And Shining Talon, refusing to leave Rags's side, even after Rags made it clear that he wanted to be alone.

The instant Rags stepped out the front door, Shining Talon was there at his side like a late-afternoon shadow, if a shadow could glow more golden than the thief who cast it. "You will have to learn how to work in unison with others when you command the Great Paragon. Is it not better to begin practice now?"

Way too much to argue with there.

"I work fine with others," Rags told him. "You want something stolen, you let me know. But sitting around and chatting? Making *friends*? It doesn't work out. I've already told you I'm not your guy. I'm not going to waste time with your fae mind exercises, or whatever you want from me."

Perfect. It was rude enough that Rags prepared himself for the blissful distraction of an argument.

He wasn't prepared for Shining Talon shoving him to the ground, palm against his chest, and crouching over him like an alleycat guarding its first meal in days.

"Ow," Rags began pointedly, only to find his mouth covered by the same hand that had pushed him down. It smelled of green grass and precious metal.

Shining Talon's silver eyes flashed with sudden danger, scanned the tree line.

"Something is amiss," the fae prince hissed.

Then a black arrow sprouted from his shoulder. Too quick for Rags to think, to react, to process what was happening, Shining Talon snatched the next one out of the air. Shouts rose from the trees. To Rags, they sounded like a charge.

"Get back inside," Shining Talon commanded. "It will be easier to defend from within."

"Mmph!" Rags yelled. For once he was glad his mouth was covered. He didn't know what would've come out otherwise.

The arrow remained fully planted in Shining Talon's shoulder. Silver blood had blossomed around the buried tip. Didn't it hurt? Or did fae not feel pain?

All living things feel pain.

Fae blood dripped onto Rags's shirt. Figures melted toward them from between the trees, faces bulging and colorful. They were wearing masks.

Where was the enormous silver lizard when you needed her?

Where was the ex-Queensguard, for that matter, presumably trained to defend and attack?

Rags wriggled out from under Shining Talon's weight. Opened his mouth to shout for Cabhan. Found he'd lost his voice.

Dane had always wondered what it would take to shut Rags up.

Shining Talon lunged away to meet the enemy, muscles coiled, an arc of pure grace and power.

"Cabhan!" Rags finally croaked, flipping onto his belly and digging his nails into the grass, heaving himself to his feet. The wall of the cottage at his back, protecting him, also made him an obvious target. "Cabhan of Kerry's-End, you'd better get your well-trained, well-muscled Queensguard ass back here, or I swear on Lady Winter's tits—"

A window squealed open from above. Bossy Brown-Curls stuck her head out. "My *sister* is still a . . . ," Inis began, then trailed off, noticing the assault on her home.

Two. Her mouth formed the word, and the silver cat appeared at her side.

Both disappeared from the window frame. Rags swiveled in time to witness Shining Talon catch the haft of an ax and wrench it away from his assailant.

Heavy, blocky, pulp-paper masks, painted deep gold with black markings. Like the ones from the theater costumes human actors wore to transform into fae. Beneath the colorful masks, the figures were dressed in black.

It must've been wild for Shining Talon to be fighting himself. Or for him to see what humans thought of his kind. So much gaudier than the real thing, the difference between paste jewels and precious stones. Even their motions were jerky, clumsy, compared to Shining Talon's speed and sinuous movement.

He caught one by the head and slammed them to the ground.

Unlike Rags, they stayed down.

Where was everyone else? Shining Talon was amazing and all, but he was one against too many.

Rags grimaced, pushed away from the house, and rushed down the green toward the fighting, cringing the entire time. He'd seen too many decent thieves ruin their livelihoods by throwing a bad punch and breaking their fingers.

But Shining Talon was badly outnumbered. If anything happened to him, Rags was as good as dead.

Anyway, if harm came to the last of the fae, it wasn't going to be because Rags had stood back to watch him die alone.

Their attackers were shouting wildly. Shining Talon was silent. Small relief. Rags didn't think he could handle a fae battle cry. If he had to bet, they'd be epic poems.

"Pissing balls of fucking fire!" As he charged the line, Rags failed to convince himself that he wasn't as small as a shed feather tossed on the wind.

He tackled a masked attacker around the waist, headbutting them in the stomach for good measure. They fell to the ground but kicked as they went, hard-toed boots winding Rags as he scrambled to pry his fingers under the edges of the heavy mask.

It was stuck. Rags fumbled. The slice-song of a knife being drawn, slashing a violent arc toward Rags's throat.

Stopped by Shining Talon's hand, palm to sharp edge.

"This is not inside the house!" Shining Talon bellowed at Rags as he grabbed the mask with his other hand, slamming it down to the earth, knocking its wearer out cold. He tossed the blade away as though it were a splinter. The skin of his palm was split, dripping more silver blood.

Like he'd forgotten the shit they were in, Shining Talon touched Rags's throat, painfully merciful, to satisfy himself that it was unharmed. Left a streak of cool fae blood on Rags's pulse.

Rags swallowed, shivered. Sensed Morien's arrival like river-flu season.

That prick must have been waiting for the most dramatic moment to show up.

"Oh dear." Though Morien's voice snapped in the air with the charged promise of lightning, boredom dripped from his syllables. "If it isn't the Resistance. Come to defend their beloved Ever-Loyals? Or to steal more of the Queen's royal assets?"

A black-swathed body fell boneless at Rags's feet, its arms and legs twisted at limp angles. Rags looked away from it, but that meant he was looking at Morien. He wished he wasn't. Couldn't look away now.

Arms lifted, thumbs drawing sharp geometric patterns, Morien turned his palms to the sky.

A foreboding in the act made Rags's heart shudder.

Morien flicked his forefingers. Rags shouted. A fine diamond spray exploded outward toward the dozen or so black-clad attackers. Shining Talon dove to the earth atop Rags, chest on chest, chill blood splashing Rags's cheek. The mirror-dust cloud enveloped the Resistance fighters like a swarm of angry mudjackets. Screaming so desperate it might never stop. Rags was ashamed to find himself cringing, sick to his stomach, sick to his heart.

He'd seen plenty of death in his time, watched it claim friends, strangers, enemies.

And he knew what the mirrorglass felt like in his heart. Couldn't imagine how much worse it'd feel piercing every part of him at once.

His arms shook. His throat ached when he swallowed. The worst was the silence, the moment every scream died. The bloody shards of mirrorglass and mirror-dust drifted back to Morien on an invisible breeze like pollen blown off a wisher-willow in spring. The air was still and thick with death.

Rags looked up, nose brushing Shining Talon's chin. Only Shining Talon's heartbeat anchored Rags in place. The arrow remained embedded in his shoulder.

Rags was gonna kill him.

But then Shining Talon pulled Rags up with him, his long hair brushing Rags's lips as he stood. He proceeded to pat Rags down in search of injury, which left Rags too scrambled to grumble in protest.

Much.

"You're the one with an arrow sticking out of him," Rags muttered. "Why don't you look after your own self?"

Shining Talon ignored that reasonable question and turned to face Morien, keeping himself between Rags and the sorcerer. "These warriors could have been questioned as honorable prisoners. I fought to incapacitate, not kill, for this reason. Now they are dead, and the dead cannot speak."

Shiny had been thinking about honor. Meanwhile, Morien the Last had downed—Rags counted quickly, breath hitching—twenty-two fighters in masks. They looked smaller now that they were unmoving.

A couple were Rags's size, if that. Meaning they might be kids. Laid out across the front garden of the Ever-Loyals' grounds, never to move again.

"I protected you from the Queen's enemies." Rags would swear later that Morien had yawned, bored by the proceedings.

The muscles in Shining Talon's back twitched and clenched under his shirt. He was about to call Morien a Lying One again.

A shout from the other side of the Ever-Loyal house kept that from happening. Inis and Two appeared—*Bit late,* Rags thought darkly— the former holding Cab's muddy shirt in one hand. The wind picked up, air finally moving, Morien's mirror bullshit no longer keeping it at bay, and twitched the corners of the garment like a peace flag.

"Cabhan of Kerry's-End is gone," Shining Talon murmured quietly, for only Rags to hear. "And One has gone with him."

"Shit," Rags said.

"Indeed," Shining Talon agreed.

Rags was clearly a bad influence on him.

Violence and slaughter had come to Inis Ever-Loyal's doorstep once again. Only she wasn't helpless this time, and she wasn't alone.

The one you don't like is missing, Two said as he shot ahead, slinking past her ankles to patter down the stairs.

"Bute!" Inis hissed. The man poked his head out of the kitchen, hands still busily drying a kettle. Hands that stilled when he saw the look in her eye. She cleared the tightness from her throat. "Find Ivy and take her to Mother's room. Barricade yourselves in and block the windows."

"And you, Miss Inis—" Bute began. Inis held up her hand, and he honored her by falling silent.

Perhaps you think it doesn't matter if the one you don't like is missing? But it does. Two was waiting patiently for Inis at the back exit, expecting Inis not to question him.

"What's *happening*?" Ivy burst from beneath the coatrack, where she'd been eavesdropping by the door. Listening in on the fae, the small thief, and especially the small thief's gutter mouth. Just as Inis had suspected.

She smiled tightly, swept Ivy up in her arms, and passed her off to Bute. Let go of her with fingers that never wanted to let go of anything. "Bute's taking you in to see Mother, little egg." Though it had been Inis's instinct to run out front and confront the charging army, Two was poised by the back exit, and Inis trusted him. He was the *only* one Inis trusted.

"Where are *you* going?" Ivy's eyes narrowed with the realization that Inis wasn't coming with them as Bute steadied her in his arms like a sack of grain. One that kicked, bit, scratched.

"It's not his fault," Inis hissed after them, insistent that loyalty not be repaid in unpleasantness. "I told him to. Don't you hurt him, Ivy!"

Worse than the struggling: Ivy going limp in submission, her tiny body laden with despair and hostility.

She'd recover from this injustice. An Ever-Loyal could recover from anything, save death.

Nonetheless, Inis winced as she turned and opened the door for Two, leaving her family safely behind.

This was her element. Constant motion. A near-impossible task. Nothing remained for herself after being mother and sister, father and two brothers, to Ivy. Her own hopes and dreams were locked away in Mother's room, lost and untouchable as Mother herself.

Two lunged sinuously through the grass with the speed of a born hunter, Inis struggling to keep apace.

The fighting was on the other side of the house. No, the *slaughtering*. Inis intimately knew the difference.

Be glad the one you don't like isn't dead. That would make things even more difficult. Two's voice startled Inis. She strove to keep him in view, his tail rising like a shimmering pussywillow through the grasslands where they bordered woods and field. They were headed away from death, possibly toward more death. *I can smell his blood where it spilled. Does the thought of his spilled blood make you smile?*

It didn't, though Inis couldn't explain why.

I think you aren't smiling because, Two continued, *despite how unpleasant it is to acknowledge this, he is a part of something greater than both of us. He is also a part of us.*

I'm following you, aren't I? Inis thought back, fighting off dueling waves of nausea and headache. She'd left Ivy alone, the one thing she'd sworn she'd never do.

Perhaps this was how the fae took people. The stories had it all wrong. They showed up one afternoon and said you had a destiny to fulfill—then they gave you the most wonderful gift—then, when your armor was off and your guard down, when you least expected it . . .

Inis didn't realize she'd caught up with Two until he nuzzled her hand, half in comfort, half because he wanted her to scratch behind his one good ear. *Thanks, master.*

Inis crouched, breathing deeply, waiting for the latest wave of nausea to pass. Helping with the wall repair had been stubborn and stupid, more than she was ready for with Two's thoughts echoing in her blood, Morien's shard in her chest, but she couldn't let the Queensguard, someone who'd destroyed her life, be the one who fixed anything for her. She had to have a hand in it, was willing to pay the price.

She shut her eyes, remembering a time when her mother's cool hands would have passed over her feverish brow, lifting her curls off her hot neck. The simplest comfort in the world, but wonderful.

Stay here a moment while I explore. It's safe. Two's weight tipped her back against the curve of a wizened tree. Inis felt like a fae child nestled amid the roots. Her eyelids were heavy.

I could almost forget you're mortal, the way you keep yourself going. But you're no good to anyone if you collapse. Two butted his big, sun-warmed metal head into her hand, brief and comforting, before he was gone.

Just three breaths, Inis told herself. She'd allow herself to rest for three breaths. And then she'd follow him.

Instead, she almost cried out when, heralded by a flicker of sunlight on grass, she saw the world despite shutting her eyes.

Don't be startled. Two's voice inside her skull again, in the pulse at her wrists and throat. *You see what I see. We're closer to each other already than One and her pretty boy because you grew up with me. Ate your breakfast off me every morning, though you didn't know it.*

Inis couldn't open her eyes, but didn't wish to. Any lingering suspicions she had melted away. Two hadn't left her behind, hadn't tricked her, was showing her more than she could have seen on her own. They were sharing one sight. Headache forgotten, she focused on the shapes and shadows of the nearby stream, looking through the silver tint of Two's eyes at the world around him.

They took in the river, the bank, the signs of struggle. The Queensguard's dirty shirt, all that remained of him. Inis couldn't unravel what it meant. Her senses were flooded, hearing every buzz from every bumblebee, every click of every beetle leg on bark, every rustle of every worm shuffling through the earth . . .

One is following him, Two explained. *But it's dark and she's taken many twists and turns. They are already a long way gone. What is the word for when humans steal another human? Kidsleeping?*

Kidnapping, Inis supplied.

Have it your way. The word itself makes no difference to those who have been taken. Inis felt Two smile, felt the dizzying rock of his tail flicking back and forth. *The assailants split up—a few took Cabhan, while the rest caused a diversion to ensure a successful nap-kid. One has followed her human at a distance. Oh, this is going to be a problem.*

The word *diversion* made Inis's heart leap, despite what Two said. *Is my sister in danger?*

No. The diverters are in danger. The Lying One is mad.

The Lying One was what Two called Morien.

So he was back, with his anger. It couldn't be as strong as Inis's anger—nothing could. But his came with mirrorcraft.

Morien's timing was impeccable, and that made it impossible to ignore what Inis had viciously hoped couldn't be true.

He was spying on them. Constantly.

Rumors had it that hearts bled their truths onto a mirrorglass shard, and none could lie to them or hide from them. But those were supposed to be exaggerated stories. Sorcerers weren't meant to wield this much power. They drew on old spells, studied the few remaining histories left behind by Oberon's children, but their work had begun as pale mimicry of legend. They were like children dressing in a parent's clothes, aping maturity beyond their ken. They could go so far as to predict blurred futures, to extract truths from the Queen's enemies. To spy, and—sometimes—to salve.

Crisiant the Questing and Siomha the Undine had been frequent guests of House Ever-Loyal while they attended to the Queen's business, and though they had been odd, they hadn't been dangerous like Morien, who was a weapon masquerading as flesh.

They didn't stick mirror shards into people's hearts and control them like hand-shadow puppets cast on a wall.

She wondered if Morien could hear her thoughts, could eavesdrop on every private conversation she had with Two.

No, Two told her. *Our connection is safe. It is beyond the Lying One's current reach.* Relief swelled in Inis's breast. It was short-lived. *He does, however, know that One and her master are missing, because the little one with the dirty mouth won't shut up about it.*

Despite Two's superior fragment senses, One and her master were too far out of reach for him to determine where they had been taken.

Inis couldn't let Ivy see any of this. So much like the night they'd lost everything.

Two said, *Open your eyes.*

Headache or no, it was time to get up.

44

RAGS

When Inis came running out of the woods with Cabhan's shirt, Rags thought it might've been a confession. She'd murdered him.

Then Rags figured Morien would've seen that coming and stopped her.

Sensible people with wicked mirrors in their hearts needed to *avoid* pissing off the guy in charge of when those wicked heart-mirrors started heart-murdering.

On the other hand, nothing Rags had seen from Inis, who'd introduced herself by decking an ex-Queensguard in the face, gave him any reason to call her sensible.

That was another problem with working in a group. You didn't always get to choose your team.

"I had thought," Morien said, perched in the seat they'd left for him at the table, "that your purpose was to gather more fragments and masters for me. Not lose ones you had already found."

"One," Rags pointed out. "We lost One, not ones." He laughed too loudly. "Get it?" With his nerves this frayed, there was no chance he'd be able to control his tongue. Morien was going to punish them. Might as well bring it on, control when it happened, if nothing else.

"I see no humor in the situation," Morien said. "And neither does my lord Faolan."

"Speaking of your lord Faolan—does *he* have that insurance you mentioned?" Rags kept talking—shouldn't have, did anyway—figuring it was the best tactic to draw Morien's irritation to himself and spare the others. He'd set all this in motion with his own two hands simply by excelling at his trade. He had some responsibility for what happened next. "*Your* insurance. Speaking of, why not do your sorcery stuff, track Cab down, and solve the problem? That's *why* you bound him to your 'cheating will'—so you could snap your fingers and bring him back."

"There are limitations to the spell." Morien's voice had hardened to the point of petrification. Rags's pulse raced while limping like a dog injured at the track. "If he has been blindfolded, or if he is unconscious—if he himself does not know where he is—then I am unable to track him."

"Cheating will these days ain't what it used to be, eh?" Rags asked.

Darkness fell too quickly, not from the setting sun, but behind Rags's eyes. He didn't know if Inis was consigned to suffer the same fate or if he'd managed to direct the burden toward himself alone. Then he stopped thinking, stopped asking questions, stopped breathing. Clutched his throat, *like that makes a fucking difference*, and dropped to the floor.

As quickly as the punishment began, it stopped.

"—will be able to find them both more easily with the assistance of the other fragments." Shining Talon was talking fast, saving Rags's ass *again*. This debt was piling up so big, he'd never be able to repay it. His eyes watered. No sound but rasping wheezes came out of his throat.

Inis remained seated, unharmed. She looked pissed, but also smart enough not to draw Morien's attention—and with it, his wrath.

They were Morien's prisoners, his pawns. Whether he'd predicted this would happen or not, the masters the fragments had found had something to live for. Family to protect, or, selfishly, their own futures to preserve. Morien had more leverage than mere mirror shards, could manipulate both with equal skill.

"Without Rags, you will have to wait another of your human lifetimes for a Master of Five to come of age," Shining Talon continued. "A shameful delay, when we are closer than ever. With Inis Fraoch Ever-Loyal and Two, we have all we need to uncover the location of Three and Three's master, who will lead us to Four—"

"And so on," Morien said, voice diamantine.

"—which means we do not currently require Cabhan of Kerry's-End and One. We will be able to find the others without them, and find them *with* the others," Shining Talon concluded.

"There, see?" Rags knew it was a mistake to speak up again, but did it anyway. Didn't like the way a simmering-with-fury Morien was focused on Shining Talon. "I might be a pain in the ass, but at least you're not changing my nappies until I'm of Mastering age, yeah?"

"I feel that perhaps I'm not being taken seriously." Morien raised his left little finger, traced a half circle in the air. Rags screamed, the noise drawn from a part of him he hadn't met until this moment, never wanted to meet again.

Not just his heart, but traveling through his right arm to his *hand*. His right fingers spasmed. Pain spread through Rags's chest to his lungs, his heart.

Shining Talon moved toward him in a golden blur. Rags shouted, stopping him in his path. Was reduced to nothing but an animal, unable to explain to Shining Talon what was happening.

Every one of his ribs felt shattered to splinters. His lungs stretched to the point of splitting. His heart was in tatters. Those were facts.

Rags had seen his first dead body when he was six. A waxy white woman, skin stretched over bone, no muscle or fat to soften her features. She'd taken refuge in one of the sewer pipes that flushed refuse out of the warehouses into the sea, and died there.

Rags had found her because that was where *he* slept three days of the week.

She'd been stiff as pressboard. Still clothed, so fresh she hadn't been stripped yet. Rags could find nothing in her pockets but a glass pipe.

Since his first, he'd seen countless more. He knew how bodies worked and had a passing familiarity with their limits, how far flesh and bone could be pushed before they gave up.

His fingers popped at the joints one by one. Worse than a thousand paper cuts, the sensation of blade-thin arrows of honed air tearing apart the muscles in his hand.

Rags neared the point of no return. Dark spots and bright spots flashed in his vision. His heart was beginning to fray, the muscle pulling apart with as little fight as the threads of an old shirt.

In a distant, dark part of him, held separate from the pain, he wondered if he was going to die.

He didn't want to.

When he came to, his hand was still twitching, not to mention stinging like he'd shoved it into a hornetsuckle bush. Morien's face loomed in his blurring vision.

Something warm and solid at his back. A steady, broad touch. *Shining Talon*. Rags glanced up to see murder flashing in the fae prince's monochrome eyes.

Rags distracted Shining Talon from trying, failing, to kill Morien the Last, by doing the only thing he could think of. His quick hands found the shaft of the arrow in Shining Talon's back. The one that still worked yanked the arrow free. His fingers twitched but held.

A wet rip of muscle. Rags winced.

"That hurt me more than it hurt you," he offered hoarsely.

Shining Talon cleared his throat, almost a cough. He sought Rags's gaze, but Rags was busy pressing his hand into Shining Talon's shoulder to stanch the sudden flow of slippery, shiny, cold fae blood.

Not Rags's best play.

But it had worked. Shining Talon hadn't done something stupid like get himself killed sparring with Morien for Rags's sake.

"Everyone here has respect for the gravity of the situation except you, thief." The scarves over Morien's mouth never moved when he spoke. "I've left you a reminder. A few needles of mirrorglass in the appropriate joints—they'll cause you significant pain, but nothing more. Now we can avoid misunderstandings in the future."

Rags's vision tunneled, black at the edges, with a center of pure white.

Morien hadn't taken Rags's hand, merely crippled its motion. This had once been Rags's greatest fear.

In recent days, his perspective had shifted to welcome a host of new, even greater fears. He was going to pass out. *Good.* He welcomed not having to think about what had just happened.

"I don't need you *whole* to find the rest of the Great Paragon." Morien straightened, looked around at his captive audience. "You won't lose track of anyone else?"

The sun dipped low on Rags's consciousness. He jolted awake to find Morien gone, then again as Inis helped him into Shining Talon's arms so Shiny could put him, little more than a collection of shivering bones, into bed. He clung to the gossamer of Shining Talon's fancy shirt, the fae fabric cool and slippery, bunched in his hot palm. The wound in Shining Talon's back was already healing. Maybe already healed.

Rags wasn't so lucky.

"You should have let me kill him," Shining Talon said, low enough that only Rags could hear. Could've imagined it. Rags was feverish, fever being the true mother of all Cheapsiders.

He shook his head again and again. Shining Talon pressed it to his chest to still him. Rags had spent so much of his life in motion that it felt good to lie still for a change. He couldn't recall the last time he'd let anyone this close. Such carelessness in the Clave got you pickpocketed. Or stabbed, *then* pickpocketed. Shining Talon's arms around Rags felt sturdy the same way a taut rope felt in his palms after he'd managed to hook a grapple on the first try: safe to rest his weight upon, while the rest of the world threatened to crumble.

Though Shining Talon made for a silent companion, no throat-clearing or irritating mouth-breathing, Rags knew he was there.

He listened to the steady lift and fall of Shining Talon's breaths. The heat rolling off Rags's skin smelled scorched, like woodburning, or the forge in a smithy. Charcoal and steel. Because he was too tired and sore to stop himself, he thought about the fae prince's silver eyes, the black bones underneath his skin, and shivered.

This ancient, powerful creature answered only to Rags's command.

Why did it feel like he'd swallowed hawkshade?

Too tired to ponder it further, Rags told himself that if Shining

Talon was going to stick close, at least this time it meant the fae would get some rest, instead of staring at Rags in the dark.

So Rags couldn't bring himself to protest.

Only this once.

45
CAB

Cabhan woke to blindfolded darkness. Excruciating echoes of pain in his chest. Before the first flash of panic set in, he learned he wasn't alone.

Shh. One's voice settled alongside the pain. Soothing it, icy-cold. Wasn't enough to take it all away, but it dulled the agony. *You are in a good place where they have taken the Lying One's black mirror from your heart. It hurts but is already beginning to heal.*

"*They*"? Cab asked.

Don't get ahead of yourself, One replied.

Is it supposed to hurt this much?

It is supposed to hurt more. I am doing what I can to help. One's voice sounded faint. Separated from Cab by a great distance, or focused on more important work than conversation. In the same way that Cab had trusted her from the start, he trusted her now. If she said he was safe, he was safe.

Although he couldn't imagine feeling worse than this.

One of the initial qualities stamped out of trainees in the Queensguard was imagination. It only got in the way of duty and obedience, of action and reaction, of drawing a blade without thought spared for defeat.

Cab focused on his breathing. Another Queensguard training

technique that still served a purpose, however little he liked to admit it. A captain's voice barking, *If you can breathe, you can take stock of your situation.*

He was lying on his back in something wet. His throat felt rough, as if he'd been shouting orders. No matter how he tried to call his mind to attention, it wouldn't heed.

He was aware of a bruise on his head. Chafing on his wrists. He'd been bound at some point. The knot on his blindfold was too tight, and his head ached beneath it. Other than that, he was unharmed.

He tried not to think about the obvious. The shard of mirrorglass in his heart—now the empty space its removal had left behind.

Whenever Cab pushed the stray thought aside, it roared back to the forefront of his mind, twice as demanding.

He heard One *tsk* in chastisement, so he left it alone. Felt like he'd swallowed a flaming bramble.

Whatever happened now to Prince Shining Talon, Rags, and the Ever-Loyal girl was beyond him.

His mirror shard was gone. No matter how much it hurt, whatever damage the extraction had done, Cab was grateful. He was free.

He didn't have to decide what to do with his freedom alone.

Left a scar. One's voice again. How much time had passed? A trickle of sweat beaded in the hollow of Cab's throat, dislodged when he swallowed. *On your heart. I'm looking forward to meeting the Lying One again, getting the chance to repay him for that.*

Where am I? Cab asked.

A dark place.

You don't know, Cab realized.

We were separated. I have decided to remain undetected for now. Try not to get into too much trouble without me, my pretty.

Prone and blindfolded on a hard surface. Where to go from there?

Cab waited. He relinquished control. Either someone would come to free him, or he'd regain his strength and make his escape. Eventually, the blindfold would come off.

When it did, he was half dozing again. Listening to an unfamiliar melody hummed with a metal edge, One sharing a fae lullaby with him. He got lost in its repetitions and only caught the last few steps approaching. Had barely a moment to brace himself before the edge of the blindfold was lifted and pale light flooded in.

Above him, an inhuman face. Black stars at both corners of its mouth. Silver eyes. A long, thick fall of stone-white hair. Golden skin.

Cab recognized the features, what they meant, but not who wore them.

Another fae. *Not* Shining Talon.

How many of them were there? And what *had* happened to them, if they hadn't been wiped out?

Cab's heart tried to race but couldn't move around its wounds.

"I am so sorry for what you have suffered," the fae said. Clear tones. Young. Very. "I have done what I can to heal your heart, but the Lying Ones have grown strong feeding on our power."

"Fae." It was all Cab could squeeze out of his tight throat.

"Yes. I am Last Beacon of Silent Burning," the fae told him. "But my human friends call me Sil. You may tell your One she is free to join us. I already know she is here."

While Rags was unconscious, Inis ran downstairs to take stock of the bodies on her lawn.

It was barren. The overgrown grass billowed in the breeze, unbent by the masked raiders she'd seen swarming her home. Gooseflesh crept up Inis's bare forearms, and she hugged herself around her chest.

Sorcerers had beaten the fae with mirrorcraft, so it made sense that they could kill a host of mere human enemies, then make all proof disappear. Inis had once trusted the joyful side of magic: the intricate displays of light and water created for Summersend; Ever-Land's fragrant fields of ever-blooming wildflowers.

But this—the eerie calm after a massacre, bodies gone, death lingering—was too much like the night the Queensguard came for Inis's family, even without the bloodstains and charred frame.

Remember, your kind needs to breathe every now and then. Two's voice plunged through the wreckage of her thoughts. Her family lived, and that was what mattered.

This time, Inis told herself, she'd seen the enemy coming, and no one had to dig any graves.

Did that make a difference?

No.

She tapped her mother's door. Behind it, Bute had barricaded himself and Ivy. Inis used the secret knock she'd made up for Ivy to memorize—two swift taps, two slow, then three more swift.

The door creaked open an inch before Ivy practically exploded from within, crashing into Inis, bunching her hands tight in the bundle of Inis's aproned skirts. She scrubbed her face angrily against Inis's abdomen, but wriggled away before Inis could return the embrace.

"I'm sorry about that, little—"

Ivy snubbed her, turning to beckon for Bute's ear instead. As he bent to indulge this display of childish stubbornness, Inis caught a glimpse of their mother in her chair. Undisturbed, hands limp rather than clutching the woven black shawl around her shoulders.

She didn't know something was amiss, or didn't care.

Inis's mother had once taken great pride in her reputation as a hostess. She glowed at a full table, seemed to possess a sixth sense for what would make the people around her most comfortable. The woman she'd been then would never have missed a Queen's sorcerer on her lawn. Would have invited him in for tea, then poisoned it before he could threaten her family.

Bute squared his shoulders, filling Inis's vision.

"The Lady Ivy wishes for me to inform you that she is very glad to see you alive." As Bute spoke, Ivy swanned past Inis as though she wasn't there, holding out her skinny arms for Two. He'd changed his size to that of a normal housecat—rearranged all his parts to a stature better suited for their small home—and leaped gladly toward Ivy with a laugh only Inis could hear.

Traitor, she thought, knowing he could feel the warmth of her approval beneath it.

"Isn't that lovely," Inis said aloud.

Bute cleared his throat. He fought a smile, evidence of his deeper loyalties. "Lady Ivy also wishes me to inform you that she will not speak to you until further notice."

Fine. Inis could handle silence better than questions at any stage. Better to let Ivy stay angry than think of this new shadow drawn across their house. Anger was shield and weapon, and the ladies of House Ever-Loyal needed both.

Inis touched Ivy's hair as she passed her little sister, teasing out a wild tangle in the back.

Can you comfort her? Inis thought at Two. That was Inis's job, but in this moment, an otherworldly fae creation would provide better company to Ivy than her own sister. *Please.*

I know my manners. Two's voice was a throaty purr, a chuckle in her mind. *You only had to ask.*

47

INIS

Inis settled in alongside the fae to keep vigil over Rags. She intended to be the first to know if anything changed, mostly because *change* meant *danger* in Inis's world.

There was also the matter of the fae prince. She didn't like taking her eyes off him. With Morien gone again, the fae was her next most dangerous houseguest and demanded rigorous supervision.

From her window in House Ever-Loyal, Inis had watched the same great-pine be struck by summer lightning storms year after year. In her girlish mind, she'd thought it romantic that this one tree had grown taller, as if to protect the others in her garden from harm.

Now she knew: attracting danger was no admirable trait.

Inis found herself desperate for a clearer image of what, exactly, she was tangled up in. When Two padded into the room, settling like a pan-warmed blanket over Inis's feet, she decided to take advantage of her time alone with the fae, without the gutter mouth running wild to distract and confuse.

Morien would still be able to eavesdrop. Nothing could be done about that.

"What happens when we find all the pieces?" Inis turned to look at Shining Talon. As the hidden strength in him grew more obvious, strangely, she found that made her *less* afraid of him, not more.

His honest hatred of Morien meant they could be allies. He rippled with reserve, a mighty weapon sheathed. Inis could do worse. "We become new soldiers in Her Majesty's royal army? Help slaughter her enemies?"

"I cannot answer that. The Great Paragon was not used in my time." But from the way the black marks at the corners of Shining Talon's mouth moved, Inis realized he was lying—or at least cleverly omitting some part of the whole truth.

She didn't ask him to elaborate.

It's more than that, Two explained. Information Morien wouldn't learn from their conversation, and might not already know. *The Great Paragon can tear open earth and sky, can unleash the same upheaval that birthed the Ancient Ones. I remember the last time . . . No, it's better if I don't go into that. Wouldn't want to overwhelm you. Your thoughts remind me of a hive of angry bees.*

Thanks for that. Very helpful, Inis shot back. Was there anything worse than knowing information was being kept from her?

Yes. It was understanding *why.*

She'd asked Two something Morien couldn't be allowed to know. He'd torture anyone who knew the truth to get at that truth, and the only way for Two to protect Inis was to keep her ignorant.

She was quick to conclude that Queen Catriona Ever-Bright wanted the Great Paragon for more than an elaborate showpiece at her next ball. The Queen was planning something. Inis pictured her with *more* than the might of the Queensguard and her sorcerers combined, then had to stop picturing it. She stared down at her sleeves instead, at her newly rough hands, callused and cracked, bruised and sunbrowned.

"Very well," she concluded. "Once the thief—Rags—is recovered from his . . . indisposition, we leave to find the next fragment."

"First, we will be brought before the Lying One's benefactor," Shining Talon said. "Although whether the Lying One is master or hound is a riddle I have yet to solve." Though he was a fae, and not inclined to straightforward communication, his meaning was clear. Someone pulled Morien's strings, provided him with coin and free passage.

Only a favored Ever-Family—or someone in the palace—would wield that much power.

Inis, about to escape her exile, didn't intend to run back to the same brandished swords that had felled her father and brothers. She'd learned freedom could come at the cost of being torn in half, meant leaving behind who she loved most in order to protect them.

"I suppose we had better get cracking," Inis said.

"I know not what we are cracking," Shining Talon replied, "but you may be assured I will crack with vigor. We must act with conviction at every turn, even if the road we tread leads us to the darkest depths imaginable."

If he had been a human prince, Inis would have assumed he'd memorized verse to impress her. But what she felt wasn't impressed. It was the faintest breath upon the guttered ember she carried within, coaxing to life a wisp of curling flame.

Inis wasn't alone. This was a nightmare, but there were others having it with her.

The gown Bute brought her to wear was one of Mother's, one Inis had once loved best. *Once.* Silk puff sleeves and a square-necked bodice, trimmed with lace in plummy shades of red, regal without ornamentation. Around her neck she wore a finely wrought chain

with the crest of House Ever-Loyal: two swords crossed over a broken blade, pinprick opals set into the hilts. One of a rare few pieces of
finery they'd held in reserve after the first year of exile. A keepsake
not yet ransacked for its parts.

If Inis was to return to the Hill, she'd have to make an impression.
Tightening the ties at her waist so the dress wouldn't gape around her
chest, she felt like a child.

She'd escaped the Hill. One day, she'd escape her mother's closet.

She said goodbye to Lady Ever-Loyal without expecting a reply.
Leaned down, kissed her mother's cool brow, found herself tickled by
curls she'd inherited. Mother didn't answer. Inis hadn't expected her
to, although that hadn't stopped her from hoping.

Foolish girl.

Tucking her mother's shawl more closely around her shoulders,
Inis made Bute promise not to let Ivy run after her when she left. It
was too dangerous. Ivy's safety was what mattered, the only thing left
to matter.

Morien knew where Inis lived, knew what—who—she loved. If
she didn't deliver what he wanted, he'd make her watch the last of her
family suffer. She had no delusions about that.

She wouldn't let him win.

"I'll be back soon," she promised Ivy.

Another lie, like the first one Inis had told while they hid in the
closet, tangled in Lady Ever-Loyal's finest ballgowns. With every soft
scrape of the gem-strewn skirts against the wood paneling, Inis had
grown more certain they'd be caught. Would be slaughtered, too. So
she had lied through her teeth. *We're going to be fine, little egg. Everything's going to be all right. Papa and Tomman will protect us.*

"You're leaving and I hate you." Ivy didn't shout. She said it coolly, eyes blazing, before she turned on her heel and ran back inside the house. "And I *won't* watch you go!"

Good. Inis preferred anger to grief. Anger would keep Ivy alive, keep her from succumbing to the same torpor of sorrow that had swallowed their mother.

Morien waited for them on the front lawn, astride a black destrier darker than thunder. He led a string of exemplary, if nervous-looking, horseflesh, two shaggy pack ponies bringing up the rear. "Only the finest mounts, provided by Lord Faolan Ever-Learning for his friends and allies," he said.

It made Inis's skin creep, her blood curdle, to think he'd known exactly when to return, had arrived with the precise number of mounts required for their party. Through his mirrorcraft, he could watch all they did, hear all they said.

She wondered if she was meant to be grateful, and offered her best grimace of obeisance. Behind her, Rags succumbed to a coughing fit.

They left, once the thief finally managed to mount his horse without falling off the other side, taking the one road Inis had refused to look at since she'd arrived at the cottage at its farthest end.

Back to the capital, so Morien the dog could report to his master. Back to the Horrible Hill.

Her nose stung with unshed tears. She didn't set them loose.

If they wanted an Ever-Loyal back on the Hill, they'd get one. Her survival *was* her rebellion. Let the Queen's Silver Court see her and remember, every day of their lives, what had been lost when House Ever-Loyal burned.

Eyes fixed on the path ahead, she doused each fresh ember of fury as it threatened to catch flame.

Shining Talon traveled on foot, easily keeping pace with the horses, while Rags, still in poor shape from Morien's punishment, slumped over the neck of his thoroughbred and bounced with every step. He clutched his right hand against his chest, a wounded bird nursing a broken wing.

Fucking Lying Ones, Two groused. When Inis lifted a brow in surprise at his language, he showed his teeth. *You don't spend as much time as I have around cooks and kitchen wenches without learning how to curse like one. You all right, sweetheart?*

I don't have to be, Inis replied. *Has One told you where they are?*

Two's head twitched in a brief shake. *Haven't heard from her. I'll let you know when I do.*

By nightfall, they'd covered good ground, and Inis noticed that Rags was even able to dismount and stand on his own, despite wobbling knees. He refused Shining Talon's help to keep him upright, cursed enough to teach Two some more colorful phrases for his collection, and dropped by the stack of firewood Inis was trying to light, falling into slumber before he even hit the ground.

Shining Talon covered him with a cloak, lifting his head to place a bedroll beneath it. Inis burrowed deeper into her own cloak and watched the fire lick the twigs.

Once, she caught the fae prince looking at her. It was impossible to read the nacreous silver of his pupilless gaze, but there was no pity there. Nor was there contempt.

She'd expected one or the other. Or both. To receive neither unnerved her.

"You wear the face of a warrior before the battlefield," Shining Talon said, just loud enough to be heard over the soft snap of the fire.

Inis understood this to mean she was scowling. Rather than soften her expression, she shifted back to watching the fire, only it reminded her too much of herself. Never steady. Burning until there was nothing left to burn. She gazed out, onto the forest beyond, finally up to the canopy of branches over their heads.

"Forgive my lack of courtly manners," she said, though her nose was pointed in the air.

Shining Talon wasn't her enemy. The entire realm was Inis's enemy most days. But one of the fae couldn't—by his very existence—share in any of that blame. Both of them, she realized with a start, were victims. Both had been stripped of home and family, consigned to the blankest pages of history.

"Your court was taken from you," Shining Talon replied. Inis, who had been raised on Hill conversation, knitting together half-truths, deceptions, and omissions, found fae honesty as clear and refreshing as creek water on a summer's day. "As mine was from me. I would rather stand next to one who has suffered than beside a loyal servant of your"—his nostrils flared—"crown."

Inis's heart flamed hot. She thought of Morien smirking underneath his scarves, and it relit the fuse within her. That monster could be watching her every move, listening to her every word. Gloating that there was nowhere for her to hide.

Shining Talon knew this and defied it anyway, like he spoke directly to Morien through Inis's heart.

She reached for Two, palm settling atop the smooth curve of a hind haunch. He rumbled.

"I won't do anything to put my family at risk," Inis said. A statement meant for *everyone* who might have been listening.

Shining Talon settled back next to the sleeping heap that was Rags. Inis hadn't recognized he'd been tense until he relaxed. The difference between frozen and running water. "I would expect noth-ing less."

Inis had no experience navigating fae conversation, but she sus-pected she'd answered a question Shining Talon hadn't asked outright, and that her answer had been the right one.

She didn't close her eyes. Even if Shining Talon could keep watch better than anyone, Inis planned to keep her own.

Sometime in the night, with Two at her back, she curled into him and slipped into his thoughts, his senses, behind two of his four eyes. The wholeness he brought her, after leaving the rest of her family behind. She cried.

Tell me a story, Inis, Two said, licking the tears off her cheeks. *The first one you think of.*

Inis wasn't sure if she was still awake or dreaming. Night bugs glowed over her head, winking on and off. Sometimes they weren't night bugs but stars. She heard every sleepy cricket, the twisting of an owl's head from back to front, and the splash of a far-distant frog as it dove underwater, the bog fly it had swallowed still writhing.

Inis's thoughts drifted back to her childhood. To an old, long-gone friend, the youngest prince—one of the Queen's many sons who had no chance at the crown, his chances even less than the others'.

His name was Somhairle Ever-Bright, a prince with a beauti-ful face and withered side. He'd told her most of the stories she still shared with Ivy on nights when memory haunted them like vengeful ghosts, chasing them from sleep.

Once upon a time, Inis started. But instead of focusing on the story—about a girl who runs across a midnight procession of the fae and must outwit them to earn back her freedom—she found herself thinking of the boy who'd told it to her.

As if the storyteller *was* the story.

Sitting beneath a pear tree with Prince Somhairle, neither of them important enough to be wanted anywhere else.

She felt Two radiate warm approval.

Inis knew where they had to go next.

48

SOMHAIRLE

Somhairle woke to banging, to his bedroom door being nearly pounded off its hinges. He fell on his way to open it, good knee and both palms stinging. Not yet awake.

He'd been dreaming of silver. Again. Still tangled in the dream's webbing, fingertips catching beams of oddly bright moonlight like they too were wrought of metal.

Somhairle unlatched and opened the door.

On the other side, Lord Faolan. His black hair tousled, loose, falling over his face in chaos. His eyes like glass—mirrorglass.

"You need to go somewhere, anywhere else," Lord Faolan suggested, brittlely calm. Outside, lightning split the sky, buried its forked tongue in the earth directly in front of Somhairle's window. Its heat charged his lips, his skin a single, continuous prickle. "On second thought, stay here and don't come out until I've given you the signal. Or don't do what I say and regret it the rest of your life." Faolan's voice cracked. "Your choice!"

"What about you—?" Somhairle began.

Faolan didn't let him finish. "Ah, Morien the Last is here." He shuddered, straightened, and dragged the door shut, Somhairle still gripping the knob on the other side.

Something screeched along the floor, probably one of the heavy hall tables being dragged into place, heaved as barricade between Somhairle and the rest of the house. The wall trembled on impact, stilled. Silence descended.

Outside, the rain had ceased to fall, the moons hidden, the night pure black.

Somhairle rubbed silver out of his eyes. Whatever job Morien had been sent to complete for Queen Catriona, whatever royal approval he bore—surely this didn't give him the right to terrorize the countryside.

The door rattled when Somhairle pushed it, pounded on it. It refused to budge.

He fought with the doorknob even though it was a futile effort, *because* it was a futile effort. One he had to make, in order to live with himself. It had happened so quickly, he hadn't realized he'd let himself be made prisoner. In his own room, in his own life.

He placed his shoulder to the door and pushed and pushed, and cried out and slipped. He tried to lever the door open with his leg brace, all the while grateful he couldn't dislodge the table.

What did he plan to do if he could escape? What power did he imagine he held over Morien the Last?

What use was a prince who didn't understand anything happening in his own kingdom?

Unable to answer these questions, Somhairle turned to the window. He imagined that, if he opened it, tried to escape his prison that way, the unrelenting night would suck him in, preserve him like a specimen in amber.

He returned to rattling the door but at last surrendered. A foregone conclusion. His arms sore, his hip throbbing, his knee protesting, his twisted foot cramping. In his head, as he sank to the floor, he composed a thunderously passionate five-page letter of outrage to his mother, tore it up, and burned it, all before putting pen to paper.

He had only his complaints, and those were neither shield nor weapon.

The silence closed like ice water over Somhairle's head. Whenever he told himself it was nothing, that he was being a child and a fool, he recalled the glassy panic in Faolan's gaze.

This terror was no nightmare, but a waking thing.

He would have to endure it.

The sun appeared a few hours later. It hadn't risen, merely winked on cautiously behind a curtain of smoky clouds. There had been eternal darkness and then it was no longer, a curtain drawn back, summer returned to the living world.

Morien was gone. This was what it meant, to have the sun back.

A mist had settled over the grounds, as though to hide its wounds.

What had Morien accomplished before he departed, while Somhairle hid and Faolan weathered this storm? Somhairle peered out the window to see black streaks slashed through the earth, bushes and flowerbeds reduced to mulch. One of the willows smoldered; another was reduced to a scorched stump.

Somhairle opened the window. He tossed his brace out first, then hauled himself after, one-armed, landing with a thump in the scarred dirt. Using his brace solely as a crutch, he entered through the open front door, following silver bootprints stamped onto the carpet and etched into the wood.

The footprints led to the library. The library was missing its door.

Shattered glass crunched beneath Somhairle's slippered feet as he stepped inside.

Faolan sat in Somhairle's favorite chair. Or slumped in it. It seemed he was using its shape to hold himself in place. His eyes flashed when they met Somhairle's.

He looked his age for the first time, older than Somhairle, but uncustomarily young for the Head of an Ever-House.

He's been alone for a long time, Somhairle thought. *Alone like me.*

"You look . . ." Somhairle didn't know how to finish the observation.

"More alive than you expected? Really, you and I were never in *real* danger. When Morien is bothered, he seeks to transfer that bother to someone else. I shouldn't have troubled you." Faolan's tongue was very red, as though in the night his mouth had been full of wine, or blood.

"And Morien . . . ?"

"Had other business to attend to!" False cheer in Faolan's voice. Flecks of blood—Somhairle still hoped it was wine—on his open collar. "He's a very busy man. I'll pay for the door, the window, that bookshelf, its books, those two Gleaming age revival vases, and . . ." He trailed off with a circular gesture.

Somhairle hadn't been thinking of reimbursement.

"I'll make some tea," he offered. How small he sounded, in the wreckage of the room.

"No need to do it yourself. Call one of the servants." Somhairle couldn't be sure if the hollowness in Faolan's words was real or due to wishful thinking. Somhairle didn't want him to be so unbothered with the lives of others. "Morien always takes care of servants,"

Faolan continued, "locking them away in some corner of their mind so they don't bear witness. *Extremely* useful spell! No *permanent* damage done! They'll be more forgetful than usual for a day or two, but better that than cowering in a corner babbling nonsense for the rest of their lives, eh?"

"My mother's enemies must be truly formidable, if Morien is tasked with so many duties." Somhairle leaned against one brocaded arm of a settee, maneuvering around his true questions. Ones he knew Faolan wouldn't answer. "Fortunately, Ever-Land was built for relaxation and abandoning your cares. You're in the right place, if you need—"

Faolan's smile sliced thinly across his face, then disappeared. The terrible gleam had faded from his eyes. "Rats make better guests."

"Lord Faolan." Somhairle gathered his courage, wrought a heart brace of its disparate parts, and held fast. "If Morien the Last has overstepped, harmed you—one of the Queen's dearest friends—she must be informed of his transgressions, and will intervene on your behalf."

"How long it's been," Faolan said wearily, "since you've been on the Hill, little prince." Somhairle stiffened in disappointment but didn't draw back until Faolan waved dismissively at him. The gesture stung like a slap. "Morien the Last is the Queen's hands and the Queen's will, swathed in red."

The words scattered like a flock of ravens when Somhairle tried to examine them. His mother—the mother he remembered—would never have allowed harm to come to her favorite courtiers.

Had the fall of House Ever-Loyal changed her so fundamentally?

How could any House trust the Queen, if there was no safety offered in return for total loyalty?

"I, too, am the Queen's most loyal servant. As you *must be*," Faolan finished, licking a fleck of red from the corner of his mouth and shuddering to his feet. "Leave us to our business, stay out of Morien's way, and you'll be happier by and by."

He lurched past Somhairle, through the door, into the hall. A shadow. A stranger. His loyalties, Somhairle thought, made plain.

Faolan didn't look back, though—to Somhairle's credit— neither did Somhairle allow his face to crumple.

He wasn't so far from the Hill that he'd forgotten that.

With his stiff, awkward gait, Somhairle maneuvered around the broken glass and books on the floor to approach his writing desk, which stood as an undamaged eye in the center of a now passed storm. Its four stout legs were carved to resemble an Ancient One's paws, furred and feathered talons. Its polished walnut surface was littered with more of Faolan's papers.

Papers he might have left behind because he thought Somhairle was too naive or too honorable to snoop through them.

But Somhairle was his mother's son. The same blazing willpower that had kept her reign's light shining for nearly two centuries flowed through his veins.

Also, he suspected Faolan was too clever by far to have left documents behind if he truly wished their contents to remain private.

A few of the pages were opened letters: correspondence from House Ever-Learning's steward about the hounds, one from the royal archives thanking Lord Faolan for the return of their city records, and an abandoned missive that read in part . . . *some connection can be presumed but not guaranteed* . . . and . . . *not a true setback* . . . amid larger sections of text that had been blacked out hastily with splashes of ink.

Faolan and Morien's business for the Queen, whatever it was, wasn't going as hoped.

On the desk, a vellum map of Ever-Land had been half copied onto parchment, the unfinished copy nearly obscured by a leather-bound book being employed as a paperweight. Recognizing it as one of his own by the gilt binding, Somhairle hefted the volume. The task required both hands.

The drawing beneath was one he knew down to the smallest detail: a tracing of a watercolor of the Lone Tower, the original image from a tome on fae history that offered multiple artists' attempts to portray its underground chambers and halls.

Someone as important as Faolan wouldn't bother mapping myths and old wives' tales.

Next, a series of recent assessments and surveys of several royal mining tunnels that spanned the city's foundations. The Queen, always digging for silver.

As a child, Somhairle had pretended she sought fae relics. Older now, he'd learned that Queen Catriona reserved no space in her heart for sentimentality without purpose. It was the same with her sons. She loved them because they were a living testament to her total defeat of Oberon's curse—not because she had any special interest in them as individuals.

Somhairle looked closer at the copied drawing. Contemplated the incomparable riches Oberon Black-Boned hid in the earth before his demise.

Perhaps the Queen was looking for something more precious than silver.

Somhairle dropped the book, snatched his hands back as though he'd burned them. Faolan had made it clear that he wouldn't share his secrets with Somhairle.

Why make such a declaration, only to leave Somhairle alone in the room with his private documents?

There was something else at play here. For the first time, as far from the Hill as could be, Somhairle Ever-Bright found himself entangled in courtly intrigue.

49

CAB

They were underground, in a damp maze that had to be a sewer. Cab was thankful it was dark. The smells were enough to emphasize where they were without a torch.

Cab had kindly requested One's presence. Being her "master" didn't seem the right term for what they shared—a partnership—and Cab wouldn't command her to do anything she didn't want to. He was desperate for her company but had practice pushing his needs aside.

She'd promised to make an appearance, but added that she might be a while.

Which left Cab alone with Sil in the sewers, on his way to being introduced to the members of Sil's dedicated Resistance.

Resistance. It was the word whispered through the Queensguard with the understanding that anyone in this category was to be executed at once. No trial. No chance for self-defense. Cut the head off the snake. Never let it lash out at the Queen.

But this Resistance didn't offer the agents of destruction such a word called to mind. When Sil introduced Cab to her fellows, they amounted to a pitifully small group of humans: one older woman, Uaine; one man barely out of boyhood, Malachy; and one slim girl with red hair, teasing green eyes, and a gaudy dress, who cut Sil off before she named her, called Cab handsome, and asked about his scar.

"What scar?" Cab's throat still felt raw. He suspected he'd been screaming, without remembering it, while Sil removed the mirror shard from his heart.

The redhead tapped the air over his chest, grinning when Cab didn't flinch. "Tough sort, are you? Could use more of those around, after thinning our numbers. Here, lift your shirt and you'll see what I mean."

Sil nodded, so Cab did as he was told—and was met with the sight of three parallel black lines raked across his chest, as though a sharp-taloned hand had reached its claws between his ribs to remove the mirrorglass.

No wonder it hurt so much.

"Suits you, though. Sexy story to tell." The redhead winked, then turned sharply to Sil without wasting a beat. "Sil, we can't trust this shitter. Not another Queensguard. You remember what happened with Baeth—"

Cab forced himself not to stand at attention at his old captain's name.

"I would not be able to forget what happened with Baeth," Sil said wearily. She sat in an alcove, tucked into the hollowed spot with room to spare and looking like a ghost child. "This one is not a spy. I crushed the mirror shard he carried into dust—our conversation with him cannot be overheard."

The redhead sighed. "I trust you, Sil—don't get me wrong. Just wish I had your otherworldly senses."

"You wouldn't be able to handle them," Malachy said, and got a swat to the back of his head for his troubles.

This was the force that had compelled the Ever-Loyals to turn on their Queen and the Queensguard to turn on the Ever-Loyals? So few in number. Raw, undisciplined. United by a common cause and nothing more. It didn't seem rational.

Living fae didn't seem rational as a concept, either. But they were real as day.

Cab cut his gaze toward Sil through the curtain of his black hair. Her small stature didn't mean she was only a child, like how One's shape didn't mean she was *only* a lizard.

Still, it was difficult to imagine this little girl as a threat to the Queen's realm, one for whom so much blood had already been spilled.

His eyes lingered on her too-long fingers, gleaming gold where her hands cradled each other in her lap. She'd freed him from a terrible fate. No two ways of looking at that true thing.

"What happened to my . . ." Cab rubbed his head, a distraction from the hitch in his wording. He didn't know what to call the fae and the thief who'd brought One to him but couldn't pretend they were strangers. ". . . the people I was with?"

Cab was thinking like a soldier. Proving them right, yet unable to stop himself. He *was* a soldier.

And they needed soldiers.

The redhead stepped half behind Sil. Not protecting her. Fortifying their position. Her cheeks flushed with flustered, spotty red, the heat of rage and sorrow. "*They're* alive. Unharmed. *Our* people staged an attack on the house to cover our retreat, and Her Majesty's royal bitch Morien stepped in and slaughtered them all."

It took more of an effort not to react to the word *slaughter*. An attack on two fronts. Cab had been caught from behind, while it sounded like another group had stormed the house. Struck down by Morien, which Cab could have warned them would happen. If they'd been smarter, more tactical, more might have survived.

Had they only been after him? From what the girl described, they hadn't hoped to rescue the others. Maybe they would have tried, if Morien hadn't gotten involved.

No point in speculating, when Cab focused on what *had* happened.

These people had gambled, and he was all there was to show for it.

Cab might've thought low of himself, but he wasn't worth nothing. He cleared his throat. Turned his face to Sil's strange fae gaze. Said what he should've from the beginning.

"Thank you"—he hesitated, hand over his chest, anticipating pain if he touched it—"for what you did for me. And for trusting me—when I've done nothing to deserve trust."

Sil's eyebrows were white. Cab caught notice of them as they rose, twin flashes of lightning against a golden sky.

"For returning you to your natural state? This is not something a man should give thanks for. Have humans truly become so diminished?"

"What you did for me . . ." Cab didn't know how to let it alone. He had to ask the real question, the one sleeping like a cat in the shadows at the back of his mind. "Can you *all* do it?"

He still thought like a soldier, wondering: Was Shining Talon not the ally he seemed? Had he merely feigned helplessness in the face of humans and their suffering?

Sil smiled crookedly. The expression was impossibly wise on her young face. Over her shoulder, the redhead scowled at him like he was worse than a beetle that ate dung.

"I was a promising young Enchantrisk, rare among my people. Our magic allowed us specialized knowledges, so while I cannot wield a sword to protect my allies, I have this." She lifted her small hands, showing her elegant, too-long fingers that tapered at the tips.

Cab imagined those fingers burrowing through skin, muscle, bone. His heart twinged in pain, but without fear or shame. Wholly different from how he'd felt after Morien's magic had burrowed into him, an invading force without respect for anything living.

He finally touched the spot on his chest through his shirt, and was surprised to find it numb. Like it had been removed—put someplace safer. He remembered what Sil had said to him about Morien and the sorcerers, before the pain had become too much.

"They're growing strong off you?" Cab rubbed his fingertips into the numb spot a moment longer, then stilled his hand. "Sorcerers like Morien. That's what you said."

Sil didn't flinch. Maybe fae couldn't—or wouldn't—show vulnerability. She ducked her head, wavy falls of hair slithering free over her shoulders like water. The older woman stepped protectively to her side. Gave Cab a look like he'd said something wrong.

"We're the ones asking the questions," the redhead snapped.

Sil shook her head. "I'd hoped he might be perceptive—and strong enough to think for himself, despite his training. He is. Doesn't that make you feel better about his past as a member of the Queensguard, Einan Remington?"

The redhead snorted in a way that meant *definitely not*, then spat onto the ground.

"I had hoped we might talk about our future rather than linger in the past." Sil's voice, calm and clear, parted Cab's thoughts. "The Lying Ones profit from the state of my people."

Cab couldn't see how anyone could profit from the dead.

There was his lack of imagination again.

"We seek to explore a place with which I fear you will find yourself all too familiar." Sil's lashes skimmed her cheeks like the sweep of Cab's scythe across Tithe Barley's fields. How had he ever imagined he could escape his past? "The Queen's catacombs."

Cab flinched. In spite of himself, all his training.

Queensguard had blank faces. They cultivated silence for the guilty to fill. They didn't react first, instead allowing others to reveal their own emotions and feelings.

If it unnerved the townspeople—well, that encouraged compliance.

Cab hadn't marched with the Queensguard in some time. Yet his memory of the anthill tunnels beneath the Queen's castle were fresh.

The inspiration behind the initiate tours was that new recruits should swear allegiance not only to the sitting Queen, but to every queen before her, now lying in their sacred vaults beneath the Hill.

No skeletons, no hanging cobwebs, no shrieking bats.

Flickering torchlight. Stone tunnels and rows of pearlescent drawers housing the remains of their glorious queens.

Captain Baeth's first joke on their tour—"If your responsibilities ever get to be too much, recruits, the quickest way to end it all's coming down here without supervision."

Not only royal remains set beneath the Hill, where fortifications were strongest, but traps peppering the tunnels to snare grave robbers and glory sellers. Fashioned after the style of the fae underground, which everyone on the Hill could appreciate only once the fae were defeated.

"You'll never hear whispers of selling Queen Thula Ever-Bright's pinky bone, or Queen Reve Ever-Bright's jewels." Captain Baeth's chest puffed like a proud gray dove. "These traps are deadly to anyone without proper clearance—only Queensguard knows how to get around 'em, see?"

Sacred knowledge. To be granted only once they'd proven themselves and been sworn in.

Cab didn't trust he could remember every twist and turn they'd taken that night. He'd been wide-eyed, in awe of the captain and the royal catacombs. He hadn't been paying attention to what mattered: How to get around the traps. How many there were. Which ones were set to maim and which to kill.

"I was never . . ." Cab's voice faltered. He pushed himself to continue. "I only passed through them once. I left the Queensguard before they initiated me into the highest ranks. If you need me to guide you, I'm sorry, but—"

Need some guidance? One's voice was like a sudden summer shower, gentle rain in the back of his mind. *Trust me to help.*

"Ah . . ." Malachy raised his voice and his hand at the same time, pointing toward the end of a tunnel, from which a faint silver light had begun to glow.

Cab felt a rush of warmth through his battered, still-beating heart, as the graceful shape of One coalesced at the end of the tunnel. He'd had good days and bad, days so dark he thought he'd never unburden himself of their weight.

There was nothing like knowing One.

"Oh," Einan whispered, "damn."

As One entered the sewer chamber—picking her way around puddles of garbage, lighting her beautiful way forward—Sil began to smile.

50
RAGS

Rags had almost recovered by the time they returned to Lord Faolan's country home.

He'd spent the whole ride trying to move his hand. Weakly coaxing his fingers out from his palm, only to halt when the stabbing pain seized control once more. Breathing through the pain, then trying again. A little farther each time.

Now they had another meeting with Morien, and he'd do what-the-fuck-ever to Rags for any damn reason.

Granted, Rags made it easy for Morien by purposefully goading him. But that felt closer to control than waiting for punishment to happen out of nowhere. He'd do it every chance he got, until Morien figured it was pointless or Rags's body gave out under the strain.

Whichever came first.

Rags walked into their meeting under his own power, deliberately kept his head down to avoid Shiny's attempts to catch his eye, and cradled his wounded hand close. If he was going to have to work without it, he'd better start practicing.

Except their meeting with Morien went smoother than Rags had anticipated, since Inis was the first one to speak up.

"I know where we have to go." She stood confidently in the middle of Lord Faolan's study, facing Morien and Faolan with all the poise and bearing of the nobly trained. No Ever-Noble could say the ex-Lady Ever-Loyal wasn't one of them by birth. In her velvet riding cloak, the hem of her gown embroidered in crossed lace swords, she was transformed—nothing like the tangled spirit of retribution Rags had seen thundering up the road to whack Cabhan in the face. Rags realized his mouth was hanging open and clamped it shut with a hard snap. "That is, if His Highness Somhairle Ever-Bright is still alive. I know his health has never been predictable, and it has been a few years since last I summered in Ever-Land."

Lord Faolan and Morien exchanged glances. Rags would've sworn that beneath the swaths of red fabric, Morien wore a smile that matched his lord's.

"Despite the unfortunate issues of ill health that plague His Highness, he is still alive," Lord Faolan replied.

Inis nodded, showing no relief or pleasure at the information. "I'd suspected. I didn't think Two would have pointed me toward a master who was no longer among the living."

Lord Faolan settled a fluttering hand on the neck of one of his hounds. "Arrangements will be made for your safe passage to Ever-Land first thing tomorrow. His Highness spends all his days there."

The silver of Shining Talon's eyes flashed in the corner of Rags's vision. Rags turned.

The fae's broad shoulders carried the tension of a criminal lineup, breaknoses and cutpurses standing side by side to await condemnation or clemency. The black crossbones at the corners of his mouth shadowed his frown.

It was killing him to be here, and yet here he was. The last of a proud people. And here Rags was, witness to Shining Talon's pain, for no reason he could imagine other than dumb luck.

"All the comforts of my home are yours for the night," Lord Faolan continued. "In the morning, you'll find new horses awaiting your next journey. Your service to the crown is commendable," he added. "The work we are doing here, though I understand it has been harrowing and has required . . . uncomfortable elements of supervision, is necessary. As evidenced by the disappearance of our friend Cabhan, the enemies of Her Majesty grow ever bolder. We race against them. Let us harbor no illusions of what terrible chaos will reign should we lose that race."

Rags could see Inis's jaw harden at the mention of their missing Queensguard, but she didn't say anything, and left without protest when Lord Faolan dismissed them.

Again, a massive, cozy bed awaited Rags for the night.

Again, he couldn't enjoy it because Shining Talon was dogging his every step.

"Don't you ever sleep?" Rags snapped, throwing his boots across the room.

They narrowly missed the drink cart, setting the crystal glasses shivering. Rags descended on it and snatched up a bottle of something tawny and expensive-looking by its neck. Out of habit, he tried to pocket a silver stirring tool, but his hand twitched so badly between the grab and the drop that it slipped free, fell to the rug.

Not that it mattered.

Faolan could have Morien tear him to pieces if he caught Rags stealing his precious hospitalities. The risk outweighed the reward.

"Forgive me," Shining Talon said—*forgive me,* like everything was his fault and not Rags's. "I thought I had explained. My people do not require rest as you do."

It took Rags a blink to remember what Shining Talon was even responding to. The not-sleeping thing: one in a long list of circumstances that had seemingly aligned themselves against Rags, ensuring he never got a second free from Shining Talon's golden supervision.

"Right, and you've been sleeping for a thousand years already, so." Rags threw himself on the bed, closed his eyes, and flung his arm over them for good measure. It took some doing to pry the stopper free from the bottle with only one good hand, but he finessed it, finally, with his shuddering thumb. The first swig he took burned down his throat into his belly, filling him with a sickly heat.

Either it took a better tongue than his to taste the difference, or the expensive stuff was as tough to swallow as the cheap swill Minty brewed under his Clave bunk.

Rags forced down the sudden longing he felt at the memories of his piss-stinking, never-warm-enough childhood. Nights spent sleeping with one eye open, expecting Mountain to wallop him and steal his last coins, or Sidle to pickpocket him the instant Rags lowered his guard.

Another swallow of Faolan's spirits. Rags didn't know the name for what he was drinking, didn't care. He was after the comforting numbness that billowed through his mind like hot steam from the city streets.

He'd felt too much in recent hours. His whole hand pulsed like a raw nerve, sensitive to every dust mote in the air. He imagined it hurt worse than when Lady Winter, an old Clave folk hero, had sewn diamonds into her palms to escape with her stolen goods.

His drinking filled the silence, though he could feel Shining Talon watching and judging him.

Finding Rags *obviously* unworthy. Even now, Rags was in bed trying to black out peacefully, instead of working with the thing that fell from the stars in his pocket.

There was no peace to be had in the dark of the crook of his elbow. Rags's pain and his cure for that pain had him feeling light-headed, and when he sat up in one smooth motion, he only made it worse. As expected, he met the silver sheen of Shining Talon's eyes.

"You might as well take your chance and get lost now." Rags gestured shakily with the bottle in his hand. He stared at the other hand, the one Morien had cursed. His palm didn't look different, but he kept expecting a shard to surge from beneath the skin like a shark's fin, betraying hidden danger. "I'm as good as dead on the streets without my hands. Pretend he's killed me, and you're free."

Shining Talon moved, was seated on the edge of the bed with both hands around Rags's damaged one before Rags could slip away.

For a moment, Rags was merely impressed. Even through his discomfort at being reminded *again* that he was hopelessly outmatched, Shining Talon had a presence, a gravity, that glowed with trustworthy brightness.

Rags didn't trust it, or he couldn't. Safer to burn out the part of him that wanted to than to let it take root and flourish.

He stayed where he was. He thought he was holding still, though it was impossible to be certain with the sway of the bed. He'd never been on a ship, but he could guess it felt like this.

Then Shining Talon pressed his thumbs into key points along the back of Rags's hand. The sharp pain in his joints lifted, reverting to a numb sort of pressure. The relief was sudden, brief, and exquisite.

Rags almost melted, only somehow avoiding giving everything away. He was aware of Shining Talon's gleaming silver gaze on him, how he seemed to want a response. Rags cast about for something. Or pretended to, until Shining Talon spoke again.

"I did not know if that would work, but I see from your expression that you are no longer in intense pain."

So much for Rags having to thank him.

"What do you mean, you 'did not know'?" Rags withdrew his hand, flexed his fingers experimentally, and nearly cried with relief when they obeyed without blinding pain. A stiffness remained, his joint movement hindered by the mirrorglass shards, but the agony had ebbed. "My hands are my livelihood, Your Majesty. I trusted you with custody of my favorite one, and you're telling me you treated it like an experiment?"

Shining Talon's eyebrows quirked. He bowed chin toward chest, again taking Rags's hand in both his own. The touch was oddly cool, making Rags wonder whether the fever in his blood was real or imagined.

A fae prince was holding his hand. Did the fae know what hand holding meant, or did it mean something else to them, like *Kiss my ass* or *Want to talk to some trees together?*

Another swallow of liquor. If Rags was sick, this would kill his fever, right? Logical.

"This generation knows so little of our kind," Shining Talon said. Hardly fair. Rags couldn't read the histories even if he wanted to. "You would no doubt have encountered fae glass in the ruins of the Lone Tower where I was awakened. Reflections, distorted by enchantments."

Rags remembered Mirror-Rags's yawning mouth, the swivel of his scrawny neck, and barely contained a shudder. "Not my favorite of your accomplishments."

It felt small to complain to Shining Talon about fae cruelties. Humans, despite more limited means, had beaten them at that game, and *how.*

"They are unsettling by nature," Shining Talon acknowledged. "They are the most powerful of our magic, and the most dangerous. Indeed, the Lying Ones based their mirrorcraft upon a perversion of fae glass. I performed what presented the most immediate solution— the same offered by the royal Enchantrisks when our warriors began to fall."

Rags's heart thrust itself against the shard slicing its red muscle, a pounding ache in his chest when he thought of the beautiful fae pierced by mirror shards. It was one thing when Morien the Worst tortured a parentless thief, but his kind had done this to Shining Talon's family, friends, brothers in arms.

Rags didn't want to think about any of it. He didn't want to learn about the ways the fae had tried to fight a war they ultimately lost. How everything and everyone Shining Talon once knew was gone, the centuries passing over their black bones.

How could one scrawny thief begin to cover the debt that was owed?

Rags did what he did best and changed the subject. "So it's *temporary*, then."

Shining Talon's strong fingers found a tender place between the roots of Rags's first and second fingers. He pushed in hard, the pressure furrowing to the center of Rags's palm before it moved to the outer edge.

Rags watched the motion carefully, intent on replicating it for himself later. He wouldn't be beholden. Though in this precise moment, he appreciated the free hand for drinking and saw no reason not to take full advantage of his situation. He meant only to lean forward enough to meet the bottle, but instead found himself with his forehead pressed to Shining Talon's broad, sturdy shoulder.

For a moment, the world was steady.

"Your ear has been damaged." Shining Talon's formerly merciless fingers brushed Rags's torn earlobe with the same fluid ease with which he'd touched the stream in the Lost-Lands. Shining Talon, fae prince, talking to water. Asking it the time of day.

Rags's whole body turned liquid and slow. Shining Talon's skin smelled of gold and blastpowder, like one of Blind Kit's explosions taking out the wall of a vault. His heart mule-kicked at the thought of treasure.

Was he sure that was all it was?

Deflection time. "You said your brother was that—uh, suit of armor. Body. Corpse I passed, in the tunnels. By the first door."

Shining Talon nodded slowly. "You speak of the Lo— the ruins. Where you woke me. Your livelihood was injured then, too, as I recall."

His strangely cool fae touch moved away from the damaged earlobe, ghosted the very corner of Rags's jaw. Dangerous.

"This is not *about* me." Rags slid down, curling against Shining Talon like a starved kitten. He gesticulated with the liquor bottle to distract from the fact that he'd shut his eyes, his face resting perilously close to Shining Talon's hip. "I wanna know what a family does to get the honor of—whatever it was. The Sleep, staying behind, being the *only one* . . ."

The question came out less sure of itself than Rags had planned, but out it was. He had to take his victories where he could.

Shining Talon's hand rested curled on Rags's shoulder. Not beckoning him closer, not pushing him off. "My father was one of Oberon's oathsworn warriors," he said. Openly answering the question asked, without skirting or weaseling. "He was granted a high position in the Bone Court after years of distinguished service. A fae promise is wrought in iron and gold. Without sorrow, beauty would mean nothing. So with the privilege came sacrifice. That is duty."

Rags's mind drifted, unwelcome, to Dane—who had parents, rules, chores, and so had imagined Rags's life to be one filled with wonders and adventures. Rags had given his old friend similar wisdom.

Sure, Rags had been a kid with no bedtime, but he'd also been a kid with no bed.

"See." Rags poked his index finger into Shining Talon's ribs, barely felt the frisson of pain that followed. "This is why I work with just me. No rewards to divide, no friends to wall you up in an underground tomb. Never had them, never will."

It made Rags angry because it should've made Shining Talon angry. He should have seen it for what it was—a burden—and didn't. What kind of value was there in being abandoned?

Never the kind of boy who liked to hit things with his fists, Rags preferred verbal sparring.

He waited for Shining Talon to object to his characterization of fae honor.

"You are lying," Shining Talon said. Which, all right, Rags had asked for it. Hadn't quite accounted for how bluntly it might come out. "You told me you had a friend, once. Before we were interrupted."

"By you getting arrowed in the shoulder."

Rags remembered every word that had come out of his mouth. He didn't appreciate that *Shining Talon* remembered them, but there was nothing he could do about it.

Nor about the flash of memory that conjured up an uncertain smile and sandy hair: a boy Rags's age, but soft and rounded where Rags had recently shot up from scrawny kid to something taller and made of all elbows.

Dane's family had owned a butcher's in the shittiest part of the city before it turned into pure Cheapside chaos, and he could be counted on to reliably slip a beef bone or some chicken necks Rags's way when called to. On lucky days there was even a liver or a heart. Despite his better instincts, Rags kept coming back for the free food. No other reason.

They'll be butchering me next, Dane used to joke, prodding his belly, as they lay stretched out side by side on a sunny rooftop.

Rags clenched his bad hand into a fist, didn't allow himself to flinch when the pain returned. Pain dissolved his focus, which had been exactly what he wanted.

"Dane," he said finally. "His name was Dane. And if you're hoping to tell me to think of him for courage, don't bother, 'cause he's dead. Like our late pal Cabhan of Kerry's-End."

"Cabhan is not dead," Shining Talon said. "The Lying One's wicked arts would have told him if the heart ceased to beat, and then his location would be known to us."

"That's . . ." Sensing the need for a clear mind, Rags pulled away, though it felt like shit not being pressed against Shiny anymore, and precisely *because* it did, perching his borrowed bottle on the polished bedside table. He settled with the pillows at his back, brushing black hair out of his eyes with a sweep of his fingers. "Okay. So where do you think he went, then?"

"I do not know," Shining Talon said. Rags's heart sank. He'd asked the question he'd been wondering all along. *How the fuck is Cab hiding?*

But the more important question was whether Rags could do the same.

Frustrated, he ran a hand through his hair, then shook out his fingers. Shoved his hands into his pockets in search of his fragment to toy with and instead recoiled when he remembered what he'd stuffed there days ago.

Morien's magic blindfolds.

He shivered.

Fear wasn't the right reaction. Rags had been walking around with tools in his pockets the whole time. Was so distracted, he hadn't thought to appraise their value or test their worth.

It wasn't like him.

Those blindfolds had shut out the world when Morien had put them around his eyes. Rags drummed his fingers against his left ribs, thinking.

Wondering if the gamble was worth it. If he turned out to be wrong, made a bad play . . . Morien would know something was up. He could kill Rags for trying to be clever, right in front of Shining Talon.

The fae prince didn't need that after losing his family. Losing everyone. Everything.

Shining Talon was still talking about Cab. "He has slipped the Lying One's net. Someone has helped him. Assistance I have not been able to provide you. Forgive me—"

Rags held up a finger, prompting Shiny to shush.

If he was going to do this, he had to do it quick, like setting a bone or jumping between rooftops the first time.

"I'm going to sleep now," Rags said, forcefully. "Because humans still do that, and with everything going on, I'm fucking tired."

He shut his eyes, ignoring Shining Talon's look of handsome bafflement, and pulled the blindfolds from his pocket. It was quick work to tie them around his chest, covering his heart.

Rags flexed his sharded right hand, covering it with his left. No reason to trust Morien when he said the shards in his hand were for causing pain and nothing more—like spying through his fingernails—except Shining Talon had seen mirrorcraft like this before being put to Sleep.

Rags trusted *him* not to get them both killed.

That was new. The whole trusting thing. Fortunately, no time to examine it.

When the final knot was tied, it felt like a boulder had settled on Rags's ribs. Had he done it right, or did the cloths sense his subterfuge and want to kill him for defying their master?

"Well," he wheezed. "It seemed like a good idea at the time."

Wonder gleamed on Shining Talon's face, which meant Rags probably wasn't about to die. And no sign of Morien appearing to tear his heart from his chest, which was always appreciated.

Shining Talon reached forward, a flicker of distaste darkening his features when he touched the cloths.

"To use a Lying One's arts against him . . . you are cunning, Rags."

"A hunch," Rags protested. He felt light-headed, though whether that was from the blindfolds or the compliment, he wasn't sure. "Now we can talk without that creep listening in. So if you've got any brilliant theories? It's time to share them."

What Shining Talon said next took the rest of Rags's breath away. He hadn't *actually* expected an answer.

"I believe that I am not the only surviving member of my kind. I told you about our Enchantrisks, yes? They performed feats of wonder for our people, and were our best defense against the sorcerers. My connection with One is weaker since she has bonded to her master, but I know this much: Cabhan of Kerry's-End is still alive, and someone has taken the poisonous mirrorglass from his heart."

Rags's thoughts tripped over one another.

There was another fae. One with control of magic, if Rags was following along correctly.

What Lord Faolan had said about enemies of the Queen was true.

Only if those enemies had the power to fix Rags's problem. . . .

Then he was pretty sure they weren't *his* enemies.

Somewhere out there, while they were being attacked and before Morien had started his slaughter, another fae had passed Shining Talon by. He wasn't the last of his kind. Wasn't doomed to remain alone.

They had to find this other fae. Set Rags free in both hand and heart. Release Shining Talon to the custody of somebody a little more appropriate.

That meant throwing himself into this quest like he really believed there was something waiting for him at the end of it.

He wasn't the guy for the Great Paragon. But he could see things through to help himself, and maybe a friend. No, an acquaintance. No: a fae he'd dug out of the ground once and was now bound to forever more, apparently.

Rags's heartbeat was slowing, fading, but dizzy relief briefly over-powered any distress at the situation.

"We should remain in possession of these foul items to exchange information freely whenever we have opportunity." Rags saw, rather than felt, Shining Talon soothe a thumb over his chest. *Morien,* Rags had to remind himself, fear gutting any hope of pleasure. They were talking about the blindfolds. "He will see nothing, hear nothing, while your heart is shrouded. But we must take care. Too long a silence, and the Lying One will notice."

"I feel a little"—Rags gestured to his chest, unsure of how to con-vey the situation—"like my heart's not beating?"

Shining Talon rested his palm on Rags's chest. His heart reared like a horse gone mad after years of being yoked to a cart. "I assure you that it is."

"Ah," Rags croaked weakly.

"There are ways to break the Lying One's control," Shining Talon continued, "and I intend to find them."

Rags meant to roll over and close his eyes, return to the preten-sion of sleep. Instead he paused halfway and rolled back, reached his thumb up to brush the crossed bones at the corner of Shining Talon's wide mouth.

The Clave had all kinds of rituals for luck, most of which had nei-ther explanation nor provenance. It was the symbol that mattered: the touching of the lintel over a doorway or the brow of a statue, till one honored spot was shining wood or burnished bronze. Rags wanted to return to this touch over and over, with the same reverence.

He let the question burning his throat die. *Shining Talon is gonna stick around.*

He closed his eyes and feigned sleep as Shining Talon untied the strips of red cloth, returned them to Rags's pockets. Slowly, skittering like prey, his heartbeat returned to normal. Shining Talon's weight shifted, settling to sit against the bed frame beside him. Rags reached for his lump, that fae puzzle, to keep from reaching out to Shining Talon instead. To keep from closing his palm around golden skin.

He might not have to solve that puzzle for Morien.

Might get to solve it for himself.

Rags should have been grinning. Instead he squeezed his eyes shut tight and willed himself to fall asleep before his hand started up with the stabbing pain again.

After everything they'd been through, he figured he deserved a break.

When Morien announced that he would not accompany them on their journey, Inis nearly believed that, after a long absence, fortune had shown her face at last.

"Although I am most eager to join you once again in the saddle, I must meet with the Queen, and will accompany Lord Faolan to the palace without delay."

"Our fondest regrets." Inis curtsied, only preserving the peace because she'd seen firsthand what happened when Rags's mouth ran wild. "We will keep you similarly informed, of course."

"Never forget that I see all," Morien intoned.

Then he was gone.

"You know a guy's the worst when he takes *all* the fun out of insulting him behind his back," Rags fired off.

Inis found herself seized with the sudden urge to laugh. She gnawed it down. There was no way Rags was taunting Morien on purpose. He couldn't possibly be that thoughtful, could he?

Thankfully, no retaliation from Morien followed, though Inis could swear Rags looked over his shoulder for it more than once.

The ride to Ever-Land took them little more than a day. Lord Faolan Ever-Learning owned preferential property, his country estate sitting as close to the royal vacationing grounds as possible without encroaching on them.

Whatever task he'd undertaken for the Queen, she was happy enough with the results that she had granted him this lovely place.

And who, Inis wondered darkly, had she stolen it from, in order to make a gift of it?

"Where'd an Ever-Lady learn to pack a wallop like the one you laid on Cabhan of Kerry's-Back-End?" Rags sat straighter in the saddle, his grip on the reins ice white.

"Stop talking. I have to concentrate in order to lead us the right way," Inis told him. Which wasn't fair, but it was true.

One could only reach Ever-Land by picturing it in their mind. An impossible task, unless one had already been there, exactly the sort of fae paradox the gentry loved to imitate.

Inis closed her eyes and let the undertow of her memories drag her down. It wasn't as difficult as she'd feared. For the past year, she'd been fighting to forget, so that it felt like the simplest thing in the world now to surrender that fight. To remember everything, how perfect it all was, and how all had been taken from her without a single breath of warning.

The charges levied against her brother Tomman were that he had allied with the Resistance and conspired to overthrow the Queen. That was so nonsensical that Inis had been forced to believe her family was banished for nothing. Some political slight, some envy simmering to the point of boiling bloodlust. Someone had wanted what her family had, and didn't mind a little murder to get it.

She could believe it because she'd seen it happen to other families.

It made more sense to her than Tomman risking everything they had, everything they knew, without telling her. Without telling anyone.

None of this was helping her picture Ever-Land. Inis forced herself to think of laughter and rippling water instead of Ainle's sharp, single, final cry. The scent of verbena flower and not fresh blood, the *clack* of practice blades instead of steel falling on bone.

Dawn in Ever-Land rose without urgency, a child without worry or care, decadently slow.

Sunlight warmed her cheeks. Tucked against Inis's back in a shawl slung around her shoulders, Two purred.

Behind her, Rags gave a startled gasp at the change in scenery, his dark bay courser snorting in annoyed reply.

In Ever-Land it was ever summer, thanks to the sorcerers under the Queen's command. The trees were full and lush, the flowers always in raucous bloom, and no unwanted clouds darkened the fair blue skies.

This had been Inis Ever-Loyal's kingdom more than the Hill had: the sun-drenched fields of rippling grass and secret ponds secluded by crookback trees.

She'd taught Ainle to swim in one of the southern lakes. Led victorious assaults in countless war games. Dug holes, raced until breathless, buried trinkets for future explorers between gnarled roots.

She remembered braiding a wreath of hare's bell and poppy for Tomman, who had refused to wear it. Wounded Inis's feelings by doing so. She'd tossed the wreath aside; even then, her instinct had been to crush her humiliation. But Prince Laisrean Ever-Bright had rescued the wreath, said, "It may be the only crown I'll ever wear," as he set it crookedly on his head. Then he'd knighted Inis as his champion in a cathedral of white birch trees.

Inis recalled uncomfortably how it was then that she'd first noticed Laisrean's black hair curling, damp with sweat against the nape of his neck. The way surprise had quickened her pulse, kneeling in the soft grass as the wooden sword kissed her shoulders. She'd been grateful to be seen, included. Glad that one of her friends still made sense, and Laisrean wasn't prey to whatever moods haunted Tomman's footsteps.

It seemed like an insult that the air in Ever-Land should still smell as grassy and warmed by sunlight as it did in her dreams, without the same turn to darkness those dreams took.

Her only relief was that the Queensguard had gone missing before she'd been forced to guide him to this sacred place.

Though there was a sliver of her that was sad for Two, who didn't get to spend more time with something, *someone*, like him.

The nudge of Two's triangular head in the small of her back, right as their horses crested a shallow hill, answered her concern.

With you, Two said, *loneliness has no meaning. Look below.*

Ever-Bright Manor and its three outbuildings lay cradled in the shimmering bowl of the Ever-Land valley, backed by a spiral of golden orchards and a crescent lake.

The first time Inis and Somhairle had found a wild apple tree on the borders of his estate, she'd filled her skirts with the hard, red fruit. But the first bite had revealed a metallic aftertaste that Somhairle blamed on magic, and though he had no proof, Inis hadn't given any of her harvest to Ivy.

Even then, nestled against the red-feathered breast of the Queen's acceptance, with a prince's friendship to shield her, Inis had been uneasy about sorcerers.

For all the good that instinct had done her.

"Do you see, Sir Rags?" Inis had no quarrel with the thief, yet couldn't seem to soften her tone, which tapered to a rapier point. "We'll make the manor before nightfall."

She urged her dappled gray palfrey forward and they descended into the valley below, where Somhairle Ever-Bright waited, not knowing how they were about to crash into his life and change it forever.

Inis should have learned by now not to anticipate a happy reunion.

52

INIS

Ever-Bright Manor's main house was exactly as Inis remembered it: quiet, haunted by melancholy, as remote as it was stunning. Its balconies facing the slowly gathering sunset were reflected in the silver-skinned lake. Something dark passed over the water's clear surface like a shadow on a mirror, but there were no clouds overhead.

"Fine, I'll say it, since no one else will: this place is creepier than the fae ruins," Rags muttered, not quietly enough to avoid being overheard. He snatched at an imaginary bug, flailing in the corner of Inis's sight.

"You too were reminded of my Folk?" Shining Talon asked.

Something in his voice made Inis angry, until she recognized it as the steely grip of self-control. It was the way her voice sounded when she was fighting not to let memories of happier times overwhelm her.

She couldn't hate the fae prince. He'd lost nearly everything, and thus reminded her of herself.

Servants awaited them in the perfectly manicured front yard, took their horses, and averted their eyes without comment on the silver cat riding with Inis.

No doubt the servants were accustomed to peculiar comings and goings, to the necessity of keeping their eyes down and their mouths shut. Queen Catriona Ever-Bright's sorcerers could snap their fingers and summon stranger companions than an exile, a thief, a fae cloaked in black to hide his ears and eyes, and a pure silver cat.

They entered the front hall while another servant hurried up the main staircase to find his master. Waiting, Inis caught sight of a round mirror hung on the wall, reflecting the summer scenery. Under her gaze, the mirror showed a sky blackened, flames licking its edges. Inis's mouth ran dry. She couldn't pull her gaze from the reflection, instead watched in horror as dark blood flooded the greenery, soaking the grass and leaves.

Unmarked mounds swelled up from the ground. The bodies of the murdered Ever-Loyals, now nothing more than food for worms, rose one by one. Father, Tomman, little Ainle missing half his face, all of his right arm.

Inis's reflection was wan, her cheeks sunken, her brown curls sparse. She lifted a hand to touch her face, and in the mirror saw her skin give way like soft cheese. Her reflection dragged its fingers down, peeling off her flesh like sloughing the skin from a rotten fruit.

Blood ran down Mirror-Inis's jaw and throat, melting her limbs into puddles at her feet.

Inis screamed.

Sudden impact, and she was flat on the floor, her gaze wrenched toward the ceiling. The terrible pressure in the air lifted.

I can't protect you from the Lying One's stain on your heart, Two said, *but I can help contain it. Don't give in to his lies.*

The silver cat was bigger and heavier than Ivy now, his silver paws planted on Inis's chest. The sudden change in his size had sent her sprawling.

Inis blinked to clear the red-stained edges of her vision. Rags stood frozen, halfway to pocketing a small Luster period vase, staring down at her.

"I've seen Ever-Noble ladies faint before." He broke his gaze and looked to Shining Talon, then back at Inis. "They're not usually that noisy."

Inis found her voice. "The *mirror.*"

Morien had never tormented one of them when he wasn't there to see its effect. Inis had known he was watching them at all times, but she'd assumed that was all he could do. She'd never heard of a sorcerer who could exert his will from afar, without being present.

A scraping sound on the steps above. A gasp. Inis was already lifting her eyes to see Somhairle on the balcony in his arm-and-leg brace, crutch attached, leaning on the railing, golden hair and golden eyes lit up in the slowly gathering "sunset." He had the Queen's face, her beauty and poise. Just not her strength or constitution. He'd grown a bare inch since the last time Inis had said goodbye to him.

"Inis?" he asked.

"It's been too long, Your Highness." Two leaped to the floor, and Inis scrambled to her feet, took the corners of her skirt in both hands to manage a not-clumsy curtsy. The memory of how deep it should be for someone of Somhairle's station, how to rise gracefully, was as much a part of her as breathing. She fell into the old routine as easily as if she'd never left it.

Beside her, Rags executed an overly dramatic bow. Two also bowed, with perfect poise, one paw extended in front of him, his tail whipping the air.

Again, Somhairle gasped, as though he'd only just now looked beyond Inis and noticed the strangeness of her companions. Next to a thief, an ornate mechanical cat, and Prince Shining Talon, an exiled old friend wasn't so shocking.

She hoped.

"Please . . ." Somhairle gestured with his good arm for them to follow him up the stairs, "introduce me to your friends."

53

CAB

Sil, One explained, though she used the phrase *the Shining One* to describe the fae at first, was diminished. She spoke the words with deep sorrow. Cab found himself breathless from the force of it.

Someone has sapped her nearly to emptiness, One went on. Replacing the sorrow was a crackling vein of anger. *She is young, too young for her hair to be all white, for the color to be taken from her. Whoever has done this . . .*

Cab didn't envy the bastard responsible for the revenge One would take.

Sil and One embraced. When Sil drew back, her eyes were silver-wet with tears.

"I've never seen one of you before," she murmured. "I was born after you were sent away." She kissed One's brow over her third eye. "Welcome, One of Many. I regret that I cannot greet you with the ceremony you deserve."

One shook off the apology, a gesture she turned into a bow. Respect passed between her and Sil. Love and understanding. Its depths were something Cab, despite his connection to One, would never know. He stepped back. Gave them their space.

In the meantime, Einan kept a wary, curious distance on the tips of her toes. Cab pretended not to notice her swaying with the force of wanting to get closer but not too close, until she grabbed him by the sleeve. "Listen," she whispered, "I've seen some wild shit in my time, but what the *fuck* is that?"

Cab held up his hands. He hadn't been trained since childhood to explain or describe. Only to take orders. It was obvious to him, through what little chance to observe he'd been given, that this Resistance could grasp the stakes. He couldn't do One justice with his stumbling tongue—and even if he could, he wasn't sure he had the right to.

"This is what the Queen has been seeking." Sil straightened. Taller somehow, with One at her side. "A piece of a terrible puzzle we cannot allow her to complete. Our remaining agent within the Silver Court alerted us that the first piece had been found, and so we moved quickly. To find *you*, One of Many. The Great Paragon was the deadliest weapon ever crafted by my Folk, and somehow, the Queen of Mirrors has learned of its existence. Her sorcerers have been bleeding us dry for decades in their attempts to find it. It seems they are closer than I thought. And they were close enough before my rescue."

Once, Cab had been a child not much larger than Sil, head crowded with cockeyed thoughts of guarding the realm. What a fool he'd been.

The name Queensguard made it clear exactly who its members defended.

Cab searched, found his voice. Met One's eyes to see if he had leave to speak and accepted her slow blink as permission. "Rescue from what, exactly?"

He already knew from his own experience with one of the Queen's sorcerers that whatever the answer was, it wouldn't bring him comfort.

54
CAB

There was a chamber of iron below the palace. In that chamber were twenty-seven fae children like Sil, all of them kept alive but helpless, the veins in their wrists cut open. Bowls made of birch collected the dripping blood.

From their blood, the sorcerers forged new, more powerful mirrors.

With those mirrors, they maintained Queen Catriona's long reign and longer life.

Cab had known sorrow, for himself and the things he'd done. Regret was an endless howling from the nameless beast in his heart. He'd passed too far into the seamy shadow-side of the queendom and glimpsed something horrible living in its darkness.

But he'd thought, foolishly, he'd seen the depths of it.

How cocksure, to presume the Ever-Loyal massacre had been the most extreme of Queen Catriona's orders.

The fae weren't all gone, as the first Ever-Bright queen had proclaimed. Perhaps she'd been lying. Perhaps she hadn't known. What mattered was this: while expanding her mines, Queen Catriona had found something more valuable and rare than silver, and she guarded this treasure more jealously than any other.

Shining Talon wasn't the last of his kind. Once Sil concluded her story, Cab would tell her about the fae prince. *There are more of you still breathing than you know.*

He couldn't begin to imagine how he'd get through the rest of it. Find Shining Talon, explain to him that he wasn't alone, tell him where the other fae were. What had happened to them.

A human himself, Cab had no answers for why humans did the things they did. Just that war made its players into madmen. The Queen had obviously been leading her own silent war for decades.

But Sil's story had only begun.

Her escape had been part of a greater plan to free all the young fae trapped with her. An Ever-Loyal had discovered the source of the Queen's power, that chamber of silver blood and silence, but he and the Resistance had managed to set only Sil free before his plot was uncovered and he was killed for his efforts.

Captain Baeth had leaked the details of their plan, having feigned dissatisfaction with the crown in order to infiltrate the Resistance's ranks and feed vital information back to Morien and the Queen. Cab remembered the day she'd revealed her role to the loyal Queensguard. Felt sickened by how they'd cheered for her as she laid out the punishment for those crow traitors the Ever-Loyals.

More Houses than Ever-Loyal had burned that night. A few of the lesser ones, diminished by the Queen's greed as she bought up land to dig and dig, had also been torched. *The usual grousers,* Baeth had explained, *with nothing to offer but complaint and treason.*

The Resistance had been larger once.

No longer.

They'd risked too much by bringing Cab here, and he'd been working against them since before they met.

Not all of the Ever-Loyals had been innocent. One of them *had* been plotting against the Queen. Only the plotting hadn't been part of a base grab for power, as the Queensguard had been told. Someone in House Ever-Loyal had learned a terrible truth, terrible enough they were willing to risk the consequences of acting against the Queen.

Cab had struck them down for that.

"Something ails you." Sil paused in her story. Her eyes burned twin holes through Cab's heart the same way he imagined her sharp nails had bored through his chest. She should have left the glass there—or torn his heart out with it. "Unburden yourself, Cabhan of Kerry's-End."

"Bet you I know what's got his tongue," Einan said, falsely bright, when Cab found himself unable to answer. Always was a coward. "Word is, they sent *every* Queensguard they had out into the streets that night. Even the recruits. No chance our man here wasn't part of the Ever-Loyal massacre." Though her tone remained light, Einan's eyes were as hard as steel. "Always liked them when they came to see my shows. They clapped loud, threw flowers, never gossiped through the monologues. Good people. You helped kill them. Did I hit the mark, soldier?"

Cab nodded. "It's as you say."

Uaine, who'd stood silent until now, let out a choked snarl. She didn't leap forward and grab Cab by the neck, though.

She clearly wanted to. But Sil held up one hand, and no one moved against him.

Cab would have welcomed it.

"Not all of the Ever-Loyals are dead," Cab managed. State the facts. *Make your report, soldier.* "One of them shares the connection with Two—Two of Many—that I share with One."

Good boy, One said.

Any clue where Two and his human are? Cab asked.

He felt, rather than saw, the flick of her tongue tasting the air around her. *Some information's too precious for communication of any sort.*

It wasn't the others she was protecting. It was *One* who'd gone silent, in order to protect Sil and her Resistance. To keep knowledge of her location hidden from those close to Morien. Cab shared the taste of his approval with her, though he had none for himself.

"And the others have not yet been found." Sil's eyes glittered brightly. "Our hope in this darkness is that the Queen does not *fully* understand what she plans to control. She does not know all the ways in which it can be used."

"Her sorcerers can control us, if they find us first. The mirrorglass in my heart, in the Ever-Loyal girl's heart—" Cab began.

"—can be removed." Sil's small hands formed tight fists. "As you have learned through experience, Cabhan of Kerry's-End. And we must only contend with them if we do not find the others before the Lying One."

"She's got more than we do already. Two masters, one fae prince, and one fae fragment."

"Then we must beat her to the rest, however we can," Sil said. "If you are with us, I will allow myself to feel hope again."

Fear, panic, the old urge to run. All these were present in the flood of adrenaline that surged through Cab at Sil's words. She hadn't posed a question. She'd given him the room to make a graceful retreat.

Back to what? Another village, not Kerry's-End, this time with a silver lizard he couldn't hope to hide? Consign this precious thing to cowardice, too?

No. Cab had stopped running from his past when he'd met One.

Am I a part of this Resistance? Cab asked her. Silly to want her approval, but it was something Cab had yet to wrap his mind around. He'd been taught to think of the Resistance as dangerous agitators, less than human, if he thought of them at all.

Seems to me you're feeling resistant, One replied.

"I won't make myself unworthy of the sacrifices your people made to bring me here." Cab hadn't knelt for the Queen, but he bent his knee easily to the pale fae child in the sewer. Funny the way things worked out. "If I can serve you with my hands or heart, I'll do it."

Einan snorted. "*Now* I've seen gallantry."

Rags hadn't given much thought to the name Ever-Bright, but now that he'd met his first member of the royal family, he wondered if they were all as luminous as this one. Somhairle Ever-Bright's hair was as curly as Inis's, but short and pale as wheat. His sharp chin looked a mite off-kilter with the rest of his softer face, but he managed to give the impression of deliberate grace in his arthritic gait.

He couldn't compare to Shining Talon's fae glow, but he had the human companion of that quality. Goodness, Rags figured. Decency. The mother's milk of kindness.

Rags didn't miss the way Inis stood straighter with Prince Somhairle in the room. Gone were the sharp words and ready fists.

Rags was the only smudge on this courtly tableau now that Inis had made her transformation. Meanwhile, Somhairle's attention had been wholly on Shining Talon since he'd laid eyes on the big fellow. He hid it badly, kept letting his glances slide into stares the way starving kids couldn't help but follow the smell of bread.

"A prince of the Lost-Lands. In my home. *Inis!*" Prince Somhairle paced excitedly, hitching his way frenetically around the room.

"They were not lost when I knew them," Shining Talon replied.

A prince, a fae prince, and an Ever-Loyal. Rags tried not to look at Shining Talon. Or, more accurately, tried not to look like he was hoping to catch Shining Talon's eye, which was easier to do than to think about.

There was a time Rags hadn't been able to turn around without tripping over his very own, very big, very shiny shadow.

Then he got too close.

Shining Talon hadn't said anything about Rags falling asleep on him last night, almost like it'd never happened. He wasn't thinking about it. Which made Rags feel rat-stupid for thinking about it, remembering it, expecting Shining Talon to talk about it because he talked about and to everything—including water and trees.

Somehow the sting cut deepest because Rags had known this would happen eventually. Expected it, deep down. Now that Shining Talon could be among finer folk with proper manners and real names, he didn't need Rags for company.

Going unseen was Rags's whole life, so why change now?

They'd let Inis handle the bulk of the explanations—what was going on and why they'd come. It seemed only right, and it gave Rags a chance to sit back and cover his hurt by appraising the room's valuables. He glanced toward open glass doors that overlooked a balcony, let himself wander from the conversation toward the night sky.

A scattering of clouds overhead as he stepped onto the balcony. A shadow rippled over the paned glass, and Rags turned, flushed and ready with a quick comment about how Shining Talon couldn't leave him alone.

But it wasn't Shining Talon. Instead, Rags saw his own reflection, without the Ever-Land trees and twin moons behind him.

The Rags in the glass stood in a dark room, one lone window near the roof to let in light, fatty sides of meat hanging on hooks from the ceiling.

A butcher's cool cellar.

Fuck no. Rags's hand tingled. He made a fist, which heightened the pain enough to give him a focal point.

He'd already dealt with a mirror devil in the fae ruins. With Rags's luck, why wouldn't Morien be able to pull a similar trick?

Knowing it was only an illusion didn't make it easier to look away. Rags's reflection touched the hanging carcasses, setting them gently swaying.

"Stop it," Rags muttered under his breath. He held his wrist to keep his injured hand from shaking.

Mirror-Rags grinned. Gestured to the last shadowy shape suspended from the ceiling. As it began to sway, it turned, and Rags saw that it had a face. Bloated, distended, his old friend Dane's soft features were nearly unrecognizable.

Shh. Mirror-Rags pressed a finger to his mouth. Flesh grew over his lips, then sealed his eyes, his nose receding until the surface of his face was smooth as a hen's egg.

"Stop that!" Rags shouted.

The image shattered, splintering to pieces. Shining Talon stood between Rags and the shower of broken glass around his feet, having destroyed the balcony door with no weapon other than his body crashing through it.

"The Lying One." Shining Talon's keen gaze swept over Rags's face, read the information he wanted from Rags's expression. "I should have known, when Lady Inis spoke of the mirror, that he had found another way to torment you."

Too startled to speak, mesmerized by the slide and clatter of glass shards falling from Shining Talon's shoulders and hair as he straightened, Rags nodded. Felt like a shitheel for not saying something.

Thanks for being my noble fae protector yet again when I wandered off and got attacked by my own reflection, the usual shit that happens to me these days.

Rags was starting to anticipate the noble-fae-protector bit. Enjoy it, even, which felt dangerous. He'd thought Shining Talon had moved on to bigger and better goals, but this was proof he was still paying attention.

"My apologies," Shining Talon said, "for the destruction."

Rags opened his mouth to tell him to shut up when Shining Talon shifted to kneel in Somhairle's direction instead of Rags's. The door was a twisted ruin of wood at his back.

Right. The fae prince acknowledging the other prince in the room. No concern for Rags, which was what Rags had wanted. Now that he had it, he needed to learn not to hate it.

"You saw something, too?" Inis's usually hard voice threatened to crack. Shadows on shadows in her eyes as her mouth twisted into a sour smile. "Why is the Last haunting us? Aren't we doing what he wanted?"

Rags's knucklebones ached. Morien's poisonous mirror shards might have wormed their way bone deep.

It said something about Inis that she thought anyone needed a reason to be cruel.

"Maybe it's how he cheers himself up at the end of a busy day." Rags shrugged, pretending to shake off Morien's mirrorcraft as easily. "Maybe he's still sore about Cabhan and wants to remind us who's in charge. Keep us from letting someone else get kidnapped."

"He's a bully," Inis said. "Hardly a surprise, considering . . ."

Her gaze drifted to Somhairle. Rags wondered if she'd been about to insult his royal mother.

"I have an idea." The prince deftly cut the knot of tension in the room with the honeyed warmth of his voice. He braced himself with his good hand on the back of his chair, composed enough to smile at his guests. "Why don't I lead you on a tour of the grounds? No glass to concern yourselves with out there."

"Sure," Rags found his voice. Grateful for the distraction. "Shining Talon here likes nature stuff. Might as well let him hug some trees."

"Trees," Shining Talon said, "do not like to be hugged."

56
RAGS

Off through the orchard, where glowbugs danced among roots in the dark, chaining their ankles like jewels. Or manacles. Somhairle kept their pace steady, probably faster than he'd go if he were taking a stroll alone, but he didn't stumble or falter. The grace of his loping stride and perfectly balanced brace and crutch were like music.

That delicate silver contraption reminded Rags of something out of the fae ruins, the metalwork so thin and fine it resembled silk in places, but was sturdy enough to bear Somhairle's weight. It twisted in interlocking geometries around his wrist and up to his elbow, and if it hadn't been for the way the prince leaned on it, it might have been a bit of jewelry, a court fashion, not a vital support.

Yeah, for the countryside, this place wasn't actually too bad. Except when the glowbugs gathered around Shining Talon, haloing his body, shimmering like the corona around the sun. It made him harder to disregard, like a great big signal fire lighting up exactly what Rags hoped to ignore.

Now that Shining Talon wasn't looking for him constantly, his silver gaze had become more precious than gold.

Sometime between their arrival at the house and their departure from it to tour the grounds, Shining Talon had twisted his hair into a high tail like a horse's, the white streak braided alongside the black and disappearing into whatever was keeping it tied up. Fae magic, Rags assumed. Why wouldn't it apply to hair the same as it applied to anything else? The fanned ends brushed the back of his golden neck.

The sight of him like that had initially stopped Rags in his tracks. He couldn't help but feel as lowly as a glowbug, pulled in by the same light that had beguiled their tiny insect brains.

Except Rags was big enough that it was obvious when he stared.

"These are new," Shining Talon said. About the bugs. Held up one finger while two of them circled each other around its tip. "I appreciate them."

There was a fruit smell on the breeze, heavy and sweet. Peaches, maybe, though it was hard to tell, because the only peaches Rags had ever tasted were rotters thrown out after swelling unsold in the full-day sun of the market.

Maybe this answered one of Rags's most burning questions: *Do fae sweat?* Maybe Shining Talon *did*, and *this* was what it smelled like.

Rags had slept on him all through the night and he still didn't know the answer. That didn't seem right.

"Are you well?"

Rags didn't realize how close Shining Talon had gotten until it was too late and there he was, fingers on Rags's chin, glowbugs halo-ing him like a theater's limelights. Rags tried not to go cross-eyed watching the bugs instead of Shining Talon.

"What?" Rags's voice betrayed him the way a squeaky hinge called out his thieving in the night. "Why wouldn't I be? I've got mirror shards in two very important parts of my body, and I'm being haunted by mirrorcraft."

Shining Talon looked at him, eyes narrowing. Rags felt himself swallow.

"You are not as skilled in concealment as I would have guessed," Shining Talon said, "for a thief."

"Say that to my face." Rags tilted his chin up, breathlessly defiant.

The furrow of confusion in Shining Talon's brow slung a jolt of heat low through Rags's belly. It also brought him to his senses. Whatever he was entertaining, he needed to stop. Shining Talon took him too seriously, followed his whims too completely.

"I am saying it to your face," he replied.

Like Rags had known he would.

"Come on." Rags rapped his knuckles against Shining Talon's shoulder, pretending it was a door. His attempt at camaraderie as they broke apart naturally. "They're gonna leave us behind, and Morien will want to know how we lost *two* masters this time. I've had about enough of being tortured by my own reflection, thanks."

Shining Talon nodded, though his gaze on Rags was piercing. Seemed pointed enough that he wanted Rags to know Rags wasn't fooling *him*.

He knew Rags was running away. He was letting him do it. Which confirmed it was the right thing to do, since the right thing was always the not-as-fun thing.

"The Lying One's powers seem to grow alongside his rage," Shining Talon confided as he drew even with Rags. "Though it goes against our nature, we must give him no reason to find further displeasure with us."

Because there was hope, if they could stay alive long enough to reach it. Another fae Enchantsy-something out there, who'd take the treacherous glass from Rags's heart and his hand, maybe take his star lump, too, set him free to live his unremarkable thief's life without the scent of fae blood on his knuckles, fae fingers in his hair.

Rags groaned and quickened his pace. The thought was supposed to make him feel better, not worse.

They came through the orchards to the edge of a crescent-moon lake, Somhairle's manse in the near distance. The final traces of sunset still stained the hills in golds, softened, spread pink like spilled wine across the sky. Confusing, until Rags realized it was another sorcerer's trick, magic always at work to frame Ever-Land as picture-perfect. He'd never missed his busy, dirty city more fiercely.

But he could agree that Ever-Land wasn't all bad.

"Magic here," Shining Talon murmured. As if they agreed with him, the glowbugs held back from the edge of the water. So did Inis, Rags noticed, like she was afraid of what she'd see in the lake's smooth surface. Not that he could blame her. He hung back for a moment longer, then risked it. In place of fine breeding, he had curiosity to feed.

Across the lake drifted the reflected shimmer of so much precious metal that Rags started to drool, had to clamp down on a gut-punch of sticky-fingered desire. At least it made for a distraction from the other kind of desire.

He didn't look at Shining Talon.

They faced a private carousel for one small prince to use, the cost of which could have gilded every room in the Clave dorms. Carved bronze garlands wove around the top, framing the wink of gold, the glitter of silver beasts affixed to ivory poles.

"My first birthday present from Her Majesty," Somhairle explained. "Inis and I used to ride it together with one of my brothers and both of hers."

Her brothers, who were now dead. Rags had to say something, quick. "What's something like that cost, anyway?"

"I know. It's extravagant, like Her Majesty." Somhairle wavered, then caught his balance. One toe dipped into the lake, staining the tip of his boot, splashing the bottom of his crutch, which slid on the shale. "My apologies. It's been a long day, with more excitement than I've seen in months, and I—"

They all moved to Somhairle's side, Two included. Rags crashed into Inis and Shining Talon's speed put him in front of them. But none of it was necessary, because one of the carousel's menagerie had unhinged itself from its pole and was already winging its way over the water toward them.

Not graceful. Lopsided. It had only one eye, and it was missing half a wing.

Kind of matched Somhairle, Rags thought.

Then it was before them, leaving ripples across the surface of the lake where its talons had dipped too low, its sharp-tipped feathers arcing to Somhairle's crippled side.

The prince's crutch melted off his arm, the rest of his brace off his body.

The last piece of Three had been with Somhairle already.

It wasn't enough to fix the missing eye, but it patched up the wing perfectly.

Without his crutch, Somhairle slipped, barely catching himself on a nearby sapling. He wouldn't keep his balance for long. Inis started toward him again, then let experience hold her back, instead reaching a hand down for Two to butt his face into.

Three, in the form of an owl, was nearly too big to land on Somhairle's shoulder, but it did, balancing him on his weak side. Instantly, panic faded from Somhairle's expression, that split-second concern replaced by a peacefulness that made Rags avert his eyes.

He knew what was coming. The beauty, the bonding.

That didn't mean he had to watch.

Or think about how that was promised for him. Some made-of-metal animal from times past invading his thoughts, making him feel better than ever, letting him know how little he'd meant in his life up until—

When Rags turned away, Shining Talon was there, facing him.

"Gonna put a bell on you." This close, Rags had to look up to meet his gaze.

"That would be inadvisable." Impossibly tall, impossibly golden, with a jaw cut sharper than a broken window. "A warrior's pride is his stealth."

Rags groaned. "Don't remind me."

Those looks, noble fae blood, *and* the ability to sneak up on a born thief? Not fair. At least before, Rags had found him too annoying for all that other stuff to matter, but now Shining Talon couldn't even do Rags the courtesy of pissing him off like he used to.

He looked away and caught sight of the massive one-eyed silver owl bending its head to nuzzle Somhairle's cheek. Somhairle held the bird's face in both hands, one whole and one withered, and didn't flinch at the hinged talons digging into his shoulder.

He was one tough nut, more so because he'd been strong enough to stay softhearted.

Morien would put an end to that with his mirrorcraft. Too bad they couldn't cover their eyes now, pretend they didn't know where they were so Morien wouldn't, either.

The blindfolds, Rags thought. If Shining Talon could wrap one around his chest and one around Inis's, maybe they'd have a shot at warning Somhairle before the sorcerer descended on them.

They'd already found Three. They had a matter of moments, if that, before Morien appeared to piss all over it.

"I'm bored," Rags announced to Shining Talon's face. Though they couldn't speak mind to mind like Somhairle and Inis and their clockwork partners, Rags was trusting him to follow along. Didn't know why. "Think I'll take a nap."

He closed his eyes and tapped his chest, tracing lines over his heart.

What was the point of Shining Talon staring at him every moment if he wasn't going to learn to read Rags's every movement?

A hand at his pocket. The blindfolds tugged free. One weight lifted, Rags's face splitting into an unstoppable grin before another weight took its place.

For all that he had no real-world instincts, Shining Talon had figured it out. He'd figured *Rags* out.

"Inis Ever-Loyal," Shining Talon said, in that voice that made everything sound like it was a precious gem from ancient times, "perhaps you would like to join him? I know human constitutions can be frail, and the ride here was long."

"What are you—" Inis began. "I can assure you, Prince Shining Talon of Vengeance Drawn in Westward Strike"—of course she knew his full name and used it; that fat cat had probably told her what it was—"I am perfectly capable—"

Just like that, she stopped.

Rags supposed Shining Talon had communicated what was happening to her, or Two had picked up on it and tipped his master off, because next thing he heard was Inis's yawn.

"No, you're right. I shouldn't let my pride get the best of me. Prince Somhairle, do you mind if we . . . ?"

"Of course, Inis," came Somhairle's soft agreement, no doubt having been clued in by Three. "I'm sure the Last will understand your need to rest, given all this excitement."

Rags had to admit, the wordless-connection thing was a pretty sweet setup.

Soft footsteps in the grass. The sound of Inis lying down. Silence followed, then the rustling of cloth. Shining Talon took Rags's hands, guided them to hold the cloth over his chest.

Time slowed. Senses dulled. Rags opened his eyes to a quiet world, what he saw separate from his now-hidden heart.

He watched as Shining Talon finished doing the same for Inis, her fingers white and gripping the blindfold tight.

"What about his hand?" Even with her heartsblood muffled by sorcery, Inis managed a glare of suspicion. The expression faltered into neutrality before recovering.

Rags shook his head, the small movement dizzying. "Think that was more about pain than spying. No, I *know* it was, since if Morien knew . . . he would've shredded us the first time I learned the knack for slipping our chains."

"If you're wrong," Inis said calmly, "and this harms my family, Morien the Last won't have the chance. I'll get to you first."

"I understand," Somhairle said before Shining Talon was forced to explain. With Three on his shoulder, Rags didn't need to guess how he knew. "Morien's been looking for you." A pause, while he listened to something Rags couldn't hear. The owl known as Three was catching Somhairle up on his destiny, giving him the quick-and-dirty.

"He seeks to complete the Great Paragon. To control it through his mirrorcraft. We can't allow that to happen. *We can't.*"

Somhairle turned his bright blue eyes on them with weighted understanding. Rags supposed it wasn't that difficult to figure out.

An impossibly powerful fae weapon was only as strong as the weak humans commanding it.

"We didn't have a choice. We had to come here." Inis didn't sound miserable, couldn't with the blindfold draped across her chest, but her jaw clenched. "I would never have done this if—"

"I know that." Somhairle sounded surprised. "It's impossible not to obey a sorcerer's commands when it comes to mirrorcraft. Besides, the gift you brought balances out any curse."

"Says the princeling who doesn't have mirrorglass in his heart," Rags said. "You'll change your tune once he—"

"Obviously, we don't intend to obey Morien's orders forever." Inis's voice, strong and sure. Rags snorted alongside it, then sobered and nodded when her accompanying glare threatened to scorch off his eyebrows. "But our other choice is death, and I can't be that selfish."

I could, Rags thought.

But that wasn't true. He owed it to himself, to Dane and every other kid who didn't make it, to hold on to his life with both hands. He had to find a way out of this so he could free Shining Talon from Morien's leash in the same slip.

Time to lay some of his cards on the table. Even if it meant throwing in his lot with the others.

"We don't have much time," Rags cut in, "before Morien figures out we've got a way to chat without him eavesdropping. But there used to be one more of us. Maybe still is. And *somebody* removed the mirror from his heart."

Again, no shock registered in Inis's eyes, but she said, "Is that possible?"

Somhairle nodded. "Another sorcerer could do it. But they're all loyal to the Queen."

"She's your own mother and you call her 'the Queen'? Woof." Rags felt the time ticking away and pushed along. "Anyway, whoever it was, we're gonna find 'em," Rags continued. It wasn't his place to bring fae Enchantrisks or any other kind of risks into the equation. Let them see for themselves who it was when their group finally tracked down Cabhan. "We're gonna ask for the same treatment. Once we know who it is."

Rags watched the realization seep from him to the others, traveling like blood through cobblestones, flowing downhill.

Surprise made even Inis look soft.

There was hope now. Something out there that could give them the power to resist Morien. Something that could free their hearts. They might be able to undo Morien the Last after all. Their future hadn't yet been sealed with his yoke around their necks.

Though Rags didn't do his best work in groups, he was powerless against the connection he felt between them. They'd gone from begrudging servants to budding rebels. The knowledge bound them together.

"And perhaps," Somhairle added quietly, "it might be different for me. Mirrorcraft takes its toll on a body, and my body is already weak. I know my blood tie to Her Majesty means little in the face of courtly paranoia, but perhaps that, coupled with my poor health, will allow me to remain unmirrored. I'll see what I can do to convince Morien the Last of my frailty."

One of the Queen's own sons plotting against a sorcerer. It was better than a money grabber at the Gilded Lily, the kind of play everyone loved because it was pure fantasy.

"Sounds like a plan." Even without a script—couldn't've read it if he had one—Rags was the one talking. "'Cause we've only got two of these blindfolds."

Three the owl was an owl in name only. She was the idea of an owl, imagined by a nobler mind to exist in a nobler time, wrought of wisdom, the hunt, and the purest fae silver.

She was worth more than a full menagerie of sightless, soundless carousel beasts, with a heart and mind and voice of her own. She was every bird that had ever alighted on Somhairle's windowsill. He was hers, and she was his.

You survived weeks with a Lying One stinking up the place. Three stood beside him, the ruined half of her face to the ruined half of Somhairle's body, as he sank into his study chair, fortified only by a tray holding two cups and a pitcher of iced barley tea. As fine a weapon as any to use in the fight against a sorcerer like Morien the Last. New understanding of him as a blight on the earth ached in Somhairle's fevered joints, shared knowledge that bristled Three's wingfeathers. *That's my boy.*

I was hardly exemplary, Somhairle replied.

I wasn't either, was I? Couldn't do a thing for the birds, but rules are rules. What are *the rules, exactly?*

Plenty of time for that when a Lying One isn't *stinking up the place,* Three offered. She'd grown smaller since they'd first met, as though she thought to diminish herself in Morien's eyes.

Somhairle intended to use a similar tactic.

Morien appeared without fanfare in the doorway, sinister, scarved, silent. Somhairle offered him a smile that trembled, channeling real fear into the role of weak cripple. "At last," he said, "I can be of use to my mother in her fight against her enemies. This is glorious news, is it not? Please, sit, and have some tea with me, and allow me to offer—"

He doubled forward. Used a napkin he'd already dipped in ice water to cover his face in a chill sheen of wet.

Does this make me a Lying One, too? Somhairle asked as the moments passed. Not too much time that the act went over the top, but enough to remain in keeping with the courtly estimation of Somhairle's bad health. He straightened stiffly, good hand braced on the table, pale from the strain of containing his excitement and letting Morien make of it what he wished.

There are two kinds of lying, Three replied.

Morien stood directly across the table from Somhairle now. He cast no shadow, was himself a shadow. The scarlet scarves around his head and shoulders had been sloppily wrapped, as if wound in a hurry, and his eyes were the endless dark tunnels of an underground ruin. His gaze rested on Three.

"A passing pain, nothing more. I intend to be strong enough to bear this honor for the crown," Somhairle continued, hoping to shift Morien's attention. His hand shook as he poured the first glass, slid it across the table. "Please, Morien the Last, for all you have done for my mother . . . sit with me awhile."

"In service to Her Majesty, I have been custodian to wonder and horror." Morien didn't sit. "Are you prepared for the same, Prince Somhairle?"

Queen Catriona wouldn't suffer weakness. If Somhairle overplayed his suffering, Morien might attempt to find Three a more durable master.

It doesn't matter what he *thinks,* Three said. *If you can call what* he *does thinking.*

"Please sit," Somhairle insisted softly. Insistence was an easy mask to don with the silver owl at his side. "Can there be any reply to your question but yes?"

Morien made no sound as he settled weightlessly into the waiting chair. His dark gaze couldn't be gauged as it passed from Somhairle to the tea he'd poured.

"When the Ever-Loyal girl directed us to Ever-Land, I raised the possibility with Her Majesty that one of her beloved sons might be honored with his own piece of the Great Paragon."

Somhairle didn't miss the way Morien referred to Inis without her title. However accurate it may have been, it felt pointed.

"So wise of you." He didn't need Three to remind him that there was more than pride on the line. Instead, Somhairle slumped slightly in his chair, looking defeated. He'd hoped to speak with his mother before Morien got the chance. Now that he'd felt his connection with Three, he could tell the Queen they had nothing to fear from the fae. He had to find the words to make her understand what he knew, to reveal fae science for the beauty it was. It would be difficult, but not impossible—for how could anything be impossible in a world where he'd found Three? "I wish I could have heard her reply in person, but my health . . ." Trailing off, he rubbed his knee, then spoke again with sudden inspiration. "It will take some time, I imagine, for the royal smiths to construct a new brace and crutch to my specifications?"

Morien inclined forward in a subtle bow. Instead of drinking, he touched his finger to the tea Somhairle had poured. Its surface rippled, then settled, mirror-bright, haloed by the earthenware cup, which trembled once, then stilled on the tabletop.

Ick, Three said. *Lying Ones had to use a real mirror in my day, couldn't make one out of any old thing.*

"Gaze into the mirror, Prince Somhairle," Morien said. "Your mother waits to speak with you."

Somhairle lifted his head and was struck dumb. Not by what he saw in the black, glassy surface of his tea, but by Morien himself.

As a prince, Somhairle had grown accustomed to mirrorcraft, having been swaddled by its cool embrace through so many fevers. But he'd never been entirely comfortable with sorcerers, shrouded in red and secrecy.

What he was seeing now was a glimpse beneath the shroud.

A long, dark sliver where neck met chest. No flesh. A thick, purple vein that twitched rhythmically next to its threadier cousins. It extended over a glister of muscle and stark white bone tucked where the hollow of Morien's throat should have been.

Where was his skin?

There was no skin.

Somhairle's hand froze, curved around the swell of his knee. He had to stop staring.

You know the story about the lady and the tiger? Remember, some people would rather kill what they love than grant it freedom, Three said. Somhairle forced a blank smile. He met Morien's eyes with a guileless expression, pretending not to notice the sorcerer adjusting the fall of his scarves and robes to obscure the skinless nightmare that lurked beneath.

Somhairle found his voice and the mirror, half paralyzed by the thought of what lay under Morien's scarves. "I'm grateful my mother has you at her side to think of everything."

Nobody thinks of everything, Three commented.

Must I do as he says? Somhairle asked.

With scum like this, you have to. Though a bird couldn't scowl, Somhairle heard the expression clearly in Three's voice. *Don't worry. I've got your back. You're as safe as you can be, even with a Lying One. 'Cause you're with me.*

Somhairle lowered his eyes to the still surface of the tea, and the world washed silver around him. He recoiled as his surroundings vanished into bare, blinding light. The air fogged his nose with steel and heat.

Breathing shallowly, he tried not to panic as he realized he was alone. No brace and crutch. No Three.

Only Queen Catriona, who sat waiting for him in a column of light, as regal in this nothing place as on her throne. She was no more than a voluminous silhouette, but she radiated authority.

"We must be brief." Catriona's voice tinkled like glass chimes. "The Last's energies are better spent elsewhere, and my time is much in demand. Approach your mother, Prince Somhairle."

In contrast with Morien, Somhairle couldn't imagine disobeying the Queen. He was before her, bare and unworthy, diminished further by the intensity of her presence. She was an inverted shadow, as was he.

Her hands were ice cold when he clasped them with his good one. White shadows on white light.

"It's everything I could have dreamed, Mother," Somhairle said to remind himself he had a purpose he couldn't abandon. "A wonder of the long-lost world. I intend to—"

"Oh, fledgling." Somhairle felt, rather than saw, her solemn, searching gaze. "You share our will, if not our constitution. Such strength, for such a little bird. Come. We have told you every tale but one. Will you sit with us to hear it?"

There was power in knowing when to kneel. Somhairle had no body here, no true form, but as he melted closer to the Queen, it was difficult not to feel like a boy again. Sitting in his mother's lap awaiting a nursery story before bedtime.

"Once upon a time," Catriona began in her flute-sweet voice, "there was a beautiful young woman, cursed by Oberon Black-Boned to wander a barren desert. She would have suffered this fate willingly herself, but she had many other mouths to feed, and many other hearts to guard against evil.

"The good woman built shelter. Every day, she tilled the bleak land and watered the mutinous soil. With her strength and cunning, with her refusal to be bested by the black-boned fae king, she brought abundance to the valley.

"In time, with great personal suffering, her labors bore fruit, and her crops grew tall in the sun. But some were sickly, stunted, damaged in the seed before they passed through the soil. They would never provide the sustenance she required for her children."

Somhairle's brow wrinkled. His tongue rested heavy and thick in his mouth.

His mother's gaze came from twin silver eyes—a result of the mirrorcraft—when she turned it on him, gone in a flash. Perhaps this column of relentless light was his mother's true form, not the woman's body she wore over that core.

What a treasonous thought.

"The young mother culled the weak season's growth," Catriona said. "She pulled each out at the roots before it had a chance to flourish and poison her other crops, though she loved each one the moment it was planted, and mourned each loss terribly. Because I would not see my children suffer for anything, Somhairle. Not even life may have that privilege, not now that I am her master. Do you understand what I am telling you?"

Somhairle's throat worked. His body, distant but real, burned and tingled as if he'd been thrown into a thicket of glorynettles.

He'd always assumed he was his mother's final attempt at pro-creation. That his less-than-perfect appearance had been deterrent enough against more children.

She hadn't culled him as a poisonous crop.

But there had been others.

"Mother," Somhairle began. "I have something to tell you, too."

If he believed there were others born crippled, like him, who she had culled, then he had no excuse for sudden boldness. Now was the time for meek acquiescence. But Three was on his mind. In his heart.

They didn't have to fear the fae. He could make Catriona understand that she had spared him for a reason. To give her an incomparable gift. To mend this rift, to heal this wound.

"There's more than beauty in the Folk," Somhairle said with pure feeling, no desire to calculate his remarks, although speaking extemporaneously in front of his mother felt uncomfortably like baring his neck for the executioner's greatsword. "I've felt it—"

His mother's sharp *ha* shattered into a thousand brittle pieces, her laughter echoing in the dark space. Their features had always been similar enough that sitting near Catriona was like looking into a broken mirror. Now he felt like a moon staring in terror at an exploding sun.

He fell silent until she subsided, lifting her golden head.

"We would call that talk treason on any other's tongue. Remember this: we will always protect you. We will not have Morien the Last use mirrorcraft on your royal person, as he has with others." Her cold fingers caressed Somhairle's cheek. He bit his tongue as they grazed his throat. "Know this also: that the fae ruin all that they touch. Do not give in to their trickery and deceit. For we would not hesitate to cut the head off the snake if a fae were to corrupt even the most precious flesh of our flesh."

A promise and a threat. Gold and iron.

How very fae, Mother, Somhairle thought. He was glad he could be seen as little more than a shining silhouette. Just now he didn't trust himself to hide his expression.

"Thank you, Mother," Somhairle said.

She was smiling when the illusion dissolved, throwing Somhairle back to his study, to Three, to a world lacking light.

To Morien the Last.

After the conference with his mother, Morien's presence was almost a relief. Somhairle sank, shaking, against the plush back of his chair.

You survived. See? You can trust me and pretty much no one else. Three craned her noble head toward Somhairle. *The Lying One's mad as a wet house cat that he can't sink his claws or his mirrorglass into you.*

Not me. Somhairle smiled so he wouldn't appear dazed or sullen. Morien watched him closely. *But how many others?*

Inis Fraoch of House Ever-Loyal. Rags the little thief. The missing ex-Queensguard Somhairle hadn't met.

And, Somhairle suspected, it could be used to ensure loyalty anywhere—not just in masters.

If it had been a point of debate to shard a prince, there was no reason to expect that Lord Faolan of House Ever-Learning would be exempt from this treatment. It was infallible insurance he could never act against the Queen's desires.

It would either explain everything, or reveal Somhairle's real weakness to be wishful thinking, not a half-withered body.

Neither is a weakness, actually, Three said. *Any weakness can be forged into weaponry.*

My mother didn't want to hear it, Somhairle said. He had to say it to make it real, but he couldn't trust the words aloud.

Not to Morien, who worked in service of the Queen.

I could've told you that, honeyflower. Even as she chided him, there was warmth in Three's voice.

Somhairle breathed. Tasted metal. Of the Queen's imperfect children, he was the only one to survive. Catriona would rather kill her own than let Oberon's curse touch them.

He'd tried to give her the key to freedom from her fears, only to have her slam the cage door in his face.

"Your skill with mirrorcraft is surely unparalleled, Morien." Strength flowed from Three into Somhairle to steady his shaking. "A pity it takes such a toll on the body."

Three's feathers ruffled as she shook her wings out in silent laughter.

"It would be ill-advised to give Her Highness a reason to regret her generosity," Morien said, in the political tone of voice that meant *If I could, I'd flay your skin from your bones.*

And also, *I might still do that.*

Somhairle's thoughts swirled. Three inspected her talons as a reminder that she had them, and they were sharp as knives. Morien's scarves remained tucked tightly in place. There was no further chance of seeing beneath them. He reached out, closing red-gloved fingers over his cup of tea, and drank through the red scarf over his mouth.

58

CAB

Sil hadn't been at full strength after pulling the mirror out of Cab's chest, and she'd begun to feel faint as they approached the catacombs.

"I'm sorry," she'd explained with a wan smile ill suited to her childish face. "It's the iron. We have a natural antipathy to it—as it is the only metal that can kill the fae."

They were close to the Hill. To that foul room of torture beneath the palace, and the catacombs below that.

"Let me go." Cab had felt the eyes of every remaining member of the Resistance on him as he knelt before Sil's small form. "I'll get whatever you need, then bring it back to you."

Einan's hand landed heavily on his shoulder. "Not without me, you won't, handsome. And we'll just be taking a look around. Nothing more."

She was nice in front of Sil. But when they were alone, she changed her tune.

"If," she said, "you fuck this up . . . if you give her hope, only to snatch it away, I'll let Uaine cut you open and use your guts to string me a fiddle."

Colorful. Threats came with Queensguard training, but they weren't so imaginative. Civilian cityfolk were about as unpredictable as it got. Cab found it remarkable that the Resistance had grown with such little experience governing their ranks.

They believed in what they were doing. Sometimes that was enough.

And sometimes it earned you death in the Far Glades at the hands of a sorcerer.

"I didn't know you played," Cab replied. He knew Einan's quarrel wasn't with him so much as what he represented, and that made it easier to bear.

He resented his association with the Queensguard, too.

"I'm a girl of many talents," Einan said.

Cab considered taking her threat more seriously.

"Sil saved me," he pointed out. "Hit me on the head first, kidnapped me, tied me up, but saved me. I don't intend to repay that with betrayal."

Einan snorted.

Then One mimicked the sound, which made Einan jump. She eyed One the way someone looked at an unfamiliar dog they badly wanted to pet.

"If you want, you can tie me up again," Cab offered. "Not that One would approve, but she likes you well enough. Probably wouldn't bite you for harming me."

"Probably."

"I don't make promises I can't keep."

"Thought you were her master." Einan took a measured step away from One, whose grin widened.

"It doesn't exactly work that way," Cab said.

It does, actually.

No, it was more than that. They belonged to each other.

Cab didn't get the chance to answer One. The floor shook beneath him, and dust filtered down from above. A reminder of what he was here for.

Not to make friends.

A cave-in near the catacombs? Or had someone accidentally triggered one of the oft-mentioned underground traps?

"Fucking diggers," Einan whispered. With quick fingers, she tied her hair back into a fiery braid. Then she reached for Cab's hand. Gripped it with surprising strength. "I can take you to the catacombs now if you swear you can guide me safely through. Actually, it doesn't matter," she added when Cab hesitated. "If we both die, then you weren't the man for the job. Clearly. And Sil lives to carry on the cause."

"I don't intend to get us killed."

Cab was making a lot of promises lately. After he'd sworn never to take another oath.

Maybe that was the first resolution he needed to break.

Einan led him swiftly down a dark length of sewer tunnel. Made a left, then a right, then a sharp V-shaped turn that took them through a hole where the stone wall had crumbled, leaving an opening large enough for an ill-fed person to squeeze through.

Cab winced at the squeal of metal on rock as One followed them.

The audacity, One said. *I've lived hundreds of your lifetimes, and you worry I'll scratch easily?*

After that, Cab shut up. Einan's freckles stood out dark against her white knuckles, white throat, and white cheeks, illuminated by One's faint glow.

Finally, Einan paused at a section of wall that was slick with green algae—or worse. "Through here."

She'd barely said it before she pulled Cab relentlessly forward and straight toward the wall. He didn't have time to shout. They passed through the stone like it was the curtain of a waterfall, came out into a steep, upward tunnel. Cab felt himself gasp. Heard One chuckling in delight as she passed through the wall behind them.

"What was that?" he asked.

Another tremor shook the earth around them. Einan swore. "That was all Sil. And we can talk about how wonderful she is later, all right?"

Without waiting for his agreement, Einan trudged up the slope. Threw her shoulder against something heavy. Stone scraped. A weak, greenish light filtered into the tunnel. Einan's long legs disappeared through the crack in the ceiling. Above, she pushed the heavy flagstone farther aside, then reached her hands down for Cab.

He knew where they were before she pulled him up. Arched hallways of cold white stone, carved without seams. And the vault drawers made of opal and milkglass.

They shimmered, reflecting One's light, just as they had before in the light of the captain's torch.

"You said something about diggers," Cab murmured.

Einan's lips twitched, more grimace than smile. "We thought the fae were gone. That's what the Queen told her people—it's what's written down in all the histories. Only that wasn't true, was it?"

Cab shook his head. *No.* He tried to orient himself. Looked left, then right. Down seemingly identical forked paths.

"The fae did disappear," Einan said, "and many of them *were* killed, but not all. Because while Her Majesty was busy turning the finest architecture left by the fae kingdom into a channel for piss and shit, she found something in the deep she *wasn't* expecting: a sleeping fae girl."

From the way she said it, reverence and reverie, Cab knew who she meant. *Sil.*

"There she was. Tucked in for a thousand-year nap. So the queen figured, where there's one, maybe there're others. Kept close guard on the treasure she'd found and set about searching for more. She destroyed whole neighborhoods. Homes, shops, whatever was in the way of the tunnels. Sent a get-out-now squad of Queensguard with a royal writ, and anyone who didn't budge conveniently disappeared before excavation began."

"Happened to you?" Cab asked.

"What's it matter? Happened to plenty."

"And they found more fae. Explains how sorcerers like Morien the Last got so powerful." Cab drew his gaze to the stony ceiling. A light was out over the right-hand path—the catacombs weren't lit by torches but by glowing spore-light, an accidental offshoot of a sorcerer's experiments with fungi. They wouldn't burn out over time, and they wouldn't blow out in a gust like fire.

It was a deliberate marker.

Left, then.

"This way." Cab directed them, all too aware of Einan breathing down his neck. He couldn't help but feel like she wanted something more from him, although Cab had already sworn his allegiance and couldn't think of what else he had to offer.

Another rumble beneath them. Cab dodged a fall of pebbles. He jerked back from touching the wall for balance. Behind him, Einan scrambled to do the same.

Among Queensguard recruits, whispers suggested that the catacombs remembered everyone who touched their stone. The walls remembered. The old queens remembered. And so every recruit kept their hands firmly to themselves on their tours, glad of the thick bootsoles between them and the stone floors.

After he'd fled the Queensguard, Cab came to suspect those rumors were probably gossip encouraged by the recruits' officers, who didn't want the rowdy youths touching everything in the royal burial chambers. He hadn't realized how deeply the old superstition still affected him.

He wasn't willing to test his theory. Not with others depending on him.

"Hands in," Cab said gruffly. "Don't touch the walls."

Einan didn't have to follow his orders, but she did follow this one, and Cab was grateful. He could only help as much as she'd let him.

He gestured reflexively with two fingers, an old Queensguard signal that meant they were to move along around the corner. Einan replied with a ruder variant.

"I'm no soldier," she said, had the good sense to get in close and keep her voice low, "and I *don't* respond to commands like a *dog*."

"Right. I'm going around the corner." Cab barely moved his mouth. When he glanced back at Einan, he had only an impression of her face. She was so alive. High color in her cheeks, the sheen in her eyes like light through a whiskey bottle. So unlike the mirror-glaze of the Queensguard's gaze. Not a soldier, and obviously terrified, but there was anger there, too. Determination.

She wanted to be here.

That was Cab's impression as he moved, nearly stepping into open air. Einan slammed solidly into his back.

For one sickening moment, Cab thought he'd swing forward and down through the hole where the floor had given way.

Someone had triggered one of the traps before them.

Then someone else had come along behind and turned the triggered trap into a passageway. Real torches stuck into the walls, casting haphazard orange light through the empty space. Steep slopes on all sides faded into almost total darkness below. The bottom wasn't visible, but Cab thought he could see something—someone—moving down there. Deep, deep down.

"We're going down," he said.

Einan was unfazed. "You afraid of heights, handsome?"

"Not that I know of," said Cab.

"Figures." Einan replied. "Why should this next bit be a nightmare for *you*?"

In the torchlight, Cab could see strange markings carved into the stone. He didn't understand them, but they were too deliberate to be claw marks from vermin. They formed a pattern.

It was nothing like the beautiful, barren halls of the queens' catacombs. And yet something about the structure of the hall below mirrored the hall above. Dark and light. Night and day.

Better hurry if you don't want to lose them, One said.

I'm going, Cab said, but didn't move yet.

Do you think I'd ask you to do anything unsafe?

Properly scolded, Cab jumped—and slid on his ass through gravel, past torches and carvings, into the dark. Panic rose, louder than the inner voice demanding to know why he was shredding his backside for a Resistance he'd fought to put down not so long ago.

The answer to that was obvious. The fullness of his heart with One in it made his transgressions impossible to ignore. There was no honor in hiding if he could use his skills to combat the Queen's brute might.

The real problem lay in trying to figure how he could stop sliding without smashing into a wall or cutting himself to pieces on debris.

Cab jerked his forearms in against his chest, squinting at the flicker of torches as they whizzed past. Behind him, Einan's soft voice muttered something that sounded part prayer and part vulgar action with a plate of mashed potatoes. Then he heard a crash of gravel that meant she was sliding down after him.

Kept going for a while, until he rolled into a wall. The impact didn't quite wind him.

Einan's secondary impact was the blow that did him in.

One followed them, picking her way through the broken shale like the steep angle meant nothing to her.

Einan helped Cab to his feet. Over her shoulder he could see three mechanical drills the size of horses. Each had two stations—one to turn the bit and one to steer. All three machines were coated in black dirt. One had fallen on its side, revealing a spiral of diamond plating down the bit. Someone had hung a pair of grimy goggles on the handlebars.

"Look," Einan counseled in a whisper. "They left their drilling equipment. They only do that when they've found something."

Do you know what's—who's—down there? Cab asked One.

One shut two of her three eyes. The center eye remained open, shimmered faintly in the darkness. Cab felt the start of a headache, vision swimming, doubling, then returning to normal.

Yes, One said.

Without elaborating, she shot forward, toward whatever awaited them.

Cab was bound to her. He had no choice but to do the same.

59
CAB

Cab didn't know Einan had followed him until they rounded the first corner, One in the lead, and found themselves face-to-face with two Queensguard. Einan crashed into Cab's back with a curse that would've made Rags the thief blush.

The Queensguard charged.

They were following orders. Bad orders. The same fate Cab had run to escape. It wasn't their fault.

It brought Cab up short, but it meant nothing to One or Einan. One knew what she was fighting to protect, and when she reared on her hind legs, Cab felt fresh, cool strength flowing through his limbs.

The Queensguard—had he known them? served with them? eaten with them or trained beside them?—didn't have time to make a sound before One was upon them.

Each blow, each snarl, each lash of claws and raking of teeth, echoed in Cab's bones. He found himself completing One's every movement, meeting her between slashes, striking out from the other side to finish whatever she had begun. He acted without thinking, without needing to think. He saw what she saw and she watched through his eyes. They were everywhere at once, in complete harmony.

It was nothing like being commanded in a drill.

The two Queensguard toppled like ninepins in a heap.

To her credit, Einan didn't miss a beat before she was relieving their bodies of weapons. Cab's guilt hadn't settled before she shoved a sword into his hand.

"Thought for a moment you might freeze and leave a poor maiden defenseless." Einan shoved two daggers into her belt, looking at the second sword with distaste before hurling it down the tunnel. "I like something with more finesse," she added by way of explanation.

"Whatever suits you," Cab agreed.

He was trying to ward off the sense of numbness that occupied him now that he had a Queensguard sword in hand. These Resistance folk were chatty, and he didn't want to give Einan any more reason to mistrust him.

"I don't like this." A burr of real anger caught in Einan's throat as she looked at Cab. "We risked everything for you, thought you could lead us through the catacombs, but you can't even do *that* reliably. What if you're bad luck?"

That's gratitude for you, One sniffed.

"Bad luck is the only luck permitted Her Majesty's enemies," Cab replied.

Einan snorted. This time it was she who went first, Cab a step behind. They followed the glow of One's body, a lantern in the dark. No one had set torches in this part of the tunnel yet. It was too fresh.

A scraping sound ahead made Cab tighten his grip on his sword.

Frightening how easily the instincts came back to him. Maybe they'd never left.

No time to dwell on that, either.

They exploded out of the mouth of the tunnel: two humans and a silver lizard too big and shiny to be natural. Cab saw three diggers and two more Queensguard, threw his shoulder into the first man and knocked him down. Einan whirled and stabbed, caught a digger in the shoulder with one of her knives, then leaped on him like a wild animal. Cab didn't have to keep track of One. He knew where she was, same as in the first fight. He let his body take over. Thinking would prove detrimental at a time like this.

He could use the skills he'd learned. He didn't have to fear them.

He kicked the man he'd knocked down, then turned away as One leaped in to parry a thrust from the next Queensguard. A third man caught him in the cheek with an armored glove and Cab staggered, face raw from the pain of a strike.

Tail thrashing, One snarled and lunged. Einan slammed the hilt of her dagger into a digger's head.

Cab's face felt tight and hot and One's claws were stained ruby when they finally lowered their weapons to silence.

"Shit." Einan's voice was hoarse.

She was closest to the dig site, so it was she who'd first seen what the Queen's men had been excavating from a nearby mound of dirt and stone: the corner of a glass coffin, threaded with silver.

Inside, a pulse. A glow that throbbed like a heartbeat.

One padded closer. The carvings on the walls brightened, lit from behind.

Through the glass, they saw it together: the top half of a golden face in repose. Asleep. Peaceful. When their shadow fell across its features, its eyes fluttered open, and they were silver through and through.

60

INIS

Between Three and Shining Talon, Somhairle made his staggering way to bed. One of the servants had a cup of strong tea waiting, smelling of bark and ginger and mint, and Somhairle nearly spilled it in his lap with shaking hands.

Inis helped him to drink.

"I fear I've overextended myself." His fingers lingered on hers for an instant, letting her know he was all right.

Should have been an actor. Two sounded impressed.

Tea finished, Somhairle collapsed on the pillows, face releasing its tension in sleep.

They left him with Three standing guard, perched on the bedpost.

When they returned to the hall, Morien awaited them. His eyes glittered with veins of silver.

Had they been that way before?

"No need to worry," he said in his steady, unimpressed voice. Each word was a pinprick in Inis's heart. "I don't intend to do to the prince what I needed to with you. He's a vulnerable spirit, too kind for court. Would he do a thing that would put *your* life in danger, Inis Fraoch Ever-Loyal?"

It was like being back on the Hill, at a ball or tea party, trading barbs with a smile. "I'm sure I don't know what you mean—" Inis began.

"Find me the next fragment." Morien held up his hand and Inis's throat shut tight. She couldn't breathe. When Rags choked on a gasp, Inis understood she wasn't the only one suffering from Morien's warning. "That is all I require."

The curtains in the hallway billowed inward, though the windows were shut.

Morien was gone when they settled.

Inis snarled and slammed her hand into the wall. She let it hold her weight as she gasped for breath, trembling and fiercely glad Somhairle hadn't seen her like that.

If she could keep her temper from getting the better of her, she could believe they'd win this battle.

So why did it taste bitter, like soft, smoldering leaf ash, reminding her of the pipe her father used to smoke?

You're a puppet who sees its own strings, Two said. *No peace until they're cut.*

One day, she'd learn how to unravel the knot in her throat.

Inis rubbed her neck as if to reassure herself that no invisible fingers still gripped it. There was no safety to be found in defying Morien.

No safety in the Queen's embrace, either.

Any mistake could spark unforgivable consequences, but Inis couldn't protect her family by merely staying out of the Queen's way.

She felt Two twine around and between her legs, momentarily getting lost in her skirts before reappearing. His eyes peered out under the fall of fabric.

The little thief has provided us with something invaluable. Not everything is lost.

Inis crouched to rub Two's head, the jagged shape where his missing ear should be. Inis didn't know why she hadn't thought of it before, but someone must have stolen a fork or spoon from the set.

"We'll have to wait for Somhairle to wake up," she said aloud, with the same false confidence she used to show for Ivy's sake. This time she wasn't trying to fool her frightened little sister but a nasty sorcerer from whom only her inner thoughts were safe. Her false certainty would have to work. She knew what awaited them if they failed. "I can tell Somhairle how to commune with Three, how to figure out where to go next, if he hasn't worked it out already. Maybe Morien will have found what we lost by then."

"Wanna bet me on it?" Rags asked.

They met each other's eyes.

"I'm not the betting kind," Inis replied.

61
CAB

Cab had to use the sword's pommel to chip at the stone around the fae coffin, dirt laid atop ancient white rock that fought them for every inch. Einan hacked away beside him, holding one stolen dagger two-handed. Neither of them was as successful as One, whose claws raked away stone and soil without pause. Cab didn't like to see her toil like that, but she told him she was happy to sharpen her nails for the next group of enemies. Cab left it at that.

All the while, the face in the coffin watched them.

The fae face.

When the fae had first opened his eyes, he'd screamed in horror, mouth open wide behind the coffin's glass lid.

Once he saw One, though, he had stopped screaming and now showed no sign of fear. The sight of the silver lizard, a fragment of the Great Paragon, was enough to earn immediate trust, though Cab wasn't sure it was something he deserved.

They had the coffin halfway out when they heard human shouting, echoing down a nearby tunnel and coming closer.

"We're not going to get it out in time." Einan cursed. Wiped dirt out of her eye. Smashed the dagger against the wall in frustration. "Fuck me! Should have waited for them to *finish* digging and *then* attacked, instead of getting caught with our pants around our ankles—"

"Something tells me there'd have been more Queensguard in place by then," Cab said. "Like the Queensguard who are coming now."

When they came, they'd bring deadly force. Moves Cab knew so well, he practiced them in his dreams.

Another shout. Almost on them.

The coffin exploded.

Einan threw her arms up to cover her face. Cab didn't, knew he didn't need to before registering *why* he knew. One wasn't afraid. And not only because she was made of silver and couldn't be cut.

The glass blasted to either side of them, leaving them unharmed. The body within slid out.

It hit the ground and the earth began to shake. Cab reached for it.

Protect him. One's voice in his head. Then, *Look out!*

Cab spun around, stepping in front of the fallen fae. The Queensguard had reached the mouth of the tunnel. They carried torches, the flames glinting off royal armor and steel swords, making it easier to see how outnumbered they were.

The odds didn't matter. Not to Cab. Not when One had no fear.

Einan shifted her weight uncertainly. A slender hand reached out and wrapped its fingers around Cab's ankle.

I will borrow your connection to One of Many, a new voice said, *and thank you for allowing me this sacred trust.*

What? Cab's palms were sweaty where he gripped the sword. If the fae needed One, then it was One he needed to ask.

"Shit," Einan said. "What are we doing? What's the plan?"

Strength, One explained. *He's been asleep for a long time. Needs a jolt to get him started.*

The Queensguard began to pour in, and Cab lunged, stepping away from the fae to knock the first Queensguard back into the tunnel with a hard, swift blow from his stolen sword. He'd create a bottleneck to better their odds.

The Queensguard dropped his torch but it didn't go out, flickering against stone. Cab smelled something singed. Hoped it wasn't his trousers.

Right, he said to the fae. *Do it.*

It happened all at once, like the arrival of a summer storm. He felt something shift, a push from the inside of his skull.

With that push, jagged stalagmites erupted from the ground, rising like stony prison bars across the mouth of the passage. The Queensguard shouted, then were silenced, the light from their torches doused. Those who couldn't move out of the way fast enough were impaled. Rock acted to protect the cave where the fae had been unearthed, lunging free of the ceiling into new formations to shield Cab, Einan, One, and the fae where they stood.

It would've made a prison for them underground, but more stone was crumbling away behind them, creating a narrow corridor through the earth. Their escape route was clear.

One's voice in Cab's head was approving as the sense of otherness receded. Then only the two of them remained in his head. Cab fought off a bout of dizziness from the strain. Stumbled, then kept moving.

Good work. Not that I expected any less.

"We have to find our way back to the others," Einan said.

Her eyes were on the fae they'd discovered. Cab could only guess at the joy she felt knowing Sil wouldn't be alone. If it was anything like what he'd felt when he'd encountered One, Cab was proud to have had a hand in it.

"Can you run?" Cab asked the fae.

The fae lifted his young, golden face. On his brow above his nose was a tattoo of a black crescent moon. He was marked with tattoos like Shining Talon's, but fewer of them. Only one bone, on the middle finger on each hand, and nothing beside his bow-curved mouth.

"I *will* run," he replied.

With cutlery in his trousers and a sleeping fragment in his pocket, Rags headed downstairs, Shining Talon dogging his heels.

It'd taken hours, and a half dozen dropped forks, before Rags had been able to get the things into his pockets. His hand shook from the exertion, fingers weak as newborn kittens.

But anything was better than focusing on Shining Talon in the room they shared. It was getting harder, impossible, even, to work up a head of steam about anything the fae prince did and said.

At least there was hope for getting the mirrorglass out of Rags's heart. But there were other things that had wormed into that organ because of this quest, more insidious things, and he didn't know how to be rid of them.

This softness would do him no favors in the street.

Inis and Somhairle were waiting by the door, one with a silver cat, one with a silver owl. Someone—Rags suspected Inis—had draped a decorative tapestry over the hall mirror to protect them from catching sight of, falling into, one of Morien's twisted pantomimes. Rags held up his hands and framed all four in the right angles of his thumbs and forefingers. "Nice portrait you lot make."

"Good. You're finally up. Three and Somhairle have a few leads," Inis said.

"What do you mean, 'a *few* leads'? Isn't it a straight shot, like how Cab led us to you and you led us here?"

"Ah." Somhairle bit his bottom lip, apologetic. "That's . . ."

"He's practically sequestered here," Inis began.

"That's all right, Inis. I can explain myself. The trouble is that I rarely see anyone out here. The last time I was in a large group was when I was still in the city, and I was only a child then. Afterward, I rarely visited. We already know who it isn't, since we've ruled out the servants and the few regular visitors I *do* get, but as for who it *is* . . ." Somhairle shrugged, still sheepish. "It's more complicated than if I were someone with more friends. Or experiences."

"Easy for you to say," Rags muttered. His anger was misplaced, as always, but knowing that didn't help the anger go away. "*You* don't have this *thing* in your chest ready to shred your heart meat if we don't do what Morien says."

"Heart is muscle," Shining Talon said, "not meat."

"Listen up, Shiny—" Rags began.

"Enough." Inis's voice practically made the chandelier rattle, but more effective was the way Two rose onto his hind legs to back her up. Rags quieted quick. "This means we're going to have to go to court. *Together.* Splitting up isn't an option. We've already lost One and her master. We can't afford to lose anyone else."

"Me and him"—Rags jerked a hand Shining Talon's way—"at court?"

"Morien can glamour Shining Talon so he doesn't look so . . ." Inis paused.

Rags snorted an ugly laugh. "So fucking fae?"

"That," Inis agreed. "Same with Two and Three. Make them look like a lap cat and a hunting bird to everyone else. Somhairle and

Three believe that if Somhairle is back in that place, something will trigger the right memory, and he can lead us to Four's master." She shrugged, hands in the air. "As you said, we need to deliver results."

"If we ever find One and her master again, *I'm* going to be the one to clout him in the face," Rags said, "as thanks for putting our dear Morien in a blacker-than-black mood and leaving the rest of us to deal with him."

"It's not a bad plan."

Everyone turned to face the new voice.

Where there had been an empty receiving chair in the corner, Morien now sat, his legs crossed, fingers steepled.

Rags rolled his eyes, then made it look like he was studying the ceiling when Morien's attention shifted his way. When he put his hands into his pockets, stolen silverware poked his palms.

"We thought you'd approve." Inis dropped into a curtsy with a readiness that had Rags resolved to watch her more closely. Smart girl. "Even if Prince Somhairle's constitution isn't robust, he's keen to help."

"You talk too much," Morien informed her.

"Now, Morien." Somhairle's voice was weedy and hoarse. "She's my friend—"

"But not a friend to Her Majesty's Silver Court, I'm afraid."

"Disguise me too, then," Inis said.

She clearly had more to say, but she bit down on it, not wanting to do anything that would put their sharded hearts, or Somhairle's unsharded heart, in greater danger.

"Start with this one," Rags said, louder than he needed to, as he pointed at Shining Talon. A little sleight of hand to draw Morien's attention from Inis, cast it elsewhere while she wrestled her mutinous feelings under control. "Something tells me he's going to need extra practice acting anything close to human."

Shining Talon blinked, shedding whatever mood had threatened to take him. The idea of traveling to the Hill, the epicenter of the power that had murdered so many of his people: not good.

His silver eyes turned to Rags, but that was what Rags wanted, for a change. Ignoring the way it made him feel thirsty like a hot day.

"I had never imagined such experiences," Shining Talon said. "Being with you is a marvel."

"Ugh." Rags ignored the twist beneath his ribs that told him he was pleased. "You ruined it."

63
RAGS

Instead of taking separate horses, they rode in a carriage to the Silver Court to arrive in style. This left Rags and Shining Talon trapped with two born Ever-Nobles, both of whom seemed convinced that mere hours before they landed at court was plenty of time to teach a common thief and a fae a lifetime's worth of manners.

Although Rags knew what Two and Three were supposed to look like, the spellcraft disguising them made his vision blurry at the edges. What he knew he should see and what he actually saw were two different things, and if his focus wandered, he ended up seeing *four* animals in the carriage, not two.

As for Shining Talon, Morien had assured them the glamour would work on anyone who didn't know who he was, but Rags had his doubts. Those innocent silver eyes shone through. He was so big, so golden. He filled a room, or a carriage, like no human could, his massive shoulders steady whenever the carriage hit a bump that sent Rags flying out of his seat to crack his head on the roof for the nineteenth time.

Whatever. Rags had other problems: like how their cover would be blown if he reached for the wrong fork at a dinner, or bowed a fraction of an inch too low for somebody who didn't deserve it, or farted in the middle of a party and cracked wise about it to a deacon.

"You're telling me there are *seven* forks to choose from at an *informal* dinner?" Rags refused to believe it. There weren't tables big enough. "Then we're fucked, and not 'cause of me; I'm a fast learner. Listen, Shiny *hates* cutlery. Went mad one time, thought a spoon was attacking me, knocked it across the room and would have fought it to the death if we hadn't been interrupted. True story."

"They're arranged in order of size for each course. It isn't difficult to remember. One new fork with every plate." Somhairle's patience hadn't worn through yet, while Inis had long since given up, staring moodily out the carriage window and refusing to acknowledge she could still hear the sound of Rags's voice.

There were bowing lessons next, then titles, and by the time Rags's head was feeling stuffed full of nonsense like a stinking etiquette book, the countryside was rolling into properly populated landscape, which could only mean one thing.

They were on the outskirts of the city.

Rags breathed in deeply, could almost smell the familiar mix of cheap food and pollution. The press of too many bodies too close together. Tenements and sewers and laundries and countless pickpockets, scoundrels who'd steal the eyes out of your head if you didn't keep watch on them.

Home.

Rags sat up straighter in his seat while Shining Talon frowned to himself. "The air smells wounded."

"Don't ruin this for me, Shiny," Rags replied.

The capital was old, built on a mass of fae ruins. The castle on the Hill perched atop the conquered, the buried. Rags didn't spend much time dreaming about that place. He'd had normal ambitions once: to own a room he could call his and fancy jewels none would be brave enough to nick, to eat whatever he pleased every night, and to sleep without somebody breathing down his neck.

The Hill could have its wonders. Rags would settle for comfort and a bad reputation.

He flexed his hand, trying not to wince. There'd be no life for him to go back to if he didn't get these shards out of his body.

The tight set of Inis's jaw told Rags she was thinking along the same lines. Thanks to Morien, Inis had lighter hair and a different mouth. The bridge of her nose was shorter, its end tilted up. No one would recognize her, but she couldn't do a damned thing about her insides. The only change Morien had made there was the shard in her heart.

Then there was Somhairle, so good-natured about everything it was impossible to imagine him feeling bad about anything. Still, he'd called the Hill his home once.

Topping it off was Shining Talon. A member of the conquered race upon whose bones the first Ever-Bright queen had built her castle.

Yeah. It was a good thing Rags didn't worry about anyone but himself. He would've been in too deep with this group.

The carriage ride passed all too quickly after that, in a blur of jostles and bumps. Somhairle tried hard to distract them, but his chosen topic of conversation—fae battle poetry, *of course*—was so boring, only Shiny was still paying attention.

As they passed through the courtyard, Shining Talon shuddered.

Rags didn't ask him what was wrong this time. But he looked over. Big mistake. Shining Talon opened his eyes, bare slivers of silver peering out at Rags from behind their glamour of simple blue.

"There are shanks of iron buried beneath the crossroads here."

"That's worse than a spoon, innit, Shiny?" Rags replied.

Without warning, the carriage rocked to a halt. Rags nearly fell forward into Somhairle's lap. Shining Talon, of course, remained statue still.

They should've spent more of the ride teaching him how to be clumsy like a human.

A rapping on the door, followed by "Out," in the official voice of the Queensguard. The kind of voice Rags used to have nightmares about before his nightmares turned fae and feral. He almost relished the icy slide of regular fight-or-flight fear, a welcome change from the new instincts he was being forced to learn to face terrors he *still* wasn't prepared to deal with.

Somhairle leaned over to the carriage window and cracked it open. "Perhaps you weren't aware, but I'm Prince—"

"Out of the carriage, Prince," the Queensguard insisted. "Her Majesty's orders. For *anyone* who passes through, no matter their bloodline."

"Yes. Of course. One moment." Somhairle shut the window again, patted Three nervously.

Rags didn't have to ask where that nervousness came from. "If Morien's sent us here to get ourselves arrested for being the shadiest group of bastards ever to approach the castle . . ."

"Say it louder, Rags." Despite her sharp tone, Inis stroked Two uncertainly. "We *are* here because the Queen commands it. Aren't we?"

"According to Morien," Rags muttered.

"Then we'll have nothing to worry about," Somhairle said.

"Except that we're glamoured in a fuck-ton of sorcery, and have a *fae prince* and two big-ass silver beasts of unknown power and origin with us," Rags replied. "Other than that, we're not suspicious in the slightest."

"Best get on with it." Somhairle opened the carriage door, raised his voice. "My apologies. My condition makes it difficult for me to move quickly, hence the delay."

With an exaggerated wince, he levered his bad leg out of the carriage and braced himself on the doorframe so as not to stumble.

The Queensguard, being gracious, good-hearted, law-keeping servants of the crown, didn't offer him one whit of assistance. Inis was behind him in a flash, taking his good arm, leaving Two behind with Three on the plush carriage seat. If Rags looked at them cross-eyed, he was almost able to convince himself they were a pair of regular Ever-Noble pets. Then he blinked, caught the silver sheen, and scowled at his own headache.

Shining Talon's face was gray-pale. Was that a side effect of the sorcery, a mixture of his golden skin with the image Morien would have the world see when the fae stood before strangers?

Rags blinked. No, definitely gray.

"You're not freaking out about the iron, are you? 'Cause you'll blow our cover if you can't keep it together."

"I am together," Shining Talon replied. "But I do feel as though I am being pulled apart."

Rags sighed and grabbed Shining Talon's arm. "You were asleep for a thousand years in an abandoned tunnel and you came out ten times better than anything else alive today. You can handle a little pat-down by a couple of clank-headed humans."

"I believe you," Shining Talon said, so fervently Rags had to make it true.

In the quiet, with Somhairle and Inis outside handling the Queens-guard, Shining Talon found Rags's hand with his.

Rags laid his head on Shining Talon's big shoulder in return. Despite the privacy of the carriage, he couldn't help his awareness that Morien could be watching every moment. That nothing was private.

"At least do that magic massage thing if you're gonna hold it," Rags said.

His mind was executing flips and back-handsprings, more skillful and acrobatic than his actual body could manage, to avoid the well-spring of want bubbling up inside him.

He could still slip this trap as long as he didn't look directly at it.

As long as he didn't name the desire for what it was.

As long as he didn't notice the perfect shape of Shining Talon's mouth between the twin sets of—regularly perplexed, where Rags was concerned—crossbones.

Rags couldn't scream or throw himself out of the carriage without ruining their subterfuge. And he had his pride as a thief to consider, proving he was good at the sneaky bits.

But that mouth.

Rags just . . . wouldn't look.

"It would be my pleasure," Shining Talon replied.

As he turned his back to the door, the better to focus on Rags's glass-filled hand, Rags thought about that hand. About his hands in general. Trained in dexterity, drilled for hours into days into months at picking pockets, opening locks, skirting sealed windows.

They were a tool, nothing more. He'd never put his hand in some-one else's—nothing to be gained from that. The only people who wanted to hold on to Rags were the ones dragging him in for arrest.

He tucked his knees up onto the carriage seat, let himself grip Shining Talon's shoulder and arm for ballast against the intense pressure in his palm that gave way to greater relief.

"Am I causing you pain?" Shining Talon asked.

"Yeah. Don't stop," Rags replied.

64
INIS

Of everything Inis remembered about the capital, this checkpoint wasn't one of them.

There was plenty she did remember all too well, that featured in her dreams or when her thoughts wandered, dangerously, to how life used to be. A swing wrought of ivory, dangling from a low-hanging bough. The rooftops of the Palisades glimpsed from a castle balcony, or flower-viewing days when the roses were in bloom. . . .

The checkpoint was definitely new.

"Prince Somhairle is tired," she said shortly, not meeting the Queensguard's eyes and hoping he thought it was deference that caused her to avert her gaze, not her shimmering hatred for everyone who wore the Queen's crest. If he looked too close, he'd see it. She couldn't hide it no matter whose face she wore. "It is unpleasant for him to stand while submitting to this search."

In the meantime, two Queensguard had him holding both arms out while they patted him over. And Somhairle wasn't swaying, but he was breathing thinly, which meant it actually *was* bothering him and he was refusing to show it.

Inis would have given anything for the ability to knock these men on their asses as she'd done with Cab. She might have given anything to be less sensible. To be more like their companions in the carriage, if only for the time it took to make herself feel better.

But she remained, stubbornly, like Inis Fraoch Ever-Loyal: someone who was too smart to toss her life out the window for one moment's sweet euphoria. For the most part, her anger made her strong, but here it would give her away.

If Two hadn't helped her to see that, she would be in trouble now.

Somhairle's arm slid through hers once more, steadying himself against her. She'd made the right choice.

But how nice it would have been to see the looks on their faces.

They'd cut your throat, dearheart. Two's voice was her brother's again, affectionate and chiding in one. *Cabhan of Kerry's-End* let *you hit him.*

One of the Queensguard moved on from Somhairle to search her instead. Inis held herself steady, tried not to wonder whether they were lingering over her backside and chest. To them, she was no one, not a member of the Ever-Lasting Houses, though being a companion of the prince should have offered her some basic consideration.

Inis told herself not to bristle. She was glad to lose herself in her connection with Two.

Thanks for the blow to my ego and my fighting skills, Two.

She felt Two's shrug, elegant shoulders more vivid than the hands patting down the sides of her corset.

Plenty of time to get more practice in. I'll teach you to bite like me.

"Girl's clean," her Queensguard said.

Inis caught Somhairle's eye from the side and dipped her chin in a quick nod, trying to communicate without words that she was all right. That they both were.

"I washed behind my ears and everything." Inis curtsied. "It isn't every day a girl's taken to the Hill."

Somhairle breathed out hard, a huff of either surprise or amusement.

Had he thought himself the only one who knew how to put on a show?

"Prince too," the other Queensguard confirmed. This one had the courtesy to bow, although the gesture was shallower than it should have been. "Apologies, sire. Just doing our jobs."

"I'll be sure to tell my mother how attentive you both were." Somhairle's voice was light and his face was kind, but Inis had to admire how he'd found another way to exhibit his theatrical skill.

For the first time, the guards looked nervous.

"We wouldn't want distinction," Inis's Queensguard said. "No reason to go to any trouble on our accounts."

"Thought I saw others in the carriage." That was the second Queensguard.

Inis felt her spine straighten. If she pushed, didn't allow the Queensguard to regain ground or their confidence, there was a chance she could keep them afraid.

Afraid enough not to search the carriage.

"It's only our servants inside." Inis's voice carried, disbelieving. "Would you paw through a lady's baggage next? Are our personal belongings to be mistrusted?"

Somhairle rested his withered hand on her elbow. "I know you're upset, but as they said, these men have a job to do." He smiled once more at the Queensguard. It wasn't the childhood smile of Inis's past, gentle and forgiving. "Don't be modest. Your dedication demands special mention. What are your names and ranks? I shall wish to speak with your captain as well as with my mother."

The nervous Queensguard glanced toward the carriage. "Perhaps we've kept you long enough."

"I'm nearly certain I won't collapse yet." Somhairle lifted his face in the direction of the castle, gleaming and forbidden, as though searching for someone in a particular window. "And since I'm so close to the castle, if I do, perhaps someone inside will notice and rush to my aid."

"Be that as it may . . ." The first Queensguard gestured them back to the carriage, offered Somhairle a hand up, which the prince ignored in favor of Inis's assistance. The door shut behind them. Two chuckled at their antics, a bell-like tinkle, purring laughter.

"We don't get the pat-down treatment?" Rags asked. There was high color in his cheeks, and he was shaking out his fingers as though he'd been stung by a bee. "I'm offended. I was looking forward to them finding the silverware in my underthings."

Inis chose not to question his final statement. "Not at all. We informed them only our servants were within. Which, conveniently, takes care of another matter."

Rags frowned as the carriage started moving again, those last, critical steps along the road to the top of the Hill. "What matter's that?"

"You bow like a broken-legged toad and talk with as much grace," Inis replied. "Now you don't have to. Simply stay behind us at all times and don't open your mouth. Ever."

Inis nursed the feeling she got at the look on Rags's face into a warm flame, burning beside the mirror shard in her heart.

65
CAB

Cab and Einan hadn't been caught by the diggers yet, but that didn't mean they could stop running.

Out of breath. Covered in dirt and sweat. Cab felt more alive than he had in a year, had assumed he'd buried that part of himself alongside his uniform. Looking a mess next to the fae they'd rescued—or who'd rescued them, a point Cab wasn't clear on—they burst into the chamber where Sil, Uaine, and Malachy were waiting.

Only Sil was asleep.

That was what One said. *Asleep.*

She looked dead.

Drawn, nearly colorless, with only the faintest luster of gold still dusting her skin. She was the size of a thirteen-year-old girl, her hair as white as a village elder's.

"We couldn't wake her," Malachy said, looking at Einan while Uaine stared at their fae guest. "She's been like this since you left. But Uaine said I shouldn't go after you."

"She was right," Einan said tartly.

Cab knelt before Sil. He could tell the fae from the coffin was staring at her, not believing his eyes. Cab knew that without their leader, what remained of the Resistance was hesitant and scared. He was the only trained soldier here.

Trained to keep his head in situations like this.

Elsewhere in the tunnel, a crash. Muted and distant, but no less real.

Better not to let it get closer.

"Forgive me," Cab murmured as he lifted Sil into his arms. He couldn't avoid the feeling that he'd break her to dust if he held her too tightly.

"Be careful with her—" Einan began.

"Or you'll gut my garters or whatever it is you like to say. I remember." Cab adjusted his hold gingerly. "Do you have a safe place? Somewhere else you meet when the sewers have been compromised?"

Einan's expression fell. "The sewers have *never* been compromised."

"Then it was only a matter of time," Cab said. "They were digging. You had to know eventually—"

"I can take Malachy to my place," Uaine said. "But they'll see us walking in the front door."

Not an option for the fae.

"Where else?" Cab turned to Einan, who seemed to gain resolve from responsibility.

"You're right." She looked at Sil in his arms, then to Uaine. "Only one place for a troupe of freaks like this. Uaine, Malachy, get yourselves to safety. We'll split up. Protecting Sil. That's what's important."

"Lead the way," Cab replied.

66
CAB

After they'd spent too long chasing Einan's twists and turns in the dark, the air finally began to smell less stale. Sounds of city life, muted but unmistakable, followed. The occasional sewer grate appeared overhead, unsteady light filtering through the bars. Carriage wheels, laughter, marketplace shouting, the scampering of small feet.

And more shit and piss. The sewers here were active.

I am disgusted, Cab heard One grouse. *I hope you can make this up to me someday with a proper adventure.*

If we make it out of this one, he replied.

Always so dire! Try not to be gloomy.

The clatter of heavy, iron-soled boots interrupted their conversation. Reminded Cab to stay focused on the present. Queensguard overhead meant he couldn't let *his* guard down.

He also had to keep checking over his shoulder to make sure their new friend was still there.

The fae remained quiet as a shadow.

Einan led them down a narrower, smellier tunnel where the light faltered. Less clamor overhead. From there she found and climbed a rusty ladder to the surface. A grated panel in the ceiling gave a *creak* as she pushed it open.

Einan disappeared through it, then reappeared, gave the hand signal for *all clear.* She held her arms out for Sil. "Be gentle!"

As he passed Sil off to Einan, Cab wondered if she might close the grate on him and disappear with Sil into the night.

But if Einan did that, she'd also be closing the grate on One and another fae.

Not everyone was as disloyal to their brothers and sisters as Cab had been the night he'd fled the Hill.

"Come *up*," Einan hissed. "What are you standing around for?"

Properly shamed, trusting that One could handle a ladder without hands, Cab settled his palm on a rusted rung and hauled himself up.

When he surfaced, he came face-to-face with the black-and-silver uniform of a Queensguard.

Trap, his instincts screamed. But One hadn't warned him of any danger.

Next to the Queensguard's uniform was a voluminous white dress. Glittering fish scales patterned the skirt, edged in blue beading. Hanging next to that was a series of masks, some of them with long, comical noses, others with frozen expressions of fear or sadness. A bureau with a mirror faced Cab, reflecting Einan to his left, settling Sil in a pile of colorful fabric and folded banners.

"Are we in a madman's wardrobe?" Cab asked.

"Close." Einan's voice hushed, her expression reverent as she touched Sil's hair, brushed it out of her face, and finally released her. "You're in my theater."

Of course. These were costumes.

A sneeze from One caught Cab's attention. When he turned, he saw that she'd already extracted herself from the sewers and was tangled in a feathered scarf. Bright fuchsia plumes floated gently in the air around her head, sticking to her body where the silver was wet.

The fae climbed out next, huffing another plume off his face.

"Used to be more jewelry, of course." Einan straightened, kneading the small of her back with her knuckles. "Bits of gold, real silver candlesticks. Until the Queensguard rounded up all our good metal to melt down into weapons. I'll bet there's more than a few family heirlooms masquerading as swords these days."

It wasn't the sights in the room that had distracted Cab. He was suddenly, overwhelmingly aware of their smell in such a small space.

Einan's nose wrinkled, having the same thought. "Right. You'd best clean up. Bathing stuff's behind that screen, and *don't* touch my perfumes and powders, thanks—they don't come cheap. After the lizard's clean and dry, she'll have to hold still if anyone drops by my dressing room. Pretend to be a prop. Go *on*," she urged, hands on Cab's back, shoving him forward.

Behind the screen were a pitcher of water and a small porcelain tub, soaps and perfume bottles lined up beside them. Cab stripped quickly, nodding at the fae to do the same, then scrubbed One down before he started on himself, using a washcloth that might have to be burned after he finished with it.

"I'm Cabhan," he said as he scraped grime off his forearms and wrung the cloth out over the tub, its water coming away black.

"I know," the fae replied. "One of Many told me."

"She didn't tell me your name."

"Names have great power. It is important for us to introduce ourselves." The fae took the washcloth from Cab's outstretched hand, which was big, rough, and callused in comparison to the fae's smooth golden skin. "I am Second Hope for Windsworn Glory."

"How's Hope for short?" Cab asked.

Second Hope for Windsworn Glory considered this, cleaning dirt from the backs of his hands, so that the black bone tattoos, few as there were, stood out more clearly. Then he nodded.

There might have been more to the conversation, but shirts appeared, flung over the screen, and Einan said, "These should fit you. If they don't, too bad. It's not like we're in the Royal Theater, but we're good enough for the lesser princes."

The shirt better suited to Cab's size was a billowy white affair with enormous sleeves that narrowed to a tight cuff, too tight to button at Cab's thick wrists. He managed to roll the sleeves up to his elbows, then looked back to find Hope tricked out in black velvet.

"You're taking your time, divas," Einan added. "I'd like to bathe before my own smell kills me, thanks."

She surveyed them mercilessly when they came out from behind the screen, gave neither of them a single compliment on their ragtag appearance, and disappeared to wash with an armful of clothing for herself. Her shadow played over the screen as she undressed, and Cab turned away respectfully.

Instead, he faced Sil, whose eyes fluttered open and traveled to him only after they'd drunk their fill of Hope.

"Thank you, Cabhan of Kerry's-End," Sil murmured.

"Cab," Cab replied, the back of his neck warm. "That's good enough for me."

"Second Hope for Windsworn Glory," Sil continued. "Welcome to the world as it now stands."

"As it now crumbles," Hope replied.

None of them could find the words—or the conviction—to correct his first impression.

67
SOMHAIRLE

Somhairle excused himself to his quarters the instant they arrived at the castle on the Hill, trembling not with pain, but overstimulation. He couldn't be there for Inis if he allowed himself to be overwhelmed.

Memories often betray us this way, Three said, because Somhairle hadn't moved or spoken for some time. He rested on the canopy bed, between the swans carved into the bedposts, their eyes dots of red and silver.

Somhairle had needed to be alone so he wouldn't feel watched by Morien through his friends' eyes, or shamed by the way he was exempt from their suffering, apart from them despite being with them. A member of the adventure but held separate, and still so lonely. As lonely as ever.

No dust had gathered on any surface of his old palace quarters, which showed no sign that they had been without an occupant for the past five years. With no piece of furniture or favorite toy out of place, all Somhairle could feel was how different it was from what he had known. It wasn't the room that had changed, but the palace around it, the Hill beneath it, the people who filled its bright halls.

Because what we think we remember and what truly was are only distorted echoes of each other, Three continued.

This is more than the distortions of nostalgia, Three, Somhairle said.

Yes, this is more than that. Three poked at a stuffed owl's pearl eyes and ruff, looking back at Somhairle as she flicked it with the tip of her wing. Amused. *So take this time to work it out. Knowledge can betray us, too, but if you can be the first to wield the weapon, that's a fine advantage.*

I was young. I don't remember it very well, he replied.

I was a brace and a crutch, so you remember better than I do, Three shot back.

You're being flippant. This is my home. You hate my mother, and you have good reason to, but I—

Three swept the stuffed owl off its chair with a swipe of her wing. *Emotions have their place. You can't afford to let yours get away from you.* She bowed her head, her one eye rolling and rolling. The taste of metal in Somhairle's mouth was worse, not better, since he'd left Ever-Land. *And neither can I. Sorry for snapping. I'm not myself here.*

I used to imagine this place was what made me sick, Somhairle admitted. He'd forgotten until now how the air on the Hill could be so heavy. *Then I'd lie awake in bed at night, expecting my own mother to storm in and lock me up for treason.*

That might still happen, Three said.

Somhairle appreciated her refusal to be tender with him, to coddle, when what he needed was the merciless truth. Catriona had as much as told him: she wouldn't hesitate to strike him down if she suspected fae corruption.

He was thinking like the members of the Resistance against the Queen. They claimed she had chosen fear to rule alongside her, forsaking good sense. He now saw their point.

She was still his mother.

Somhairle fought for a deep breath. *It's worse here than in Ever-Land, and Morien was the cause of the trouble there. So it's sorcery that's bothering me,* he reasoned.

Owls couldn't smile. Three did. *And lots of it.*

I have to do something, don't I?

Plenty of places you can go that the others can't.

That's not usually how things are for me, Somhairle admitted. He couldn't hide from Three what she'd learned already.

Cane's by the door. With one beat of her great wings, Three was aloft. Somhairle followed in less-spectacular fashion, shuffling across the floor. *I can't promise you'll be comfortable, but you'll be necessary.*

That's all I've ever wanted, he replied.

Three chuckled. *Time to dream bigger, birdie.*

The sharp pleasure of her humor infected him. It wasn't the pure joy he'd felt when they'd found one another in Ever-Land, her lightning-crackle laughter melting through his mind, but it helped.

Somhairle fingered the silver grip of his rosewood cane, its ornate head carved in the shape of a falcon midstrike. If he looked at Three from the corner of his vision, he could see Morien's glamour on her clearly. No one would think it strange that Prince Somhairle had adopted a wild bird after years of caring for them in Ever-Land.

He understood now that he'd spent those years waiting, not living. Waiting for his mother to give him purpose, or for one of his brothers to tell him his role. Now he was acting without anyone's direction. He might even be taking action against his mother.

Did that make him a traitor to the Crown?

Better that than a traitor to himself.

He couldn't let fear stop him. What he'd felt when Three became a part of him was too big to ignore.

Somhairle held out his arm and Three landed on it, lighter than a sparrow. *I believe a trip to the court seneschal is in order.*

68
SOMHAIRLE

According to Seneschal Tarlach, who had managed the royal family's affairs since the birth of Prince Adamnan, three of the five princes in residence were currently attending court. Lochlainn was north of the Hill surveying their land. Berach had gone into hiding with a pirate's daughter. He could go on. The elderly seneschal was only half as old as Queen Catriona—however, he looked it.

Somhairle barely managed to get him to continue.

"Prince Murchadh is often in the Hall of Mirrors with Her Majesty's sorcerers, attending to important—and private—matters of state." The years had stooped Tarlach's shoulders, turned his hair and flesh the same faded paper white, but the most troublesome change in the man was that he no longer appeared to relish gossip. His voice droned on dully. "Prince Adamnan will be hearing council with Her Majesty much of the morning. Do not be troubled if you cannot locate Prince Laisrean until well into the afternoon, as he keeps strange hours and is often abed. The court celebrates the Queen's many triumphs, none more devotedly than Prince Laisrean."

The Seneschal Tarlach who Somhairle used to know would have leaped at the opportunity to share his unfavorable thoughts on parties, liquors, new styles of dance, current fashions, Laisrean raiding the kitchens for midnight picnics—until Somhairle began to visibly sway on his feet.

The Seneschal Tarlach in front of Somhairle, though, began to nervously list the Queen's latest, greatest accomplishments and future plans to turn the ruins of Eastside into a garden that would rival Oberon's forest of legends.

He smells of lies, Three commented.

Most people at court do, Somhairle cautioned.

But this is more than that.

It was. Again. Somhairle made his excuses to the seneschal, went to find the cooks next. He had once known each by name—Marnoch, who smelled of dry rosemary; Garvie, with flour always under his fingernails; Magh the butcher, who saved him summer strawberries from the countryside, since they didn't have the tang of metal beneath their sweetness. Their gossip was what truly fed the lords and ladies on the Hill.

But no one at the stoves knew any servants by those names. Somhairle would have asked more questions, answered a few in return, and laughed awhile with the new cooks, but he was too aware of their desire to have him out of the way. They had work to attend to, work they couldn't manage while down on both knees, praising his mother to him.

He gave it a solid try, but wasn't granted entry to the Hall of Mirrors to "enjoy a warm reunion" with his "beloved brother." The Queensguard stationed by the doors smelled of more lies, according to Three.

Somhairle could ask his mother for her seal of approval to enter the Hall, but that would alert her to his interests, give her reason to watch him more closely, and he couldn't risk that.

So we're finally able to think of her as the enemy? Three asked as Somhairle limped away to make the rounds outside of council instead. There, he could gauge the tone of the court, catch some of the gossip he still hadn't managed to glean. Prove himself necessary to the group. Continue to betray his mother.

I can't be certain yet. This may prove to be the work of Morien the Last. He could have asked them not to speak with me. Or done worse than asked.

Don't lie to yourself too often, Three suggested. *One Lying One to deal with is plenty.*

Outside of council: the lingering petty Ever-Nobles who roamed the place daily, hoping to ingratiate themselves. The occasional member of an Ever-House swanning past, showing off, getting to feel big after Catriona had made them feel small. Those were the tableaux Somhairle expected, though he told himself it would likely look less enormous than his childhood perspective would remember.

A dazzling reception hall lined with little mirrors—there were mirrors everywhere now, not just in the Hall of Mirrors where they belonged—awaited him. It held fewer guests than Somhairle had prepared to encounter, though at first it appeared that there were more, a trick of reflection layered upon reflection.

Some of the mirrors were reflecting Three as she truly was. A young woman caught sight of Three in the glass and opened her mouth to scream, but no sound came out.

Somhairle stumbled, slamming into a mirror at his back he could have sworn hadn't been there before. It rattled in its frame. Three swung her wings in a wide arc. Eyes were turning toward him; he was making a scene.

"Sorley?" A familiar voice speaking a familiar nickname, a familiar hand landing on Somhairle's back a moment later.

He's handsome, Three said. *And unlike most of the humans around here, he* doesn't *stink.*

Somhairle turned to face Laisrean Ever-Bright. His favorite half brother.

"Sorcerers have been redecorating since you left the Hill." Laisrean slung an arm around Somhairle's shoulders and heaved him out from between two mirrors, out of the hallway, out of the false mirror-light. Though he had the strength of a bear, his touch was courtly gentle. His strong jaw was dusted with dark stubble, his hair uncombed, his eyes darkened by sleepless undercircles, though they brightened when he grinned. "What brings you back to this wicked place?"

"I hoped we might catch a play." Somhairle offered his true smile, the one dazzling thing he'd inherited undamaged from his mother. "No. It isn't that. Ever-Land hasn't been very peaceful since Lord Faolan arrived with Morien the Last."

"Best not have any truck with them." Laisrean forced a steely smile. His tone was bluff and cheery. "These aren't your regular bed-time warnings for naughty children. Whatever Faolan's looking into has the court on the edge of a knife. Better you don't find yourself caught on—"

Prince Adamnan interrupted him by striding through the main doors in a sudden burst of purposeful activity, his favored courtiers providing a buffer between him and the lesser crowds. He ignored everyone vying for his attention, pausing only when he noticed Somhairle tucked against Laisrean's side.

"You"—Adamnan skidded to a halt, his expression blacker than his boots—"shouldn't be here."

Before Somhairle could form a stunned expression, Adamnan had moved on, swept away again by eager attendants to decide matters of state.

"He's like that these days. Nothing personal. Ignore him." Laisrean squinted, staring hard at Three on Somhairle's arm. "Did you tame an owl? Big one. Never seen a bird that color."

"I found her in Ever-Land," Somhairle explained.

"Maybe sorcery changed her," Laisrean said. "Hey there, girl. You got magic in you?"

He reached to touch Three's round head, slow and tentative, like he was sure the bird would snap at him for trying but was compelled to do it anyway. Three allowed Laisrean's hand to settle and began to preen under the touch, angling into it.

Somhairle let out a breath. Even he hadn't been sure whether Three would allow someone else to get that close.

I have manners, Three said. *And I know which hand wants a biting and which doesn't.*

"Glad you've got something fierce to look out for you." Only Laisrean ever appeared satisfied when he looked at Somhairle. Like he was glad for who Somhairle was, instead of thinking about what he might have been. "Do me a favor, since everyone's being so serious, and stick to your rooms while you're here, will you?"

Somhairle stepped back, bringing Three with him. "I don't need anyone looking out for me."

"That wasn't coddling. Life on the Hill's not like it used to be, Sorley." Laisrean looked past Somhairle for a moment—spotting someone attractive, Somhairle guessed—before refocusing his gaze. "Why don't I meet you later near the Palisades, in the fall garden? Our favorite spot. Always nice to get some fresh air."

Somhairle took in his brother's handsome, if distracted, profile.

He was larger than life, like the heroes of old.

Somhairle's heartbeat quickened. What if Laisrean was the master they sought? His behavior could be called eccentric, had been described as feckless, but it remained more faithful to the past than anything else in the palace Somhairle recalled from childhood.

Time was running out. Somhairle had to find the next master for Morien while simultaneously gathering enough resources to thwart him. Success hinged on finding the right piece or pieces of silver, the fragment of the Great Paragon possibly hidden directly under the Queen's nose. Not exactly a simple task.

A walk in a garden had helped Somhairle find Three. Perhaps it would do the same for Laisrean.

"I'll meet you there this evening," Somhairle promised.

Nothing is beyond possibility, Three agreed.

I know, Somhairle told her. *I found you, didn't I?*

69
RAGS

Even back in the city, Rags was still out of his element. It didn't smell right on top of the Hill, didn't smell of the city he knew. Didn't smell dirty, of fires and blood, of sweaty bodies and cheap perfumes and garbage baking in the sunlight, of piss running over cobblestones after dark.

It smelled spotless and unsoiled. Blood lurked beneath the pretense, but it'd been buried under layers of polish, hidden behind curtains and below floors tiled with black bone.

"Are you listening?" Inis asked in a tone that implied she already knew Rags wasn't.

Rags turned away from the massive window affording him a view of the moat, called Old Drowner by everyone who knew what it was *really* used for.

"I'm *looking*." Eyes staring wide for emphasis. "Thought that was why we came here. To find Four's master."

"Yes." Inis, or the unassuming blonde Morien had glamoured over her skin, crossed her arms. "That's what I'm telling you. Prince Somhairle thinks he might have a lead. It's royal company, so no need for our loyal servants to attend."

"Afraid we'll embarrass you?" Rags asked, but his accompanying smirk was cut down before it could flourish.

"Stay or go, it makes no difference," Shining Talon intoned from the other end of the room, where he'd been keeping silent vigil. "The heart of this Hill is as rotten as its wretched ruler. No matter where one puts their feet, the ground is poisoned."

". . . right. I'll ask you to stay out of sight for now." Inis bowed to Shining Talon, eyes lowered, like she'd have agreed with him—if their every move wasn't under surveillance by a murderous sorcerer. They'd flipped the hinged oval dressing mirrors in every room so the glass now faced the walls. Less chance of Morien's reminding them of his impatience whenever they glanced in the wrong direction.

Then Inis was gone and Rags was left alone with the fae. Between Shining Talon and the open window he couldn't leap out of to make a quick, clean escape.

What shook him was how easily he shushed the urge. How limp and half-hearted it'd grown.

Past the moat was the city Rags knew and loved, the city he wanted to return to. If you lived in the bad parts of town, you had to watch out for a sack over your head and a knife in your guts around every corner, while the Queensguard, running marching drills in the courtyard, didn't give a fuck.

The rules were simple. *Look out for yourself.*

Rags rubbed his chest. Caught Shining Talon watching him. Stuck out his tongue.

"In my time," Shining Talon said, "we did not allow our tongues to be free of our mouths so carelessly. Often the windlings would snatch them for their private collection."

"Don't know what a windling is."

"Yes. I slew the last of them."

Rags replied with a groan, pacing the length of the gold-threaded carpet while the fork and knife he'd stolen poked his thigh. Inis and Somhairle had passed off the servant story, then shut them away, the better to keep them from getting into trouble. Arrest in a fancier cell, as far as Rags was concerned.

It gave him too much time to think, for starters. Was Shining Talon teasing him? Was he finally learning from Rags how to be a sarcastic ass?

Without looking down, Rags reached for the fragment in his pocket. He felt his way along the etched curves of the thing, fitting his fingernails into each groove he came across.

There was a crease in the casing that seemed to run the length of the fragment. Like a seam, a catch. Did that mean it opened?

Rags faced the window again. Felt Shining Talon at his back, touching his hip. Reaching for the blindfold, Rags understood, though not before he sucked in a breath, fought the inclination to arch back against the fae. He closed his eyes, guiding Shining Talon's hand into his pocket and up to his chest with the cloth in tow. He drew it over his heart and darkness settled over the mirrorglass shard; he was safe from Morien, if only for a few stolen moments.

"What is it?" Rags allowed himself to lean back against Shining Talon's chest. His voice sounded so serious when the blindfold was in play.

"I sense something here," Shining Talon replied. "Something terrible."

Oh. Rags straightened, eyes snapping open. This was about more than Shining Talon wanting to get close. Of course it was. Rags bit the inside of his lip, lingering pain from Morien's torture flaring through his knuckles. Sending him back into the hard, real edges of his world. "Sounds like the whole damn place to me."

"No. It is more than that." Something in Shining Talon's voice made Rags turn to face the fae. Found his eyes had darkened and his golden face had paled. "When I stray too close, I . . . hurt."

Rags felt an emotion unnamed brewing in the distance like clouds rolling in. From the city rooftops, you could see a storm coming from miles away, from out over the countryside or the ocean.

Was there still time for him to outrun the downpour?

Shining Talon looked different with his hair tied up. Sharper. Harsher and less fluid. Rags's fingers twitched. Before he could command them to stop, he'd reached out to touch the braided white streak in Shining Talon's hair. Had to practically go up on tiptoes to reach, which was a blow to his ego and then some.

Shining Talon's throat bobbed. "I should not command your attention in such a way. Not when your fragment remains unsolved."

He looked like he might be sick at any second. Did fae get sick?

"Stuff it," Rags said helpfully. "Maybe you should sit down. Try and tell me more than 'it hurts.' Listen, I've been there."

Shining Talon shook his head. Or was he tilting it, trying to listen to things Rags couldn't hear?

It was weird, not in the usual weird way that Shining Talon had, and *that* had Rags shaken. Worse, it didn't seem like they were going to get anywhere by talking it out. They didn't have enough time, could only steal a couple of moments before they had to remove the blindfold. Unless . . .

"Listen," Rags said, "I'm gonna take this thing off and leave it over there. Then I'm gonna lie down and close my eyes, pretend to sleep. After that, you're gonna take the blindfold back out and put it on my chest again, so quietly that I don't hear you do it. And *then* I'm gonna do some snooping."

Shining Talon's face regained its faintly quizzical blankness. "What is 'snooping'?"

"*Investigating.* I'll try to find this 'something terrible' you've mentioned, 'cause what the fuck, why not, this is my year of bad decisions." Rags forced a grin, then wheeled away to follow his own idiot plan.

"For one who doubts his own character at each turn, you act with bravery at every chance presented."

Rags pretended not to hear him. He couldn't let that kind of distraction in, not now. The blindfold would slow his heart, but he was ready for that. If he didn't overextend himself, it would be fine.

Shining Talon had never asked Rags for anything before. Rags was giving this to him.

It went smoothly. He only knew Shining Talon had draped the cloth over his heart a second time because he felt it, not because he heard it or saw it. Morien wouldn't know anything was amiss, would think Rags was lazy or beat down or both.

As long as nobody saw him knocking around.

But nobody would see him. He was made for this.

It was what had landed him in all this trouble in the first place.

70
RAGS

Out in the hall, Rags was back to his old life: lingering around a corner or behind a column to avoid servants in a house too fine and too big to be his, sticking to the shadows, casing the joint for a wicked heist.

Only this time, the house in question was a castle. *The* castle.

Well, he'd bested fae ruins, so the home of Her Majesty should be a breeze by comparison.

Never mind that he had someone with him, because Shining Talon could be quiet as a cat after the cream and ten times as graceful.

No poisoned arrows. No doors whispering Rags's darkest secrets back to him. They left their room behind, no note for Inis in case she read it with Morien over her shoulder.

Shining Talon could sense when they were about to pass by a mirror, and that was a handy talent. Couldn't be too sure which mirrors were Morien's and which weren't. Maybe they all were.

The two of them worked well together. Better than if Rags had been on this job alone.

Twice the fae heard someone coming when Rags didn't, gripped him by the shirt and pulled him backward to avoid being caught. Rags chalked it up to his instincts being off, to having too much on his mind. *Too much in his* heart. He couldn't blame himself for not having the same eagle-sharp reflexes as a fae prince, so he nodded shaky thanks, told himself he didn't have the words because he was conserving energy for sneaking around.

With both of them huddled together in an alcove or behind a corner, Shining Talon holding him by his shirt until it was safe to proceed, Rags kept his mind on the mission.

He couldn't afford to let his breath run ragged or his pulse quicken in the shelter of Shining Talon's tattooed arms.

After they'd taken three sets of servants' staircases, all of them down, it was Rags's turn to return the favor, gripping Shining Talon by the shirt and dragging him into a dark alcove so he wouldn't barge into a fancy footman wearing silver gloves.

The guy passed them. Rags bent into a crouch, willing the dizzy spell—it had cropped up after winding down, down, down all those stairs—to pass. His heart had to labor twice as hard against the silencing effect of the blindfold.

"Just gotta catch my breath," he wheezed.

Shining Talon didn't answer him, mouth drawn, eyes dull.

Rags gripped the fae's elbow, pulling himself straight. "Whoa, hey. Snap out of it."

"We are closer," Shining Talon explained. "I hear sorrowful voices."

While Rags could've turned back, or asked for more time, the suddenly ashen color of Shining Talon's silver eyes told him what he already knew.

No chance of that.

His chest felt tight, like he'd been running in a dead sprint with the Queensguard on his heels. If he left the blindfold on too long, would it kill him? Probably not, since the magic was Morien's, and Morien needed him alive.

Then again, Morien didn't know he was using the blindfolds for this. There went that theory.

Onward, looking after Shining Talon to make sure there were no more missteps, no more too-close calls. Another flight of stairs down, three more footmen, a butler, two cooks, five maids. None of them gossiped, Rags noted, or laughed or smiled or wasted time. Most of them were a step short of running. Wherever they were headed, they were taking their duties seriously. Too damn seriously.

Whenever there was a mirror nearby, Shining Talon would flinch, hiss. So he was still useful for that, although each time, Rags found himself gripping Shining Talon's hand, squeezing it to bring him back to the present.

Rags had to take another break eventually, leaning back against the wall with his eyes shut while Shining Talon kept watch.

He counted a few slow cycles of his heartbeat. Then pushed on.

They were one floor below ground level, having descended what felt like the entire Hill on the inside. But that was where the servants' staircases ended. Rags and Shining Talon circled the perimeter once, and it took ages. The castle was massive, round to fit atop the Hill, and unnaturally quiet. There were no idle comings and goings, no men and women of state milling on the white tile inlaid with black bone. Rags didn't like it. Gave him the crawlies.

"Below," Shining Talon murmured.

Rags looked down, saw that they were standing on a black hand. More fae bones. He made a face, but it was time for him to be useful, to find a way down for Shining Talon. If he was leading them straight into some bad shit, at least he was leading at all. Right?

Easier thought than done.

Still, Rags had experience with tricky architecture and getting into places he wasn't meant to find. He also saw another hand inlaid into the floor, about ten paces from where they stood, and noted that its fingers were pointing the same way as the first.

Another ten paces, another hand. Rags crept from one set of black bones to the next, which kept him close to the wall. That was good. He was starting to feel faint. He counted off eleven hands in total before the trail stopped. A hand was missing beneath a high, narrow window with a plush velvet seat built into the sill.

No, scratch that. There *was* a hand, but it was white bone, *human bone*, and almost impossible to see against the surrounding white tile. Rags crouched to inspect it, then found himself grinning as he set his palm against the outline. Sure enough, the top of the window seat hinged open soundlessly, revealing a space wide enough for Shining Talon to crawl through, which meant Rags could fit, no trouble.

Beneath the window seat: a ladder. Rags sent a prayer to Lady Winter and gripped the rungs for dear life. Miraculously, he managed not to plummet straight down.

Shining Talon had no difficulty following him.

The window seat snapped shut after them, plunged them into darkness. Or it would have, if not for that faint glow of Shining Talon's skin.

Rags counted the rungs as they went, although he started to harbor a worm of panic when he came to fifty. How far down were they going? And how much of an idiot was he for wanting to reach the bottom without knowing what he'd find there?

He forced himself to slow his breathing. If he panicked between the castle and what lay beneath, he'd black out and fall to his death for sure.

He just had to remind himself that after weeks of being out of control, he could control this. Going down was his choice.

Whether or not it was a terrible one.

Finally, after seventy rungs, Rags's heel hit solid ground. Shining Talon dismounted the ladder after him, and Rags groped his way one-handed along a dark tunnel that curved inward toward the Hill's center.

They had to be below the Hill at this point, surrounded by fae bones. Shining Talon's breath shivered audibly. Rags didn't know what to do for him, settled for doing nothing. He wouldn't tell him it was gonna be all right, because Rags wouldn't make a promise that could be so easily broken. And unlike in the carriage, they were on the move, not the place to touch Shining Talon's arm or take his hand. Rags recalled the warmth of smooth fae skin against his own before he banished the thought. No distractions.

In front of them, a sliver of silvery light shone from around a final curve in the tunnel. Rags slowed, let his eyes adjust, and kept himself tucked against the wall so he wouldn't bust in on—

What he saw around the corner nearly blinded him. He drew back, squinting and wincing, biting down curses. Light *everywhere*, it seemed, like the chamber they'd found held a sun. Only there was no heat, so it couldn't be fire. The place was cold, sucked warmth from Rags's fingertips, his chin, his nose.

He had to look in there again, try to resolve the overpowering light into a set of images. He couldn't ask Shining Talon to do it, because Shining Talon had gone still as stone after edging away from the light. Rags could barely see the glint of his gaze in the shadow.

He wasn't glowing anymore.

Steeling himself, narrowing his eyes, Rags peered out into the burning white space a second time. It was dizzying. His vision swam. He was seeing too much at once, too many of the same shapes, like he'd stumbled into Whisper William's Horrific House's Room of Mirrors.

Mirrors.

That was what Rags saw: countless mirrors set at different angles. A mirrored wall. A mirrored floor and ceiling. The bright light in the room's center was reflected a thousand times, had blinded Rags when he first looked in.

There was more than light at the center of the room. There were bodies, unmoving—dead?—lying side by side, black hair like crows' wings and silk, pale silver eyes open but unseeing.

A better person would've retched. Had tears prickling at the corners of their eyes. Their knees would've buckled.

But Rags only felt a roaring in his ears, the rush of Old Drowner separating him from the shock someone was meant to feel when they saw something like this.

Of course, whispered the boy in his head, the one who'd kept Rags alive all those years on the street. The hard cockroach shell of protection he'd donned to survive. *Of course this shit exists in the world.*

Acceptance trickled down his spine like runoff from a stalactite overhead. But it was a different kind of dirty, rippling underneath his skin and staying there, becoming a part of him.

Rags wasn't surprised by the sight. No disbelief, but *belief.* Undistilled.

Mirrorcraft.

And at least twenty small fae trapped by it. They'd found more of Shining Talon's people alive, all right.

Only Rags wasn't sure this counted as living.

71

INIS

After exile to the Far Glades, Inis had imagined there would be nothing more difficult than a return to the Hill.

But that had been before Somhairle told her who they were meeting in the fall garden by the Palisades.

Laisrean Ever-Bright. Tomman Ever-Loyal's best friend, when Tomman had still been alive to have one; before his best friend's mother had ordered him killed. Laisrean had been Inis's friend, too, up until he wasn't.

The depth of Inis's fury held no room for distinctions, like if Laisrean had known about the attack on House Ever-Loyal before it had happened, or if he could have warned his friend and didn't. Even if he could have done nothing to prevent it, where had he been all this time? What had he done to honor Tomman's memory? If he'd missed Inis or mourned with her, what had he done to show it?

Nothing.

Is that why you never wrote your little summer prince? Even knowing he couldn't have been aware of his mother's plans? Two's voice was wry in her mind. *Easier to blame them all by association, I know. But there's strength to be found in focusing your anger where it truly belongs. Where it can strike its deadliest blow.*

I'm trying, Inis promised.

So she accompanied Somhairle to the fall garden, leaving the thief and the fae behind, if not her worries.

Because she didn't want to make Somhairle uncomfortable, she couldn't stare at him.

Because she didn't want to fall into a pit of grief, she couldn't stare at anything other than her feet on the grass.

Summer parties she had attended here once upon a lost time. Garlands of light and silk ribbons threaded through trees. Ivy's first time to one, clutching Inis's hand. The swish and laughter of skirts, a favorite pair of silver shoes, being complimented by princes who'd suddenly grown taller and broader of shoulder and looked like strangers, not the children she'd chased between rows of flame-colored lilies.

Impossible not to remember all of it when she smelled the roses.

They stopped to rest beneath the Oak, the Hill's oldest tree. Its roots had grown around the bodies of the conquered fae where they fell, twisted in the shapes of their bones. A few of those bones, black and bare, peeked out from the soil.

Strange to be back. Two curled up at Inis's side. *At least no one's eating hot porridge out of me.*

"I'm sorry," Somhairle said.

"For what?"

"I don't know what we'll find here. And it can't be easy for you, being back, but not yourself."

Inis shrugged, fixing her focus on her hands. Not a proper lady's hands anymore, although Morien's glamour had made them look like they were.

"And the longer it takes me, the longer you have to stay here," Somhairle added.

"Don't," Inis began.

Someone's coming, Two said. *Never ate porridge out of me, though, so I don't know who he is.*

Somhairle's head flew up at the same time as Inis's did. Three must have warned him, too.

Laisrean had Somhairle's eyes and chin, but that was where any resemblance ended. He was tall, dark-skinned, and heavyset, and wearing a smile that made Inis want to swallow a rosebush, thorns and all. "Sorley! Did I keep you waiting?"

Prince Laisrean must have been twenty now. Inis rose, keeping her head down despite the disguise she wore like a second skin. He wouldn't recognize her, but that didn't mean she wanted to look at him or see the man he was becoming, picture the men her brothers would never be.

"Laisrean!" Somhairle struggled to his feet while his half brother broke into a run, making it to Somhairle's side in time to offer him a hand. "I feared you might be too busy to meet us."

"Never!" Laisrean pulled Somhairle into one of his massive yet surprisingly tender hugs. Somhairle practically disappeared in his arms. Inis's vision wavered, threatened by tears. The threat passed. The hug ended. "And who's this?"

"Ah . . ." Somhairle paused.

"Ailis, Your Highness," Inis said smoothly, dropping into a deep curtsy. "Accompanying His Highness Somhairle Ever-Bright on his travels."

Laisrean had once carried Ivy on his shoulders when her short legs had tired ahead of theirs. He'd threatened to give Inis the same treatment when they'd splashed in the Queen's lake together, scattering panicked copper-and-black-scaled fish, the heat of the summer's sun reflected by the luster of their skin.

If he took her hand, would he find it rough? Did the glamour cover other senses than sight?

Inis reached for her anger to ground her, only to find more than the anger in that bottomless well. Other, older feelings, alongside precious slivers of hope. Stowaway dreams she thought she'd jettisoned along the road to the Far Glades, deadweight cast off so she wouldn't drown.

It didn't matter. Laisrean was a stranger now.

Inis kept her eyes on the grass beneath her feet. *She* was the stranger. Unwelcome in lands that had once been hers.

Was this what Shining Talon felt in the home of his enemy? As the last of his people?

"Ailis and I met at the theater many years ago," Somhairle confided, doing his best to dispel the tension. "We've been friends since. She tells me of all the new plays at the Gilded Lily."

Laisrean chuckled and ruffled his brother's hair with one of his enormous hands. Inis shifted instinctively toward Somhairle to brace him if he lost his balance, but he didn't. Laisrean's touch was considerate. He'd always been bigger than his brothers, so he'd needed to know his limits, how to carry himself.

"I'm being rude." Laisrean knelt in the grass in front of Inis and held out his hand. From the years of etiquette instruction in her youth, she knew she was meant to give him hers, and she complied with the barest hesitation. "Forgive me, Lady Ailis. I was so surprised to find my brother *with company* that I thought you were a trick of the light. Now I realize you're more solid than that."

Inis smiled despite herself, because it was impossible not to. Endless roses reflected in the green of his eyes. Looking away, she glimpsed twin leather friendship bands knotted around Laisrean's wrist, tucked beneath the twin suns of his cufflink. Tomman had worn his faithfully, had kept them until they frayed into scraps and fell off his arm.

Inis gripped Laisrean's hand tight. He squinted at her.

"Pardon," Inis said quickly. She was supposed to play silent and cool, draw no attention to herself. She was already mucking it up. "Compared to such fine company, I'm nothing."

"Seldom true," Laisrean assured her. Inis made herself release him, and he watched her for a second longer than he might have if she hadn't tried to crush his knuckles. She cursed herself. "But I have to admit, you'd be hard-pressed to find better company than Somhairle."

"*Lais.*" Somhairle's cheeks were red, although whether from embarrassment or exhaustion, Inis couldn't tell. "I don't need your recommendation. I *can* make my own friends."

Laisrean rose, blithe and unbothered. His attention to Inis faded and she breathed a sigh of relief. "That's what you get for bringing pretty girls to the castle. Wait till she meets Berach."

Three flapped her wings, as if preparing to take flight. Inis tensed, but nothing came of the movement. It was only a Queensguard strolling past, armor gleaming in the afternoon sun. Inis's stomach turned at the sight, at the sound of clanking armor.

Laisrean glanced over his shoulder as the Queensguard continued on his patrol. "Often I think Sorley *might* have the right idea, keeping away from the capital. Something about too much armor and weaponry spoils the ambience."

Had he noticed her discomfort? Or was this a test? Every

conversation at court was a little battle.

No matter how much Somhairle wanted to believe his brother was one of the masters, Inis couldn't allow herself to forget Laisrean's position.

"Some might call that talk treason," Inis murmured.

"Would you?" Laisrean stared at her—through her, she felt—and she had to look away or risk him seeing *her*, not the glamour she wore. He was squinting again, as though he could pick out places where it had faded or faltered.

"I'd not say a word." Inis tutted at Two, who rose and stretched lazily. "I ought to give you some privacy with your good brother, Prince Somhairle. I've been most uncouth."

She ignored the princes' protests, walking too quickly away from the roses and the memories, the leather cords of friendship Laisrean still wore, the real possibility she was about to give herself away.

Friendship with Tomman or no, Laisrean hadn't stood between his mother's Queensguard and the Ever-Loyals.

No one could stop the Queen from getting what she wanted. Inis's blame was misplaced, and she knew it. But her cheeks were still flushed, her throat tight, her eyes burning, when she made it back to Somhairle's rooms to find that Shining Talon and Rags were gone.

72
CAB

Cab spent the day proving useful around the theater. "Have to make some excuse for you to hang about," Einan had muttered, giving him a less-fancy shirt to wear from her collection before introducing him to the owner of the Gilded Lily. According to a faded poster by the front door, it was the oldest entertainment establishment in Northside.

It looked and smelled like it.

"He might not be that smart," Einan had explained, referencing Cab, "and it's best if you don't talk to him at all, it only mixes him up, but he follows orders and can lift heavy objects. Didn't you mention we were short a stagehand?"

Carrying props, splashing paint on backdrops, and carting costume chests from one side of the old building to another kept Cab occupied, kept him from worrying about nightfall.

Because when night fell and Einan took to the stage, Cab had to meet with one of Sil's contacts. Her most important contact. Einan didn't trust him with this responsibility, made that clear by storming out of the room in an actress's melodramatic huff after Sil proposed the plan.

Cab didn't blame her.

But he wanted to do this for them. For Sil, who'd saved his life and granted his freedom. For Einan, who'd taken him in. (However grudgingly.)

For all the innocents he'd once hoped to defend.

When he'd fled the Queensguard, he'd lost the part of himself that had made him join Queensguard in the first place: the strength and the will to protect. The massacre on the Hill had taken that from him. He hadn't fully realized it was missing until he'd felt it slip back into place.

That evening, as he dressed for the part, One told him, *This is very dangerous.*

Cab shrugged into a bulky coat, another Gilded Lily costume special, and turned up the collar. *No wonder I like it.*

The plan was simple, but it had plenty of room for failure and loss. It had been almost a month, Sil said, since they'd been able to meet with their contact from the Hill. They needed to learn what the Queen was planning. What new tricks Morien had up his red sleeves. They needed to know how many other fae had been excavated and what fae secrets had been discovered.

Cab hadn't asked who their contact was. Sil hadn't offered the information. The less he knew, the better.

Meet him—or her—at the designated spot. Get the information the Resistance needed to keep limping forward. Leave without being caught.

He could follow those orders.

There was someone waiting for Cab beneath a streetlamp when he rounded the corner, approaching the address he'd been given. It was close to the theater, which had drawn a respectable crowd.

One kept to the shadows, which was easy in the dark.

Also, she explained, *it's my specialty.*

Cab approached the waiting figure. He'd been rehearsing internally the line he was meant to recite. How to make it sound casual and organic in case of mistaken identity.

"Could use a light," he murmured, stepping under the lamp.

"Dark times," the young man agreed. "So could we all."

When he turned, Cab saw that he was dressed like a gravedigger in a black coat with a black rag tied over the lower section of his face. The outfit had two advantages. It concealed anything about his identity that might have stood out. And it made most decent folk look the other way.

Gravedigging was necessary work, but necessity didn't stop people from wanting to avoid grave curses and grave sickness.

They shared a moment of staring at each other. Cab felt himself being measured and did the same in turn. The contact was big, heavyset. For a second, Cab allowed himself to think there might be something familiar about his green eyes. Then he shut down the wondering before it took root.

"You're not my usual," the young man said.

"She got held up at the theater," Cab replied.

Einan hadn't told him how to manage the contact, how to allay the man's mistrust of an unknown entity. Maybe that was a test, too, of his meager instincts.

But One hadn't warned him yet. He had to assume he was doing well.

"Shit." His contact looked down the street toward the crowded theater. He seemed to be weighing a decision. "All right. You'd better come with me."

Don't lose him, One cautioned.

Although the contact was built like a brick storehouse, he moved like one of the Queen's trained horses: fleet as the wind and with little regard for whoever he left in the dust. He melted into the dark mouth of a narrow alleyway and Cab stepped quickly to follow him, trusting One to keep up.

So far, she'd never let him down.

Cab was twitchy without a decent blade for protection, but no one jumped them from the shadows. He followed the contact down the next open street, past a vendor selling grilled chestnuts, through a crowd of glittering young ladies moving from one coffeehouse to the next on their way back to the university. Cab realized they were making for the cemetery as they cut a jagged path through the city's backways, edging onto the main streets only when they needed to.

It was a good route to take if you needed a giant silver lizard with three eyes to keep pace unseen, although the gravedigger couldn't have known about that.

But there were no screams of awe and terror yet. One hadn't been noticed.

Finally, the iron gates of the cemetery rose into view. Cab was shrugging out of his coat to throw it over the spikes—so they could hop the fence—when his contact dug a key out of his pocket and opened the gate. It groaned shut behind them.

Inside, Cab tried not to look at the neat array of stones, old and new. He didn't wonder if he was responsible for any of the graves. Despite their Ever-Noble status, the Ever-Loyals had been named traitors to the crown. They would've been buried as traitors.

They walked past countless silent, mossy markers, stopped at a rickety shack on the edge of the grounds. No light shone through the windows and no key was needed to enter. Cab listened, but One was silent, wherever she was.

Anxiety hummed in his bones, but it hadn't transformed into fear.

"Shut the door behind you," the contact said.

Cab did as ordered. Kept his hand on the knob.

The gravedigger outfit gave nothing away. Hid everything save for the contact's eyes, except where a torn sleeve revealed a brown wrist wrapped with leather straps. "You're new?" The only light in the shack was moonlight, which the contact had angled Cab into, so he saw Cab's nod in response. "Nothing personal, but it isn't easy to trust the new ones."

Cab licked his lips. Knew he couldn't speak straightforwardly, but knew he'd sound a fool trying to code his responses. "Our . . . mutual connections saved my life. I owe everything to them."

"Loyal, are you? Hah." A muffled sigh beneath the bandana. "But it makes sense that a new face would be sent. There's barely anyone left. Excavation groups have tripled in the past few days. They're digging deeper, harder, like they're looking for something specific, not whatever they can find, as they have in the past."

The Great Paragon. Cab nodded again. He wasn't supposed to share the information he had until he got everything the contact knew.

"Another point of interest for our 'mutual connections'"—the contact's voice was tinged with a flash of gallows humor—"is that one of the princes has returned to the castle with friends. Reason it's worth pointing out is that this prince doesn't have friends. Not since the Ever-Loyals were killed and their eldest daughter exiled a little over a year ago. Oh, and *he arrived wearing red*."

"Friends?" Cab asked.

Not casually enough. Einan's acting background made her better for this job.

"Right, friends. Three of them. Two of them pretending to be servants. I'll learn more, find out what I can, and report back when I'm able. The usual signal. Which you don't know, because you're new, but you don't have to. Our mutual connections will understand."

There was a lot more Cab felt he didn't know. He didn't see why it mattered what the prince had been wearing. Why the contact had bothered to mention it. Unless it was the color, *red*, that mattered.

Only one person in red came to Cab's mind, accompanied by a cold, grim weight on his chest. Morien the Last.

If the youngest prince had come to the castle with Morien, then his three friends might well be the thief, the fae, and Inis Fraoch Ever-Loyal.

Close enough that Sil could help them with their mirror problem.

Cab couldn't ask the Resistance to risk all a second time, not when they'd lost so many of their forces taking him.

But if they had a chance to free the other masters of the Great Paragon, shouldn't they try?

It wasn't Cab's decision. Sil would know what to do.

"Listen," the contact continued.

Cab was listening. But it was to One's voice, clear as sentry bells: *Break it up with the big boy. Company's coming.*

Cab held up his hand, one finger to his lips. To his credit, the contact had excellent reflexes. Dropped into a silent crouch the instant Cab signaled him for quiet.

In the cemetery outside, the rhythmic crunch of heavy boots, faint but unmistakable.

Queensguard, Cab mouthed.

The contact nodded, whispered, "Get out of here. No, don't

worry about me. I'll be fine. Back door. Stick to the shadows, and don't get caught."

Cab didn't know how the contact would be fine but didn't hang around for clarification. He knew a clear order when he heard it. When corroborated by One, he had no reason to disobey.

73
RAGS

Inis was spitting mad when Rags and Shining Talon got back to Somhairle's quarters, though apparently she didn't like being told she was actually spitting.

Both Inis and Rags held blindfolds to their chesst. Rags lay on the floor to get ahead of what felt like imminent collapse. Reckless this, foolish that, and a whole slew of new vocabulary words Rags figured meant "stupid" but with extra syllables.

"If you'd quit hollering about us leaving the room, I'd have the chance to tell you what we found when we did." In comparison to the rows and rows of fae bodies—twenty-seven by Rags's count, in lines of three, with bare slabs waiting for more—Inis's fiery eyes didn't give him pause. What scared him was a bunch of fae hooked up to mirrors, trapped between them, eyes open and seeing nothing, skin so pale their black bones showed through.

What scared him was the noise Shining Talon had made, a broken gasp, at the sight. It was like *he'd* broken. After weathering the extinction of his people and making peace with them putting him to Sleep, this was the final blow.

Shining Talon hadn't said a word since Rags had hauled him out of the secret fae torture room, or whatever it was, back to where Somhairle and Angry Inis were waiting.

It was terrifying, and Rags had to make it stop.

"You have every right to be upset," Somhairle told Inis. "It's awful for you to be back on the Hill, and we're all grateful that you've come." A pointed look at Rags, like the prince thought he could perform gratitude on command. "However, I think we need to hear what Master Rags has found."

Somhairle's kindness stung worse than Inis and her shrieking. Rags would've withstood the headache if it meant fewer soft words and concern for his well-being when, yeah, he deserved shouting. With Shining Talon too distressed to back him up, he was as alone as he'd been before he'd awoken the fae.

Even though he'd been steeling himself against this moment all along, he didn't want it to come.

"We went snooping under the Hill." Rags glanced toward Shining Talon, checking to see if he'd chime in, share some fae insight. He was seated in a chair, his silver eyes blank. Two had left Inis's side to twine around his ankles, and Three was perched nearby on the mantel over the empty fireplace. There was something tender about the way the fae creatures clustered close. Like they needed to protect their own.

Inis pressed her lips together, nostrils flaring with the effort it took her to contain another outburst. But she did it, which meant she had a shred of respect for Rags.

All eyes on him, the last place a thief ever wanted to be. In the light, center of attention.

He was making a habit of this.

"Continue," Inis said.

"There's more than catacombs underneath the palace." The words spilled from his mouth in a jumble. Rags hadn't thought about what he wanted to say, because then he'd have to think about what they'd seen. "I noticed this pattern on the floor. Bones. Hands, forefingers all pointing the same way. We followed them to a hidden passage."

"You're not making any sense," Inis told him.

"Oh, you'll want to save that comment for what comes next," Rags said.

He told the story as best he could, feeling uncomfortably aware of Shining Talon's attention on him, his lack of contribution. When Rags got to the part about the fae being held captive by mirrorcraft, Inis sat down hard, and Somhairle's knuckles grew white where he was holding on to a chair.

Rags felt another stab of guilt.

Maybe the voice behind the door back in the fae ruins had been right. He was caught up in something so much grander than his means, and yet no one seemed willing to acknowledge that and turn him loose.

When he'd finished talking, his throat felt dry.

"Forgive me." That was Somhairle, his voice so thin it might snap at any moment. His gaze rested on Shining Talon. "I didn't know. That my mother could— I truly believed you to be the last of your kind. To realize you aren't . . ."

He trailed off, casting about for somewhere to sit, then chose the edge of the bed, looking like an old man. Three left Shining Talon to land on Somhairle's shoulder and comb his hair with her beak. Preening him for comfort.

Rags shrugged. "Guess we all thought wrong." Shining Talon was practically back to his sleep-for-a-thousand-years state, Somhairle's pale skin looked ashen, and Inis was fussing with the hem of her sleeve, pulling so hard on the threads that she'd soon tear the fabric.

Rags couldn't join them in their shock. His brain was working overtime. Seemed likely that the only reason Shining Talon hadn't joined his kind in the chamber of miserable mirrors was because he was leading Morien toward this other, greater power. Otherwise he'd be down there with the rest, color being sucked out of him to feed some no-good sorcerer plot.

Because of course Morien had to know about this, had to be behind it. Maybe it was how he'd learned about the fae ruins, why he'd sent Rags and the other thieves before him after this mysterious treasure he couldn't explain.

Another stroke of insight: The collection of fae beneath the castle *had* to be why Morien was so damn powerful. Why he could pop in and out of rooms without warning, practice sorcery that shouldn't have been humanly possible.

He had a whole room full of paralyzed fae at his disposal, to replenish his power by draining theirs.

"He's doing it. Morien," Rags said. Wished he hadn't, but there it was, plain as day. Let the others look at him like he was paranoid until they realized he was deadly right. "It's why he can do the shit he does to us, and maybe why he doesn't feel like he needs to bother putting the same insurance on *you*, Somhairle. Prince. Your Lordship. Oh, what-the-fuck-ever. He's got *so much* he can draw on. He's collecting these fae wherever he can find them—not like *I* know where, but he seems to have plenty of intel about fae ruins, so he's searching them out one by one—to suck them dry. He takes what they've got, uses it for himself. And the mirrors are a part of that . . . uh . . . somehow."

Another thought dawned on him. More like smacked him in the head with how bad it'd be if he were right.

"He's using us, too," Rags continued. "But not like we think.

We're going to help him find all the pieces of the Great Paragon, right? Or else he'll tear us to shreds, murder the rest of Inis's family while she watches, blah blah. But what if, once we get the piece that's *supposed* to be Shiny's, Morien's figured out how to put a shard in a fae? What if he transfers our connections so *he's* the one in charge of them? With enough fae power, what couldn't he do?"

After a long, wretched silence, Inis let out a shaky breath. "I hate that you're not as stupid as you look," she said.

She wasn't the only one.

But if Rags was in this, *really* in it, then he was going to throw everything he had at it. Morien would regret finding someone clever enough to beat the traps the fae had set.

Rags had slipped every snare but the last one, Shining Talon himself, who had landed him here. And he'd had nothing in the weeks since but experience and time to work out how to avoid repeating the same mistakes.

From here on, when he worked to free himself of Morien's machinations, he'd make sure to dodge that final hook.

74

SOMHAIRLE

There were, by Rags the thief's count, twenty-seven fae trapped underneath the palace. Twenty-seven fae gathered and imprisoned on Queen Catriona's command. Twenty-seven fae exploited, suffering, as Somhairle drew free breath after free breath.

Mm-hmm, Three agreed. *Things are worse than I feared. And what I feared wasn't pretty.*

Twenty-seven fae, and Somhairle still hadn't made the connection with Three that he needed in order to find the next master. The next fragment of the Great Paragon. The next step in the path to rescuing the cruelly enslaved fae.

That was treason. Unquestionable.

Equally unquestionable was that it had to be done.

A yet more complicated prospect when the Crown was one's mother.

"You're quiet," Inis said. "You're . . . suffering."

Somhairle blinked. He stood, drawing Inis after him. Rags was sleeping off the effect of the blindfold, Shining Talon sat unmoving as an inanimate relic, and Somhairle was ready to return to Morien's sight. He pulled Inis's blindfold free, tucking it into a pocket. "Time is of the essence, Inis. We *must* find the next master." Now that Morien was listening, he added, "I shall redouble my efforts. We'll leave the thief to rest. The Last awaits our success, and I'd rather not disappoint him."

His only lead, however, had been a spark of hope that it might be Laisrean. Someone he cared for, one of the few people truly connected to him.

Finding the next master had come easily to Inis.

Never assume anything comes easily to anybody, summer lad, Three cautioned.

Inis had scarcely lifted her head since they'd arrived on the Hill, as though a blade hung over the back of her neck.

Faced with Rags's discovery, a prince—Somhairle—had chosen treason. It was no longer unthinkable that the Ever-Loyals might have done the same, with the same knowledge.

"I shall find Laisrean." Somhairle found his voice as they entered his inner rooms. This was similar to fighting through a day of pain. He had to keep moving. If he settled, grief and shock would catch him, and those were more dangerous than his mother's silver eyes. "It could still be him. We just have to find the silver, too."

Trust me, Three said. *Be patient.*

Somhairle did trust her, but patience wasn't implicit in that trust.

"You aren't tired?" Inis's voice held no judgment.

"Not yet." With Three's weight on one shoulder, Somhairle's gait was lighter, more even than it had been with the crutch and the brace. "Well, tired of being a disappointment to those around me, perhaps."

He smiled, small and fey, so Inis would know he was poking fun. Plagued with doubts as he was, they were another price to pay for adventure.

Though there was a stinging familiarity to his current position. Once again, not made to the standard of his fellows.

Less familiar was the silence, interrupted only by the sound of their footfalls, in the Ivory Wing of the palace. Floors tiled in opals and pearl. The neat click of Inis's heels. No Ever-Ladies lunching in the solarium, no Ever-Lords raucously debating in the drawing room. What few servants passed did so with their heads lowered like Inis's, none of them greeting Somhairle as their prince other than to step widely out of his way.

Inis slipped her arm through Somhairle's as they took the moon-stone stairs down, sideways, then slowly upward.

Laisrean's rooms were in the Crystal Wing, where the iridescent gleam of white stones battled diamond-bright patterns of paned glass.

Hanging mirrors decorated the walls, their glittering frames wrought in the twisted shapes of brambles, antlers, and bones.

A swift flicker of blue reflected in a panel down the hall. Somhairle hesitated by the nearest open door, which led to one of the palace's many libraries. Inis came to a halt alongside him, Two's silver tail poking out from beneath her skirts.

Is now really the time for a story? Inis's expression said.

"Laisrean?" Somhairle called out, stepping over the threshold. The mirrors could see him doing what looked like Morien's bidding.

But it wasn't Laisrean dressed in blue. It was Lord Faolan Ever-Learning, slouched in a handsome chair, and he didn't look happy to greet an old friend. Not even one whose home he'd recently invaded.

"Your Highness!" Faolan didn't stand, though his gaze slurred warmly from Somhairle to Inis. "And *treasured guest*! Please, sit, if you'd like. I can't say much for the company, but the drinks are excellent."

"We really can't stay." The edge of hostility in Inis's voice, the arch of one of Faolan's dark brows over his long, sharp nose, the glare of mirrors set along every paneled bookshelf, made Somhairle light-headed.

"Speaking for a prince? Even a mostly exiled one? *Tut.*" Faolan swept a gloved hand over the books in front of him, spilling a glass of wine in the process and splattering his nearby papers. Old, precious maps, sections of fae designs, the stuff Somhairle's dreams were made of, blotted at with a silky handkerchief, smeared rich red. Destroyed. "You forget your manners. Too long from court. Well then! Don't allow *me* to detain you in your *important business.*"

Faolan stood, swaying and clasping Somhairle's shoulder to do so. His breath wine-sweet, then wine-sour. Inis looked away in disgust and missed the intimate press of paper from Faolan's palm to Somhairle's.

Faolan staggered away, deeper into the library.

"Ah, another shining example of Queen Catriona Ever-Bright's court," Inis muttered.

Somhairle turned his back to her for the moment it took to fumble open Faolan's note. Written not in the impeccable hand Somhairle recalled, but hurriedly, almost blindly. As though he hadn't been looking at the words as he wrote them. Or as though he couldn't, for fear of who might see them through his eyes.

It was signed only with a fingerprint in red, a smudge from the spilled wine.

> *JUST BECAUSE THERE IS NO SHARD IN YOUR
> HEART DOES NOT MEAN SHE IS NOT WATCHING.
> THERE ARE EYES ON EVERY PRINCE. ALWAYS.*

Somhairle twisted the note away into a fold of one sleeve, to be burned later. After he decided how to share Faolan's warning with the others.

Preferably once he'd figured out what it meant.

"We should find Laisrean," Somhairle said, cheeks hot, "without further distraction."

75
INIS

Laisrean was only available for dinner later that night, though the delay heartened Somhairle greatly once he learned of Two's origins. He seemed hopeful that Laisrean's silverware would undergo a similar transformation.

"Eat extra for me," Rags said sulkily, flopping down on the arm of the chair in which Shining Talon sat silent. "I'll keep an eye on this one. Show *him* how it feels to have somebody clucking and fussing and not letting him breathe."

Inis reached out to Shining Talon, thinking to take his hand. To show him compassion. To explain that she was afraid they would be easily defeated if they weren't in this together, that she was afraid they would never leave the palace if they didn't act quickly.

What she saw in his eyes was a reflection of her own loss, and she recoiled.

Yet away from them, alone inside her dressing room, without Rags and his loud mouth filling her head with noise, there was nothing to distract Inis from the promise of seeing Laisrean again.

There was no way he could recognize her.

A piece of her wished he would. Managing her rage was as much a part of her day-to-day as breathing, but the beast that stirred when Laisrean took her hand was an enemy she no longer understood.

Maybe, if he had to look her in the eye, he'd explain to her why her brothers and father had been taken from her, murdered in cold blood in the middle of the night. How he could still wear those leather cords around his wrist when his mother's Queensguard had been the ones to execute—

Inis shook her head, dabbing extra powder over her nose. Her hand shook, a dusting of snow white spilling onto her chemise.

It was next to impossible to get dressed without a mirror, but she couldn't trust her own reflection these days.

"Are you sure this isn't asking too much of you?" asked Somhairle at her back, as he watched her fumble in front of the cloak-obscured vanity. He looked so concerned for her. Had the face she was making been that awful?

She turned and dusted his nose with her powder brush. He sneezed. "I'll be fine. You know, no matter how much you wish for it, it might not be Laisrean."

"Then we'll have had the excuse to dine with pleasant company," Somhairle said, turning the coin queen-side up, as he always managed to do.

Inis kept her mouth shut. In a mood like this, she'd start a fight with anyone. Even Somhairle, who didn't deserve it.

"I'll see you there," she told him instead. She needed a minute to clear her head, to be free of princes both friendly and foreign.

If you did *want to fight, there are plenty of bones around here worth crunching,* Two said lazily, without looking up from where he was curled at the foot of her bed.

I need you to stay where you are, Inis replied. *Keep an eye on Rags and Shining Talon while Somhairle and I are gone. Make sure they don't do anything stupid.*

Could chomp on the little thief's bones for you. When Inis shook her head, Two sighed. *You say no, but you'd smile if I did it.*

Inis pursed her lips. There was a dress on the bed, skirts and bodice the color of the sky between the moons at twilight, a ghostly purple-blue that shimmered nearly silver in low light. A gift from Morien, another costume to help her play her part. It was extravagant, not Inis's usual style. Certainly not what she'd grown accustomed to during House Ever-Loyal's banishment.

Dressing like an Ever-Noble lady without the assistance of Ever-Noble servants took more than one attempt, but she managed to secure the laces and adjust the neckline of the dress, making certain everything settled in the right places.

The gown made her skin glow like fresh cow's milk. Or maybe that was Morien's glamour.

She gave Two a final pat on the head and left.

Laisrean might be able to see through the glamour if they were alone for too long. And there was another issue Inis couldn't shove aside, which was whether she'd make it through a meal with Laisrean without giving herself away.

Chomp chomp, Two called to her as she made her way to Laisrean's wing of the castle.

A servant guided her through the rooms until they reached one lit with handsome candlelight, a steady fire in the fireplace, and a table set with the latest delicacies.

The rooms had changed since the last time Inis had—

She swallowed, ignored the flash of memory better this round than the last. Somhairle hadn't arrived yet. She should never have sent him away, should have known arriving in numbers was the safer bet.

"Ah." Laisrean, who'd been reading on a couch by the fire, shut his book and stood. His broad face broke into a smile, banishing the hint of shadows beneath his eyes, as though he'd been up too late the night before. Attending a fancy ball, no doubt. Inis dropped into a quick, deep curtsy. "No need to be so formal. Sit, please. I'm sure my brother will be along any moment."

"It's not like him to be late," Inis agreed. In the firelight, Laisrean was more golden than brown. There was kindness in his eyes: polite but distant, meant to keep guests at arm's length. His black hair had been wetted, then combed to keep it in place.

Inis remained standing and cast her gaze to the fire in front of her. Slowly, she unclenched her hands and used them to smooth out her billowing skirts.

You are not Inis Fraoch Ever-Loyal, she told herself. Ailis was uncomplicated, with no history to weigh her down. She cast about for something to discuss before silence settled and suffocated.

What was he reading?

"You look tired," she said.

Laisrean laughed, then startled at the sound coming from himself. He gazed into the fire as though he sought what Inis saw there, and Inis looked away toward the mantel, where one of the servants had placed a bouquet of red and orange lilies.

"Forgive me." Her cheeks were hot, her expression horrified. "I spoke out of turn. Prince Somhairle told me how hard his brothers work on the Hill, and I . . ." Inis did her best not to choke on the words. If Somhairle didn't arrive soon, Inis didn't trust herself to maintain this deception.

The first time she'd repaired the thatching of the cottage roof with Bute, it had taken her hours to learn how to prevent the sharp stalks from slicing her hands. It had been a hard-won lesson, paid with a hundred tiny cuts.

She felt the same trying to maintain her composure alone in Laisrean's room, trying not to think about his mother's role in the ruin of her family.

Trying not to notice the way his shoulders strained at the fabric of his fine tunic. Would he ever stop growing?

"It's far from nonstop balls and banquets, if that's what you're asking," Laisrean answered.

The words alone were easy, friendly, but there was a sharp look in Laisrean's eyes. He knew Inis had said the wrong thing and was trying to figure out how to proceed. He took a step toward her, and like it was a dance, Inis stepped away.

The fire burned at her back. Any further retreat and she'd singe her skirts. She smelled smoke and lilies and imagined the Lost-Lands burning again.

Queen Catriona liked beautiful things. Unless they stood in her way.

"I fear I've forgotten my place." Inis lifted a hand, restless, to brush a stray lock of glamoured blond hair from her forehead.

Laisrean touched her wrist, fingers gentle against the place where it narrowed to meet the heel of her hand. "I don't mind it myself. But it's best not to speak out of turn in front of your friend Morien the Last. I warned my brother, but he trusts people."

Threat? Or joke? If Inis fought his hold, she'd know by whether he hung on or let go. Defiant, she lifted her chin, daring him to be the one to crack the veneer between them.

Laisrean didn't tighten his hold. He looked at her, not through her. So focused on her that she became the only true thing in the room.

The fire blazed. Her skin thrummed with its heat, its orange reflection in Laisrean's eyes. For one scant moment, it was as if he knew her. The same quality had drawn her to Somhairle: he made her feel seen. But what anchored Inis to one prince cast her out to sea from another.

"There's something about your eyes," Laisrean said.

He couldn't see her. He couldn't know her.

"Your Highness, please . . ." Inis demurred as her words curled, turning to white ash on her tongue.

A faint knock at the door. Laisrean dropped her hand as if it were a hot iron and went to answer. Inis wanted to open the windows and let the cold night air rip her chignon loose from its careful pinnings. She wanted to press her hands to her face, to rend her skin and scream, become the Morien-warped reflection she saw in every mirror.

Instead, she stepped away from the mantel and folded her hands politely in front of her. Somhairle and Three stepped inside, the former with sincere apologies and a bashful explanation—"I used to turn right at the mirrors to find your wing, but there are mirrors everywhere now, aren't there?"—for his delay.

Again, she took in Somhairle's newfound grace. It was remarkable. All he'd needed was a giant silver hunting bird to balance him out.

"Welcome, little one." Laisrean patted Somhairle on the shoulder, his smile bright again for his brother. "I'm not sure I have anything that's to your owl's liking, but no matter. Plenty for the rest of us."

Somhairle paused for only the briefest of seconds when he caught sight of Inis. She didn't know what she looked like, and she didn't want to know. Cheeks hot, she offered Somhairle a tight smile.

"You look lovely," Somhairle said, his discretion a continued blessing. "Is that a new dress?"

Inis told herself not to look at Laisrean as she turned in a slow spin. How could she succeed at being someone else when the sharpest parts of her kept poking through?

All she had to do was breathe to the end of this dinner. Whatever came next, she'd breathe through that, too.

"Let's sit—eat. I don't know about you—well, *your* appetite could always use some encouragement, Somhairle—but I'm ravenous."

Laisrean held out a chair for Inis first, then helped his brother sit, giving Three a companionable pat, which she arched into.

Traitor. How could she like him?

And how could Inis want him to look at her again, to see her, while knowing what she knew?

Inis focused on her food, and Laisrean and Somhairle shouldered the brunt of the conversation. Mostly Laisrean did the talking, sharing news about their other brothers, about shifting court politics, about his latest job inspecting the Queensguard in search of traitors. Inis sat up straight and took small bites.

She'd aroused his suspicion before, couldn't afford to draw further attention.

"That must mean you've been working with Lord Faolan." Somhairle frowned, stole a glance in Inis's direction. The silverware hadn't transformed, they were on their fourth course, and they had crossed into dangerous territory in the conversation. "Fighting the . . . what was it?" An impressive touch, since Somhairle knew full well. "Ah, the Resistance."

Laisrean waved a spoonful of herbed potatoes before pausing to eat it. "You know how Mother is. She sees spies and traitors everywhere. She has me chasing down little leads and putting in my time to show she values the Queensguard. It's a sensitive subject, since the fall of House Ever-Loyal."

Was it Inis's imagination, or had Laisrean been looking straight at her when he said that last part? He'd turned her blood to shards of glass as easily as a sorcerer with his spells.

"Can't say I get the opportunity to spend much time with any of her sorcerers, though." Laisrean's attention was back on Somhairle. "How'd you meet Morien the Last? The man's always busy."

"I've had his unique company at Ever-Bright Manor for weeks now." Inis had to admire how smoothly Somhairle could insult someone while stirring a bowl of soup, waiting for the broth to cool.

"Hm. And he invited you back to court with him, did he? Think it has something to do with Her Majesty? Nice surprise for Mother, that sort of thing? Or because she asked him to bring you?"

"I'd never presume to know her thoughts."

"Haven't seen her lately?"

"Only her reflection in mirrorcraft. Gifts come from the castle, but of course she doesn't have time to visit. I'm not here to take over your job, if you're worried about that. I couldn't do it. Roaming about with the guards, talking to them man-to-man . . . I doubt they'd be convinced."

Laisrean tore into a hunk of buttered bread with a snort. Inis rearranged the vegetables on her plate. Her appetite had departed for good when she again saw the leather cords around Laisrean's thick wrist, on display after he'd rolled up his sleeves to eat. She had to keep from staring at them and willing them to burst into flames on Laisrean's arm. Instead, she stabbed a carrot, sliced it in half, and went in search of something else to dismember.

"—carrot ever do to you?" Laisrean was asking.

"My apologies," Inis murmured. "I've never been in such royal company. Is it impolite to eat in front of people one wishes to impress?"

Laisrean laughed. "She's fascinating, Somhairle. Where'd you find her?"

Somhairle didn't have to come up with another quick lie. Three fluttered her wings and knocked over his glass. It landed in Inis's lap, wine spattered like fresh blood on the pale silk.

Inis leaped to her feet amid a flurry of Somhairle's apologies. Laisrean lunged across the table with a handful of cloth napkins, while Three took off and flew in circles overhead. Somhairle's attention shifted to his owl and his expression barely changed. Inis was too busy mopping the red stains off her skirts to notice Somhairle snatching the blindfold from her pocket, until he'd pressed it to her chest.

He must have heard something from Three. But what?

Inis reached behind herself to finish the deed. She tied the knot without hesitation.

Laisrean froze when he saw the blindfold. Not another napkin to sop up the damage, and he knew it instantly. His face changed. Inis recognized his new expression before he managed to cover it, almost immediately, with perfect courtly training.

It was fear.

But why would a loyal prince be frightened of a sorcerer's blindfold?

"Little brother. Where'd you get that?" Laisrean asked.

"You." Somhairle's cheeks were flushed and feverish. "*You're* a—"

He didn't get the chance to finish. Laisrean clapped a big hand over Somhairle's mouth, moving with unexpected speed for someone so big. There was grace, agility, muscle under his weight.

Shh, he mouthed. Inis realized he'd angled them so he was between Somhairle and the mirror over the fireplace. As though he didn't want them to be seen. As though someone were watching through the glass.

"Little brother!" Laisrean spoke loudly. "Why, you're choking! Shouldn't try to talk with a full mouth! What manners are they teaching you out there in Ever-Land? Come, let me take care of you!" He hauled Somhairle along, remained between Inis and the mirror, indicated with his eyes that she should follow him.

His body shielding her, she went with him into the next room, where the only mirror in sight was covered with a red cloth.

A red cloth exactly like the one Inis still clutched to her chest.

Laisrean kicked the door shut behind them and released Somhairle gently, setting him on the edge of the bed.

This was Laisrean's bedroom.

"Sorry for the manhandling," he said, very quietly. "Couldn't let you say what I suspected you were about to when you could be overhead. Almost had my cover blown once today, and I couldn't risk it a second time."

"—you're a *spy*," Somhairle concluded.

"What gave it away?" Laisrean eyed Three as he said it, already suspected it had to do with the owl.

"You met with someone she knows last night. It's—complicated," Somhairle said.

Laisrean folded his arms over his chest and leaned back against the door. "I'll try to follow along," he replied.

Since the moment they'd met, Shining Talon had been impossible. Rags couldn't take a step without the fae in his shadow, couldn't rise on a stormy day without Shining Talon shielding him from the rain. There was no telling him different. He was stubborn as he was regal, and it drove Rags to distraction that he couldn't make the big lug see reason.

In earlier days, seized by extreme frustration, Rags had even wished that Shining Talon would climb back into the coffin where Rags had found him and *go to sleep*.

Until Shining Talon started doing his best impression of a Sleeping fae all over again.

Rags never thought he'd actually see this. But now Shining Talon didn't speak. He didn't move. He was so caught in his private misery that Rags suspected he could throw himself out the window and Shining Talon wouldn't look up.

Which was fine. Really. Rags should've known better than to get used to something. Everything, good and bad, got snatched away in the end, since time was the greatest thief of them all.

That didn't mean he was happy about it.

"You know, this is the last thing we need." Rags paced back and forth in front of Shining Talon, barefoot on the fancy rug. On top of everything that was making him itch with frustration, there was *another* added weight: he couldn't talk about what they'd seen. Not directly. Using the nap-and-blindfold trick required two people, and Rags's partner in crime was currently out of commission.

Maybe permanently. This was why Rags *always* worked alone.

"You're looking queasy. We should see if Prince Sunshine or Lady Fury can order you some soup. Do your people eat soup? Or is that impossible, given the way they feel about spoons?"

Rags had given up looking for any change in Silent Talon's expression. The crossbones at the corners of his mouth stayed put. And what was the point of staring at what once had been animated, only to be confronted with the equivalent of a tragic oil painting?

So Rags looked out the window instead. Watched the Queensguard in their shiny plate armor running drills in the courtyard. Thought about how *Shiny* needed a better nickname. Forget stealing: this was the first job Rags had done where he was hoping to make it out of the place with what little he'd had when he arrived. Like still-breathing lungs. He wondered if Angry Inis was going to get through this in one piece after everything she'd lost. And if Somhairle was truly willing to throw his family over for the fae, because fuck what was right, he had blood *and* money to protect.

Rags belonged here least of anyone, and he'd enjoyed a lifetime of being stepped on to enforce that knowledge. Inis was new to it. She'd been born Ever-Noble, then had her world shoved into a smaller box, shuttering its bright expanse when it was packed away.

There'd been a time when Rags never would've worried about any of this shit. The fact that he did now had to be Shining Talon's fault.

Evening passed into night, and the Queensguard drills ended late.

Rags turned away from the window, disgusted with himself and the state of his life.

"Gonna lie down for the night," he said, expecting nothing in response. "Make sure I don't catch whatever's got your tongue. Maybe the windlings are making a comeback."

It wasn't a ruse. He was exhausted by the prospect of throwing himself against Shining Talon's stony grief for the rest of the evening while Inis and Somhairle were at a fancy dinner.

Rags, for the first time in his life, wasn't hungry.

After closing his eyes, he had barely enough time to inhale before he felt the blindfold being pulled from his pocket and tied around his chest.

When Rags opened his eyes again, Shining Talon wasn't looming over him. Instead, he was stretched out next to Rags, lying on his back with his hands folded over his stomach.

He looked like he had in the coffin. Like those fae they'd found trapped in the mirror room. The thought of him under the ground without Rags to come dig him out made Rags shiver.

Shining Talon had to *quit this shit* or Rags was going to lose it.

"I am causing you distress." Shining Talon's voice was soft. "This is not my intention."

"*You're* distressed," Rags said. "You get to be. I'd say I get it, but I don't. I don't have an entire people to mourn."

"I cannot leave this place," Shining Talon said. "I've sworn an oath to you, an oath I would not break, but abandoning those trapped . . . it would be a crime of the highest order."

"I know." Rags licked his chapped lips like a snake testing the ground in front of him. He didn't want the earth to crumble under his feet like it had in that fae maze. "Listen. Remember Dane? I told you about him. Only . . ." Only not really. He hadn't told Shining Talon everything. Hadn't told anybody.

Silence followed. Rags let himself believe it was his duty to fill it.

"I was ten. Maybe twelve. The years blur together when you don't know how old you are, you know?" Shining Talon knew. He'd needed to ask the water how many years had passed while he'd been sleeping. "I used to rummage through the butcher's garbage for scraps. And there was this kid. He caught me once. Offered to bring me better cuts, if he could sneak 'em away." Rags laughed through his nose. "Obviously not meant for the street life. But that's exactly what he wanted. We'd sit in that alley and he'd beg me to tell him stories about the Clave, the other thieves there, what I'd stolen that day, how I almost got caught, how I'd hidden for hours in a pile of laundry, like it was all some kinda game. Sometimes, when he showed, he'd have these big purple bruises on his arms or his face. Said he fell, or walked into the meat slicer. Clumsy kid."

Rags rolled his eyes. Sometimes they'd stayed on the roof all day, watching the sun sink like a fat golden coin beneath the Hill. The heat of the roof tiles against his back, sunlight in Dane's hair, the goofy wheeze of his laugh: it was all as vibrant as ever. "Used to listen to me like I was the royal bard mouthing off about princesses in Storyteller Square."

Rags looked at Shining Talon out of the corner of his eye, but he was staring up at the bed canopy. Impossible to know whether he was listening. But Rags had started telling the story. He had to finish it.

"It wasn't long before he was saying he wanted to join me. I'd train him in the thief's life, and we'd live free on the streets." Rags scratched an itch on his nose. "I don't gotta tell you that a butcher's kid's never gone hungry. He was soft, inside and out. I was using him for food and that clapboard never suspected. I told him he was an idiot. No way I was taking any apprentice, and especially not one so green."

Rags's throat clenched, tight and hot.

"But he wouldn't leave it alone. Kept nagging. Going on and on about how great it'd be. Eventually, I got fed up. I was settling into the city, making my mark, and I didn't need a starry-eyed kid dragging me down. The next time he talked about running away from home to pick pockets with me, I stopped coming around. No more back-alley butcher's shop visits. The meals weren't worth the hassle."

Rags waited for something, anything, from Shining Talon. A disapproving look, a wrinkled nose. Nothing. Probably he wasn't listening, and Rags was telling this story for no one but himself.

Rags kept telling it.

"Life happened. I got pinched selling off an old lady's prized emerald brooch, and I did six months in lockup. After that, I had to build myself back up again, practically from scratch. Didn't have time to think about Dane. It was over a year before I went back to the butcher's shop to check on the kid. Felt bad, you know? Wanted him to see that I was still kicking, in case he was worried."

Rags was cursing himself for starting this. He'd never thought about how awful it'd feel to share this part with someone else.

"When I finally made it back, the butcher's shop was boarded up. Full of squatters. I fished the story out of one of them. The butcher and his wife left one night, split town without telling anyone where they were going. Locals waited the respectful amount of time before they started looting, and meat spoils something awful. Nobody thought much of the stink. Took a while before they found Dane's body in the cold room, stacked between sides of beef." Rags coughed a nervous laugh, though the story wasn't funny. "They had to stop and call in the Queensguard after that. Law said his head was knocked in. Could've fallen. Always was a clumsy kid."

Dane had been running from something, from someone hurting him, and Rags had been too caught up in his own worries to notice. He wasn't anybody's savior.

He didn't want to fail Shining Talon the way he'd failed Dane.

"What I'm saying is"—Rags stared burning holes into the canopy over the bed, unblinking, until his vision blurred—"we don't have to take off. Who said anything about leaving?"

"You have been moving." Shining Talon spoke at last. "You have not stopped moving. I assumed this implied more travel was imminent."

Rags groaned.

"And there are orders from the Lying One to find Four, Five, and Six," Shining Talon continued. "When those orders change, they may require a new journey—"

"In case you haven't noticed, Prince Sweetheart hasn't figured out where he's supposed to go next. We're stuck here until he does. I guess we're gonna have to use the opportunity to bust your buddies out."

"They are children." Shining Talon released a long breath that sounded like he'd been holding it since their discovery of the mirror chamber.

"Shit," Rags said.

"Yes, it is shit," Shining Talon agreed. Rags didn't laugh at the curse on his perfect fae tongue. "I know I am young. I am a warrior who has not proven himself. I was unable to protect you from the Lying One. Neither am I able to protect them. They are dying."

"Quit feeling sorry for yourself, Tal." Rags tried out the new nickname, let it roll around behind his teeth. Couldn't call him *Shiny* after they'd found that glittering torture chamber, all silver blood and polished glass. "Clouds the mind. Gotta keep that clear for working out how to pull off the craziest jailbreak in . . . well, ever. Thriftlamb the Unstoppable wouldn't even try this. But we're gonna save those kids."

For Dane, and all the others like him ground up by the city.

Rags felt something tug at his wrist. Tal's fingers hooked under his sleeve, drawing him close. Their fingers interlaced like a key turning in its lock, the bolts sliding seamlessly into place. Rags stared at the ceiling, aware of his palm pressed to Tal's as they lay side by side. The fragment in Rags's pocket warmed with approval.

"You are exactly who I knew you would be," Tal said, "from the moment I opened my eyes."

"You like the nickname, then?" Rags asked, because his throat was tight again, his cheeks hot.

He half turned on the bed, aware of the hard, bony press of Tal's hip against his own. Did fae have bones of iron? No, it was iron they despised. The Ancient Ones, giant beasts, had skeletons of stone, which Oberon Black-Boned had used to build his court.

Their palaces were the bodies of age-old creatures. And here was Tal, a prince of his people.

Rags's head swam with possibility, with the desire to climb on top of Tal and try to wrestle some of the impossible grief out of him. But there was a shadow in the beat of his heart. Pain like a splinter deeply embedded.

This wasn't the time. *Daring as ravens,* Rags reminded himself. He'd found something more important than snatching what he wanted.

"You can stay, if you want," he said, "while I sleep."

Slowly, carefully, he settled into Tal's side. He set the palm of his free hand on Tal's shoulder. Then he closed his eyes, because looking at Tal while he suffered was too much from up close.

"I would like that," Tal agreed.

Never a moment of stillness until this. Rags knew it couldn't last. But for a few deep breaths, he let peace wash over him, holding the warmth of Tal's body against his.

77

CAB

Cab told Sil everything he'd learned from her contact while, a flight of stairs down in the Gilded Lily, Einan died onstage.

She returned covered in a paste that smelled suspiciously like red wine and didn't bother going behind the screen to change out of her soiled costume. Cab accidentally saw a flash of her slim, flat chest before scrambling to look away.

"Well, you survived." Einan came back into Cab's line of sight wearing a simple shift dress, whipping her red hair out of her face into a braid. Her lips were stained berry-dark, shapely against the ghost white of her freckled face. "That's something. Betray us all yet?"

Cab didn't know where to rest his eyes. At least he'd spent enough time with Einan that her barbs no longer hooked into his skin. "I swore myself to your cause and I meant it. I'll do whatever it takes to earn your trust."

Einan snorted in reply, then crouched at Sil's side. Took her hand, finger-combed Sil's hair out of her face.

I think I can help with earning their trust. One's voice, coming from far off. She hadn't returned with Cab to the theater. The distance didn't quiet her voice, simply colored it. He trusted her to make the right tactical decisions. Knew she wouldn't linger somewhere unless she had good reason. *I'll check in with the others.*

Others? Cab asked.

Some old friends, One replied.

Then she went silent, leaving Cab to rise to the occasion and figure things out.

Sleep didn't come easily after Cab shared the news from Sil's contact: that the Queensguard was patrolling more ruthlessly, that the excavation efforts had tripled, and—this last being a suspicion One had confirmed earlier—that Three of Many had been found and was currently at the castle.

Morien now had two pieces of the Great Paragon under his control to the Resistance's one.

"Quit tossing and turning," Einan hissed at Cab sometime near to dawn. "Is this how you plan on taking down the Resistance? By making sure we can't get a decent night's sleep?"

Cab was startled to find her so close. His old instincts should have measured better. He didn't know how to apologize.

In the end, he remained on his back with his arms crossed over his chest to avoid bothering Einan again, listening to her breathing as it steadied and softened into sleep.

In the far corner of the dressing room, Hope's open eyes glowed faintly through the night.

Come morning, Cab helped out around the Gilded Lily, hammering up a new piece of the set, while Einan took it on herself to check on the other members of the Resistance.

When she returned, her hands were shaking. Cab tried to steady her, and she didn't shake him off. Instead she pulled him into a hidden spot below the stage where there was no chance of being overheard.

Her cheeks and throat were red with anger and she still smelled of the wine-paste stage blood.

"Queensguard caught Malachy." She slammed her hand into a wooden beam that didn't look strong enough to withstand a second onslaught. Cab caught her arm, would stop her from breaking her hand if he had to. She stared at his fingers on her elbow. "I'm only telling *you* because telling Sil . . ."

"Malachy," Cab repeated. "The boy from the tunnels?"

Einan nodded. Her head rested briefly on Cab's shoulder. "He's only fourteen. Young, but his father's lands were taken by the Queen so she could search the grounds below. Found four fae buried there. Had to discredit Malachy's family to do it. Ruined their name and reputation to seize their estates. His father killed himself." She lifted her head and opened her eyes. They were burning. "Two years ago. Might've been *you* in the squad that served the papers."

Two years ago, it might have been.

"Einan," Cab said, because there was nothing else to say.

"Oh, *don't*—" Einan began.

The doors of the theater blew open and a company of Her Majesty's finest marched in, clanking down the aisles in perfect formation.

Cab's heart stuttered. The Queensguard in the lead held the theater's owner by the arm. Similar, but not similar at all, to the way Cab had gripped Einan's just now.

"This is a raid, conducted in the name of Her Majesty, Queen Catriona Ever-Bright, Shining Star of the Silver Court."

Legally, that was all they were required to say. The Queensguard captain shoved the theater owner to his knees.

Cab shifted his hammer in his hand, holding it not like a tool, but like a weapon. "Go," he told Einan.

He didn't need to elaborate. *Get Sil and Hope.*

Get what's important out of here.

To her credit, Einan hesitated. Then she dragged Cab toward her and kissed him fiercely on the mouth.

Cab had never kissed anyone. He'd buried such thoughts beneath layers of survival and duty, what it took to put one foot in front of the other.

He found he didn't mind the idea that Einan would be his first kiss and his last.

She'd appreciate the story. He wasn't going to get a chance to share it.

"*Go.*" Cab picked up an awl in his other hand and strode out of the hidden stage compartment, came forward to meet the Queensguard. Seven of them. Impossible odds. But he might be able to make a difference if he acted quickly, might be able to slow them down long enough for Einan to lead the others to escape. "Remember what matters."

"The *balls* on you," Einan sniffed, already leaping onto the stage with an acrobat's grace, "thinking you need to tell *me* what's important!"

The Queensguard clattered along the aisle toward him, then descended on him. Cab pierced one in the throat, through the joint where helmet met gorget. He took the sword out of the wounded Queensguard's hands as another elbowed him, knocking him down. That same Queensguard impaled himself as Cab thrust his stolen sword upward and lurched back to his feet.

Five against one.

The actors were screaming and fleeing. The theater owner had disappeared in the struggle. Cab hoped they'd make it out unscathed. In the background, Einan hollered something about how he had to survive this so she could give him what for, for overplaying the hero.

This wasn't a play. And if it were, it would be a tragedy.

A third Queensguard lunged at him and Cab swung the hammer into his wrist, dove backward into the seats.

He was messing up Einan's theater, but if he could lead the Queensguard out of the aisles and into the tighter, cramped audience quarters, he'd be able to use their numbers against them like he had in the sewers.

Another Queensguard swung at him, chunks of a wooden seat flying up from where his sword raked them loose.

"Go after the girl!" the captain bellowed. "We'll deal with this one."

"Not a chance." Cab jumped onto the seat backs, leaping across two aisles, lunging for the Queensguard who'd managed to break away. Tackled him around the neck. Sent them both crashing to the floor.

Since the Queensguard was in armor and Cab wasn't, it hurt Cab worse. He caught a steel elbow to the gut and sputtered, the wind knocked out of him. Another Queensguard rushed over while Cab was down, kicked him in the head and chest. Red blood sprayed from his nose. Cab saw stars.

Had he bought the others enough time?

Sorry, One, Cab thought. *Was looking forward to getting to know you better. To forming something bigger than myself.* The boot caught his cheek. Bone crunched. Instincts kicked in and Cab swung the hammer around, caught the Queensguard in the knee, metal plate smashed into his leg. The Queensguard howled and dropped, but another wrenched the hammer from Cab's hand, lifted it high.

Cab watched it rise, swore to himself he wouldn't shut his eyes against the blow when it fell.

It didn't fall.

Instead, silver raked across steel. The Queensguard over Cab whipped around as claws batted him aside. He was thrown hard into the far wall, taking half a row of seats with him as he flew across the theater. In his place, One rose on her hind legs, opened her mouth, and screamed a grinding snarl.

You look terrible. Your pretty face, she told Cab.

New strength surged through his limbs, as though he was also made of unbreakable fae silver. She offered him her power, letting it flow between them. The agony in his beaten body faded to a hum.

Cab rose as Hope appeared, braced his hands on One's back, launched himself over her head into the Queensguard's midst.

There were only three Queensguard left fighting, but watching Hope move, a gold-and-black blur, Cab realized that if there'd been thirty, the outcome would have been the same. In a flash they were down, Hope pummeling them through their armor with his bare hands.

His knuckles left dents in the metal.

He broke bones through plate, crushed helmets into skulls. Cab caught his breath while leaning on One for support, thought he heard her whistle with approval.

"That's enough." Cab's voice came out sticky with blood and

ragged with exertion. "They're down. They won't follow. And we have to get away before they send more."

Hope froze, fist in midair. He wavered. Wanted to keep going until the metal before him was pounded flat, the bodies inside nothing but pulp.

Then he lowered his arm and stood. Raced back toward Cab and One, vaulted over both of them. "This way," he said, "to Sil's side."

Hop on, One added.

She carried Cab out of the Gilded Lily—or what remained of it—his broken cheek pressed to her neck, his other wounds leaking blood over her silver shoulders and back.

He still had the Queensguard's sword gripped in his swollen-knuckled hand.

78
CAB

Einan led them through back alleys. Kept them out of sight as best she could. She had cloaks for Sil and Hope and an extra one she draped over Cab. They didn't dare use the sewers.

But they couldn't stay on the streets forever. Twice One's head perked up, agreeing with Hope and Sil that they needed to change their course. The Queensguard was out in full force. Busting down doors, kicking over tables, breaking bones.

If the Queensguard didn't find them first, someone else would take note of their odd-looking group and turn them in, seeking a reward.

For Cab, strategizing through the haze of pain that had returned in his throbbing head was a challenge. One could only numb his pain and bolster his strength for so long.

The bleeding had mostly dried up. He was damp with sweat and sore to the point of total collapse when Einan finally held up a hand. Cab took stock of their surroundings. He'd been concentrating so hard on not falling off One's back that he'd lost track of where Einan was leading them. Through one swollen eye and one good, he saw that they'd come around a back alley and into a garden, a sparse wooden fence separating it from the house behind it and the neighbors on either side. Glowbugs bobbed in the air around tall hollyhocks. Einan rapped twice on the back door.

Am I going to die? Cab asked One.

Not while I still live, One replied. *I'd never attach myself to someone so rude.*

Cab's arm trembled where he held on to One for support. He flinched when the door opened and golden light spilled out onto him.

Uaine stood in the open doorway, gray hair tied back with a red rag.

She surveyed the group. Cab, broken and bleeding; his silver lizard, who still looked like a dog in company; two short fae draped in black cloaks; and Einan. Without a word, Uaine stood aside, holding the door open to let them in.

Cab murmured his thanks, tasting blood on his teeth. Einan took him by the arm, more gentle than he'd thought her capable of, and steered him toward the kitchen sink.

"Sit." She pointed to a three-legged footstool. Cab sank onto it gratefully. One curled up at his feet. Sil and Hope were led to the table. Uaine went about the business of closing her shutters, putting out the lights one by one, until only three candles on the table remained lit, flickering.

By that bare light, Einan tipped Cab's face up toward hers and began to clean it, dabbing his cheeks with a wet rag that smelled of lemon soap. She wouldn't meet his eyes, too focused on the task at hand. Cab stared at her pursed lips, the bow curve soothing, distracting.

"I heard about Malachy," Uaine said. "Thought the safest thing might be to lie low. If anyone was watching and I led them to you . . ."

"No. You thought right. It was the sensible thing to do." Einan swiped the rag over the broken skin on the bridge of Cab's nose. It hurt. So did the rest of him. So much that he didn't think he'd be able to hold it together if it weren't for One at his feet. "Sadly, we've had a change of plans."

"I can see that." Uaine turned her attention to Hope. "I'm honored to welcome another of your kind into my home."

"They raided the Lily." Einan continued to work at Cab's wounds while she spoke. "Chin up, soldier, I didn't bring you here to die on Uaine's floor."

"Are you sure?" Cab winced, the words more painful than they were worth.

Einan met his eyes at last, and for a moment he wanted to smile. Even if he couldn't.

"I apologize for losing control of my fury." Hope stood, then knelt at Sil's feet. "Forgive me. In my rage, I may have cost us valuable time."

Sil rested a slim hand on Hope's head. Her expression was sorrowful, but at peace.

"Rise, Second Hope for Windsworn Glory," she said. "You have done nothing wrong."

"Saved my life," Cab agreed. *"Ow."*

"Hold still," Einan commanded.

Tell her that if she ruins your handsome face, I'll return the favor in kind. One's tail lashed over the floor.

"One says to be careful with me." Cab let Einan guide his hand to his face, holding the rag to his lip. The soap on it stung, which meant it was doing its job, but that didn't make the experience any less unpleasant.

"One should tell *you* to be careful with *your own damn self.*" Einan went for a cupboard like she owned the place. She fished out a few jars and returned to work. The first jar's jellied contents smelled of honey and the second's of cinnamon as she spread them on Cab's face, including over his split lip. He soon discovered they didn't taste as good as honey and cinnamon, but he weathered the treatment.

"Used to be a healer," Uaine explained as she fished beneath a loose floorboard for something. "That was before the digging started— and before the Queen wrote laws against us. Too dangerous to have anyone practicing the old ways. Only sorcerers allowed to practice magic. Try to heal a friend, and suddenly you're in Coward's Silence for five years, a menace to the crown. When I got out, everything I'd built, my business, my home—gone. And more of us common folk dying every day because healers can't do other than stitch and patch them and send them on their way."

Uaine found whatever she'd been looking for and popped it into an apron pocket. Einan finished tending to Cab's face with more of Uaine's salves. Wiped the muck off her hands with another rag. He had to admit that the throbbing and swelling in his face had eased. It was manageable now.

One yawned. *We can't stay.*

Yes. I won't bring any more trouble to innocent people, Cab agreed.

That's not what I meant, handsome, but it's sweet of you to care. Queensguard are already executing a full sweep of the city. There's nowhere safe for us here.

"What is it?" Einan squinted into Cab's face. Her hand was big and rough against his cheek. "You haven't lost *that* much blood. Aren't you as strong as you look? Weren't you trained by the bastards in black? Don't pass out on me."

"He isn't fading," Sil said. "The masters can commune with their fragments mind to mind. It is a connection only they can understand, though the fae are able to hear and share a little with all the fragments. It is the deepest of bonds."

"She gossiping about me?" Einan asked, nodding in One's direction.

Conceited little actress, One said. *Anyway, don't you think it's time for a plan?*

They need one. Badly, Cab agreed. *There aren't enough of them and they haven't been trained. They're barely holding it together.*

So are you. One rose, stretched, and flicked her tail, eyes locked on Einan. Teasing her, Cab realized. *Here's the news, master. I've been talking with Two and Three, and there are a few things you should know.*

After Somhairle explained, with Inis supplying any details he didn't know, why they'd come to the castle, what the owl really was, and who Inis really was, Laisrean put his head in his hands, sat down heavily on the floor.

He didn't look up for a long time.

At last, pushing his hair out of his broad, dark face, he met Inis's eyes. "I recognized you. I knew I did. Morien must be stretched thin to let his glamour flicker so carelessly. But then, he's planning something, and it's taking most of his attention. If you've got the mirror treatment, he must figure he doesn't have to worry about keeping too tight a rein on you." Laisrean swallowed, touched the leather cords around his wrist absently. He clearly wanted to say more.

Didn't.

Instead he faced Somhairle again. "The bastard didn't hurt you, though?"

Somhairle shook his head. "Not any more than I'm already hurt. No one looks at me and sees a threat."

"Right." Laisrean drew himself to his feet and rolled out his shoulders. "Better go back to your rooms, put that thing"—a dark look at the blindfold on Inis's chest—"away. I'll meet you there, and your friends. I have contacts. I might be able to get you to them, if—"

Three began to shriek, a high, heartrending sound.

Somhairle's face drained horror white, contorted with fear. Inis had never seen him so affected, and it pierced her like Morien's shard of mirrorglass. She froze in the center of the room. Laisrean moved before she could clear her mind, before she could ask Two what was happening, slung one arm around her shoulders and hoisted Somhairle nearly off his feet with the other. He pushed aside the velvet curtains next to his bed to reveal a narrow stone balcony shuttered behind glass doors, then dragged the red cover off his mirror while Inis opened the balcony doors.

Laisrean threw the red blanket around them like a cloak and pushed them outside, Three circling above their heads.

"Lais—" Somhairle began.

"Sorry." Laisrean snapped the doors shut between them. The *snick* of a lock followed. "Looks like I won't have time to introduce you to my friends."

Inis pounded the glass with her palm. Laisrean held a finger to his lips, touching the door on the other side.

Then he turned away, drawing the velvet curtains and hiding them from the room and the room from them.

Inside echoed a mighty splintering crash. Inis reached for Somhairle's hand. The glass wasn't so thick that they couldn't hear everything happening beyond. Footsteps—a group of Queensguard—and a voice that Inis knew well.

"Prince Laisrean Ever-Bright. I regret having to interrupt your dinner."

"Morien the Last," Laisrean said. "Didn't the swamp hags who raised you teach you any manners?"

Inis was aware of Somhairle trembling where they stood shoulder to shoulder, of Three wheeling furiously overhead. Two's silence chilled her. A bare sliver of light between the curtains, not enough to see much by.

Laisrean let out a strangled yell and fell to his knees. Inis caught sight of movement, Morien lifting his hand. The mirror Laisrean had uncovered glowed.

"I'm afraid there won't be any concern for etiquette where you're going, Prince Laisrean." Silver armor flashed past the crack in the curtains: Queensguard, surrounding Laisrean. "You're under arrest for consorting with enemies of the Crown."

No clever comebacks from Laisrean this time. Somhairle clutched the red fabric tight and Inis peered forward despite herself. Laisrean lay on the ground, curled up and twitching like a dying insect. He cried out once, growled a curse. Then he was silent.

Rage coursed through Inis's veins, a siren song that would dash her on the rocks. She couldn't rush to Laisrean's side no matter how much she wanted to.

This was like hiding with Ivy in the closet while—

"Search his rooms." Morien said. "I want to know how this treason was able to fester."

Somhairle covered his face with his weak hand. Inis risked a glance over her shoulder, calculating how high up they were. They couldn't jump and they couldn't overpower Morien and his Queensguard. Not with Somhairle's condition. Not with the shard in Inis's heart.

The crashes continued as the Queensguard searched Laisrean's room, overturning furniture, tearing pillows open with their swords.

The beat of wings above made Inis look up. Three was swelling in shape, rearranging her metal components, stretching from a normal-sized owl to a bird the size of a small horse. Somhairle sucked in a breath, his gaze suddenly glassy. A flash of silver in his eyes.

"Yes," Somhairle said. The frailty in his voice was almost unbearable. "Do it."

Three hovered low and picked them up in her claws. Together they rose along the outside of the castle, heading back to Somhairle's wing.

80
RAGS

Rags was drawing a map of the castle with a sooty finger on the floor when shit literally hit his window.

The only thing Rags could think as Inis, Somhairle, and Three crashed onto the balcony, shattering the glass to burst into the room, was how lucky he was that he still had the sorcerer's cloth over his heart.

Rags tried to calm said heart. It hadn't reacted well to the surprise, his first thought being, *Fuck, they've found us plotting crazy treason*; his second, *If Morien's mirrorcraft isn't what kills me, a surprise like this is gonna do the trick.*

Inis was the first to her feet, Two bounding to her side from the other room. Flash of silver in her eyes, and she nodded.

"We have to get out of here," she said.

"Right, except there's Morien to consider—" Rags began.

Inis shook her head. "This fabric—it can keep us hidden." Something caught her attention and she cursed, a gutter phrase she'd definitely picked up from Rags. Couldn't have learned that one with her fine upbringing.

Rags would've mentioned it if she hadn't lost her mind and started breaking all the turned-around mirrors in the room. One hanging over the fireplace instead of artwork, a second, small one on a tea table. When she was done with the ones in that room, she went storming into the next, and the sound of shattering glass continued.

Meanwhile, Somhairle was still dragging himself to his feet, Three at his shoulder to help.

"Want to explain why she's gone mad?" Rags asked. Paused. "Madder than usual, and not at me, I mean."

"She's blowing off steam." Somhairle gasped for air, cheeks flushed in red spots, wincing as he straightened his bad leg. "But she's right. We need to get out of here. It isn't safe. Morien's distracted"—now he winced from more than physical pain—"but he won't be for long."

"No fucking kidding. We've known that since—"

"There's a Resistance against the Crown," Somhairle explained. "I know it's troubled Her Majesty for some time, but I never knew it was serious. We've just discovered that Prince Laisrean is helping it. If he is, he has good reason to."

"Yeah." Rags bent down, smeared his diagrams into nothing with his palm, then wiped the soot off his skin and onto the rug. "No offense, *again*, but your mother's a power-hungry kidnapper who's keeping fae *kids* hostage so her sorcerers can have near unlimited power. I'd say that's good enough reason." Rags took a deep breath. "We can't leave. Not while those kids are still captive. They're dying and it's—" A glance at Tal showed he was watching Rags with a glow in his eyes, the first time he'd started shining again since they'd arrived at the castle and he'd sensed his people crying out for a savior. Tal's gaze was so bright, so trusting. Rags's skin burned. "Stop it," he muttered. "Just—want to make a name for myself by breaking into a royal and royally-fucked-up secret castle chamber and steal the Queen's greatest treasure. Don't look at me like that. It's not for you."

"Morien knows there are traitors within the castle." Somhairle glanced over his shoulder like he could see his half brother, or a ghost of him. "Knows that a prince was acting against Her Majesty. Security's bound to be higher than ever. Besides . . ." Somhairle reached out with his good hand to touch the cloth on Rags's chest. "We don't know that this is enough to stop him from killing you—"

"Yeah, yeah. Maybe he'll be busy checking on the other princes for a while, won't bother with us right away. Probably wants to see how deep the conspiracy goes. That'd give us enough time to free the kids . . . if nothing else."

Another flash of silver, this time in Somhairle's eyes, as Inis returned, little cuts on her hands. By her side, Two was crunching happily on a mouthful of mirrorglass.

"Enough standing around. We need to—" Inis began.

"What the fuck?" Rags interrupted. Her eyes were glazed silver, too. Rags looked to Tal for explanation.

Tal nodded knowingly. "They are speaking with One and, through One, with her master. I do not know what they are saying—"

"Wait, you mean with *Cab?*"

Another nod. "I cannot eavesdrop. It is not my place, without a fragment of my own. But if they are communing, it must be important."

"Sure. Important," Rags muttered, left out as ever from the creepy-silver-connection cabal. He patted the thing in his pocket. Since his conversation with Tal, it had warmed to the temperature of his skin. Did that mean it was alive in there? That it was finally waking up, now that Rags had done something worth waking for?

Only a little longer, he thought in its direction.

81

CAB

Inis Fraoch Ever-Loyal? Cab thought the name, on One's instructions, "as loudly as possible," though it seemed like madness.

The silence that followed, long and awkward, nearly confirmed that.

Then, when Cab was about to open his eyes and ask One if pranks made sense at a time like this, he heard it: like a stretching of muscles. Like a cat rising in a nearby room, arching its back after a long sleep, yawning.

You. It was Inis's voice and also One's voice and also nothing like either. *What is it you want?*

Cab hadn't expected her to be pleased to hear from him. *There's a way to help you. Free you from Morien's control. But I'm with people who also need help—your help.*

In some trouble of our own at the moment, actually, Inis replied. Clipped, irritated, sounding more like herself. *Morien's uncovered conspiracy at the castle.*

The news hit Cab heavier than the blows from the Queensguard, and they'd threatened to split him open. A face sprang immediately to mind. Sil's contact.

Einan was going to be furious.

We'll come to you, Cab said. Making decisions without thinking, nothing like the good soldier he'd been trained to be.

Don't come to the Hill. Even Inis's caution sounded annoyed, like speaking in favor of Cab's well-being rankled her. *We can't stay, we're going— Shut up!*

Cab got the sense that this last bit wasn't directed at him. It had to have been one of the others in the room, either the thief or the fae prince, because Inis had cut off their connection, presumably to handle the interruption.

Cab wasn't left alone.

Hello?

Cab didn't recognize the new voice. Male. Gentle. Threaded with anger he was fighting to keep at bay.

Still here, Cab said.

Oh! So you are. Cabhan of Kerry's-End, isn't it? We're going underground, the young man's voice said. *Three says she'll be able to guide One, so don't worry about how to find us.*

The newcomer: another master for the silver fae creatures.

Don't suppose you'd be willing to tell me what we're walking into? Cab asked.

I wish I knew, the voice replied. *My name is Somhairle Ever-Bright.* A prince was one of the masters? That was nearly as unlikely as one of the loyal Queensguard joining the Resistance. *If only we were meeting under different—*

Be ready for a fight. Inis again. *It would take too much time to describe.*

Sadness colored her explanation, tied so tightly to her connection with Two that Cab couldn't determine who was the true owner of the emotion.

There you have it, One concluded. *They're off, about to act. We should do the same.*

It took Cab a moment to recover. When he opened his eyes, the world was tinged in fading silver. He blinked, blinked again, and finally his sight returned to normal. Einan stood in front of him, arms crossed over her chest.

"We have to move," Cab said.

Einan tutted. "That much was obvious the second we got here. You're telling me that's all you got from your mystical communications? *I* could've told you that for free."

Cab stood. He ached from head to toe, ribs bruised, knuckles and face bandaged where they'd been bleeding. He needed a healer's undivided attention, and to sleep for a week. Einan gave him a look like she wanted to help him stay upright, then clenched her jaw and stayed where she was.

Cab appreciated that. He needed to see if he could do this on his own. If not, he had to be jettisoned. He'd only slow the group down.

But he'd been taught to ignore pain, to ignore his needs, in favor of the greater good. Which wasn't service to the Crown. It was moving against it.

"We have to go to the castle," Cab explained. When Einan scoffed again, a raw whip of laughter and a roll of her eyes, he breathed out heavily. "Your man on the Hill's been compromised. He's being held in Coward's Silence. Likely getting tortured. If we don't break him out, they'll kill him."

Sil pressed her small hands to her cheeks, then covered her face in despair. Hope touched her shoulder. Einan calmly kicked one of Uaine's chairs over.

"I'd thank you not to take it out on the furniture," Uaine said. "Although I get the feeling I won't be returning to this old house."

"We have other allies on the inside," Cab continued. "Including the Masters of Two and Three. I spoke with them." *Don't ask how,* Cab willed, because damned if he could explain it. No one asked, although Einan's sharp green gaze narrowed. "Two of them have mirrorglass in their hearts. The Master of Two, and—Rags, the thief who started this." Sil nodded. She'd known, must have learned that from One. "If we can get Sil to them—if she can help others the way she helped me—then we might be able to turn the sorcerer's control. We might be able to make a stand."

Or escape with some of their lives.

They'd need to get real lucky, and soldiers weren't supposed to believe in luck.

Where they'd go—if they survived—was another matter. He'd figure that out if they managed to mount a successful break-in—and out again—of the castle. Cab focused, recalled what he knew of the castle's layout: the grounds, the barracks, the little he'd been shown of the Queen's sanctum. He'd been a promising young soldier, but no Queensguard was allowed to know everything about the castle they protected. Only about the points they were meant to protect.

"I must save the others who are trapped," Sil said. Einan's face tightened. The danger was a knife hanging over Sil's head. "Or die in the attempt. I cannot leave them to suffer what I have suffered. Some are close to death."

Hope touched his brow as though he felt it, too. "I will defend you in this task. They *will* be saved."

"So that's it, is it?" Einan choked back a dark laugh. "Here's our plot: We march up to the one place that's least safe for us, where the entire Queensguard is stationed, and find some way to sneak into the fucking castle, despite every last soldier *and* sorcerer being on the alert for us. Then we storm Coward's Silence, because making it to the castle without being caught isn't impossible enough, and break out our compromised agent—though he's probably dead already. Then, while we're not too busy, we rescue the most heavily guarded group of hostages in the place, hostages *probably* too weak to stand on their own, when saving *one* a year ago lost us too many good people. On top of that, we're *also* looking for someone who's got mirrorcraft in her, and once we find her, we have to remove that spell so she can fight on our side. That's *if* she doesn't turn on us with her ancient fae weapon first, when Morien the Last snaps his fingers and *makes her do it*. Plus, there's only two of us who've been trained to fight, and one's already pounded into mincemeat, so we're down a man."

"That's the long of it," Cab agreed. "The pain's not terrible, though. I'll manage."

When he met her eyes, Einan was the first to look away. Cab understood. Laypeople did funny things in the presence of death. Like kiss a person, then never mention it again.

*Also—*One padded lithely to the door—*we're about to have company. How many?*

Thirty, all told, patrolling the streets, sniffing us out. Two Lying Ones. The rest are armed Queensguard with mirrorglass in their hearts. They'll have to capture us or die. And they're close. Can we stay and fight them?

So it was true. The Queensguard were controlled by mirrorcraft.

The weight of the truth, the confirmation, stilled Cab for a beat.

Cab had suspected it but never given form to his suspicions. Had Captain Baeth been sharded before she infiltrated the Resistance?

He could think about it when they weren't in mortal danger. When he didn't have to focus around the pain of his bones knitting back together.

We can't take them. Not when I'm in this condition, he told One. *Can't risk anyone else getting hurt.*

One pouted but bowed, tongue flicking past her lips, almost as if she was tasting the air. *As you say, Master Handsome.*

Cab drew a breath, refused to grunt when it jostled his aching ribs, and shared what One had told him. "We've been discovered. Not sure how close they are, but we need to leave."

"Kick all the chairs you like, Einan, if you're quiet about it." Uaine grabbed a few packets of herbs from her cupboards, stashing them in pouches and attaching them to her belt. She rolled up her skirt and stuck some in there as well, revealing her scarred legs. "And I'd finally made the place proper cozy."

82
INIS

Finally, Two said, flashing his teeth and sharpening his claws on the marble fireplace. He left deep gouges, perfectly parallel, through the stone. *We get to hurt the fuckers who hurt you.*

There were a thousand things that could, and probably would, go wrong. Their plan was foolish. Was it even a plan? Cab had offered his ideas of how best to coordinate their attack, but Inis still had trouble thinking of him as an ally, not an enemy.

Despite that, Inis smiled.

Tomman was never innocent. The charges against him hadn't been false.

Inis had once viewed them through the eyes of someone accustomed to a world reflected by the Hill's warped mirrors. Treason was unthinkable, and therefore her family had been innocent.

So what happened when treason was no longer unthinkable, but unavoidable? When it became necessary to rebel against the Crown by denying the Queen her vile source of power?

Tomman had been killed for the Resistance. Killed before he'd been able to see their task through.

Inis would finish it for him.

For her family, those who hadn't survived. For those who had. For herself. For everyone else in the Resistance, since Tomman had been so committed he'd staked his life on it. Father's life. Ainle's. *Everything.*

Inis gave the red fabric from Laisrean's room to Rags. He had mirror shards in his hand, didn't have a fragment of his own, *and* wasn't an unstoppable fae warrior prince, so he was the most in need of it.

Inis had Two and Somhairle had Three.

They'd free the fae. They'd make it to Coward's Silence; meet Cabhan and the others there, if they weren't killed along the way; and get Laisrean, if he was there, and if he was still breathing.

Then, if *she* was still breathing, she'd tear out Morien's heart.

With my teeth or your hands? Two asked, still grinning, showing off every tooth in his head.

Let's see how inspiration takes us when the moment comes, Inis replied.

There was the Queen behind Morien, always the Queen at the center of things. She was a problem without a solution, but Inis couldn't get ahead of herself. She had to remain steady and stealthy, keep a level head and heart. With the blindfold tied around her chest and Rags cloaked in the sheet of red cloth, they filed out of Somhairle's quarters and into the quiet halls.

She expected Queensguard at every step. But, Two told her, they were busy elsewhere. Striking early, when Morien was dealing with Laisrean and the Resistance threat, was their best chance.

Rags took the lead, shepherding them down the same path he'd taken before, while Shining Talon stayed at the rear, to protect them from the odd servant or Queensguard on nighttime patrol.

He's angry, Two commented. Inis didn't need to ask, could tell from the distaste in his voice that he meant Morien. *The Queen wouldn't allow shards in her sons, and this is what came of it. Ooh, he blames her, but he's too scared to say it.*

Good, Inis replied. *Let him taste fear for a change.*

Clanky guard friends, Two added.

Rags must have heard them.

He'd pulled Somhairle into a corner, throwing up the red cloth to further obscure them in shadow. Inis and Shining Talon ducked into an alcove opposite them and waited for the metallic stamping of the patrol to pass. Fat lot of good it'd do them to be caught huddling together under a sheet in an ill-used hallway, but waiting was torment. Every moment that passed was precious time squandered.

The Queen had chosen to protect her princes from mirrorcraft. That meant she still cared for them, in her own way, and there was a chance Laisrean hadn't been executed. *Yet.* Inis's heart soared, but she pushed the feeling away for later, once her surprise at the reaction had registered.

Deeming it safe to move on, Rags motioned for them to continue, then set off down the hall. Inis had an inkling Morien would know soon that something was wrong. They'd hidden from him for too long.

But preserving that secret no longer mattered. Nothing mattered, except for freeing the trapped fae children.

Inis knew what it was like to be driven by a single purpose. Ivy had been her lone focus this long year in exile. Now she had Tomman's memory to lead her forward, Tomman's cause to champion. She'd finish what he'd started, what he'd died for.

You're not alone anymore. Not even in your headstrong pursuits, Two reminded her.

He was right, for better or worse. Not only was she linked to Two, a piece of her she'd always missed, but she was tied to the other masters of the fragments, too. Somhairle and Cab. One her old friend, one her old enemy.

Fate laughing at yet another Ever-Loyal.

Rags led them to the path of hands, black bones set into the tiles, fingers outstretched. Pointing, or pleading? They set the hairs on Inis's arms on end, but she followed them.

Once, Shining Talon disappeared from the rear of their group, returned after subduing a Queensguard or a servant who'd been unlucky enough to stumble into the wrong place at the wrong time.

Inis was *fairly* sure he hadn't killed them. The bleak look on his face made it difficult to be certain. The blindfold around her chest made it difficult to breathe.

With Shining Talon as their rear guard, they passed through the secret compartment in the window seat one at a time. In the dark beneath the Hill, Inis reached for Somhairle's hand, so she wouldn't feel as though the Queen's castle was swallowing her.

Then her vision shifted. She saw with Two's eyes, forms taking shape in shadows she shouldn't be able to see. Carvings on the walls that were supposed to glow, but their power had been drained, no magic left to light the way. They made her sad—or made Two sad, and Inis by extension—then stoked her anger.

Down, down. Two smelled something that Inis couldn't name, a foreign taste on her lips: black bones and blood that ran silver.

The fae children.

Inis and Two began to move faster, until they rounded a sharp corner and came into the chamber Rags had described.

It was worse than she'd imagined. She tumbled out into a room filled with mirrors, angled against each other, reflecting and capturing the natural light that shone from the imprisoned fae, who rested on white stone slabs. Eyes open but empty.

Unlike in the scene Rags had described, they weren't alone.

Of course the Queensguard had been sent to secure the place—Inis and the others had expected as much. Except they'd anticipated a smaller contingent they could overpower, relieve of their weapons. Not this many.

Not this.

Not possible to count how many Queensguard filled the room. Light on armor, reflected hundreds of times in hundreds of panes of polished, silver-backed glass. How many Queensguard were real, and how many were mirror images? All of them raised their swords in unison. Inis yelled a wordless challenge, and Rags ducked behind the nearest high slab of white stone that was a fae bed. Somhairle braced himself, while Two, Three, and Shining Talon leaped forward at the same time.

Glass shattered. Someone screamed. Inis ducked a falling blade with instincts that weren't hers. Two in her blood, in her head, behind her eyes.

They moved together, Two's strength behind her, feeding her. Her palm connected with a metal breastplate, sent the Queensguard who'd attacked her sprawling. When he dropped his sword, she picked it up with little idea what to do with it, letting Two guide her. As Two's tail swiped another Queensguard off his feet, Inis swung her stolen blade in the same motion, catching a third Queensguard in the flank. He stumbled but didn't go down, and Inis braced herself, blocked him when he lunged again.

She was grinning, showing all her teeth.

What of Somhairle? Was that golden blur in the corner of her vision Shining Talon, racing from Queensguard to Queensguard, breaking mirrors along the way?

Tell that to superstitious fools who thought breaking a mirror heralded bad luck.

Movement by the nearest fae. Rags was trying to pull the child's unmoving body off the white stone slab and having some difficulty.

No more taking stock. Three Queensguard rushed Inis at the same time, seeming to materialize out of nowhere—no, out of the mirrors—and Inis would have gone down if Two hadn't been at her side.

Let me in, Two said.

Inis didn't know what he meant. A fist caught her in the chest, slammed her against a mirror. It broke against her elbows, hurt like fire. *Let you in where?*

No time to explain. Have to get it done. Trust me.

A heavy weight crashed into Inis from the side. She almost thought it was another Queensguard tackling her, until the weight disappeared and warmth surrounded her, numbing her the instant she acknowledged it. When she looked down, she saw silver coating her hands, her arms, creeping across her chest to coat her entirely. She nearly dropped the stolen sword but lifted her arm to block a lunging Queensguard.

His steel glanced off her wrist.

All of a sudden, she felt like she could breathe again, even under Morien's blindfold. Her outside finally reflected her insides. Cold. Hard. Implacable. A newfound strength flooded her. She heard Rags swear. Inis kicked the fallen Queensguard, tore off his helmet, and punched him in the face with her steel fist. She grabbed his sword next.

One blade in each hand, she snarled—or maybe it was Two, or both of them together—and leaped into the fray beside Shining Talon.

Side by side, they were silver and gold.

Inis knew there were too many Queensguard. For every one she took down, two more appeared in their place. Some had to be mere reflections. She threw one Queensguard into a mirror; it smashed like a rush of joy. Out of the corner of her eye, she saw Somhairle struggling to help Rags, Rags struggling to help the fae children. Lifting and dragging them off their slabs and away, out of the direct and reflected gazes of the mirrors—to a place behind them, by the farthest wall.

Inis had to protect them. That was her role.

Four Queensguard faced her. Where were they coming from?

A stutter of fear entered her heart. She couldn't lose here.

Shining Talon dove low, kicking a Queensguard from where he was about to strike. Inis swung both her blades, cutting down the one next to him. With Two in her veins, her muscles didn't have to strain. He was a constant flow of strength where once she might have been weak.

She knew it couldn't last forever.

Someone struck her between the shoulders. Two yowled and she spun, slamming her elbow into the helmet of the Queensguard who'd hit her. She left a dent in the Queensguard's faceplate, had enough time to register the impact before Shining Talon slashed at him, knocking him down with a borrowed sword.

Behind the fallen Queensguard stood Lord Faolan Ever-Learning.

He wore no helmet, his black hair braided over one shoulder and shot through with gold. Inis would have recognized the quill crest on his breastplate even if his face had been covered. He squinted, fighting to make sense of the scene before him.

Inis didn't know what she looked like with Two draped over her, coating her, a living armor that covered every feature.

Inis stepped toward Faolan over a fallen Queensguard.

"You shouldn't have come." He hefted his weapon: a lean silver long sword. Inis wondered if it, like so much of the silver they'd come across, had been crafted from destroyed fae relics. "You shouldn't have done this. I rather liked you, Inis Fraoch Ever-Loyal."

Behind her, Shining Talon smashed another mirror. Armored footsteps marching in time broke through Inis's fractured thoughts. More soldiers. Faolan's personal Queensguard, perhaps, in addition to those stationed at the palace. Inis's side couldn't withstand a wave of reinforcements. They hadn't secured the area, were simply buying time—

"Not too late to change sides," Inis told Faolan.

He smiled. A strange expression. It wasn't happy. It was downright bleak.

"My heart isn't so easily swayed these days." Faolan lifted his free hand to tap against his chest. "I believe you know what that's like."

Implying he'd been Morien's *unwilling* puppet in this all along.

Blinding pain erupted beneath Inis's ribs. She dropped to her knees in time to glimpse Morien stepping through one of the unbroken mirrors. Two snapped back into his old form, wrenched forcibly free. It felt like her skin was being flayed from her bones. She wasn't alone, but they were separated again.

Inis was sure she was dying, except she continued to draw breath.

"Someone's learned a new trick," Morien commented.

"I could say the same for you." Inis struggled to get the words out, her voice thin. "A hound putting the leash on his master. You must be very proud."

"He is, actually," Faolan said. His arm shook, but he kept his sword up and trained on Inis. She noticed he took a step away from the sorcerer, kept a wary eye on him at all times.

Morien's hands moved in the air between them. He was drawing the signs he needed to call on his mirrorcraft and stop Inis's heart. The next breath she drew would be her last, and she couldn't even savor it. Rags cried out, feeling the same torture. Only Somhairle and Shining Talon were unaffected. Somhairle could continue helping the fae, continue dragging them one by one to safety, while Shining Talon continued to break the mirrors that held them captive.

Had they managed to free them all?

Where would the fae children go now that they were free? Would they even get to leave this horrible room?

Look after the children, Inis thought, not sure if Two could hear her. *And don't stay connected to me when the Lying One kills me. Don't let him hurt you. Tear out his throat the moment you can.*

No answer from Two. Inis did the only thing she could: she braced herself, faced Morien, drew in a breath, and spat on his boots. If this was the end, she wanted the sorcerer to know her exact estimation of his character.

But the end didn't come.

She drew a second breath, which hurt like every inch of her was screaming, but alive, *alive*, you couldn't ache this badly when you were dead. Then a third. Morien's hands worked faster, fingers twisting, turning, drawing lines and glyphs and sigils too quickly for Inis to keep track, and with each one, a new flash of incapacitating pain shocked Inis's body, branching outward from her chest. Pain, but not death.

Morien's eyes glittered. Inis couldn't see his mouth under the swaths of red fabric, but she guessed he was frowning, gritting his teeth, on the verge of cursing.

It had to be the little scrap of blindfold standing between them that kept him from killing her.

Granted, if this kept up much longer, she'd tear the blindfold off herself, would die rather than suffer more of this impossible agony.

With a grunt, Morien threw one gesture toward Faolan instead, and he started forward with a lurch, sword raised. The first time he hadn't been graceful in their presence. The first sign he was completely under Morien's control. "Sorry it came to this. Nothing personal. Although it's incredibly unfair that you're able to resist him when I can't, eh?"

His long sword slashed, beautiful and precise and unstoppable, through the air. Inis's arms hurt so badly that she couldn't lift them to serve as shield between her throat and Faolan's blade.

Morien didn't need to have full control of her heart in order to kill her. All he had to do was bring her to her knees, unable to move, and have one of his other pets finish her off.

A blaze of gold streaked between her and the weapon. Someone grunted. Inis looked up into shadow to see the fall of Shining Talon's dark hair over one shoulder, the single shock of white.

He'd taken the blow for her on his forearm. The blade had sliced so deeply into his flesh that Inis saw a flash of black bone beneath golden skin.

Faolan stumbled backward from the impact. Shining Talon didn't seem to register his own pain. Or he felt it and didn't care. He twisted his arm around, catching the long sword in the crook of his elbow. Wrenched it back, out of Faolan's grip. Raised it high, blood-drenched, and turned it on Morien.

The agony in Inis's chest dulled with Morien's surprise.

The reprieve didn't last long.

Morien flickered before them, one moment with the tip of the long sword at his throat, the next reappearing deeper in the chamber. Light on the unbroken mirrors blinded Inis, forced her to blink. In that instant, Morien was again elsewhere.

He held a shard from another mirror in one hand, his other arm snaked tight around one of the fae children. He pressed the shard to the fae's cheek, slicing through skin as if it were paper.

Shining Talon cried out, would have lunged if something, someone, hadn't jumped on him to hold him back. Rags's skinny arms, his tangle of dark hair, his skin clammy and his knuckles white.

"What now, princeling?" Again, Inis didn't have to see the sorcerer's mouth to know he was grinning, an ugly twist of the scarves across his jaw.

Shining Talon strained against Rags's arms, not because Rags was strong enough to prevent him from doing anything he wished, but because for whatever stubborn reason, he respected Rags's will.

"I've loosed six of them from their bonds." Somhairle spoke in a whisper at Inis's back, breathing heavily. Inis turned slowly, saw the streak of blood cutting across the prince's jaw, the bruise blooming on his brow, the split in his lip. He shook his head, *don't worry about me,* then continued, "Tried to wake another, but she won't—"

Faolan lunged a second time, weaponless, hopeless. Inis saw only despair in his eyes. He was frightened, didn't think he'd manage to do anything except sacrifice himself, but he moved because he had no choice. Morien was pulling the strings.

He met Shining Talon's arm with a *crack*. Shining Talon swept him away as though he were an irritating fly. He slammed into the wall, rattled it with the force of Shining Talon's blow. Slid down the stone. Crumpled.

Didn't get up.

Morien still had a vulnerable hostage, the upper hand. "We're at an impasse. One step closer to me, and I spill this child's blood on the stones."

"You wouldn't." Rags, wheezing as he spat out the words. "You need them, don't you? They keep you powerful. Help you do the nasty, fuck-everyone-else *bullshit* you love so much."

"I only need their blood," Morien replied simply. "I don't need *all* of them alive."

Rags faltered, half laughed. "You're a fucking nightmare, you know that?"

Morien's eyes flashed, reflecting Rags not as he was at the moment but as the sorcerer wanted him. Dead. Torn to ribbons, bones crunched by wolves, flesh pecked and plundered and carried off by crows.

To his credit, Rags didn't flinch. "You think that scares me, asshole? So many people want me dead, you'd better take your place in the back of the line."

Three and Somhairle have come up with a plan. The suddenness of Two's voice made Inis twitch. Morien was so busy with Rags that he didn't notice. *In fact, I'm jealous. It gives Three all the glory. If she pulls it off, she'll never let me live it down.*

Inis kept her gaze level on Morien. He'd cut the fae's cheek deeper, glass disappearing into flesh. Inis could barely get enough breath into her lungs, past the living wound he'd made of her. *Better get it done, then. And quick.*

Somhairle's hand fell on her shoulder, pulled her back against his chest. Three swept forward, wings battering the air. They grew as she flew, slicing through mirrors, sending shards sparking and glittering over their heads, taking Morien by surprise, knocking the injured fae from his arms.

Shining Talon and Rags caught the girl before she hit the floor, dragging her away from harm.

We have to run, Two said. *While he's distracted. While Three buys us time.*

We can't—

No. But we have *to.*

Somhairle winced, so close to Inis that it rocked her. Two was right, as much as it wasn't what they'd wanted. Only six freed fae—seven, including the one Morien had further injured—and Three distracting Morien, keeping his hands busy long enough for them to run. How many were left to save? Too many. Inis rose, leaning against Somhairle to draw as much support from him as he drew from her.

This way. Two bounded off, herding the rescued fae children at the same time. *Leave Shining Talon to the mouthy thief.*

Breaking glass. Mirror shards falling all around. Three still growing and growing, lashing out at Morien with talons and sharpened feathers, shrieking as she fought.

Without a glance behind, Inis let Two lead them away. She did what she had to, and that was run.

83

RAGS

Prince Shining Talon of Vengeance Drawn in Westward Strike—impossibly beautiful fae prince, Ever-Living pain in Rags's ass, now otherwise known as Tal—needed to move.

But he was heavy as solid gold and stubborn as an ox, and Rags's whole body was spent, throbbing, barely recovered from the shit Morien had just put it through. His hand especially. It might've turned to stone—swollen stiff with pain and useless from the sting of the mirrorglass needles, a sick dead color Rags liked to call "corpse in the summer."

A giant silver owl was fighting a murderous, heartless sorcerer in front of Rags's eyes. The rest of their group, along with the fae kids they'd set free, were doing the smart thing and getting their asses out of harm's way. But Tal wouldn't budge.

Rags dug his heels into the floor, dodged a fresh shower of shattered glass, wrapped his arms tighter around the big fae's waist, and pulled.

Couldn't make the idiot give an inch.

Rags swore, barely audible over the chaos caused by Three's pounding wings. He pressed himself close to Tal, knew that not only would they lose Inis, Somhairle, and the others, but if Three kept at it, the whole chamber was going to collapse, killing the very fae Tal was determined to save.

"You've gotta *move*, Tal! We've gotta get out of here while we can!"

"I cannot leave my people." Tal's blood dripped onto Rags's body, soaking through his shirt. It was cool, not warm. Rags shuddered. "I *must* save them."

"Yeah, some other time, okay? They'll understand. Quit thinking with your heart for a change and use your brain!"

"I—" Tal's voice broke. Morien countered Three's onslaught, managing to pierce her solid silver skin with a handful of mirror shards. She howled in fury and Morien nearly got one hand free, started to trace a new glyph, before Three smacked his fingers with a wildly flapping wing.

There was nothing else to be done. Rags had tried everything but the *one* thing he didn't want to do, and this was what it had come to.

Fine. Let the dirtiest jobs fall to Rags. They were what he was best at.

"I command you," Rags said.

He hated himself for it, but what else was new?

Wondered, regretful, if Tal would ever forgive him for saving his life.

The expression on Tal's face was terrible. Like a blood red dawn sky, the sign of a storm coming.

"Is that your will?" Tal turned to look at Rags. The motion unnaturally, unbearably slow.

"Yes, damn it!" Rags tugged hard on Tal's arm. His grip slipped from all the blood and he slid on more of the same, fell on his ass. It stung. *"I command you to retreat."*

"Then," Tal whispered, "I will obey."

He held a hand over his heart. No place for him to kneel.

Saving him shouldn't have felt this shitty. But as Tal turned and loped past him, heading for the far end of the tunnel, Rags couldn't shake his misery at what he'd done.

Was it right? It had to be right.

"Come on!" He struggled to his feet and waved his arms at Three, hoping to grab her attention before Morien did her any further damage, beyond the eye she was already missing. None of them needed to lose more than they already had. "We're leaving! Get going!"

Three raked Morien with her talons, bowling him over with a final beat of her furious wings. Without waiting to see what happened next, Rags stumbled and ran crookedly after Tal, trying not to think about what it meant that Tal hadn't waited for him. Or about what he might've broken in the service of something bigger than himself.

Any trust that had been built between them.

The way that Tal had looked at Rags like he was the key to every lock the world had ever known.

Rags had told himself from day one that it wouldn't last.

Most of all, he was trying not to think about those sleeping fae children. The ones they hadn't been able to rescue. He couldn't afford a last glance in their direction, not when he was too busy running at full tilt, chased by the screeching of Three's fury and Morien's cursing. He was half expecting, half hoping to run straight into Tal, waiting for Rags in the passage, but he didn't.

Instead, Tal was a golden glimmer disappearing around another dark corner. Did he believe Rags would keep up? Or could he not bear to face Rags after—

Fuck it. Had to run.

He ran so fast, his feet nearly went out from under him. Slapped the stone wall under one hand to course correct when he veered too close to it. A sudden wind pushed him from behind, and he realized Three was there, at the mouth of the tunnel, holding it for their escape.

How to thank an enormous silver bird sacrificing itself for short-lived, petty flesh-suits who caused most of their own problems? Would Morien tear her to pieces? Use those pieces for mirrorcraft? *Fuck.*

Rags rounded the corner Tal had disappeared around and nearly tripped on his borrowed red sheet. Ahead in the dark, Tal radiated faint golden light. Like a giant glowbug. A few steps past him, Somhairle, Inis, and Two were shepherding the procession of terrified, tortured fae children.

They were never going to make it out of there. They were too battered, too weakened, too slow. There was no way they could travel back up to the palace in this state, much less escape the Hill. If more Queensguard arrived—more sorcerers—

Shit, shit, shit. Rags went over a mental list of their assets, came up with squat. All he had was that he'd been here before. Under the castle, trapped in its dungeons. He knew exactly how hard it was to escape.

He'd been here before. Rags whistled sharply into the dark.

Maybe he could guide them toward Coward's Silence, avoid the castle for another way out.

Somhairle was the first to turn, hope in his eyes when they caught Tal's light. He must've thought Rags was signaling something about Three, and when he saw no sign of her, his face fell and he stumbled.

Tal caught him, propped him up, having done the same for any of the little fae who tripped or lagged. He kept close to them the way he'd once kept close to Rags, fussing and watching and caring. Despite having a wound in his arm that cut through to black bone, he was too busy looking after others to remember himself.

Figured.

That perfect idiot.

"Better make Three's stand count." Rags swallowed down the snare in his throat to sound like an authority on the matter. "I think we're close to Coward's Silence. You know, the prison where they're probably keeping that other prince—the one who got caught 'cause we fuck up everything we touch?"

"Walk right into the prison like this?" Inis asked. As tired as she looked, her hair in disarray, her clothes torn—parts burned where hot silver had eaten away at the threads when she had *turned into one of those silver things*, Rags was doing his best not to remember that part—she hadn't faltered. "Might as well turn ourselves over, lock ourselves in the cells, and do Morien's job for him!"

Rags shook his head. "Maybe. Or maybe not. *Maybe* the bulk of the Queensguard are looking for us in the castle, and us going to the dungeons is the *last* thing they'd expect from us. Maybe we'll have better luck there."

"And if we don't?" Inis wiped sweat off her brow with her knuckles, leaving a streak of blood in its place.

Rags shrugged. "You have a better idea? We can't stay here. Going back up into the castle's a bad bet. But if we keep going down . . ."

Inis bit her lip. Rags could see her thinking, wanting to call him a muttonhead, but also weighing their limited options.

As she thought, Two stepped nimbly to the side, directly under one of the fae—the one with the cut cheek from Morien's glass—a moment before she fell. Swooned, more like. Instead of cracking her head on stone, she sagged into Two's strength, and managed to continue with his help.

Rags risked a glance at Tal. His arm was a mess. If they were going to stand around debating, then maybe Rags could fashion a sling for him out of the red sheet. He was about to start ripping when Tal lifted his good hand, resting it against the wall.

Rags squinted.

Was that—?

Yeah.

It wasn't Tal behind *all* the glowing. There were faint carvings somewhere beneath the stone, reacting to him, pulsing, alive. Like in the fae ruins.

Rags had figured this was nothing more than a Queen-made tunnel under the palace, part of the system of dungeons and fae torture chambers Morien and the Queen had set up. But there were fae workings here, workings that couldn't be seen unless you had fae with you to light them up.

More fucking fae mysteries. As if there weren't enough in Rags's life already.

Rags was still squinting when he heard a commotion from the other end of the tunnel, the opposite direction from where they'd left Morien, the mirror chamber, the other fae.

Queensguard reinforcements, had to be. Coming straight for the kids, who were out front. Unprotected.

Rags was the first to act. Two must have been distracted caring for the hurt fae, and anyway, *nobody* had Rags's instincts for trouble. He scrambled forward, hands balled into aching, shaky, but still sharp-knuckled fists, ready to take the new wave of opposition on.

He met a massive silver lizard instead, a familiar face beside it.

Their missing Queensguard. Ex-Queensguard. The one who was on their side. And damn, but he looked like someone'd tried to mince his head for meat pies.

Then again, Rags couldn't imagine that what Cab saw looked any better.

"Shit!" Rags nearly laughed with relief, arms jellying. "Did anyone know *he* was close?"

It was Inis's turn to shrug. "Two was guiding One." She peered into the semidarkness behind Cab. "And he said there were others, but I wasn't expecting . . ."

"Here to rescue you lot." It was a skinny redhead who spoke up, with a street accent, someone Rags could finally relate to. And there were two fae beside her, which had stopped surprising Rags somewhere around *chamber of mirrors filled with dozens of little ones.* They looked in marginally better shape than the recently liberated fae kids.

"Right," he said. "Follow me, knucklebrains."

84
CAB

They'd killed five Queensguard on their way to the sewers. Another six inside the tunnels. Most of that was Hope's doing, if Cab was being honest. Uaine did well for herself, too.

Cab tried his best, finishing off the wounded, but he was the rear guard this time around.

With his injuries, he had to hang back. Protect Sil. Die for her if he needed to. In the meantime, he had to trust that Hope was the best person—best *fae*—for the hardest job.

And he was. He fought like a wildfire. So angry, there was no getting past his offense to put him on the defense. Ever. The Queensguard didn't stand a chance.

Many of them had been stationed in the sewers, but they'd only been expecting a ragtag group of rebels, not their furious fae bodyguard.

Or One the lizard, her tail as swift and deadly as her claws. She shared some of the thrill of the fight with Cab, along with assurances that one day, they'd fight together the proper way.

Cab would have to ask her later: What way was that?

Hope finished off another pair of sentries, and One was sweeping them aside to clear the path for the others when her voice swished into Cab's head. She was following instructions only she heard, communicating silently with the other fragments.

We're close, darling, One said. *And we don't have much time. We're going to need a leader. Think you're the one?*

A serpentine laugh followed that. Was that a pun?

Cab looked around, but no one else had heard it.

They ran into Rags the thief and his group barely a moment later, and Cab had stepped forward to meet them.

After that, time swelled dizzily as Cab drifted in and out of consciousness—in and out of One's consciousness. The lilt of Einan's husky voice sounded different, less musical, through One's unimpressed ears.

Hush, little baby, don't say a word, One crooned. *Building up your strength. Be a good boy and take your medicine.*

Cab rested, taken outside of his body so One could encourage it to heal. When he returned to himself, they were headed to Coward's Silence.

"Been this way before," Rags was explaining as he led the charge. Shining Talon wasn't dogging his footsteps, so plenty had changed since they'd last been together. "Once we're in the dungeon, if we're not overwhelmed by your brothers in steel, the folks who *don't* have mirrors in their hearts can look for Prince I'm-a-Traitor, while the folks who *do* have shards sit back and get those nasties *out of our bodies.*"

"This plan is—" Cab began.

"Terrible?" Inis supplied.

"I was going to say unlikely to succeed," Cab said.

"Terrible," Inis agreed.

"Everybody fucking criticizes, but nobody brings something

better to the table." Rags laughed hoarsely. Cab recognized the sound. It was gallows humor. The giddiness that flooded a man when he'd been on the move for too long, had to treat the possibility of dying like a joke in order to keep going. Cab managed to clap Rags on the shoulder, making him jump midstep before he realized it wasn't an attack. A gesture of solidarity. Something a Queensguard captain would do for his recruits.

He was no Queensguard anymore, but he'd fight to protect these people. They were his brothers and sisters in arms now.

"We'll back you up," Cab said. "Sil, can you manage—"

Sil nodded firmly. No choice. She *would* manage.

As ever, Cab was astounded and inspired by her bravery.

They moved on in silence, save for the unsteady breathing of the rescued fae. The occasional skitter of loose rock as someone slipped. A gasp as One or Two darted to their side to support them.

"You *sure* you know the way?" Einan asked Rags. Time had stuttered to a nervous spiral. They knew the fate that awaited them: trapped underground, ambushed by Queensguard, by sorcerers. "Who are you, anyway, Skinny?"

"I've got this," Rags insisted.

Tell him to get it faster, One said.

Her anxiety threaded its way through Cab's nerves, but he was used to it.

This state of constant attention. Fear. Always keeping watch over his shoulder. It had been his sole companion in Tithe Barley's barn. Not the best friend, but one he'd learned to manage. He could teach the others how to live with the burden.

If they survived long enough.

That won't be helpful, Cab chided her. He knew from experience how telling someone to rush only helped them to be clumsy. Judging by their tattered group, a collective of dirt and sweat, blood and torn clothing, they'd met with their share of opposition.

"No offense," Einan chimed in, though she couldn't have known there was a conversation already in progress, "but I was hoping your friends might be . . . bigger. More impressive."

"I'm not impressive enough for you?" Cab asked.

Einan looked him up and down, then surprised him with a wolfish grin, which kindled some of the old fire behind her tired eyes. "Not the first word that comes to mind."

Dull heat spread under Cab's skin. He let himself wonder what *did* come to Einan's mind when she thought of him. Might explain why she'd kissed him in the Gilded Lily.

The distraction kept his mind from screaming that they were heading ever deeper with no hope of escape.

Rags still had a shard in his heart. What if Morien was controlling his actions even now?

That's enough of that, One broke in. *Plenty to worry about without you imagining extra horrors.*

She was right. Cab didn't know what he'd do without her, would've lost his way if she'd stayed behind to stand against Morien so the rest could escape, as Three had done.

Ahead, the flickering of torches set into the walls. Rags held up a hand and their untidy group shuffled to a halt.

"This is it," Rags whispered. "Or . . . it should be. I was led through here the first time I— Never mind. Anyway, see? No Queensguard. I'm guessing they got called over to deal with our rescue mission."

He winced as he said it. Cab didn't need One to inform him that the attempt hadn't gone as well as they'd hoped.

"You're bleeding, master." Uaine inclined her head in Shining Talon's direction. "I could see to that, if you're willing."

"Here's where those who need medical attention and shards removed from our hearts should stop," Rags agreed. "The rest can go in and bust out our royal ally."

"We can't split up," Inis said. "What if some of us get captured? There's no way of knowing."

"One and Two can still communicate," Cab pointed out. "They'll be our eyes and ears."

"I'm going to get Lais," Inis insisted. She glanced at the young man next to her, his face dark with sorrow and tight with pain. "The Queen wouldn't let the Last kill her own flesh and blood, Somhairle."

Somhairle. The prince Cab had spoken to when they were planning this madness.

Enemies, One warned.

Cab turned, weary arm hefting a sword he'd stolen from a downed Queensguard and held on to just in case. How much damage would he be able to do? His fingers felt like sausages. Still, he'd have to try.

But it was only an owl winging toward them, bursting out of the darkness, nearly barreling into Somhairle's chest. Despite how weak the young prince looked, the impact didn't knock him over.

It was no normal owl. Its entire body was wrought of silver.

Three.

She'd seen better days, missing a chunk of feathers from one wing, an eye, and half her lower beak. Blood on her talons, a splash across her breast, and Cab could have sworn she was grinning.

Turned herself into a hundred daggers, One explained approvingly, *all of them aimed at the Lying One. Would have cut him to shreds, too, if he hadn't grown so powerful on the blood of fae children. She scared him, although she left a few of those daggers behind.*

What of Morien? Cab asked.

Escaped, unfortunately. Likely displeased. Probably coming for us.

"Quickly," Cab said. "We have to remove the mirror shards. If we don't—"

In answer, before Cab could finish the thought, Rags cried out, sagging against the wall. "Oh yeah, he's looking for us." A stream of curses followed. "But he can't find us. And hey, we already know we have insurance and he can't kill us. Make us *wish* we were dead, though. . . ."

"Inis, Rags, stay behind. Hope, guard them and Sil. And the rest of the children. Two will stand with you." A lot to ask of one man, not too much to ask of one fae. Cab stepped forward, pushing through his pain. "Shining Talon, Uaine, Einan, and I will rescue the prisoner with One. Somhairle and Three should lead us."

Somhairle nodded, jaw hard and tight.

"Do me a favor?" Rags looked up as Cab neared him. His skin was gray. "Open as many cell doors as you can on your way. I want to piss these fuckers off, *really* ruin their day."

The boy Cab had been would have balked at the indiscriminate freeing of prisoners. But under the Hill, right was wrong and up was down.

He could buy a few vital minutes by stirring up chaos. It was his sworn duty to Sil.

"I think it's ruined already," Cab replied, "but I'll do my best."

He expected Shining Talon to protest. To insist on remaining behind with Rags, who was clearly in pain, in trouble. But he followed Cab into the heart of Coward's Silence as behind them, Sil began to work on Inis first.

Cab heard Inis shout once.

Then nothing.

As Cab and the others, Somhairle at their head, moved along the rows of cells, they heard no banging on the bars or pleas from the prisoners inside—until Somhairle whispered, "Laisrean?"

"No point," someone behind a solid metal door moaned. "Never going to get out of here. Never—"

Cab nodded at One. She understood, sliced through the metal easily with a single swipe. Sparks flew. The door swung open and the moaning stopped.

That was how they continued, opening every door they passed. Letting murderers and thieves free. One man blew kisses as he fled. The next hollered, "Death to the Queen!"

The third man passed in silence, as though he didn't see the people in front of his face. Cab felt a chill. They were allowing criminals back onto the streets.

But if they could slow Morien down for a single breath, that was the kind of sacrifice he had to be willing to make.

The fourth door One destroyed fell inward to reveal Malachy, three bloody stumps on his right hand where fingers ought to be. He winced, crawled away from the door, flattened himself against the far wall. He was expecting more Queensguard, not an ill-advised rescue party.

Einan yelped and ran forward.

"Don't fall behind," Cab warned. Softened. "If you can bring him—"

Einan was already kneeling at his trembling side. "Hush, Malachy. I won't hurt you."

Uaine dropped to the back of the group. "Give him to me," she said. "I'll do what I'm able."

Malachy seemed to be in shock, but he smiled thinly at the sight of his comrades.

"We can't wait for you," Cab whispered urgently. Einan would hate him for it, but he'd weathered worse.

Uaine knelt in the tunnel with Malachy at her side. "We'll find our way back to the others. Go ahead. You'll only distract me if you stay."

This last was directed at Einan, who seemed poised to grit her teeth and dig in her heels. Cab surprised himself by lagging behind with her. He grabbed Einan around one arm and pulled her onward.

"Let Uaine work," he suggested. "Everyone's doing what they can."

"And these hands are built more for clonking someone over the head than they are healing?" Einan scowled, but she let Cab steer her away. "Point taken."

They turned a sharp corner. There, Three and One stopped as Somhairle lunged forward, into a room at the end of the corridor that reeked of sweat and blood.

The big man, Prince Laisrean, was strapped to a table that stood on its end, meaning he hung from it, rather than being supported. His right eye was swollen like an apple, the skin black and purple, with only dark red blood crusting in the slit between his lids. The eye itself was damaged, maybe beyond repair. He'd been left with one good one, like Three. The tips of his fingers oozed blood, which coated his hands, dried black in the lines of his palms. Someone had taken his shirt. Bright pink burn scars marred his brown skin in wormy crescents.

"Shit." Einan stopped dead, her nails digging into Cab's arm.

Prince Laisrean breathed in raggedly as his rescue party filed into the torture room. When he lifted his head, he didn't seem to see them.

Somhairle made a choked noise of rage and sorrow, then set to cutting the leather straps that held his brother in place. What Cab had taken for a knife in his hands was, on closer inspection, a single silver feather.

"You shouldn't have come." Laisrean found his voice, enough to disapprove. "The Last will be back. If he doesn't know you're here already, it's only a matter of—"

Somhairle hushed him and kept at his work, beckoned for Cab to come forward so he could catch Prince Laisrean when his bonds were cut. At last, with a snap of taut leather, the big man fell forward, and Cab caught him on one side, Einan on the other.

"Scars *are* sexy," Einan told him, "but you're pushing it, big boy."

Laisrean choked out a laugh. The warmth and humor that should have been in the chuckle still lingered beneath its surface, no more than an echo. "You lot are another sorcerer's illusion," he mumbled.

"We are real, Prince Laisrean." Shining Talon had been so quiet that Cab was almost startled by the sound of his voice. But now he spoke with conviction, firmly enough that Laisrean blinked his remaining eye, nodded, and hissed in pain.

"We've got to move," Cab said, couldn't let the giant prince dwell on his pain and fear. From somewhere down the hall came a whoop and a howl. The other criminals causing chaos, no doubt.

If the night went in their favor, that chaos would help disguise their escape. If it didn't, it would slow them down long enough for Morien to catch them.

One more gamble in a venture too full of the same.

"I'll try not to slow you down." Laisrean swallowed, snorted, and spat out something bloody. A tooth. "Least he didn't get around to putting glass in my heart—don't think he intended for me to live past tonight—"

"Hush," Einan soothed.

They made it through the door and into the hall. Back the way they'd come, Laisrean staggering with them, determined not to lean too much of his weight on his supporters. Cab wasn't sure how he managed to stay on his feet.

Malachy and Uaine weren't where they'd been. A nasty-looking bloodstain in their stead. Also, someone had set fire to the cots in the now-open cells, and smoke thickened the already wretched air. Another reason not to delay.

"Shit rescue," Einan muttered.

She wasn't wrong.

They hurried to retrace their steps. One swept any lingering ex-prisoners out of their path without care for broken bones or knocked heads. Cab didn't spare his thoughts for their well-being.

Look after your own men first and anyone else only after the fighting was done and the field secure. One of the first rules of combat.

But he did come up short when they arrived again at the sharp fork in the hallway, the spot where they'd left Sil tending to Inis and Rags, to discover it empty. Only more blood, and a series of footprints stamped in red on the stone leading away and down.

"Least we know which way to go," Einan said.

Yes, One agreed. *And if we don't hurry, we're going to miss the best part.*

Even with their injured, with a young prince and his lame leg, they knew what they had to do.

They ran.

85

INIS

"You will have to remove the cloth from your heart," Sil explained, rolling up her sleeves to reveal her delicate hands. They were graceful and lithe, without a hint of callus. "And I will have to do this quickly."

"So Morien doesn't kill me the moment the cloth's off," Inis said.

Sil nodded sadly. Inis took a deep breath and shut her eyes, mouthing the words: *Do it.*

What she hadn't expected was to be knocked unconscious first.

She came to, not sure how much later, to chaos, an aching lump on the back of her head, pain blooming in thorned vines throughout her chest, and Two breathing steadily beneath her. Carrying her. Herding the fae children ahead of them, while they carried Rags.

Fresh air. They weren't underground anymore. The sky overhead. Looking up at it, rocked by the barest jostling of Two's silver muscles as his chest swelled and narrowed, made Inis's vision go black with agony.

Sorry to wake you. Two's voice cooled some of the bright explosions of pain, but not enough. Not nearly enough. *Had to. We've got a bit of a situation. Ideally, you'd get days to recover, but this isn't ideal.*

Inis squinted to see what had happened, what was still happening, through Two's eyes.

Our Shining One, the Enchantrisk, removed the mirror from Rags's heart,

Two explained for her benefit. *We were nearly interrupted, so she had to rush the slivers in his hand.*

Through Two's eyes, Inis saw the Queensguard flooding the tunnel and forcing the hapless band of runaways lower, into the sewers.

Hope, the big fae who wasn't Prince Shining Talon, paused only once—to gather Sil into his arms.

It was too much too fast. For the first time, Inis heard sorrow tinge Two's voice. *She is young, one small Enchantrisk against many sorcerers. That put us down another fighter. We ran, in order to add to our numbers.*

Inis felt Two's hope then, as surely as if it were her own. If they could regroup with the others, they'd have a chance.

A shitty chance, but better than none.

Halfway toward the sewer exit they'd been joined by Uaine and a boy Inis didn't recognize, barely older than fourteen and newly missing three fingers. From there, they had chased the smell of fresh air.

Emerging from underground, Queensguard close on their heels, they found themselves in the middle of the castle courtyard where the Queensguard trained.

Where countless fresh Queensguard stood now, awaiting them.

This was when Inis had awoken and rejoined the picture. She slid out of Two's mind and back into her own.

Rags was unconscious, his right hand looking like it'd been attacked by carrion birds. Inis was barely awake. The fae children were unable to fight, in need of protection, and now holding a too-pale Sil in their arms so Hope could stand alone between them and hundreds of armored Queensguard. The fae warrior bled from countless slashes, some mere grazes, some deeper. Not nearly enough to prevent him from fighting for his life, for all their lives, but eventually he'd be taken down, no matter how fast he was, no matter how strong and determined.

Inis stumbled to her feet.

Join me, she told Two. *Do the—whatever it was you did. Make me stronger.*

We probably shouldn't, Two replied. Grinned. *Doesn't mean we won't.*

Silver flooded her, filled her, surrounded her. It made her so much more powerful, not erasing the pain but allowing her to ignore it. Her fingers shone as she leaped forward, joined Hope in the fray, tore Queensguard apart with nothing more than her hands.

Their hands.

Every blow glanced off their skin. Queensguard toppled, screamed—kept coming, but they were beginning to falter. Inis lost count of how many they'd felled, went through each motion before agony had a chance to catch up with them. Two laughed, howled through Inis's throat, as they battled.

They might have made it, might have killed every last Queensguard, if it hadn't been for the reinforcements.

With Morien, robes torn and redder with his blood, at their head.

He shouted, held up his arms. The skies opened. Rain and lightning licked across a sudden roiling of black clouds. A bolt lanced through the air and caught Inis at the back of her neck, shocking Two into separating from her. Silver melted, sizzled. Inis screamed and hit the ground. The fresh surge of Queensguard swarmed Hope, and he disappeared amid their armor and weapons.

Sil. Where was Sil? And what about the children? Not older than Ivy. They needed protection.

Inis tried to rise but couldn't. The fight, Hope refusing to surrender, raged on, blows connecting, the shrieks of rending armor. Cool rain pattered down onto her face and body. She dug her fingers into the hard-packed training-ground soil and gripped tight, but she couldn't make herself move.

The whole world swam when she tried.

Two's pain was her own. More than the pain was the terrible silence, blank quiet between her ears. Was this what Tomman had felt the instant before he'd died? The vital need to rise, only to find himself unable to? Had he thought about them, wondered if Inis and Ivy yet survived, or had he thought only about himself?

Inis would ask him when she saw him. Her head felt like it had been replaced by one sculpted from solid iron.

She screamed, unable to move or think or do anything to help her friends. She let her rage loose, howling like a wolf at the moon. Let Morien see that she wasn't afraid of him anymore.

Red flooded her vision. She tried to blink it clear, then realized it was Morien the Last, soaked to the bone, draped red fabric near black and clinging to his hard angles, his looming body. Inis's heart pounded, drowning out the noise in her ears. She fought to sit, though it made the ground beneath her tilt.

"You Ever-Loyals," Morien said, "always trying to get back on your feet when you've been beaten."

"You . . ." Inis's mouth was dry. Her lips stuck to her teeth when she spoke. It was hardly a glorious moment, but she was upright. "You wouldn't understand."

She didn't have the moisture to spit at him, but she made the gesture with her lips anyway. Felt Two's glowing approval some-where behind her, wherever he'd landed. Injured, but alive. *Alive.* She grinned like he would have, showing teeth.

And a curious calm overtook her, with Morien staring her down and Hope battling the Queensguard alone. They were finished, but there was no despair. It was as if the lightning strike had burned any last traces of fear from her body. She swayed onto her feet. Morien might cut her down before she rose, but she'd die with her heart belonging to herself and no one else.

"It's over," she said. "You can't hide what's happened here. There'll be questions. Investigations. Some might stand for it, turn a blind eye, but you'll never silence everyone."

"You don't understand," Morien replied. "I already have."

He snapped his fingers, and the courtyard fell silent. The Queensguard stopped fighting at once, obeying his command. Inis couldn't make out Hope's golden aura, hidden behind too much steel. The ground slick with rain and blood.

So those darker rumors and fears were true. There were shards in the heart of every Queensguard, maybe every servant. Maybe every courtier. Maybe every Ever-Noble. Maybe every prince would be sharded too, now that the Queen's children had proven they weren't inherently loyal.

The knowledge hit Inis like a new blow.

Morien saw its impact and laughed. "Little girl, what you've accomplished here is *nothing*. No, I speak too soon. You've helped me, brought me someone who escaped my grasp. She'll die here with you."

If there was no other way for Inis to fight, she could still strike back.

Two, you have to tell Sil and the others to run. They can still escape—

I can tell the others, Two said. *But not Sil.*

Don't be stubborn— Inis began.

Didn't get to finish. Morien's hand rose, tracing murderous glyphs in the air, and the world whitened. This time, the pain came from without instead of within. The air around Inis scorched her skin while her heart beat its shuddering pulse in her chest.

It was battered, wounded, but her heart still worked. Though Inis's eyes burned, she kept them fixed on Morien, refusing to look away. She stared him down, would keep staring him down as he killed her. She'd make him see her.

Then, a snap of power, like more lightning. It didn't strike Inis this time. A chaos of clattering metal shattered Morien's silence. Two's voice in Inis's head, panting wearily, carried a delighted cackle.

Finally, he said. *Our reinforcements are here.*

For a time, Cathair Remington thought he had a son who'd inherit his name—and the centuries-old family trade of barrel making. Until, shortly after her tenth birthday, Einan told him different. She was no son but his daughter. This he could understand and accept. What he couldn't bear was that she loved the theater and not barrels.

Cathair had predicted ruin and disaster for Einan should she run off like a fool to chase glory on the stage, but even his direst warnings had never placed her in a situation quite this grim.

Soaked with royal blood, she stumbled out of the tunnels of Coward's Silence, into the open air and pouring rain.

The scene below was worse than the bloodiest histories she'd enacted onstage.

So many Queensguard, she couldn't see past them at first to what they'd surrounded. A handful of kids, all of them glowing faintly. *Fae.*

Einan strained but didn't see Sil. Didn't see Hope, either, though now and then a yowl rose from a tighter knot of Queensguard, which might've been where the enemy swarmed him. And there was the girl they'd met, pretty in an angry way, on the ground: her silver beast half melted next to her, the sorcerer standing over her, all of them royally fucked.

If ever there was a time for a grand entrance, this was it.

But someone needed to stay behind and help Prince Laisrean, who was on his last legs. Their group was too badly injured already. And sure, they had two silver beasties of their own, but would that be enough?

It wasn't enough, but it was all they had. Einan balled her fists.

Cab at her side, his bruises still fresh. He'd been so stupidly brave that Einan had forgotten how much she hated the Queensguard. She couldn't ask him for more. He'd given all.

Prince Somhairle, who'd visited her theater years ago, sweet thing, stood beside the fae named Shining Talon. Laisrean sagged, propped against the wall. Having a prince in the Resistance was always bound to be dangerous. *I'll pay the price,* he'd told them, *when the bill arrives.*

They hadn't protested. They'd needed their man on the inside, chosen not to dwell on his personal risk.

Einan wiped rain out of her eyes. White-hot energy crackled around the sorcerer, gathering, narrowing to a point, heading straight for Inis. Behind her, the kids. He'd tear them apart next. No question.

Einan started forward and shouted something brave like "Over here, you shitting son of a donkey's rear end!" Not that it'd distract a seasoned sorcerer, or do a thing to stop the countless Queensguard from getting to *her* before she got to *him,* but.

Didn't matter. It was the attempt that counted.

As Einan ran, the air around her changed, charged with new energy. She guessed it was part of Morien's sorcery, but it was so warm. So friendly. It shocked her from fingertips to chest, and when it hit her heart, the Queensguard swords flew out of their hands and rose into the air.

Shooting straight toward her.

Einan froze, though she wasn't frightened. She should have

winced, ducked, run, *anything* to keep the blades from impaling her—only she was certain they wouldn't harm her. The swords cut a song out of the air. It sounded like her father's flute music, like the tinkle of her old jewelry before it had been taken from her and melted down into brutish Queensguard murder tools.

The swords formed into a single glittering shape as they flew.

A silver beast. A hound. Chipped and dented from years of practice, his hackles up, his eyes wild with stormlight.

Hey there, master! His voice, had to be his voice, lanced through her. *Let's cause some trouble, yeah?*

Despite how very fucked they were, Einan threw her head back and laughed. Then, taking advantage of the general shock and the sudden lack of weapons in the Queensguard's hands, she dove forward into the fray.

The hound moved like river water, fierce and drowning-fast. He jumped the first Queensguard with no hesitation or hint of his former existence, but then, a sword had no allegiance to its wielder, could switch hands and sides as easily as a tossed coin. The silver hound barreled over the first Queensguard, then the next, buffeting this way and that, landing on chests, knocking legs at the knees. Wherever he went, when the Queensguard went down, they stayed down.

Hope emerged from where he'd been mobbed, battered and bleeding. On his knees. Morien's attention spun from Inis to the silver hound and the chaos he was sowing. Einan rushed into the opening, kneeling to drag Inis up.

"I'm dead." Inis sounded matter-of-fact, like she couldn't find a reason to mourn the thing once it had happened.

"If that's true, then you've spawned a nightmare of an afterlife," Einan replied.

She stopped short of touching the half-melted creature at Inis's side, not sure what she could do for him, not wanting to harm him further.

Another crack of lightning split the courtyard. Annoyance followed a flare of pain.

Her dog yipped. Einan stood, Inis next to her.

This Lying One has got *to go,* the dog said.

Einan turned, not sure how to agree with him other than to act.

But it was Shining Talon who moved into position in a blur of gold, streaking toward the sorcerer. Einan's hound broke away to join him, as did Prince Somhairle's enormous one-eyed owl, missing feathers and a section of her beak. Cab's lizard creature shot forward along the ground, and Inis's silver companion coalesced, if vaguely, his limbs loose and limping but functional, in order to follow.

Been a long time coming, Einan's dog said.

White heat scorched the ground where Morien stood. He'd erected a barrier around himself, a cocoon of living lightning. Shining Talon didn't slow before he struck it. A ferocious *crack*. The stench of sizzling metal. Black burns ran up both the fae's arms, but he kept his palms to the barrier.

He was moving through it.

The little thief fellow cried out from where the fae children had gathered. Something dirty sounding. Einan didn't know whether the knowledge was hers or the hound's, but his name suddenly appeared in her head: *Rags*.

"That shiny idiot's going to get himself killed!" Rags shouted.

His words galvanized Hope. One moment the fae was kneeling, panting, bleeding; the next he was on his feet, thrusting his hands through Morien's barrier with Shining Talon. The silver animals threw themselves against it one after another. Each time, it crackled and flashed, a little less bright than the time before.

Einan held her breath, prayed to whoever was listening. Got no answer, except a silvery snort in the back of her head.

Not—enough—to make it, her dog snarled.

Einan started forward.

She wasn't a fae. She was barely a decent actor. She didn't know what she could do, only that she'd have to do it. Give her life to bring that barrier down, sure. Her greatest role yet. Her last one.

But someone grabbed her by the back of her shirt and pulled her out of the way. Stepped in front of her and blocked her path.

Sil, hair whiter than ever, so white it was practically translucent, skin thinner than wet paper, every vein showing beneath. No, those were her black bones. As Sil lurched forward, Einan understood that whatever she was about to do, she didn't have the strength to do it. Not after performing two of those heart-saving maneuvers in a row. Not when she'd been so drained to begin with.

A human life is a short little thing compared to ours. Sil's voice in Einan's head. She'd never done that before. It had to be because of the dog creature that she could, borrowing their shared connection. *But that does not mean it holds no value.*

"No!" Einan jumped after her, had to stop her. Sil was exhausted and talking nonsense. Of course Einan's life didn't matter. Not compared to hers.

Thank you, Einan Remington, Master of Four. Sil's smile, gentle as spring rain. *With you at my side, I have seen more than I ever imagined.*

Einan shouted, but Sil pushed her back a final time and took her place between Hope and Shining Talon.

I would not have this be your final performance. Goodbye, my friend.

Sil's hands set against the barrier, Einan hollering, Rags hollering with her, and the Queensguard brought low not by their lack of weapons or the fresh assault, but by the blinding, endless, incinerating light—

It filled Einan's vision. She had to throw up her arm to keep from going blind.

And then Morien was gone, and with him the burning light. The air stank of melted metal. Her dog growled at a black streak on the ground where Morien had previously stood, sniffing at it like he could find the sorcerer by scent alone, follow him wherever he'd escaped to.

The Queensguard around them were groaning, crying out, clutching themselves where metal armor had fused to their skin from the intensity of the blast.

None of that mattered.

Sil collapsed into Hope's arms. Inis leaned against Einan for support, must have grabbed her sometime between Sil's *stupid, crazy, awful* decision to sacrifice herself and Morien's lightning burst. Einan realized she was sobbing and Inis was holding her back, Hope was howling, and—

And Sil was unmoving.

"Now," Inis whispered hoarsely.

Einan shook her head, took a trembling step forward. Reached out for Sil, but Hope wouldn't let go of her, bared his teeth at Einan and growled. Tears stained Shining Talon's cheeks like the blood staining his injured arm.

"Now," Inis repeated. Einan kept trying to shake the noise away, to shake the truth away, but Inis gripped Einan's wrist and squeezed. Hard.

It broke the spell.

Einan whirled on her, then softened when she saw the tension in

Inis's jaw, the blank, glassy sheen over her eyes. *"What?"*

"If we're going to escape, it can only be now." Inis gestured to the carnage. "They won't be able to follow us—the Queensguard—and the Last is gone—we have to escape."

She was right. There might be Queensguard yet capable of giving chase. And the Queen had more sorcerers than Morien at her command. They would follow the Queen's enemies in Morien's stead, now that he had disappeared. Einan sucked in a breath between her clenched teeth, shook off Inis's grip, and rolled up her sleeves. (What the director used to do at the Gilded Lily when the actors were messing around during practice.) She raised herself to her full, short height.

When she called for the rest to follow her, Cab was the first to fall in line.

87
SOMHAIRLE

With the sound of Laisrean's ragged breath roaring in his ears, Somhairle did his best to keep the story going.

He didn't know *where* they were headed. It didn't seem to matter.

Don't think I'd let you stumble into anything dangerous. Three's voice, deep and musical, high above. She was surveying their path from beyond the tree line, looking ahead with her bird's-eye view.

Like a rebellion against a remorseless sorcerer and a mother too proud to die? Never, Somhairle agreed.

Properly chastised.

Let's never be apart again. There was a hint of no-nonsense in Three's tone that reminded Somhairle of Inis, but that was the only overlap between his silver fragment and his strongest friend. Inis was more serious than fae silver, glittering and clever and laughing not at pain, but at death itself.

Thank you for coming back, Somhairle replied.

Thank you for letting me go.

It had to be done.

It had to be us, Three agreed. *Because you have lived with pain every day of your life, like me. Like our Creators. Your shape is different, but no matter. We do not fear pain, not like those who haven't lived inside it. We* are *pain.*

Somhairle let his eyes close for a breath. The broad beat of Three's wings, the warmth of an undercurrent in the air keeping her aloft. Was Three right? (*I'm always right,* she reassured him.) Was it possible he'd found the one, the *only* thing that might be easy for him?

Strength in a role other than the kindly, suffering cripple. To be Somhairle first, not Somhairle's weakness.

They were soaking wet from their escape. A dead sprint through the courtyard had ended in a dip in "Old Drowner," as Rags had called it. They had floated down to a more secluded spot to avoid the main roads, then swum to the desolate shores of the bank, where only blind beggars and starving urchins marked their passing. From there, they clambered out of the dirty water and into a scrubby forest too bare for the Queen's men to bother hunting in.

Somhairle stuck to his brother's side. Laisrean was heavy, and Somhairle couldn't let Shining Talon bear his weight alone.

He had finally come off the shelf, to live as he wished. Or not at all.

His stiff right leg ached all the way up to his hip, where bright-hot pain lanced in rhythm to his steps. Somhairle longed for a soft bed, a place to sit. Neither awaited him. No matter where they were headed. With every sag of his eyelids, damp golden hair trickling water into his eyes, Somhairle recalled the crack of lightning through the sky.

He saw it strike Inis, again and again.

At the time, he'd cried out, electric heat scorching his throat bone-dry. He'd imagined he was looking at a dead woman, the statue erected in a martyr's honor, the silver and human shape of the only best friend he'd ever known.

But Inis lived. Two and Three lived. Somhairle lived.

And what of Faolan? He shouldn't have, but Somhairle wondered.

Limping along, he took stock of the group. The fae girl who had freed Rags and Inis from the mirrorcraft had stopped breathing back in the courtyard, but the fae named Hope still bore her in his arms. He wouldn't release her, or allow anyone close enough to suggest it.

They were a sorry, sorrowful group.

Somhairle's fine boots were soggy; everything was sore. Stray branches slapped and stung his face as their path cut deeper through the wood. He watched Laisrean out of the corner of his eye. Was this like a hunting trip? He'd never gone hunting with his brothers.

Laisrean caught him looking.

"I warned you, little brother." His grin was a wince. The sweat coating his dark skin suggested he was feverish. Somhairle could teach him how to weather fever and missing parts. The phantom aches, the night sweats, a body that wouldn't obey. "Life on the Hill is too exciting."

Exciting wasn't powerful enough for what Somhairle had found. A group of strangers who could be friends. A group of friends who might become heroes.

They'd lost the fae girl who could save them from Morien's mirror-craft. Without her, it was up to Somhairle to find a way to free Faolan from the shard in his heart.

If the Head of House Ever-Learning still lived.

Who could say how long he'd been Morien's instrument?

What Somhairle remembered most was the wild light in Faolan's eyes that night in the Ever-Land Manor before the door had slammed shut on Somhairle's nose. His curiously cheerful demeanor after Morien's fit of pique.

His wasn't a fight anyone should have to soldier alone. Faolan didn't have a fragment to share his burdens, so it was all the more important to bring him to their side.

Or at least allow him to have a real choice.

Somhairle let Laisrean lean on him, let Three lead them onward; and despite the weariness in his bones, he didn't stumble.

88
RAGS

Rags didn't know where they were going. He also didn't know how they kept moving when they were probably already dead.

Then he told himself to quit grousing. How dare he make light of living, no matter how painful it was, when there were some among them who weren't alive? He'd share a bed with goats and wouldn't complain, he swore it, if only his hand would stop throbbing.

If only Tal would look at him again.

He'd lost track of the time when he felt lithe fingers against his damaged palm. The cool touch soothed the burning and aching left behind by Sil's rushed mirrorglass removal. He startled, nearly slapping the hand away.

He looked down instead, met two silver eyes staring up at him from the innocent face of a fae urchin. Another nipped close on his other side, the braver children in the group coming forward to cluster around him.

Rags wrestled with the urge to tell them to get lost. To look to somebody else. But the truth of the matter was, there *wasn't* anybody else. The stronger fae had other burdens, and all the stronger people had someone weaker leaning on them. One of the silver animals would've made a better nanny than Rags, but he couldn't bring himself to shake the kids loose after they'd reached for him specifically.

He'd fucked up by watching over them during the fight. They thought he was a brave warrior, a hero.

He couldn't even figure out the fragment in his pocket. Some hero that made him.

"You all right?" Rags asked the nearest fae kid. Boy or girl, he couldn't tell. They all had long hair, black streaked with white, and beautiful, blank-slate faces that'd make your eyes swim if you stared at them too long, like gazing directly at an eclipse. The other fae, the fragments, and the children's desperation explained how they could possibly trust any human to help after everything humans had already done to hurt them.

"The castle walls told me of the sky at night," the little fae explained, "but I have never seen the stars for myself."

"Lucky you." If Rags could spin this into something positive, could make them feel better, then he could spin gold out of shit. "There's a whole mess of them up there to discover."

"Of course." Another little fae, the one holding Rags's other hand. "Because we could not see them does not mean we did not believe they were real."

"But they are so much brighter than we had hoped," the first fae said.

Rags decided he was going to call that one Happy and the other one Smartass. He focused on them instead of on Tal, his broad back and powerful shoulders, his bloody arm and his inability to meet Rags's eye. Or the way his own right hand kept twitching unbidden, something damaged deep in the muscle tissue.

"I call that one the Big Asshole." Rags jerked his head toward one of the constellations.

"What is asshole?" Happy asked.

Smartass didn't have a clever explanation. He stared at Rags expectantly. "Yes. What is the meaning of asshole?"

Rags cleared his throat. What would Dane have said? "Not important. Forget that word. Uh, I call that one Ugly Dog Without a Tail. And that one's the Dirty Spoon."

He kept them moving, chatting about the stupid stars, distracted from the big mess they were in. They were weak and kept stumbling, so if they could laugh at Rags's babble, it was better than nothing.

Plus, they had to keep walking.

Rags was pretty sure his feet were bleeding, but there were cool hands clutching his, a swarm of fae kiddies looking to him to get them through.

They stayed on their feet, pushing onward and away from the castle, straight through another dawn. Rags couldn't tell one kind of tree from the next, but he suspected they were in what he thought of as the Badwoods, although its official name was the Forest of Never-Leaving.

Since people only ever went in, didn't ever come out.

Good thing they were traveling with fae and the fragments. The trees didn't attack or try to eat them or whatever it was they usually did. In fact, Rags could've sworn that the trees were bowing aside, leading them toward something.

Somewhere?

The problem with morning was there were no more stars to jabber about, so Rags worked on showing the kids some tricks, like making a coin appear behind their ears or out of their nostrils, then disappearing it again in midair with sleight of hand. He gritted his teeth and forced his brittle fingers through the motions.

Only breathed when he didn't drop the coin in the grass.

"Are you a Lying One?" Smartass asked dubiously.

"I lie," Rags admitted. "But not the way you mean it." He made the coin appear again. Happy's smile could have lit up the whole forest. Rags hid his answering grin by hiding the coin in his sleeve, then pretending to cough it up.

So it went.

Rags assumed they'd walk until they dropped. When they stopped, he swayed on his feet. He'd nearly forgotten what it was like to be still.

The scraping of stone. Rags peered over some shoulders, one of which was covered with bruising lashes, all of them dirty and torn-up and bloody, to see the fragments pushing a boulder between two great oaks. The silver cat was still re-forming after it'd been struck by lightning and slightly melted, the owl had clumps of feathers and chunks of beak missing, and the dog was *really* into sniffing trees, but the lizard had them working together smoothly to push this huge rock from one spot to another.

Rags saw why.

It had covered a hole, dark inside until Tal stepped forward and those same swirly patterns from the fae ruins began to glow around the edges.

"The Queen's people know about the tunnels," Einan, or Scrappy Redhead, as Rags thought of her, warned them. "Who's to say they don't know about these?"

"This will take us to the True Palace, the Heart of the Bone Court." The way Tal said it, Rags knew it was an official name. "Once we are there, we can defend it from any intruder. Even those who know the way."

There was no arguing with someone who sounded that sure. Tal could be hilarious when he was protecting Rags from the threat of a spoon, but in moments like this, it was most obvious that he came from someplace other.

A fae prince with a fae palace. Rags should've known from the beginning where he'd wind up in the mix. He wasn't palace people.

"Here." Rags loosed Happy's hand, fished in his pocket for the old, raw silver lump. It sat cupped in his palm, stretched the length to the tips of his fingers. "Your queen put this *in* the stars, so I guess it's kinda like a star? Go on. Take it. It's yours."

Happy took one look at the thing, then peered around to glance at Smartass. After a second's wordless interaction, which was eerie at best, she shook her head.

"It is not for us to bear," Happy said gravely. "But if you like, we will keep it with us for a time."

"Until we reach our destination," Smartass confirmed.

Rags slipped the lump into their tiny, golden hands. Too tired to think any more about who was doing who a favor. So he missed what he should've caught: a faint glow, pulsing from within, a slender seam of sunlight around the lump's middle.

Then, with exquisite precision, it split open. Rags sprang back to cup his hands around the spilling light. *Beacon,* his senses screamed.

They couldn't let anyone find them.

Nothing happened. Rags peered between his fingers, aware of Happy and Smartass doing the same. In his mind's eye he pictured Inis's dishware exploding through a wall, the Queensguard swords flashing through the air, and he hoped—

"Maybe we'd better stand back," he murmured nervously. Held his breath.

The light faded. The egg-sized fragment had taken no animal shape but was now opened and flat instead of closed and round. Rags touched its surface with shaking fingers. Etchings in the metal. Like a drawing, or a diagram, carved with only straight lines. Rags nonetheless saw what looked like trees, and little ships, and a concentric, geometric symbol in the upper-right-hand corner. Like one of those impossible fae knots.

Not a diagram. A map. Rags craned his head for Tal's input, only to remember Tal wasn't there. He was helping the group. Rags was the one dawdling behind.

It figured. He'd finally solved step one of the puzzle, but he'd lost the guy he wanted to solve it for. The guy who could explain what to do with it next.

"Would you hang on to it for now?" Rags thrust the silver map back at the fae kiddies. It was light and supple, despite being made of solid metal.

Happy and Smartass shared another glance, then nodded.

"Don't think I missed that look," Rags grumbled, but he didn't object when the fae children clung to him again, taking up their positions on either side of him like watchful sentinel hounds.

Rags's hands might be clever, but when it came to this kind of heavy lifting, the job *was* easier in a group.

89
INIS

Inis was still alive, which was more than she'd hoped for. It hurt to live, but this pain was different and new. It was hers and no one else's, the molten core of her anger. She'd carry it as surely as she carried Two.

During their escape from the Hill, she'd torn the Queen's sunburst flag from a parapet, formed the silken fabric into a sling, and put Two inside it, tucked him close to her chest. He'd shrunk to the size of a scrawny barn tom, which made Inis think of Ivy holding the big silver cat in her arms. He didn't speak but remained there silent, save for his purring, the rumble a healing warmth that vibrated through Inis's ribs and let her know he'd be all right.

In time, they both would. Inis knew too well how to be patient, biding the months until an ache became a living part of her.

She was glad Morien hadn't killed her. It meant she hadn't left Ivy alone to fend for herself with Mother and Bute.

She thought about Ivy whenever the pain in her skin became too great, whenever her weary muscles shuddered and threatened to snap and seize. She had to survive, because there was a chance Morien had survived, too. Her family's cottage in the Far Glades might not be his first stop on a tour of revenge—but if he lived, he would use her family to hurt her.

She was still sodden from their swim in the moat the day before, no sunlight underground to dry her. Would these fae tunnels never end?

It was hours of stumbling, sweaty travel before she could look at Laisrean. Before she could gather enough willpower to glance outside herself and see the ruin of the boy who'd been her friend, the brave, battered young man he'd become.

She approached Somhairle first, brushing his shoulder with hers to let him know she was there for support. She knew he was tired when he let her take his arm under the elbow, supporting him like he supported his brother on the other side.

"I'm sorry." Somhairle's chin tipped down, his gaze on his boots. "I couldn't do anything. If I'd been able to fight—"

"Keep talking like that and I'll knock you down and leave you in the tunnels." Inis kept her voice steady, her eyes fixed on the darkness ahead. "You helped free the little ones. That's why we came."

"Still." Somhairle let the word stretch on into silence. Then he brightened, lifting his head, his mouth a crooked glint in the other-worldly light from the fae glyphs wrought in the stone. "*You* were magnificent. Like a legend out of the Lost-Lands."

The soft thunder of Two's purr grew louder at the praise.

"You as well," Somhairle added in his direction. Two grinned.

When they stopped to let those of them with shorter legs rest and give the injured a chance to do the same, Shining Talon, Cabhan, and Einan left to gather mushrooms for sustenance while the others licked their bloody wounds. Inis put her back to the stone wall, lowered herself to the ground with Two cradled in her arms.

She didn't remember falling asleep, but she must have, because she dreamed of fire and silver and Two's eyes guiding her through the darkness. In the dream, she wasn't afraid, though she was in pain. She knew where she was going and what she had to do.

No one can stop us when we fight, Two said.

No one can stop us because of what we fight for, Inis replied.

Much later, when she woke, Laisrean was sitting at her side. His right eye was a shuttered mess, a feverish stink seeping from beneath its bandage.

Unbidden, Inis reached to touch his face, tracing the prominent arch of his cheekbone to his strong jaw. She didn't allow her hand to shake.

Two stirred in his sling when Laisrean shifted. Inis let her hand fall away, but Laisrean took her gently by the wrist, fingers pressed to her fluttering pulse.

"Wanted to give you something." His voice was rough. With his free hand, he reached to tug at the knot in the leather cords around his wrist, then winced, pulling away as though he'd been burned.

The ends of his index and middle fingers were bloodied and raw.

They'd started to pull out his nails in Coward's Silence.

Lucky, Inis thought. In a way, her brothers, her father, had been lucky to die before enduring weeks of torture.

"Let me help," Inis said. Not a question, no coy protestation at the thought of a gift. They were beyond courtly artifices.

There was a time when she might have imagined Laisrean taking her hand to give her a lover's token. The smell of roses would have been heavy in the air, the last breath of summer still clinging to the evening like vines to their stakes, the sky deepening pink and gold.

Miles underground and far from the Hill, Inis smelling of moat water and charred with lightning, Laisrean's blood and rot tainting every breath, the gift was far from fantasy.

Expectations and reality. They somehow intersected.

Lais tapped one of the two leather cords braided around his wrist and Inis dutifully untied it. The knot had frayed from years of wear, and it took some doing to pick it apart, but she managed it with broken nails and stubborn will.

"Here." Lais took the cord when she'd finished and clumsily looped it around her bare wrist. It was large enough to fit nearly double. Inis watched in silence. Her heart swelled with sorrow at the look of concentration on Lais's face, the care it took for him to tie a simple knot.

An ember of her old anger glowed to life between her ribs.

If they ever met the Last again, she'd make him pay. Then, she'd make the Queen pay, too.

When the task was done, Lais held up his wrist with its single cord to match Inis's. She took his hand in both of hers.

"I couldn't save him. He told me, if it came to that, I shouldn't try. Shouldn't compromise myself." Lais tipped his head back, staring at the bedrock above their heads. Inis didn't need to ask who he meant. "It's no excuse. I don't want you to forgive me. I wanted you to know. . . ." A low grunt of pain, followed by a hissed sigh. "Thought I could make up for that with Malachy. Keep Morien's anger on me, buy the boy some time. Yet we're all missing bits and pieces."

Suddenly wearier than she'd ever been, Inis rested her head on Lais's shoulder. She couldn't speak around the lump that had formed in her throat, but she wanted to show him it was all right. She understood: Tomman hadn't told her his secrets not because he hadn't trusted her. He'd kept them from her because he'd hoped to save her life that night, protect her from the massacre on the Hill.

She couldn't blame her brother for the path he'd chosen, not when she wore his trust bracelet and now fought for the same cause he'd died to champion.

They sat together in silence, the darkness swaddling them, Laisrean's breathing deepening, finally evening out. Inis thought he'd fallen asleep when, unexpectedly, he spoke again.

"Do you remember the last time we talked? Your family was returning from Ever-Land, and your sister had made us all wreaths of laurel flowers." Lais's eyes were closed, but the tight set of his mouth had eased. "When you got out of that carriage, crowned in pink and gold, I thought . . . I've *still* never seen anything more beautiful in my life."

Inis hadn't come this far by letting herself daydream about the past. She never paused to wonder what might have happened in another life.

If Tomman hadn't discovered the decay rotting beneath the Hill.

Things were horrible but honest. Inis laid a hand on Lais's chest and leaned in to press her mouth to his soft lips.

Lais sucked in a breath and his lashes fluttered. When he looked at her with his good eye, Inis was shocked to find herself nervous. *Her.* After everything they'd dealt with. After she'd been struck by lightning, tormented by the Last.

"We should have done that a long time ago," Lais said.

"Speak for yourself." A certain sensible tartness appeared in Inis's reply. With it, she felt more like herself than she had in days. "*I've* been busy saving *your* Resistance."

Lais's answering laugh was choked and soft, but satisfying. He put an arm around her shoulders and she let him keep it there. When Somhairle approached them to see what was so funny, a warm rush of gratitude settled deep in Inis's bones.

She'd regained a part of herself when she'd gone back to the Hill, something she'd believed was lost forever. She couldn't know when she'd get to see Ivy again, or their mother, or Bute.

She could manage that because she wasn't fighting alone anymore.

Two had done more than bring Inis back to these princes. He'd brought her back to herself.

90
RAGS

Time lost all meaning in the tunnels. They stopped only for brief spurts of rest, always with a fae keeping watch. They survived on mushrooms that Shining Talon insisted weren't poisonous. Rags never wanted to see another, had dreams that he was turning into one.

Had it been weeks? Hadn't they passed those same glyphs a hundred times? Had the sun ever been real?

After days of walking, they finally entered a broader tunnel and from there made their way into a massive chamber. The True Palace wasn't anything like what Rags had expected.

This was a black castle beneath the earth, tall spires wrought from the stone they stood beneath. It was attached at the floor and ceiling, delicate towers piercing downward from the dome in which they stood. Inlaid silver made patterns within the rock. Fae lights beckoned from the windows, steady and unflickering.

It looked haunted as *fuck*. A place no one in their right mind would ever call a *safe haven*. But they were out of options, and they were following four silver fragments and a fae prince. Their right mind had already left the party.

"Are we home?" Happy asked.

Smartass squeezed Rags's hand and said nothing. The wearier he got, the more Rags found himself missing the *ass* part of the little fae's personality.

They were far under the earth, but the curved walls around them stood high in a space so cavernous that Rags itched to shout to hear his own echo. He didn't—what if he made the ceiling cave in on them? But still.

A staircase had been hewn into the stone, polished steps leading toward the palace. The rocks set into the cave around them glowed like torches, lighting the way so it didn't feel impossibly dark.

Tal led them through the palace doors. Down a level. Past parallel feasting tables set with silver cups and plates, waiting for an absent court. Again, creepy, but the kids didn't seem to think so. They rushed forward gladly, settling onto benches, picking up plates and inspecting them. Rags set Happy and Smartass free to join their— friends? Brothers and sisters?

After what they'd been through together, maybe the distinction didn't matter.

"Sil would've loved this," Rags heard Einan whisper.

"We need beds for the wounded," Cab replied.

Rags rubbed his chest. The pain had faded over time, had been mostly replaced by the sting of the blisters on the soles of his feet, but he still felt its phantom traces, the scars left on his heart. He'd checked the real scar on the flesh over his ribs only once, then decided to avoid looking at it for the rest of his life.

Dirty and beaten down as he was from days of traveling and forced mushroom consumption, he was in better shape than most.

Hope still held the fae girl's corpse, had barely eaten a bite on the trek. The big guy, Prince Laisrean, had needed to be half dragged the last day, the bandage over his missing eye clotted and stinking some-thing fierce, and Somhairle wasn't much better, although he and Inis had done the majority of the dragging. Old lady Uaine was taking care of Malachy. The kids were being kids. Cab's injuries could've been worse, but could've been better. That left Tal, with his slashed arm, and Einan, who'd assigned herself to looking after Cab and Hope in equal measure.

And Rags.

The last three on that list were the best of a fucked-up lot.

"I'll do the searching." Rags hid a yawn in his shoulder. "'Cause I want a bed pretty bad myself, not 'cause I'm . . . ah, fuck it."

Smartass returned to him. He held out the silver fae fragment with both hands. Seeing it in the light of the hall, Rags had to admit: it looked an awful lot like a map.

"Do not forget your star," Smartass counseled.

"Thanks," Rags said.

"In the meantime, get the grievously injured on the tables," Cab added. "Those who can, clear off the plates, then help those who can't to lie down."

"That means you, stalwart moron." Einan steered Cab in the direction of the table while Happy, Smartass, and their crew stacked plates and set them aside.

"I will accompany you on the search," Tal said, suddenly at Rags's side.

Rags was too bone-tired to jump, but when he looked up into Tal's face, he met the fae prince's shining eyes for the first time in . . .

How long had it been? Felt like ages.

Rags shivered. "Gonna take revenge on me when we're separated from the others, huh?" He attempted a laugh, failed miserably. "All I ask is, make it quick."

Tal shook his head, the briefest memory of confusion darkening his features before he set off through one of many arched doorways that surrounded the main room. Not wanting to linger or get lost in the fae maze—if there were more fae traps around, Rags didn't want to meet them in this condition—Rags hurried after him. There were holes in his boots and blisters on his blisters, but he limped fast enough to keep up with Tal's unfaltering pace.

All the while, the map rested heavy in his hands. Tal hadn't said anything about it.

"My lump cracked," Rags said. He'd spent so much time around Tal that he'd become used to the conversation. "But it didn't turn into a beastie or even part of a beastie. It's a map . . . I think."

Tal looked at him. Maybe it was a trick of the light, and Rags hated himself for hoping, but there was a moment's trace of the old warmth on his face.

"I knew you would prove yourself worthy. It was only a matter of time."

No mention of going with him to wherever the map led. Rags let the conversation die.

Chambers after chambers. Rags got the impression that there were plenty more Tal wasn't leading them through. Some held empty bed frames or empty chests, while others held nothing but shadows stamped upon the walls. Rags would have preferred a ghost jumping out to the stifling silence, the walls glowing in response to Tal's presence.

"Hey," Rags said, distracting himself, "how come you have beds and feasting rooms and stuff if you don't need to eat?"

"We do not need to eat or sleep," Tal said, "but that does not mean we cannot enjoy both."

Great. All this time Rags had thought Tal was being normal, he was being noble. Putting off enjoyment in service of—what? Devoting his time and energy to keeping Rags safe?

Ridiculous. Tal needed someone a little more sneaky and selfish around to keep an eye on him. He wasn't ready for Rags to excuse himself from the picture.

"I must fortify the defenses," Tal said as they stopped in another room with a bed frame and an abandoned chair. "This will take time. But we need that time to recover."

"Speaking of." Rags nodded to Tal's arm. "Should get somebody to take a look at that wound."

"Unnecessary." Tal didn't acknowledge that this was the most they'd spoken since Rags had betrayed him, commanded him to leave fae children behind in order to save the few they'd freed. To save themselves. *Himself.* "It is already healing." Then he turned to Rags, a fresh streak of white in his hair held against his palm as evidence.

"Your hair changes color when you're healing?" Rags asked. He'd believe anything about the fae at this point.

Tal shook his head. "Our hair is darkest when we have all our strength. If we are diminished over time, sapped, it turns white. As I heal myself, I must sacrifice some of my immortal strength."

"Uh-huh," Rags said. "Sure. Why not." He took a deep breath. "So you're talking to me again?"

"I did not have the words for all I wished to say." Tal paused, confusion shadowing his face, mixed with something darker, like concern. After a long and uncertain silence, he knelt in front of Rags and bowed his head. "Forgive me. I lost my way when I saw the children in need. I almost sacrificed you because of my indecision—my stubborn insistence that I could save them all."

"What?" Rags heard himself say it, the nervous laughter that followed. He backed away from where Tal knelt, like that would make him get up. "No. *You're* mad at *me*."

Tal lifted his head. Blinked. That steady, pupilless gaze was extra freaky in the underground light.

"You believe I harbor feelings of anger for you?" Tal asked. "Never."

It was the spoon incident all over again. Tal needed Rags to explain things step by step. "*Yes*, you're mad at me. Because I made you leave. I did what a thief's supposed to do. I cut and I ran. You finally got that I'm not a hero and I'm not worth your time."

Tal did rise then, but he didn't look away from Rags. Instead, he reached over to grip Rags's shoulder. Not too tight. Sturdy, strong. He was still someone Rags could lean on if he wanted to, despite Tal's injuries.

"You saved all of us," Tal said. "If I had succumbed to my fever to rescue every child, then all of them would have remained captured. The Lying One would have taken us. Those who are here, whole and healthy, have you to thank for their freedom."

Rags did his impression of a gaping trout head tossed out with the scraps.

A tug at the old scar on his upper lip signaled that he was smiling. He reached to touch Tal's arm where it was whole and undamaged.

"You're an idiot," Rags said.

"And you have helped me to do something unimaginable," Tal countered. "I shall never be able to repay you, though what is left of my lifetime shall be devoted to it."

Devoted to you.

Rags shook his head. "Uh-uh. We're free. No Morien watching over our shoulders or through my chest. You can take the last fragments for yourself, if you want. You probably should. They're yours, and all we've managed to do so far is hurt them."

He didn't say what he was thinking: that with Hope and the other fae awakened, there was little doubt the Weapon would choose more preferable masters. There was no need to settle for paltry human substitutes.

Rags didn't know why, but Tal got to his knees again. He reached for Rags's scarred, freezing hands. Took the injured one, black with bruising and dried blood. He kissed Rags's fingers at the knuckles, warm lips, cool breath. Soft, but unmistakably that. *Kissing.*

"What are you doing?" Rags demanded, the words coming out hoarser than he'd intended. Scratchy. Young. Nervous.

"Your hands are precious to you," Tal replied. "They are precious to me."

"No." Rags's voice, independent of his instructions, coming from his mouth.

"No," Tal repeated, though he didn't pull away. "I should not have done this?"

"Shit, no, that's not—" Rags wasn't mad, he was happy. But every time he tried to show it, it flickered away like a flea between his fingers. When he tried to catch it head-on, he ended up with his hands holding empty air.

Rags didn't know how to show it, much less share it. He swallowed. His throat was molten silver, and he knew what that was like because he'd seen it. He also knew what it could become, which was something more lovely, more powerful, than anything else. His voice was hoarse, reaching a buried place that should have stayed buried but wasn't. It wouldn't go back to being buried, not now that it'd been unearthed.

"You're free, too," Rags said. "*I release you*—or whatever."

How Tal managed to look calm and in control when he was on his knees was but one of the infuriating and beautiful things about him. His bright gaze burned.

"Have I disappointed you?"

"What? No, I'm not *disappointed*."

Daring as ravens, Rags reminded himself. But there was the second part. *Rich as magpies.* Tal was a treasure, just not the kind Morien and Lord Faolan had anticipated.

With only one good hand, Rags nabbed him.

"I want to kiss you." The words screamed from under his skin, rooted him to the floor. No comparing it to the pain of mirrorcraft. The pain was natural to him, if brand-new. "But I can't know if *you* want to kiss *me*. Not really. Not when you do everything I tell you to. Obey my every command."

"Truly?" Tal arched one black brow. "But I have never lied to you."

"That's not what I mean." Tal's shirt was as slippery as it looked when Rags seized it. He tugged, but Tal stayed in place. It was Rags who came forward. Tal's hands caught him above the hips and Rags tilted his face up. Like colliding chest-first with an oak tree, so it was totally reasonable he felt winded.

He couldn't tell who kissed who. Maybe that didn't matter. Relief and sorrow broke over Rags like the first shock of cold when they'd jumped into Old Drowner. They were free, but they'd lost people. Fae children were still under the Queen's control. One of them had died to get the shards out of their hearts. They'd be hunted until the end of their days, probably.

But they'd slipped Morien's grip, and Tal was holding Rags up. Rags's fingers slid into Tal's silky hair, mouth softening under his. For one long honey-drop moment, Rags stopped thinking, and everything inside him turned to want.

Fucking fae.

It was Rags who found the breathless will to break away first, though really, he was on fire with the desire to go back and give in.

"Listen," Rags said sharply, though he was still using Tal for balance, "*listen.* I want you bound to me by choice. Not circumstance or fae prophecy."

"You object to our bond?" The restraint in Tal's voice, the disarray of black hair, the heat in his silver eyes: striking match after match in Rags's gut.

He thought he'd already been set ablaze.

"Yes." Rags nodded deliberately. Tal didn't have to know he was trying to convince himself in the same measure. "I can't kiss someone under my command. It's *creepy.*"

Tal frowned. "To the fae it is not creepy."

Rags buried his face in Tal's shoulder. "To the fae it *should* be creepy, Tal. We're gonna work on that. Together, I guess."

Everything shifted as they faced each other. Rags felt like all the pieces of him had been there all along, obviously, but he'd been waiting for something else, a big lug who had perfect shoulders, to bring those pieces together the way they were meant to be. To feel so damn right. So powerful.

Ready to make his world a better place.

"When the remaining fragments of the Great Paragon are located," Tal said, "my duty will be fulfilled."

"And we won't be bound by anything then?" Rags squinted. Fae were tricky, trickier than Cheapsiders during a lean year.

"Nothing but our personal will." Tal brought Rags's scarred hand to his mouth.

Against the rules. Rags allowed it.

They only had to find two more fragments: the one destined for Tal and the one for Rags, which maybe Rags's map could lead him to. Considering they'd started with one and now had four, those weren't overwhelming numbers.

Planning that far ahead should have made Rags want to bolt. It meant a lifetime sentence of working together. Rags wouldn't have believed it if he hadn't passed the verdict himself.

With the pad of his thumb, he smoothed back Tal's stray white hairs, the streak that had only just formed.

"Humans have a saying about this," Rags said. "Stress makes our hair turn gray. Your people probably don't know shit about stress, so I'll call it *trouble*. And since your Folk aren't around to disapprove of me, I'm telling you before you hear it from someone else: *I'm* trouble. *That's* why you're getting all this white hair."

Tal frowned. "The loss of color is due to a healing ritual of my people. I thought I explained—"

Rags sighed. "Easier not to kiss you when I remember you have no sense of humor."

Tal touched the back of Rags's head, making him straighten up. There was either a faint sheen of sweat coating Tal's skin or Rags had never noticed the way the gold glimmered below the surface.

"We are free," Tal said, "but there are yet those who lack the same freedom."

"Yeah," Rags agreed. No time to relax. Letting his guard down meant getting pinched, no matter who was doing the pinching. And he was looking out for more than himself now. "You might need an expert thief to track the last two fragments down, so."

"Have you forgotten that you are the one who saved me? This means you are Master of Five." Tal's hand settled big and warm on Rags's shoulder. Was he imagining it, or was that warmth and strength flowing from his body into Rags's, making him want to do crazy, wonderful, heroic deeds?

Master of Five. Yeah, right. Even with a map, it didn't seem possible.

But with Tal gazing at him and glowing bright as molten gold, holding Rags and gleaming at him, he could believe it. Whatever that map led to, it was up to Rags to make sure it blossomed into its fullest potential.

"Gotta help the rest of those kids, too," Rags added casually. "Good thing busting prisoners out is one of my many illegal specialties." Penance for leaving them in the first place. They'd also have to track down Tal's fragment while they were at it. Once they could. Once they'd recovered and it was safe.

Safer.

Tal smiled like Rags had told a joke. "It is a strange thief who seeks to steal something of little value."

"Aw, come on." Rags shoved him. The motion didn't budge Tal one bit. "Don't make me say it."

He didn't have a silver fragment of his own yet, but he'd begun forming another connection. One that explained how he understood, without either of them speaking, what they both knew: those kids were worth more than anything Rags's clever fingers had ever snatched.

They were the score of a lifetime.

The scar over his heart throbbed with his pulse. They'd only survived because they'd gotten lucky. When their luck would run out was anyone's guess.

Good thing for everyone that Rags was damn good at slipping into—and out of—too-tight situations.

He flexed his weary fingers, forcing strength into the trembling bones. The odds were against him, but when weren't they? He had a fae map to follow, a fae prince for a friend, a fae stronghold to fortify. Give him sixteen days, and he'd make Morien regret the day he brought a thief named Rags to Coward's Silence.

PRONUNCIATION GUIDE

Aibhilin: EV-lin

Ailis: EY-lish

Ainle: EN-lyeh

Baeth: Beth

Diancecht: Dee-un-KAY-k

Dyfed: Da-VED

Cabhan: Cah-VAN (Cab is
pronounced with a soft
vh sound, not a hard *b*)

Coinneach: Ker-NAH-k

Comhghall: KOW-aal

Crisiant: CRAY-shant

Einan: EYE-nan

Faolan: FWAY-lahn

Guaire: GOO-ruh

Inis Fraoch: IN-ish Free

Laisrean: LASH-rawn

Lochlainn: Lock-lin

Murchadh: MOOR-hah

Saraid: SOR-id

Siomha: SHEE-va

Somhairle: SORE-luh

Uaine: WEN-ya

ACKNOWLEDGMENTS

Years back, we planned to dedicate the next book we published—if there ever was a next book published—to everything we'd lost along the way. As the years added up, so did the losses, until we realized this was both too depressing and too unwieldy a way to begin a book. Better, then, to (sort of) end it this way: by acknowledging what was lost, grieving it, and honoring it. As of now, the official Lost List includes three childhood cats (R and S and M); Grandpa Terry; Grandma Wint; Great-Grandma Nain; Ephraim Peretz; Paul Singer; Dani's two cancer buddies, Carol Peretz and Jon Sholle; the incomparable Ric Menello, gone far too soon; the impossible Richie Shulberg, likewise; Great-Uncle Mickey; Great-Aunt Yudis; Natalia A.; Bob Jones's left ear; Dani's right breast.

Goodbye, goodbye. Thank you for everything.

You will not be forgotten. You will always be missed.

As for the rest, we wrote much of this book between chemo visits and radiation appointments, between trips to the oncologist and mastectomy surgery and follow-up. We're very grateful to Dani's oncology team and her surgeons, with deep-abiding fondness ever reserved for PJ.

We finished the first draft of this story in the Poconos with our beloved old writing group: Jean-Paul Bass drove us there, Denise Wallner cooked like a pro, Adelle Pica slept much-needed sleep, and all five of us wrote from dawn until dusk. We took breaks only to train a pregnant squirrel, three displeased deer, and one unimpressed groundhog to attack humankind in exchange for snacks. Without Jean, Denise, and Adelle, this book would not exist.

To Jean especially, our first editor on this story, we owe our everything. We love you, Jean!

Huge thanks must also be extended to our friends in the Grief Coven—Tea, Tori, Bridget, Caroline, Caitlyn, Katy, Kaylen, and Hannah. Everyone should have their own Grief Coven. We highly recommend you find or create one. For the insight to institute it, to open that door, and the gift of the room within: Thank you, Tea. You are the realest. (Love you too, Pickett!)

Thanks also to the tattoo artists who helped both of us reclaim our bodies from dysphoria and dysmorphic anxiety—Danielle's from breast cancer; Jaida's from gender confusion. Superspecial shout-outs to Anka Lavriv for being both superhero and superfriend, and all the artists at Black Iris Tattoo for providing a home, a space, a place for magic to grow (especially John and Leslie!); to Cate Webb and Meagan Blackwood and Ilwol Hongdam, for their incredible art; to our precious pal and magical Yukito, Ligia, for inspiring us nonstop in terms of sheer talent, sharp humor, and work ethic; to Studio Muscat in Shinjuku, specifically Asao and Haruka, for giving us our first machine tattoo experiences; and to Courtney, who gave us our first tattoos in her kitchen a couple of years before that, thus beginning our tattoo journeys, showing us the way.

Thank you to all our freaking amazing friends—those who stuck with us for the long haul as well as the new ones we made while in the trenches. You teach us every day how to better show up for the people we love. The best part about publishing a book may be getting to write as many of their names as we can, so here goes: Miranda, we adore you; Marc, we adore you; Alain, we adore you; Cressa and Julia, we adore you; Amy, we adore you; Helen and Robin and Anthea and Tommy, coworkers at the Art & Writing office once and future, we adore you; little Lily L., we adore you; National Student Poets, you angels, artists, dreamers, darlings, we adore you; Sky, we adore you; Nycki, thanks for all the incredible haircuts, we adore you; Tara and Claire and Gregory and all the rescuers of Brooklyn Animal Action, we adore you.

To Kelsey of I Do Declare and the team at Blood Milk (especially Jess, Miguel, and Jen): Thank you for being eternal inspirations and such real, great friends. Kelsey and Jess, your creativity and vision as artists are matched only by your kindness and generosity as people. We are so grateful and lucky to know you. And to Ana of Nuit Clothing Atelier too, for your art, your warmth, your internal and external beauty. Mia of Plutonia Blue, you and your work are utterly captivating. Thank you all for creating the fashion, the adornments, and the fantasy we were always seeking.

Sarah Potter, you gave us readings that allowed us to trust and look forward to the possibility of selling this book. And then it happened. You're pretty magical.

Thank you to our amazing families in New York and Victoria and everywhere between—putting up with us writing through reunions, dinners, obligations, conversations. You endured a lot for our fiction aspirations, even during the lean times, and *most* of you didn't disown us, and we're greatly grateful.

Thanks to our therapists! Wow, this gratitude can't be overstated enough.

To Colleen and Michaela, early readers who gave invaluable feedback: Thank you for taking the time and the care to make sure this book was saying what we wanted it to say. To Clare: You have been outright magnificent throughout this whole process. To the copy editors, who fought their way through the constant tangle of our sometimes-it's-the-British-spelling-sometimes-it's-the-American-one inconsistencies: Thank you for your careful eyes and awe-worthy attention to detail.

To Tamar, our agent, who believed in us through years of rejections, as we got closer and closer and still, it seemed, further and further away from actually getting another book out there: Thank you for never giving up on us, for helping us with every idea fully baked and half-baked and not-baked-at-all, for championing our stories, and for keeping our hope fires alight when we were too weary to stoke them, when we were all burned out.

To Alice, our editor, who is literally perfect: Thank you for taking a chance on us, for getting excited with us, for showing us how to shape this book into the one we actually wanted to write. Obviously, without you, this book would not exist—not in its current form, its final form, the form it always wanted to take. You allowed us to mold this story into its truest self and, more than that, you showed us the way. You lit the darkened path. You mapped the maze. We're your servants for life, and you will never be rid of us.